Damage Noted - Circulate as is
10/25/10 Au

DATE DUE

AUG 2 6 2005	
NOV 0 9 2009	
JUL 1 4 2010	
JUL 2 8 2010	
OCT 1 9 2010	
OCT 1 0 2013	

BRODART, CO.   Cat. No. 23-221-003

Modern
Ranch
Living

Modern Ranch Living

A Novel

Mark Jude Poirier

miramax books

HYPERION

NEW YORK

ISBN 1-4013-0042-1

First Edition

10 9 8 7 6 5 4 3 2 1

For Manuel

Prologue

KENDRA LUMM LIFTED HER UNCLE'S OLD DUMBBELLS FOR THE FIRST TIME when she was nine years old.

By ten, she had her own set of weights and a bench on the back porch—and pretty decent biceps. She was out there most afternoons, even the hottest ones when the aggressive Arizona sun beat her silly and tanned her skin until it matched the dark brown of her sweat-stained leather lifting belt. Inside, when she watched television, she'd do curls. During commercials, she'd do crunches. By the time she hit junior high, she was worked, thick with muscle and intimidating to some of her teachers. Her abdominals were like six caramel apples, and her shoulders were as wide as an Olympic swimmer's. At home, she walked around in her sports bra, on display, pausing to flex in mirrors and snack on protein.

In seventh grade, she nearly lost her virginity to Petey Vaccarino. Petey was one day younger than Kendra, and lived across the arroyo with his mother in a sprawling stucco house. Back then, Kendra liked how Petey wore his ball cap redneck-style, propped up high. It made his head look elongated, watermelon-shaped, cute. They attempted sex after school in the Vaccarinos' living room on a pile of unfolded laundry, Vince Gill on the stereo. Petey ejaculated seconds after Kendra touched his penis. She wondered why it wasn't as big as the ones she'd seen in the faded magazines she once found in the arroyo next to a rotten mattress. But she figured her breasts weren't as big as the women's in the magazine either.

On the bus the next morning, Petey pulled a University of Arizona Wildcats sweatshirt from his backpack and flaunted the stain. "Proof," he bragged to the kids sitting near him.

Kendra stood when she heard him, and plowed to the back of the moving bus. "It was dumb," she announced to everyone there. "Plussing as how Petey came on the rug and stepped in it when he stood up."

Petey slapped her then, so hard his cap tumbled to the floor of the bus.

An eighth-grade girl screamed, "Hit her again!" as the bus rolled through a dip on River Road.

Kendra could have killed Petey—he was skinny-armed and short for his age—but she didn't. She was just glad that Petey had been courageous enough to slap her. Good for him, she thought. She wobbled back to her seat and licked a smile face on the dusty bus window.

Kendra made it to tenth grade, and for almost a year, she seemed calm and happy. Her eyes grew wide like she had figured out a puzzle, like she was anticipating something spiritual. She still lifted weights and flexed, and continued sex play with Petey, who had cultivated a sketchy mustache and had long since abandoned Garth Brooks and a few other trends to mumble gangsta rap songs under his breath, but she began to move through life a little more gracefully and softly. She used a napkin instead of her shirt to wipe her mouth as she sipped her protein shake in the morning, and she held her chin self-assuredly as she strolled through the shiny halls at Catalina Foothills High School. She combed out the snarls in her golden hair with cream rinse, and sometimes wore Heidi braids with girlish pink ribbons. She grew taller: five feet seven inches—a miracle, according to her pediatrician, who had warned Kendra and her parents for years that weight training would permanently damage her bones and stunt her growth.

In March, soon after Kendra's parents threw her a sweet six-teen party crowded with kids from the subdivision she didn't really know or like, her guidance counselor switched her from special-ed math to pre-algebra, and her teacher sent home a note saying how Kendra was *not only an ace on the tests, but a delight in the classroom.* Her mother taped the note to the refrigerator. When her father read it, he said, "Looks like this long nightmare has ended—knock on wood," and he knocked his head.

But a month later, Kendra pushed her older brother Thomas down the tile stairs that led from the kitchen to the den. She had caught him in her bedroom looking at her muscle maga-zines, and the two of them began a teasing game of tag, racing through the house, squealing, skidding in their socks on the polished floors.

She meant only to grab his shoulders and shake him a little, but he stopped abruptly at the top of the stairs, and the grab turned into a shove. She almost fell after him, but she caught the banister. When Thomas hit the den's floor, both his arms broke, one of them audibly—a wet crack that made Kendra's stomach twist in fear and guilt.

Thomas missed his senior prom because of the accident. He stayed home and watched videos. His mother ordered him a pizza. She cut it up and fed it to him with a plastic fork. Kendra had spied from the top of the stairs. She had been restricted to her room, where she did push-ups and styled her hair with an old set of curlers she'd found in the garage, until Petey Vaccarino busted through the oleanders and climbed the ve-randa. He appeared at her window, smiling coyly, twirling a marking pen through his fingers, looking anywhere but into Kendra's eyes.

Kendra would wet the washcloth, then squirt a few pumps of pearlescent soap, as Thomas maneuvered into the tepid water and propped his arms on either side of the tub. His casts were wrapped in plastic bread bags, cinched with rubber bands above his elbows. The ends of Kendra's braids dipped in the water as she leaned over. Sometimes they'd brush Thomas's skinny white legs, causing him to squirm. Sweat beaded on Kendra's upper lip and coursed down her sinewy neck as she went to work on Thomas with the washcloth and the soap. Her arms shone in the afternoon light that seeped through the clouded window, each muscle defined and glistening. She was conscious of her arms, and she moved to accentuate their bulk.

"Stop looking at my dick," Thomas said.

"I don't have a microscope," Kendra said. She wasn't looking at his dick, anyway. She had seen it a million times.

Kendra knew Thomas was washed in a similar manner by their mother every night after dinner, but she didn't care. The bathing was the least she could do after breaking both his arms. Their mother brushed his teeth and wiped him—two things Kendra began to think she should do for him. Kendra would hear Thomas's muffled complaints that worked their way through the bathroom walls, and many times she was close to going in there to help him herself, close to telling their mother to get the hell out, to leave him alone, that it was *her* job to help Thomas because she was the one who broke his arms.

This continued until his casts were removed in late May. Kendra never did tell her mother what she thought, even after her mother began to complain that her work—leasing retail properties—was suffering from all the time she had to spend tending to Thomas.

Thomas was able to attend his graduation ceremony cast-free, baking in the bleachers with the rest of his class, wearing his green-and-white robe. Kendra screamed and whistled for him when they announced his name and handed him his diploma.

When Merv Hunter turned thirty, a few of his coworkers from Splash World, mostly security guys, liquored him up at the Saddlehorn Saloon and brought him across Tucson to Les Girls, where he was treated to a lap dance from a woman with a mane of wild red hair and stationary breasts the size of softballs. After the dance, his old buddies from prep school, Jason and Rusty, forced him into Rusty's new Volvo and drove him into the foothills, near the neighborhoods where they all grew up, the neighborhood where Merv still lived with his mother.

When Rusty pulled over onto the dirt shoulder of Skyline Drive, Merv knew what they had planned for him, and he was annoyed. Ice-blocking. Annoyed not because he didn't want to ride the ice block down the hill onto the eighth hole of La Paloma Country Club's world-renowned golf course, but annoyed because he had to pretend to be more enthusiastic about it than he was. It had been fun when he was younger. The loss of control, the speed, the thrill of destroying priceless greens and trespassing on clearly marked private property. But Merv was thirty now, and he was sick of how predictable Rusty and Jason had become.

On Merv's eighteenth birthday, they had introduced him to ice-blocking. The three of them drove down to a huge meat-packing plant in South Tucson and bought two blocks of ice the size of tombstones for five bucks each. On their way back up to the foothills, they bought a case of Coors from a clerk at 7-Eleven whose eyes were so bloodshot they looked as if they might drip. The clerk didn't ask for I.D., just told Jason he had a real sweet ass. They began to drink the beers on the way to the golf course, and by the time they got there, Merv had a nice buzz going. They placed folded beach towels on top of each block of ice, and soon the three drunk boys were gliding down the hill, wiping out, tumbling in the perfectly moist grass.

Merv was able to forget himself the night of his eighteenth birthday, was able to forget for a while that Rusty and Jason would be heading off to distant colleges in the fall—Rusty to Baltimore, and Jason to New Hampshire. Merv concentrated only on his aerodynamic tuck, on speeding down the hill and catching air before being hurtled into the sand trap. The beer gave him confidence enough to try to surf down the hill. He stood on the block, but he slipped and landed on his ass right away. In the moonlight, he could see that his buddies were streaked in mud. He watched as they tackled each other and wrestled on the green.

He knew it was corny, but back then he had wanted to thank them for taking him ice-blocking, thank them for being so cool when his father died, tell them they were his best friends and that he was going to miss them when they went away for college. He didn't say any of it, though. He just finished off the beer and lay flat on the green, allowing the alcohol to mess with his equilibrium, watching the moon drift, then float back to its actual location.

When a groundskeeper showed up and shined a flashlight on Merv, Merv jumped up and raised his hands in the please-don't-shoot-me position. Rusty yelled, "Run!" and without hesitation, Merv booked up the hill, his tennis shoes slipping in the wet grass.

The three of them made it back to Rusty's car and sped off. There was a small article in the *Tucson Citizen* the following day: VANDALS HIT LA PALOMA. Two thousand dollars' worth of damage to the eighth hole. The groundskeeper had come upon three teenage boys who were able to escape. The article also mentioned the beer cans and blocks of ice. For a week or so after that, Merv jumped whenever the phone rang.

The three of them relived that night on Merv's twenty-first birthday. This time, they slid only a few times, abandoning the ice blocks for bong hits on the green. They sat down there, passing the bong around, drinking cheap red wine, not saying much to each other. Jason had gotten the pot from his brother, who went to college in California, and he was generous, packing bowl after bowl as the moon rose over the Santa Catalina Mountains.

Merv grew sick, threw up the third-rate wine and the birthday cake his mother had made for him. Rusty was asleep, wasn't awakened by Merv's violent coughing and choking sounds. Jason had wandered off toward the ninth hole. When Merv's stomach finally stopping heaving, he remained on his hands and knees, afraid to move, gripping the grass so the world would stop tilting.

That night, at age twenty-one, wiping the vomit from his

lips, he swore to himself he wouldn't fuck up anymore. Rusty and Jason and his other friends from prep school had finished their third year at good colleges, made new friends from all over the country, and here was Merv, gagging, staring at the grass of the eighth hole on a golf course only a few miles from where he had always lived.

He had tried a few semesters at the University of Arizona, but it was so easy not to go to class when the weather was always perfect. Sometimes he'd make it to campus, but he'd sit on the richly watered lawn in front of the student union, soak in the sun, and watch the girls hurry by. Before he'd realize it, it was too late for class, and he'd walk down to Mamma's Pizza for a slice the size of a magazine. By second semester, after having earned a 2.3 grade point average for his half-assed efforts during first semester, it became more difficult to wake up before double digits, and to do tedious things like go to the language lab or stand in line for registration.

He had visited Rusty at Johns Hopkins in Baltimore, and he had been amazed at how hard everyone studied, even Rusty, who left Merv alone the first night and hurried off to the library to cram for a history test. Everyone at Hopkins had a plan. They all seemed driven, unlike any group of people Merv had ever met. Rusty's friends talked about Titian and Nabokov and Churchill— people Merv sensed he should know about but didn't. They dressed differently, too, in dark overcoats and big logger boots. On the white marble steps in front of the Gilman Building, Rusty's friends competed with each other for speaking time. Some quoted philosophers and poets. A few mumbled cynically between draws on their smelly European cigarettes. They all read and complained about *The New York Times*. Each of Rusty's friends was self-important and pretentious, but—and Merv hated it when he realized this—each was also interesting, smart, and ambitious, three adjectives Merv figured no one applied to him.

Now, nine years later, here he was again, faced with the task of unloading heavy blocks of ice from the trunk of Rusty's car, knowing that he hadn't changed much since age twenty-one, realizing that he hadn't done much in nine years.

"Hey," Merv said, as Jason lifted a block, "this really isn't fun anymore."

Jason dropped the block into the dirt. "You got something better planned?" he said.

"Let's just go to the Tap Room before they close," Merv said. He knew Jason was pissed. He braced himself for an indignant speech, wished he had downed six or seven more beers at the Saddlehorn so he could abide it.

"Not all of us work at a waterslide park and sit in the sun sipping Gatorade all day," Jason said. "Some of us sit in an office all day, under artificial light, breathing artificial air. Why don't you indulge Rusty and me and join us for a few slides down the hill?"

"It's *my* birthday," Merv said. "You should indulge me."

"You've been nothing but indulged since high school," Jason said louder. "Rusty and I work, pay our own bills, drive cars we pay for. What do you do? Blow your whistle at a few kids who misbehave on the slides, live at home with your mother, don't pay rent, watch television, exercise a little."

"Feel free to shut up," Merv said.

"Jason's sort of right," Rusty said meekly. "I mean, come on, Merv, you're thirty."

"So sliding down a hill on a block of ice is somehow going to help me mature?" Merv said. He lifted the other block from the trunk and heaved it into a small mesquite tree, his fingers stinging with the cold. "You guys can vent your cubicle frustrations to someone else," he said. "I'm leaving."

Cars flew past Merv as he walked on the dirt shoulder along Skyline Boulevard. To the south, he could see the lights of Tucson, gathered between the mountains like a bowl of gold dust. Even up there, in the supposedly affluent part of Tucson, beer cans, fast-food bags, and other trash lined the street, clinging to dry saltbushes and ocotillos.

A pickup slowed and pulled onto the shoulder in front of

Merv. He fanned away the dust as he walked toward the passenger window. He knew he should probably cross the street, maybe run into the desert, but his birthday made him feel he was impervious to danger. It would be too ironic or poetic or whatever to get knifed to death or kidnapped or shot on your thirtieth birthday.

In the truck there were two guys, high school jocks with short hair and fresh faces slightly aglow in the dim light of the dashboard. Their loud stereo blared Korn or some other abrasive rock until Merv asked them what they needed, and one of them lowered the volume.

"You know where a bar called 'The Biz' is?" the passenger asked, rolling down his window.

Merv could smell the whiskey on the kid's breath, sweet and ripe. The driver drummed the steering wheel along to the music.

"No," Merv said.

"How about a place called 'It's 'bout Time'?"

"Never heard of it," Merv lied. He knew the drill. He had heard about it or read about it. They'd ask him where each of the gay bars was, and if he knew, they'd beat the hell out of him. He knew where It's 'bout Time was. Right down there on Fourth Avenue near all the college bars he frequented. He'd been in there once to piss, plowed through brawny shirtless men on the dance floor to get to the rest room.

"I don't go to many bars," Merv told the kid. "Most are down near the U of A, I think."

"Okay," the passenger said.

"You sure you don't know where It's 'bout Time is?" the driver said.

"Sorry," Merv said. "Can't help you."

"Later," said the passenger, and the truck rolled into drive.

A few minutes later, the same truck sped by, and the passenger chucked a beer bottle at Merv: direct hit. It broke on his forehead. Merv was more shocked than hurt, although the blood came right away, stinging his eye and wetting his lips with a nasty metallic flavor. He pulled off his T-shirt, and used it to apply pressure to the stinging wound, treated it routinely, like he had learned in the first aid classes he had to take to get the job at the water park.

Merv figured he almost deserved a bleeding head. He should never even have talked to the kids in the truck. Stupid. But if he had run off into the desert or across the street, they would have chased him, would have eventually caught up and beaten him up. Fuckers. Fucking aggressive bored teenage trash.

He felt bad about leaving Rusty and Jason. They deserved a little fun, and he should have stayed and indulged them, like Jason said. They did work their asses off: ridiculous hours spent under fluorescent lights in East Scottsdale prefab office parks. Each had lost almost everything the year before. Jason had been working for a company that wrote Internet credit card processing software, and Jason had been a web consultant. Now Merv wasn't sure what they did, but he knew they didn't make half as much as they had the previous year. Each was forced to sell his condo, and had moved into an apartment.

Before tonight, they had told Merv that they envied his lifestyle, but he had suspected that they actually pitied him—or resented him—for living at home with his mother, working a mindless job, going out too much, and still having plenty of time to use the StairMaster and hit the weights at the Racquet Club. Rusty and Jason looked older than their ages, each having thick bags under his eyes, Rusty's red hair thinning to nothing, and Jason's gut sagging over his belt. Merv, with his smooth face and full head of light brown curls, still got carded almost every night he went out drinking.

Brian was working the gate at Rancho Sin Vacas tonight. He sat outside on a lawn chair, reading a magazine under the yellow bug light. He wore his dumb uniform: khaki shorts and a park ranger shirt. Back in high school, Merv used to get stoned with Brian once in a while. But then Brian met Kara, the woman who eventually became his wife. She introduced Brian to Jesus, and the pot-smoking stopped.

Merv crouched behind some bushes, sneaked up to Brian, and panted loudly.

Brian jumped, knocked over his lounge chair, dropped his magazine. "Lords of light! You scared me. What the heck happened to your head?"

Merv had forgotten about his wound. He realized he must look a little scary. The blood was drying, sticky. "Some fuckers threw a bottle at me," Merv said.

Brian mashed his lips, like he was holding something back, like he wanted to curse. Then he took a deep breath. "I can drive you up to your house," he said. "It'll only take a minute. And you should call the police."

"I'll walk," Merv said. "I want to."

It was only half a mile, and he did want to walk. He enjoyed the cool night air that rolled off the mountains, the smell of desert.

Saturday. June 2. 2001

Warmer

High 96 / Low 62

Clear

KENDRA WOKE AT FIVE LIKE SHE ALWAYS DID. SHE SWISHED HER MOUTH with Scope, sniffed a sports bra she found on her floor and pulled it on. She never sniff-tested her running shorts; she wore only clean ones ever since she'd read an article about yeast infections in a fitness magazine. A yeast infection could seriously impede her training.

The sky was a fiery haze, and the air was cool and dry. Quail cooed, and a few cicadas warmed up their buzzers. After April, this was the only comfortable time to run. It was too hot to get a good workout later in the day. Today, as she began her run, hitting the hill, she saw a small pack of coyotes loping back to wherever they hid during daylight hours. One of them carried a floppy, car-smashed jackrabbit in its mouth. The coyotes' small size and skinniness always surprised her. The flattened rabbit was almost as big as the coyote carrying it.

Kendra welcomed the sensation that burned through her quads and calves the first five or so times she ran up the hill. It felt like her legs were yawning. She had stretched this morning, but there were areas deep in her muscles that didn't ignite until she was really running, bounding up the hill. She ran the same length of road forty times—a stretch of faded asphalt that wound up a sharply angled foothill at the base of the Santa Catalina Mountains—but she rarely became bored. There were often new things to see, subtle changes: a skid mark, an ant-covered dead lizard, new trash, a burst of wildflowers or blooming cacti.

But there were no noticeable changes along the road today. No neighbors were awake yet. Just yellow porch lights. Some mornings, Mrs. Hunter was out walking, wearing a stupid flowered housedress and old Keds sneakers, sometimes carrying a toaster or iron. But that was only if she hadn't slept at all the night before. She'd smile at Kendra sheepishly, and say, "I couldn't sleep." Kendra never had the time or the patience to talk with the crazy insomniac woman. Kendra would only nod, force a smile, and continue running up or down the hill.

Kendra finished her forty hills quickly today, and chugged a protein shake before she went back to sleep, still wearing her sweaty workout gear.

She had planned on waking at nine, working her chest and back, and later swimming laps at the club, but her mother, Joyce, woke her thirty minutes into her deep slumber, shaking her shoulder.

Kendra saw Joyce's face, loose and sagging, and she breathed in her familiar scent of baby powder and Camel Lights, but somehow it didn't all quite coalesce into reality, and she reached up and grabbed a handful of Joyce's dry hair. Kendra tugged and shook Joyce's head. Joyce screamed. She saw Joyce's dental work, the small hairs in her nose. Kendra knew she was hurting Joyce, that it was wrong, that it was abnormal, but she didn't want to stop. She didn't stop until Gene, her father, grabbed her wrists and pinned them against her headboard.

"Kendra," he said calmly, staring into her eyes, "you hurt your mother."

"Kendra, you hurt me," Joyce added from across the room.

"But," Kendra said, relaxing her arms, no longer fighting her father's grasp, "you totally scared the shit out of me, waking me like that."

"I yelled your name and you didn't budge," Joyce said. "I thought for a second you were dead."

Gene released her and stood above her bed. Kendra saw he

had nicked himself on the underside of his chin while shaving. His face and neck were very tanned from spending hours on the golf course at La Paloma, where he gave golf lessons to guests, most of whom were senior citizens from New Jersey or Canada. The non-inked parts of his arms were ghostly white, in startling contrast to his face and hands. He had to wear long sleeves at work to hide the blue and green smears of tattoos left over from his days as the drummer of U.P.S., an early eighties punk band whose full name was "Useless Pieces of Shit."

"If you don't start hitting the weights, Gene," Kendra told him, "I'll be able to take you by August, I swear."

He laughed. "Oh, really?" he said.

"Can I have privacy?" Kendra said, pulling her comforter up to her neck. "Could you two get out and let me sleep? You're screwing my schedule way up." She flipped her pillow, exposing the cool side, and hugged it. She sighed.

"The toy show starts in two hours," Joyce said. "Get up."

"Get up," Gene said, "and help her load the van."

"You help her," Kendra said. "Or Thomas. Make him."

"Thomas has been packing the board games and lunch boxes for over an hour," Joyce said. "Get up."

"Ten minutes," Kendra moaned. "I swear."

As Kendra and Joyce walked into the bustling convention center, each carrying a plastic crate of collectible toys, a man approached them. He was stout, and sported a trimmed Vandyke beard.

As he rocked from his heels to his toes, he pointed his chubby finger at Joyce, and said above the din of haggling toy dealers, "You've been trashing my name all over the *Star Wars* community."

"If you want to sell touched-up R2D2s with bogus stickers, that's your business," Joyce said, "but don't bitch to me about trashing your name."

"Plussing as how," Kendra added, "move your ass so we can set up." She gripped the crate and flexed her forearms.

"I could have you banned from this show," he said.

"Go set up your shoddy swap-meet crap and let us alone," Joyce said. She pushed by him, knocking his shoulder with the crate.

Kendra followed her, also knocking the man's shoulder, only more forcefully than her mother had.

"Lesbos," he mumbled.

Kendra placed the crate on the floor and turned to the man. "What'd you say?"

"Nothing," he said.

"I thought so," Kendra said. "She's my mother, asshole."

Just as Kendra and Joyce finished setting up the table, snapping together the plastic shelves and unpacking several boxes of toys, a spidery woman hurried over and began to examine the goods. Kendra recognized the woman, probably from a previous show. She moved in nervous jerks, always ricocheting from table to table. Skin clung to her bones like she was desiccated. Her lazy eye made her look deranged. Kendra could never look her in the eye because she didn't know which one to look in.

The woman picked up a Liddle Kiddles coloring book. "How much?" she asked Kendra. The woman's voice was deep and froggy, incongruous with her frail appearance.

"Twenty," Kendra said.

"You give a dealer discount, honey?"

Joyce looked up from the floor where she was assembling a Barbie Jeep. "It's thirty without the discount, Glynnis. It's Liddle Kiddles."

"I know what it is, but half the pages are colored in," Glynnis said, flipping through the book. "This one's torn."

Glynnis held it up. The page depicted two big-headed midget dolls jumping rope. Kendra hated Liddle Kiddles. Of all the creepy doll lines from the sixties Joyce had versed her in, Liddle Kiddles were the creepiest. Their eyes were too big, and often their hair was scented—a rancid stink, like a two-week-old bouquet or a sick old woman. Once, Kendra discovered a shoe box full of Liddle Kiddles at a yard sale. They were good ones, even a few of the rare Kozmic Kiddles. She stuffed the box under a picnic table before Joyce could see it.

"It's over thirty years old," Joyce said to Glynnis. "They're scarce."

"I'll give you fifteen," Glynnis said. "I saw one on the Internet for less than that."

"Eighteen," Kendra said. "Is that okay, Joyce?"

"Eighteen," Joyce said. "And that's only because I've seen you at a lot of shows."

Glynnis handed Kendra the eighteen dollars and walked off with the coloring book.

Before the show opened for the public at nine, Kendra and Joyce had sold over eight hundred dollars worth of toys: a set of three Monkees Halloween masks, a *Man From U.N.C.L.E.* lunch box, a Donny and Marie record player, a *Major Matt Mason* puzzle, a *Brady Bunch* board game, a Cher styling head . . .

Joyce had spent countless hours cruising dusty thrift stores in South Tucson, picking through the junk, searching for anything she could sell at one of these shows. She often dragged Kendra with her. It was getting tougher to find anything at the thrift stores within the city limits. The thrift store employees were on to it; they knew what things were worth, they knew the market value of even the most obscure collectible toys.

The Tanque Verde Swap Meet was somewhat better—if you got there when the clueless families were unloading their vans and station wagons. Dealers descended upon any new sellers that drove up to the Swap Meet, and rifled through their stuff, often before it was unloaded from their vehicle. Kendra accompanied Joyce to the Swap Meet and to the toy shows; Kendra's counselor had said it might be a good way for Kendra to become involved in her mother's life, to better understand her mother. In return, Joyce took Kendra to the movies every Sunday afternoon, and bought her fat-free frozen yogurt afterward.

Kendra hated the Swap Meet most of the time, especially during the summer, when everything was covered in hot dust and everyone was sweating out cheap beer. But she liked to elbow her way into someone's van and find all the good stuff first. She was well-hated by the other Swap Meet vultures, and she preferred it that way, proud that she had established a reputation and intimidated people.

When Kendra announced to her counselor that she and Joyce could sell all the toys on the Internet much easier than by going to toy shows, her counselor asked, "Why do you think your mother would rather not do it that way?"

"Because she's sometimes retarded," Kendra said. "And I don't mean that as an insult, because it's true. And her name is 'Joyce' not 'your mother.'"

"You never call her 'Mom' or 'Mommy' or anything like that?"

"Why?" Kendra said. Even as a toddler, she had called her mother by her name.

"She might prefer that. Have you discussed it with her?"

"Um, no," Kendra said. "If she had a problem with it, I think she would have said something by now, don't you?"

Today, Kendra quickly became sick of dealing with customers at the toy show. They'd either try to bargain down the prices, or pick up a toy, exclaim, "I had this when I was a kid," and move on. Kendra knew most of the sales were clinched to the other dealers in the morning, which made her day-long sentence behind the table less bearable. She could be at the Tucson Racquet and Fitness Club, at the preacher bench, working her biceps. But she had pulled Joyce's hair that morning. She had to behave rationally and kindly. If Gene brought it up later, she'd work harder to convince him that she'd been half-asleep when she attacked Joyce.

Joyce wasn't any fun at these toy shows. She said Kendra needed practice in relating to customers, so she'd kick back and read true-crime paperbacks—until something sold. Then she'd tell Kendra the history of the sold toy: "I got that at a yard sale in Marana for a dollar. . . . That was in the box of Barbie stuff from that estate sale on Sabino Canyon. . . . I ordered that from that crook in Michigan. . . ."

A man approached the table. Kendra stupidly made eye-contact with him. He wore a *Star Trek* shirt, a velour V-neck like the crew of the *Enterprise*. "You have any *Trek* stuff?" he asked. Predictable.

"Just a few loose Megos," she said, pointing to them, "and some figures from the *Next Generation,* still mint on cards."

"I have a Kirk Mego, mint in box," he said, grinning, standing excitedly on his toes.

"Am I supposed to be all impressed?" Kendra asked.

He didn't respond. Instead, he looked over the displayed toys. He touched everything, made faces when he read the price tags. He picked up a Bozo the Clown gumball bank, and said, "They have this a few tables over for five dollars less, and it's in better condition."

"Then go buy it," Kendra said.

"I don't want it," he said.

"Then shut up," Kendra said. She stood, and stared deeply into his wide eyes, until he shuffled away.

She had learned to stare down people from a homeboy, a real one, Miguel. During lunch periods, she and Miguel used to sneak off campus to Dairy Queen, where they'd sit at a red plastic table and smile at each other. He'd eat a chili dog and fries. Kendra would chew through two or three protein bars and enjoy watching him devour his real food. He had the best teeth, so white they nearly glowed. Whenever some other homeboy or redneck would look twice at Kendra, or have the audacity to approach her, Miguel's face would tense, his lip would curl a little, and he'd stare at the guy until the guy walked away. It worked every time, and soon Kendra began to stare down the Latina chicks who were into Miguel. Their fanned up bangs and black lipstick didn't intimidate her. The stare-down worked every time on them, too. After eating, Kendra and Miguel would get high, or have sex in the tall weeds behind the bagel shop. Kendra could taste his meal on his warm tongue. Too bad he had stopped coming to school.

* * *

"He might've bought something," Joyce said without looking up from her book. "You were rude."

"Sorry," Kendra said. "I'm gonna walk around now. You want a drink?"

"No. Hurry back."

When Kendra first started working at the toy shows, she was vaguely interested in it all. She thought it was cool that Joyce could buy a toy for fifty cents and sell it for fifty dollars. The toys from the sixties or seventies were funny, but they held no honest nostalgia for her. She had watched hours of reruns— *Happy Days, The Brady Bunch, Eight Is Enough*—but she never connected with them. Watching them was a way of staying out of trouble for the three hours after she got off the school bus, until Joyce or Gene made dinner. The reruns were something to look at while she worked out. Even the toys from her own childhood didn't mean much to her. She had learned what toys were worth, and like Joyce, she wasn't sentimental about them.

Kendra felt it in her gut when she saw the Liddle Kiddles coloring book displayed at Glynnis's table. Glynnis had propped it up with a small stand, and placed it under a Lucite box. A little pink sign read, SUPER RARE $100.

Kendra muscled through a few women looking at some Barbie clothes, and said, "You're trying to rip my mom off."

"What are you talking about?" Glynnis said.

"You know," Kendra said.

"The coloring book?" Glynnis stepped back and crossed her thin arms over her chest like a mummy.

"I could kick your ass so easy," Kendra said.

The two women customers dropped the Barbie clothes and rushed away.

Glynnis stepped back farther, leaned against another dealer's table. "I don't have to take this," she said. Her deep voice quavered a little. "I don't have to take this at all."

Kendra clenched her fists, flexed her forearms. She breathed deeply through her teeth and closed her eyes. She wanted to chuck the Lucite box at Glynnis. She wanted to do it so bad, her fingertips tingled. Glynnis would topple onto the floor with a bloodied head. She'd kick and squirm, expose her weak, pale legs from under that tired Prairie skirt. Kendra might shove the whole table of toys on top of her. Then a rent-a-cop would run over, the rubber soles of his shiny boots squeaking on the floor like hungry puppies. Kendra would kick his ass, too. Maybe she'd twist his arm until she heard it crack like Thomas's. She'd stuff a Barbie in his mouth, ask him if he played with Barbies—Malibu Tan Barbie, Dentist Barbie, Glitter Magic Barbie—or maybe Ken. She'd ask him if he played with Ken like the fag he was. Did he undress Ken? Check for a dick? *Yes, I play with Ken,* she'd make him say, *and I always check for a dick.*

When Kendra opened her eyes, Glynnis was cowering behind another dealer, a guy who sold only Hot Wheels. The guy was pretty thick, Kendra noticed. His muscles were big, and he had the right frame, but he needed some aerobic work to rid himself of his outer layer of fat. He needed some sun, too, and to maybe shave his furry arms to fully expose muscle definition.

Kendra looked past the Hot Wheels guy and told Glynnis, "Being as which I pulled her hair this morning, you're lucky. Real lucky."

"What are you talking about?" Glynnis said.

Merv had to fish a turd from the Kid Corner Splash Pool thirty minutes after he opened it. Children were screaming, fighting their way out of the knee-high water like there was a man-eating shark in there. A few kids clung to the pirate ship in the middle and cried. He ferried the crying kids across the water in a rubber boat, and gave their mothers and baby-sitters refund coupons. In addition to adhering to several other regulations, Merv was required to close the area for twenty-four hours after the turd was removed. In addition, he had to fill out a long checklist and a form on which he wrote, *Pool evacuated and human fecal matter extracted with skimmer net and placed in biohaz-*

ard bag at 10:36 A.M. This meant that there would be hundreds of smaller kids in the giant wave pool. His lifeguards had to stay alert. He cut across the bright green grass to warn them.

Annie sat on top of her lifeguard chair, hiding her golden skin from the killer sun under an umbrella, a ball cap, and the coconut SPF 40 sunscreen Merv could smell from where he stood below.

"What the hell happened to your head?" she asked Merv, removing her sunglasses.

"I bumped it," he said.

"Did you go out after the Saddlehorn?"

"I got home a few hours ago," Merv said.

"I won't ask," she said. She slid her sunglasses back on.

"The piss pond was turded again, so there'll be tons of little kids over here. Don't space out, and tell Timmy and Brett, too."

"There's hydrogen peroxide in the office," Annie said. "For your head."

"Thanks," he said. He jogged away, but turned around and added, "Watch those kids."

Annie smiled and waved.

If he were younger or she were older, he'd ask her out. She was smart, athletic, always in a good mood. She had this look about her, like she was tough, or like she knew something secret about Merv and was waiting for the most embarrassing time to bring it up. Always making an edge for Merv. He liked the way she handled herself around the other workers at Splash World. She had fit in with the group just a few days after she began working, knowing who she could tease and who to avoid. Merv had hired her sight unseen because he liked her voice on the phone; she made him laugh. She had called him in April from her college in Maine, said she was spending the summer in Tucson with her parents and she needed to make money. "Either you hire me at Splash World," she had joked, "or I'm a subject in another medical study, and I just got rid of the burning rash from last summer."

Merv stopped at Raymond, who had rolled his wheelchair to the edge of the wave pool so the water lapped over his twisted ankles. Raymond sat there every day, smiling, blocking the sun with his golf visor, greeting people who passed him with a dignified "Good day" in his vaguely British accent. He was a fixture at the park, and each morning, one of the Splash World employees helped him switch from his battery-powered deluxe wheelchair, to the more basic nonelectric one that he used when he enjoyed the wave pool. Merv was often the one who helped Raymond, first by hanging his sport coat on a hook in the employee locker room, careful not to wrinkle the fine silk or wool. Then he'd slide off Raymond's shoes: black Gucci loafers, never scuffed, always well shined. Finally, he'd roll up Raymond's trouser cuffs, neatly, four folds, about two inches each fold, exposing his white hairless legs. Raymond always produced a crisp twenty for Merv, a bill that seemed to come out of nowhere.

"How's the water, Raymond?" Merv asked him today, placing his hand on Raymond's shoulder.

"Perfect, Merv," he said. "It's so very lovely, despite the fact that one of those ruffians from security had to help me prepare this morning."

"I'm sorry about that," Merv said. "Rough night."

"I noticed that horrible gash on your head," Raymond said, "but decided it would be untoward to ask about it."

A bit of drool had worked its way out the corner of Raymond's mouth. Merv didn't comment on it, figured it had something to do with the degenerative muscle disease Raymond suffered.

"An angry teenager threw a bottle at me from a truck," Merv said. "He had good aim."

"I'm starting to believe we all should carry pistols with us wherever we go," Raymond said. "I never thought I would utter such a thing. I guess I'm a real American now."

Merv climbed the wet metal stairs and took his post atop the Kamikaze, a 150-foot water slide—a straight-on steep lunge without any turns or twists. The sliders plunged head-first on their stomachs, rode special mats. If they pulled up on the front of their mats as they took off, they could catch air and heighten the detached, near-death feeling in their guts. While he was up there, it was Merv's job to safely space each slider, and remind each of them not to pull up.

But some days Merv didn't care. He'd robotically repeat, "Don't pull up on the mat, keep your head down, and exit to the left." He didn't watch to see if they abided by the rules. They spaced themselves, they weren't stupid about that, even the little kids, so there was no real chance of a collision at the bottom. And no one could catch enough air to flip over the sides of the slide, not even with a push-off from a friend at the top. He'd look at his watch and surprise himself. Hours slipped away unnoticed. Hundreds of sliders went by, and he warned them all, but he hadn't been aware of any of them.

Today, as the sliders filed past him down the Kamikaze, he touched his sore head and thought of his mother as he had seen her early that morning: asleep on the couch in front of the snowy television, still wearing her work shoes. He had arrived home at three A.M., and she was snoring lightly in the living room, her mouth open unnaturally wide, like a frozen scream. She couldn't sleep well—she hadn't since Merv's father died years ago. She fought sleeping-pill addiction twice, tried herbal concoctions, intense exercise, cutting all processed sugar from her diet. And Merv was right alongside her, installing lightproof shutters in her bedroom, clipping articles from magazines, fixing chamomile tea at night. Sometimes, at the end of the week, she'd be shuffling around the kitchen like a zombie, yawning, rubbing her eyes, nodding off as she stood at the counter making dinner, so ravaged-looking that Merv had to leave the house. Her sad, sunken eyes were frightening reminders of her mortality. He'd feel awful doing it, but at times like these, he'd escape to downtown Tucson, where he'd pull a stool up to the bar in the smoky Tap Room at Hotel Congress, and plug back Coors until he felt like walking through the spray-painted underpasses to Fourth Avenue, where he'd find someone he knew.

He'd probably do that tonight.

Tuesday, June 5, 2001

Warmer

High 103 / Low 67

Clear

KENDRA FINISHED HER WORKOUT EARLY. WHEN SHE WALKED INTO THE heavily air-conditioned house to find Thomas watching professional wrestling, she wished she hadn't. She wished she had stayed at the club and used the rowing machines or done a spin class. She hated to see Thomas like this, wasting his last summer before college, getting weaker. Kendra had run the hill in the morning—bumped into Mrs. Hunter, who jittered as she trudged along the road—skipped her morning nap and gone right into pyramid sets on the back porch. She had chugged her protein shake and eaten two bananas, and finally driven to the club to swim laps.

It was past noon, and Thomas was still in his underwear, sitting crossed-legged on the floor a few feet from the television screen. The television cast a blue light over his white chest and stomach. With the shutters closed and the room darkened, Thomas looked cadaverous, the color of the little fetal pig Kendra had dissected in biology class earlier that year.

"You need something," Kendra told him.

"What?" he asked without turning from the screen, where a wrestler dressed like a hillbilly in frayed overalls was being fake-pummeled by a greased-up guy with huge pecs. Like most wrestlers, Kendra noticed, the ones on the screen needed some serious ab work.

"Do something," she said. She opened a shutter, and white light spilled into the room.

Thomas turned toward her, squinting. "I'm relaxing," he said.

"You could follow me on my workouts and be buff by fall," Kendra said, sitting down on the cool tiles next to him. "You could do something."

"Why would I want to be buff?"

The hillbilly made a miraculous comeback, climbed on the ropes, and swan-dived onto his opponent with a loud "Hee-haw!" The spectators roared. Thomas grinned and chuckled softly, rocked on his butt excitedly.

"Seeing as plus you could get a girlfriend."

"What?" Thomas snapped. "You're not making sense. What does 'seeing as plus' mean?"

"You could go on a date," she said.

"I had a date for the prom," Thomas said, "but someone broke my arms."

"Brooke Luter is a bitch, anyway," Kendra said. "No one else asked her."

"Shut up," Thomas said.

"This wrestling is fake."

"No duh," Thomas said.

"Why do you watch it?"

"Shut up," Thomas said. The hillbilly won the match. The referee held up the hillbilly's wet, meaty arm, and loud hoe-down banjo music started. Thomas clicked off the television and gazed into the blank screen.

Kendra stood. She smoothed her shorts and pulled up her socks. "I'm bored," she said. She mussed Thomas's light brown hair and walked up the tiled stairs into the kitchen to make an egg-white omelet.

As she ate lunch, Thomas walked in and sat across the table from her. "You're supposed to vacuum or sweep the whole up-stairs," he said, scratching his chest, leaving pink trails with his fingertips.

"Who says?"

"Mom," he said. "There's a note for you on the fridge."

"I didn't see it," Kendra said, "so it doesn't count."

"I told you about it." Thomas stood and walked to the refrigerator. He pulled down the note and read aloud: "Kendra, I need you to do the upstairs floors. Your room and Thomas's room, too. Love, Joyce."

"She didn't write that," Kendra said. "Let me see." She sprang up and ran after Thomas, who had already bolted down the steps to the family room.

She tackled him on the sofa, sat on his stomach and straddled his chest. She tickled his bare armpits and sides. He giggled madly, begged her to stop, squirmed and kicked.

"You're gonna wet your pants," Kendra said, digging her fingers deeply into his sides, into the space between his ribs. So fragile. She could pry his ribs apart without any effort if she wanted to. "You're gonna wet."

"Stop," he begged between laughs. "Please."

She went at him for a few more seconds, then said, "Okay," and she stopped. She got off him, patting him softly on his stomach. "No tone," she said. "Sad."

Thomas remained supine, caught his breath, his pale stomach moving up and down like a membrane. "You'll miss me when I'm gone," he said.

"Probably might," Kendra said.

As usual, Kendra could hear the bumping bass from the end of Petey's driveway. She could feel the vibrations on his front stoop. His mom's car wasn't in the carport, so she walked right into the house, down the dark hall, feeling the cool adobe walls, to Petey's room where he sat with Brooke Luter on his unmade bed, bobbing his head to the blaring stereo. Brooke's presence didn't faze Kendra. Both Brooke and Petey knew if they screwed around, Kendra would kick their asses. Kendra shuffled through the clothes and basketball shoes and porno magazines, stepped over an unused Christmas snowboard. She turned down the stereo and held up her palm for Petey to punch. His punch was weak. She knew if she pulled off his sunglasses, she'd see his heavy lids and vibrating eyes.

"We were listening to that," Brooke said. She brought her knees to her chest and leaned against a Colorado Rockies poster. Kendra could have predicted Brooke's outfit: A big black Raiders coat over a wife-beater T-shirt with jeans and Adidas pool sandals—generic homegirl from four years ago.

"I don't care," Kendra said. "Being as how it's too hot for that jacket."

"You don't even make sense," Brooke said.

Kendra sat on Petey's lap to make Brooke jealous. Petey hid his face in her hair and nibbled at the back of her ears with his dry lips. He mumbled something she couldn't hear, and wrapped his arms around her. His marker pens were spilled over his desk. Their odor was palpable, like you could wrestle with it. The stink made her dizzy. "You already huff?" she asked.

"Duh," Brooke said. "A lot. He's all wasted."

"Why didn't you?" Kendra asked Brooke. "You in training for something?"

"Yeah," Brooke said, "I'm in training to get all buff and look like a muscle dyke like you."

"You gotta get rid of all that cellulite first," Kendra said. "And that homegirl outfit doesn't hide it. And don't forget you're white."

"You should get a crew cut and finish off your look," Brooke said. "Give all your girl stuff to your fag brother."

Kendra could have reached over and grabbed Brooke's neck, felt the blood skipping through her jugular and the warm sweat under her hair in the back. She didn't, though. She stopped her fantasy of killing Brooke before it got too detailed. Her counselor had told her to do this, told her to think of weight lifting or something else she liked instead. Besides, the pen fumes were making her sick. She could taste them. They coated her mouth and throat.

She stood, let Petey flop onto his bed. "Keep the pens away from him," she told Brooke. "And put the lids on them. And open a window."

"Petey's having a party tonight," Brooke said. "He told me to call you."

"I'll be busy sleeping," Kendra said. "I'll call him tomorrow. You watch his ass, or I'll kick your fat one."

Kendra walked out before Brooke could respond.

"Did you go to work today?" Merv asked his mother. He dropped his gym bag on the couch next to her.

She didn't look up from the television, continued to watch *Wheel of Fortune* with the sound turned off. "I went," she said. "I was on time, too."

"I heard you stomping around last night," Merv said.

"Did I wake you?"

"I was up," Merv said, "going to the bathroom."

"We can warm up those enchiladas from El Charro."

"I'll do it," Merv said, already walking to the kitchen. He put the Mexican leftovers in the oven, climbed the stairs, and turned on the shower.

He washed away the waxy sunscreen and rinsed the dirt from his hair. The cut from the bottle, even though it had scabbed over, still hurt. A dust devil had hit the water park today, kicked up dirt and whirled trash hundreds of feet into the sky. Merv closed the Kamikaze for a few minutes to let all the grit wash down, and radioed the other slide operators to do the same. A wall of nine giant palm trees stood between the park and its neighboring dirt lot, but the skinny trees never blocked the wind from pelting everyone with dust. When the wind hit them, the palm trees would bend and occasionally a dry frond would blow off into the park. Merv had heard the fronds' loud crumbling noises, so he wasn't surprised to see the giant brown dust devil easing its way toward the park. A few crazy kids, wet and shirtless from the wave pool, ran right into the heart of the dust devil, emerged from it sand-blasted, brown, and laughing.

Annie had radioed Merv then, said she needed to wash her

contact lenses, that the dust was making her crazy and she couldn't see a thing. Merv found her a stand-in and sent her on an hour break. "You need to mellow," he had said to her into the radio. "Go get yourself a Coke and hang out inside while your eyes flush out."

"Thanks," she had radioed back. "And could you find someone to help Raymond?"

"What's wrong?"

"He was hit by the dust pretty hard."

"I'll be down there in a second," Merv said. "Tell him I'll be there in a second."

He found Raymond in his usual spot, only a small crowd of young kids had gathered around him. Raymond rubbed his eyes with his twisted wrists. "I didn't see it coming," Raymond said, "and now I can't see a thing."

A little blond kid said, "His eyes hurt bad."

"Thanks," Merv said to the kid. He then squatted down in front of Raymond's wheelchair. "You all right? Do you need me to call someone?"

"Thank you, Merv. No, no need to call anyone. Perhaps you could take me out of the wind?"

Merv rolled him up to the locker room, stopped directly in front of the sink lowered for the handicapped. "Rinse your eyes with cool water, Raymond. Okay?" Merv turned on the cold water.

Raymond reached for the water, but couldn't make a cup with his hands, so Merv did. He flushed out Raymond's eyes after placing his large towel on his lap.

"That's beautiful, Merv. So beautiful," Raymond said.

After shampooing twice, Merv's scalp still felt a little gritty. Maybe he'd swim later, turn off the back porch lights, float around in the dark pool, look at the stars. He had done that often as a kid, knew the names of the constellations. At night he couldn't see how badly the pool needed a cleaning. He couldn't see the crumbling pool deck or the dry and gray landscaping plants.

Theirs was one of the first houses built in Rancho Sin Vacas, a subdivision of once upscale homes pushed against the Santa Catalina Mountains. Now the carpeting in the living room was worn flat and smelled of dust no matter how often it was vacuumed. It all needed to be pulled up, replaced with tiles or wood. Every wall wanted a fresh coat of paint. The linoleum in the kitchen had rotted around the sink and trash compactor and was peeling upward. Rounded Mexican roof tiles flew from the ramada whenever the wind blew hard enough.

When Merv was in sixth grade, his friends would beg to go over to his house. Merv's house was the biggest, as was his pool, and he had a computer and a VCR in his bedroom. By the time he was a sophomore in high school and his father had died, his computer was an obsolete embarrassment, a slow antique. His pool was spotted with black algae, the tiles around the edge were thick with white mineral deposits. The rest of the house, with its brown carpeting and long tan curtains, took on a tired feel that Merv came to hate.

Soon after he dropped out of the University of Arizona for the last time, Merv took a job selling pagers and made enough money to replace the tan curtains with venetian blinds and wooden shutters. He had special tinting put on his mother's bedroom windows so she could sleep in. The pager money had been good. He made almost four thousand that first month, but, after just six weeks, when he drove down Grant Road to check his client list at the office—which was just a double-wide trailer in a gravel lot behind a florist—there were no signs of a pager business, only an empty trailer, a few curls of adding machine tape on the floor.

Merv served the reheated enchiladas to his mother in front of the television and sat down beside her on the old couch. "We had over twelve hundred people at the park today," he told her. "And just two skinned knees and a few kids with dust in their eyes."

"They should pay you more," she said.

"They will," Merv said. "If we have more days like today." He wanted to ask his mother about her insomnia, about the two-hundred-dollar white-noise machine he had bought for her a few weeks earlier. But he didn't. He turned up the volume on the television and the two of them watched sitcoms until ten, when his mother went off to bed and Merv headed to the back porch for fresh air.

He heard the thumping bass as soon as he opened the sliding glass door. When he stepped outside, he could feel the planks under his feet vibrating. His dad's old metal tool box under the patio table rattled. Petey Vaccarino lived a few hundred yards across the arroyo, and from the sound of it, he and his white gangsta wannabe friends were having a party.

Last year, Petey had been a skater with Windex blue hair. Before that, a Deadhead in tie-dyes and Jesus sandals. And before that, a redneck who spat tobacco and listened to Merle Haggard and Kenny Rogers. These days, he drove his dented and scraped Nissan too fast on the curving streets of Rancho Sin Vacas, his car stereo blasting bullshit ghetto rap that didn't pertain to him or his privileged lifestyle. Last month, Merv had walked across the desert and talked to Petey about his loud music, and the kid had looked so vacant, so stupid, with wide zigzagging eyes. His mouth twitched out noises: vaguely comprehensible affected gangsta mumbles about the South Side, automatic weapons, bitches, blunts, a couple of *yos*. A few days later, Merv heard the thumping again.

Now he wondered if he should go over to the Vaccarinos', break up the party, send all the kids home. Maybe just call the police, let them deal with it. He worried that his mother could hear the bumping bass through her earplugs and the waves of white noise. He went back inside and slipped on his old hiking boots.

Ten or so shined and lowered Asian sedans crowded the Vaccarinos' gravel driveway, their mag wheels catching the moon and the glow of the yellow bug light from the porch. A few kids in ball caps and baggy shorts smoked cigarettes by a mass of prickly pear cacti. They eyed Merv coolly as he approached the front door. "You're stupit late, homey," one said. "The beer's almost gone." The kid wore a gold tooth sleeve. A tattoo, *Old School,* in gothic lettering, spanned his gaunt white chest.

"You know where Petey is?" Merv asked him.

"Inside."

Merv pushed through the front door, an antique carved Mexican church door, most likely bought from their husky neighbor, Hetta, who drove her Range Rover deep into Sonora, Mexico, to tiny secluded pueblos, and swindled villagers into selling her anything that looked old—ladders, wheelbarrows, hitches—and sold them to her rich friends in Tucson. She had called Merv once, invited him and his mother to a party where she displayed and sold her booty. He had told her he wasn't interested, and she told him the neighborhood association *needed* him to fix his roof and paint his mailbox. "Need?" Merv said, right before he hung up. She hadn't called since.

Through the smoke and milling people, he spotted Petey, who sat at the dining-room table with a few girls, a bunch of silver nitrous-oxide cartridges scattered in front of him like candy. Petey clutched a big marking pen in his fist. He had ink spots around his nostrils where he had sniffed too closely, and in the smoky haze, it looked a little like his nose was bleeding. Merv would have thought it was a bloody nose if he hadn't seen Petey with pen marks before.

"Petey!" Merv yelled. He kneeled next to Petey's chair and yelled again. "Could you and your friends turn it down?"

Petey mumbled nothing Merv could understand except, ". . . know what'm saying?"

But before Merv yelled again, the music was lowered. Merv looked across the room to the console, where a guy wearing a huge medallion smiled and flashed him a peace sign. Merv flashed him one back and walked home, breathing in the dry, sweet air of the arroyo.

"I HAVEN'T DONE ANYTHING SINCE I BY-MISTAKE PUSHED THOMAS DOWN the stairs," Kendra told her counselor, Franny.

Franny's voice was monotone, devoid of emotion. Her arms were flabby. A dainty antique watch cinched the blubber on her wrist. Kendra hated Franny's boring office and the office chair Franny made her sit in—it never adjusted right, always hurt her lower back. Kendra felt like she was perched up on display because Franny's chair was lower than hers. In Franny's trashcan: a few wrappers from the day's lunch—nothing else, never anything else. Today Franny had eaten at Burger King. And Franny's office always stunk like a candle shop unless onions or garlic overpowered the faux-floral odor, like they did now. The fluorescent light buzzed.

"Your mother mentioned that you pulled her hair pretty hard last week," Franny said. "Do you want to tell me about that?"

Kendra thought she could hear Franny's sticky lips separating with a sickening moist pop with every word she uttered.

"I was asleep," Kendra said, "and I was dreaming I was being attacked. When I woke up, I let go of her hair."

To hell with Franny today. Kendra would have rather been at the gym, doing squats, thinking about what she had discovered that morning, and what she should do about it.

After she had finished her run, the sun just peeking over the smooth mountains in the east, Kendra sat on the back porch, watching the sky turn from deep purple to pink to electric orange. She walked over to the pool, dipped her toes in the warm water, stood at the end of the diving board, bounced a little. A vague breeze spilled down from the mountains. The air was dry, but slightly cooler than normal, maybe eighty degrees. She sprawled flat on the diving board, face to the sky, and began to plan her day.

It was then that she had heard the rustling under the porch. When she was a kid, she had once discovered a rattlesnake under the porch, first heard its fake-sounding rattle, then, with a flashlight, seen its thickness and blandly colored scales. She had wanted to kill the snake herself, skin it, but Joyce called an exterminator after Thomas had told her about it, and Kendra was left only with the mild excitement of watching someone else, a humane animal relocator, trap the snake with a noose and drop it in a burlap sack.

"Aren't you going to kill it?" Kendra had asked him.

"Of course not," he said. "I'll free him down in the arroyo."

"That sucks," Kendra had said.

The guy looked at her confusedly. "Rattlesnakes keep the packrat population at a manageable level."

"You can't just kill this one snake?" Kendra asked.

"No," he said. "I can't."

"You could hold the bag up and I could hit it with a shovel."

"Snakes aren't evil," the man said. "I don't know what your problem is." And with that, he walked toward his van.

The rustling today was louder. Maybe a neighbor's cat or a coyote, or maybe a roadrunner. Kendra walked over to the porch, pushed away some thick cat's claw growing up the latticework, and peered into the shadows. No glowing eyes.

She crawled under the porch at that point, her knees hurting in the gravel and hard dirt, and soon found her hands in a pile of plastic bags about ten feet into the shadows.

At first, she had thought the plastic she felt was just trash that had somehow blown under the porch, but she quickly realized it was something more. Each bag, she could see in the weak light spilling in from behind her and from the cracks between the planks above her, contained a garment: a sock, a T-shirt, a pair of underpants, a jockstrap—mostly jockstraps. Each baggie had also been labeled in black pen, in Thomas's loopy writing. *Mike Celan, 12/6/00, 4:36 PM. David Sneed, 3/8/01, 11:53 AM. Douglas Dorst, 4/4/01, 12:25 PM* . . . Football players, a few basketball players. Kendra knew half the guys, trained with some of them at the gym. She had been in two classes with David Sneed, even had a crush on him first semester, until she heard him talking about some girl who had "great suckable tits but a face like a train wreck." Boring. Just another asshole.

"Your mother said your eyes were open," Franny said. "Do you remember pulling her hair?"

"I only remember stopping," Kendra lied. "Gene grabbed me."

"Are you concerned about pulling your mother's hair?"

Those disgusting moist pops again. Was it just lunch residue? Mayonnaise? Ketchup? Milk shake?

"You can't control what you dream," Kendra said. "And I didn't kick that woman's ass at the toy show. Plussing as which, she deserved it."

"Why?"

"She ripped off Joyce," Kendra said, "and I could have beat the shit out of her." Kendra knew then that she shouldn't have brought up the toy show. She knew Franny would hit her with hundreds of questions about it, so before she could start, Kendra said, "But I did what you said, and I thought about working out. I imagined I was running on top of Mount Lemmon. And it was sunny and cool at the same time, and there were butterflies and squirrels and other nice things up there." Like a douche commercial, Kendra thought.

"And how did you feel about not attacking the woman?"

"I felt good because I didn't get in trouble."

"How did you feel about the woman after you calmed down?"

"I felt like she was lucky," Kendra said. "Plus I felt like she knows not to rip off my mother anymore."

"How would you have felt if you had hurt her?"

"Like she wasn't lucky," Kendra said. "Like it was easy to hurt her."

"Would you have felt anything else?" Franny asked.

Kendra thought for a second. "I would have felt bad for hurting her," she lied. And she lied further: "I would have been disappointed for not controlling myself."

"How could you have avoided getting to the point where you wanted to hurt the woman?" Franny asked.

"I could have seen that she had ripped off Joyce and maybe told her that wasn't fair without saying I was going to kick her ass. And I maybe could have gone to the gym like I wanted to and not gone to the toy show in the first place but that would have made you and my mom pissed off at me for not being a part of my mom's life."

"How do you feel when you're at the toy shows with your mother?" Franny asked.

Kendra sighed. "How many more minutes are left?" she asked. She craned her neck to get a look at Franny's watch. "Why is your watch so small?"

Merv sucked in a deep breath when he saw Annie getting into her Jeep after work. He knew he should ask her out. He hadn't been on a date since the fall, hadn't had sex since then. Almost nine months. Back in September he had met a woman named Deena at Club Congress. She was adorable, with her worked body and blond bob. Even though she was twenty-six, she looked to be about seventeen. And the sex with her was a kick, aerobic. Merv loved how Deena enjoyed every moment she spent outside her cubicle at the huge HMO where she worked. She told Merv that she liked the fact that he didn't know exactly what an HMO was, and that he worked outside in the sun. After a few weeks, though, she started asking Merv about his goals, told him he should be more motivated. She went sort of psycho, and declared she wouldn't even think about supporting him, so don't even try. He told her she was delusional and paranoid, and that maybe she should think about seeing a psychiatrist. She left hateful messages on his answering machine for a week, then she stopped.

The monastic nine months since Deena seemed to sneak up on him, and when he realized it that morning, he told himself he had to ask Annie out. He wasn't bothered so much by the lack of sex as he was with the feelings of social ineptitude, knowing he hadn't met anyone new, gone anywhere different, in too long.

He jogged across the parking lot and knocked on the hood of Annie's Jeep. "Hey," he said.

"Hey, Merv."

"How's it going?"

Annie pushed her sunglasses up on her head. "Fine," she said. "But you know that because you asked me the same thing about five minutes ago when I was punching out."

"Sorry," Merv said.

"That's okay." She started her Jeep. "See you."

"Look," Merv said. "Want to go for beers at City Grille or something?"

Annie looked at her watch. A big black digital watch. Her arms were tan, the color of butterscotch. "I smell like chlorine and co-conut sunscreen and my hair is dirty, but okay, I'll meet you there in ten minutes." She tilted her head forward, and her glasses fell to her nose.

"Cool," Merv said.

The waiters and waitresses at City Grille wore denim shirts, khakis, and K-Swiss tennis shoes—a boring mid-'80s preppy look that recalled to Merv the way high school kids dressed when he was in elementary school. Whenever Merv walked into the place and was seated or waited on, the waitstaff gave him the impression that he had just interrupted something private and important, like he was disturbing their clique. But the City Grille was close to Splash World. Mostly innocuous and neutral if you concentrated on your drinking and ignored the employees.

Today he ordered a beer at the bar before the preoccupied hostess led him to his seat. He sat at a thick wooden table and sipped his bottle of Bud until Annie showed up.

Annie had pulled a BOWDOIN SWIMMING T-shirt and jogging shorts over her swimsuit. As she sat across from Merv, she said, "I can only have like two, because I have to meet my parents for dinner at that place downtown near the police station."

"Cushing Street?"

"Yeah."

"What do you want to drink?" Merv said. He reached for his wallet in his back pocket, ripped the Velcro, checked to see how much cash he had. Thirty-seven. More than he had thought.

"Same as you," she said. "Unless they card me. Then, I'll have a Coke."

"How old are you?" he asked.

"Twenty," she said, grabbing his wallet from his hand. "Let's see your I.D." She pulled out his driver's license. "Your photo's pretty good except the shadow makes it look like you have a mullet." She looked down at his license again. "You're thirty!" she yelled. "Oh, my God! I thought you were my age."

"I'm thirty," he said.

"So, you're done with college?" she asked.

"In a sense."

"You look much younger."

No one asked Annie if she had an I.D., and the two of them had a few beers. Annie talked. She told Merv about college in Maine, how they had lobster in the cafeteria, how the snowdrifts were ten feet high in March. She snowshoed and cross-country skied. Annie was headed to Australia for a semester in January. She bragged about duping her dean into letting her go. She had told the dean about fish and other sea life indigenous to Australia's eastern shores, fish and other creatures she just made up. "Beaked fish," she said to Merv. "I told him I really wanted to study this specific species of beaked fish that peck open clams to eat, and he bought it. Next thing I know, all the papers are signed, and I'm calling my mom to have her start shopping for plane tickets on the Internet."

Merv decided he had nothing to talk about. He had known she was younger—had guessed maybe twenty-two—and he had thought she knew his age. He didn't think she'd react like she had. Most people at the water park knew his age, especially since his birthday fiasco had been so recent. Besides, there were three people older than Merv working at the park, and Merv was their manager. He imagined Annie thought he was a loser now. She was studying at her perfect little New England college for smart rich kids, and he was a hapless bum who managed a water park—at age thirty—in Tucson, Arizona. At least she didn't know he lived at home with his mother. Unless someone at work had told her.

He listened to her talk about the future: graduate school in English or history at "some sunny, but good university," then law school at the best one she could get into regardless of its location and weather. "I have friends who are already beating themselves up in LSAT courses, so I figure I'll chill in some bullshit master's program for a few years and prepare for the LSAT casually." She squinted at Merv. "The LSAT is the standardized test you take to get into law school."

"I know that," Merv said.

Friday, June 15, 2001

Warmer

High 102 / Low 69

Clear

KENDRA HAD SLEPT IN AN EXTRA HALF AN HOUR AND DIDN'T MAKE IT OUT to the hill until nearly six. Almost too hot. It had cracked 100 the day before, and the old weatherman on Channel Four, the guy who Joyce had said was the most accurate but heard was a pervert, had said today would be hotter by a few degrees. Still, she had to do her hills.

She had watched a Miss Fitness America competition on ESPN the afternoon before. Those chicks were buff and aerobically fit, but most were ugly: that sickening man-face phenomenon from too many protein shakes and vitamin injections, and too many hours in the tanning booth. Like creepy rubber Halloween masks. Kendra decided that the day she looked in the mirror and saw a man face, she'd quit lifting. She'd stopped with the heavy stuff last year, and concentrated on tone rather than size. Her shoulders weren't so macho, and people—even girls at school who had never deigned to talk to Kendra—told her that they wished they had her body.

But the Miss Fitness America contestants were aerobically fit, most of them more so than Kendra, and that pissed her off. Some had nasty fake tits that rested up near their shoulders and barely moved when the women hopped around on stage or turned cartwheels. But even the fake-titted chicks were aerobically fit and seemed to be full of an enthusiasm that Kendra lacked.

Mrs. Hunter was out today, standing in the desert by the side of the road in the shade two mesquite trees, clutching a toaster, an iron, and a small portable heater. On her way up the hill, Kendra waved at her. No response. Not even a nod. On her way down, Kendra looked over, and Mrs. Hunter was still there.

On her fifth time up the hill, as her quads were starting to burn, Kendra slowed as she passed Mrs. Hunter, who was still standing there, looking at nothing, rocking lightly, tightly clutching the small appliances into her terry-cloth robe. Bare pink ankles and big, white walking shoes—no more Keds. "Hey," Kendra said to her, but she didn't respond.

Something more than usual was wrong with Mrs. Hunter today, and this annoyed Kendra. She'd have to suspend her workout and escort the psycho home or maybe just go home herself and tell Joyce. If she didn't, Mrs. Hunter could get dehydrated, or some freak could drive by and kidnap her and stab her or strangle her with the electrical cords from the small appliances she was carrying and leave her in the desert for the coyotes to eat. On her way down the hill, Kendra stopped and grabbed Mrs. Hunter's elbow.

"We need to get you home," she huffed. "Come on."

Mrs. Hunter didn't resist, just stared confusedly into Kendra's eyes. The two women walked slowly up the hill, Kendra trying unsuccessfully to make idle conversation, and around the corner into the white morning sun. Kendra carried the iron; Mrs. Hunter held on to her heater and toaster.

The Hunters' front door was locked. Kendra thought about just ringing the doorbell and leaving Mrs. Hunter on the front step, but she wasn't sure if Mrs. Hunter's loser son was around or not, and Mrs. Hunter could just as well become dehydrated and die right in front of her own house as she could have back on the side of the road. So she rang the doorbell about twenty times and pounded on the door until Merv opened it.

"What the hell?" he said. His plaid boxer shorts rested a little low on his hips and his hair was mussed.

"I found your mom by the side of the road, and she's like a

zombie," Kendra said. "Plussing as which, she doesn't talk. And she's carrying all these." She handed Merv the iron.

"What?" He hitched up his boxers.

"You should make her drink or something," Kendra said. "I got out there late this morning. She was probably out there all night."

Mrs. Hunter stared wide-eyed at the doorjamb. Kendra and Merv led her inside and sat her on the couch. She looked at the floor between her feet, still held the toaster and the portable heater.

"Thanks for bringing her home," Merv said to Kendra. "You don't have to stay, though. If you're working out."

"I know about your mother," Kendra said. "I know she's fucked-up and can't ever sleep."

"She's not fucked-up."

"I meant fucked in the head," Kendra said.

"She's not fucked in the head."

"Ask her," Kendra said. "She won't hear you."

"Feel free to leave," Merv said, sitting next to his mother, gently prying the appliances from her grasp, and setting them on the floor. "Like, now."

"I'm not being mean," Kendra said. "Plus, I'm nice to your mother. I saved her ass this morning. She could have dehydrated or been murdered."

"Don't be so dramatic," Merv said. "I'll call her doctor at nine."

"You should call her doctor now. She can't even talk. And you should get her a glass of water."

Mrs. Hunter sighed. Both Merv and Kendra looked at her, but she only continued to stare at the floor.

"I'll leave," Kendra said, "when I see her drink some water." She sat on the floor next to the appliances, at Mrs. Hunter's feet.

"Who the hell do you think you are?" Merv said on his way to the kitchen.

Kendra spoke loudly so Merv could hear: "I see her, like, at least once a week, and I sort of know her."

Merv returned to the room with a plastic tumbler of water. He held it to his mother's mouth, but she didn't drink any. She did lick her lips.

"This is pathetic," Merv said.

It wasn't his mother's zombielike state or insomniac wandering that bothered Merv; it was the fact that she had brought the toaster, iron, and portable heater. When he was a teenager, he had first noticed his mother's obsession with anything that heated up. He'd find the toaster unplugged, its electrical cord taped to the countertop, like if it weren't taped down, it would plug itself back in. All the knobs for the stove were stored in a plastic Baggie in a drawer in the family room. An index card where Merv's mother kept track of the stove was taped on the refrigerator: *January 22—off, off, off, off, off; March 3—off, off, off, off, off. . . .* After Merv's father had died, he noticed his mother began to take the smaller appliances with her everywhere, filling the trunk of her car every time she went out. But she had stopped, Merv had thought, about six or seven years ago.

"Try again," Kendra said. She admired Merv's shoulders. He had a good frame. A few more hours per week in the gym would do the trick. He had the beginnings of some musculature, and he had a tan. Not much body hair to shave. "Plus," Kendra said, "if you worked your lats even a little you'd see results quick."

"What the hell are you talking about?" Merv said.

Merv held the cup to his mother's lips again. She began to sip meekly. But Kendra's presence suddenly made him nervous, and he found it difficult to hold the cup still. He felt the agitation at the bottom of his spine and behind his ears—a warm, sharp tingle.

Merv looked at Kendra. "You can leave now," he said.

"Do you even know what lats are?" Kendra asked.

"I don't care," Merv said.

"You work at Splash World."

"So?"

"Could you get me in for free?" Kendra asked.

"If I wanted to."

* * *

Kendra and Thomas sat on the porch later that night. Thomas sipped a Mexican beer, Kendra drank Gatorade. Even though the sun had set hours earlier, it was still 98 degrees; the heat was thick and oppressive. The two of them had gone outside to escape Hetta, their loud neighbor who had come over to try to sell some Navajo blankets to their mother. Hetta said the same thing to Kendra every time she saw her: "You have bigger muscles than my son Billy, and he plays football for NAU!"

Back in February, Kendra had told Hetta that she needed to lose some weight. "Excuse me?" Hetta had said. They had bumped into each other in the supermarket, in the cereal aisle. "You're fat," Kendra said, the words just rolling from her tongue, "and look at all that crap in your cart." Twenty or so frozen dinners—not even diet ones—doughnuts, a few boxes of sugary kids' cereal, several pints of premium ice cream, a gallon of whole milk, bacon, a canned ham. Hetta didn't respond; she only took a deep breath and pushed her cart past Kendra. But the next day, when Kendra returned home from school, Joyce informed her that she had a special counseling session scheduled with Franny to discuss what she had said to Hetta in the supermarket. With the help of Franny, Kendra composed an apology:

Dear Hetta, I'm so sorry I called you fat in Safeway the other night. I need to learn that not everyone is into fitness like me. Some people may enjoy different foods than me. You have the right to eat whatever you want. I hope you forgive my rudeness. Sincerely, Kendra Lumm.

Now, like tonight, Kendra just avoided Hetta. One hello and a phony embarrassed laugh when Hetta complimented her physique, and that was it. Kendra also loathed Hetta because she always told Thomas that he looked wan, and that he should think about taking up an organized sport like her sons did when they were in high school. Tonight, Thomas had reminded Hetta that he had just graduated from high school.

"Congratulations," Hetta had said. "Would you like to look at a few rugs for your dorm room?"

The moon was full, bathing the arroyo in silver light. Kendra and Thomas watched three skinny guys on small BMX bikes riding around the Vaccarinos' driveway. "They're meth-heads," Thomas told Kendra. "I think they're like thirty or forty years old and they spend all their money on crystal so they can't afford cars and have to ride bikes."

"That's stupid," Kendra said. "That's a lie."

"I swear to God. They have purple gums and they're all skinny and they're always scratching themselves. I see them all over town. I saw them down near the university the other day."

"Why would they ride those little bikes?" Kendra said.

"I don't know. They probably stole them."

The Vaccarinos' garage door opened slowly, and light poured over the meth-heads, catching the shinier parts of their bicycles. From two hundred yards or so, Kendra could see that the guys were emaciated. Knobby knees and elbows. Pale. Scabbed.

"You think they rode those bikes all the way up here?" Kendra asked.

"I told you I've seen them all over town," Thomas said.

Petey walked out of the garage. He greeted the tallest one, a straggly-haired guy, with a four-phased handshake that ended with a knock of fists. The guys followed Petey into the garage, pushing their little bikes, and the garage door closed.

"Do you still fuck around with Petey?" Thomas asked Kendra. He finished his beer, crunched the can.

"I haven't in a while," Kendra said. "He's always high, and I'm too busy."

She thought of the jockstrap collection under the porch they were sitting on. It had been clear that Thomas had worked hard on it, diligently stealing the sweaty gym clothes and marking each bag. Tomorrow, when Thomas wasn't around,

Kendra would read all the dates on the Baggies and see how long Thomas has been doing it.

"Being as which," she said, "it's none of your business."

"Petey's an idiot," Thomas said. "He spent most of his own party barfing in his mom's bathtub."

"Did you go?"

"No."

"Then how do you know?"

"Brooke told me."

"You shouldn't *even* talk to her," Kendra said. "Plussing, she's got genital warts like cauliflower, so don't be messing around with her ass."

"You don't even know her," Thomas said. "She's all scared that you'll kick her ass; that's why she acts all tough around you."

"I would kick her ass," Kendra said.

"She's cool," Thomas said.

"Some guy thought she was the substitute in math and asked her to sign a hall pass and she got all pissed and started to cry."

"So?"

"She does look like a substitute," Kendra said, "like she's gotten too much sun and not enough sleep."

"I hardly ever say shit about Petey," Thomas said. "I never said shit about Miguel."

"Miguel was cool," Kendra said. "I know Petey's an asshole."

"You have another boyfriend?"

"Petey's never been my boyfriend, so how could I have another one?" Kendra said. "Plussing as which, I might like a few guys at the gym."

A lie. Kendra knew the guys at the gym were too into themselves and envious of her physique, or gay, or both. Most were both.

When Merv spotted the BMX meth-heads on the Vaccarinos' driveway, he recognized them immediately, and he was about to call the police, when Petey emerged from the garage and greeted them. Merv had seen the meth-heads often in the parking lot at Splash World. They'd bump up against cars until they set off a chorus of alarms, then they'd pedal away. They were rumored to live in drainage tunnels under Tucson Mall.

He had once caught up with them out there in the lot, told them to leave. They had been riding their little bikes around in circles on the hot asphalt, laughing stupidly, and they hadn't noticed Merv until he was right next to them. They hadn't touched any cars that day. One guy was drooling: a glistening stream working its way down his emaciated and sunburned chest. The tallest guy, the one Petey had greeted so eagerly tonight, wore a spiked dog collar around his thin pink neck and was missing a few teeth.

His gums looked gray when he stopped pedaling, straddled his bike, and said, "We're not doing anything. Just riding around, watching the girls pick their bathing suits from their butts when they get to the bottom of that slide." He looked to the Lemon Drop, a tall yellow slide, and whistled through his cracked, rotten teeth.

"I'm going to have to ask you to leave," Merv said.

The two other guys stopped riding. "Why?" the tallest guy said.

"You're loitering," Merv said. "I'm going to have to ask you to leave." He thought he should have called a few security guys to come with him out to the parking lot. This was dumb. A waste of his lunch break.

"You don't *have* to do anything," the guy said. He rolled closer to Merv. "You don't *have* to ask us to leave."

Merv could smell him—or them—sharp, caustic, like concentrated urine or rotten flowers. The heat was burning through the soles of his river sandals, and he was eager to get some food in him and get back to his place on top of the Kamikaze.

"That's my job," Merv said. His throat bunched, and his voice cracked a little. "Now, please leave."

"Okay, Mr. Tan-Guy-Lifeguard-Guy," the tallest one said, feigning submission to Merv's authority.

They pedaled away, laughing.

Next time, Merv decided, he'd let a few of the security guys deal with them. That was their job, and they were good at intimidation.

The security team Merv had hired was great. Seven muscular ex-football skull-busters from the U of A who knew their job at Splash World was easy and paid well, so they didn't screw it up. They acted professional as they escorted surly teens off the premises, or busted underage drinkers in the parking lot. The seven of them wore their hair in crewcuts and hid their eyes behind identical wrap-around sunglasses. They were permitted to dress as they wanted, but they chose to dress alike, in uniforms like the downtown bicycle cops: blue shorts, shirts, and ball caps, each emblazoned with the words SECURITY TEAM. On their feet, they wore river sandals like Merv's. They had developed their own schedule for maximum efficiency, changing posts on the hour, keeping in constant check via radios clipped to their shirts. The troublemakers gravitated to the Kamikaze, and it was easy to deal with them from up there—Merv would radio down to security, describe the offending kid, and be done with it.

Now Merv wondered if Mrs. Vaccarino, Petey's mother, was ever home. He knew she worked for the school district or the electric company or something vaguely governmental downtown. Maybe she was home, and just didn't give a shit who Petey brought into the house. She had probably stopped caring a long time ago.

Merv pulled a lounge chair over to the edge of the pool deck and watched the Vaccarinos' house, waited for the meth-heads to leave. How did they get past the gate at the entrance to Rancho Sin Vacas, anyway? Brian would have never allowed them to pass. Probably just cut through the desert, or maybe Brian was asleep, dozing with his head under a magazine like Merv had seen before.

Merv's mother had fallen asleep a few hours earlier, at nine.

Merv had called her doctor right after Kendra left that morning, told him about his mother's weird catatonic state, about her carrying the toaster, iron, and portable heater with her on her desert trudge. Dr. Grossman prescribed Ambien, only enough for a few days, something to break the cycle of insomnia. He told Merv to give her two pills at 8:30 P.M.—no earlier. She wasn't supposed to sleep at all until the sun went down, and if she did, Merv was instructed to wake her at 8:30 to give her the pills. She hadn't slept during the day, though. She sat in the family room and watched television. Merv called Splash World, told them he wasn't coming in, and sat with his mother for hours, making her drink water and later, milk. She wouldn't eat anything, not even ice cream or pudding.

During *Judge Judy*, as the slutty Asian plaintiff was being scolded for speaking out of turn, Merv's mother began to weep and rock her head from side to side, like a spring-necked toy. Merv didn't know what to do. He wet a towel and held it to her forehead. She stopped rocking, but continued to cry. He wanted to give her the Ambien and let her sleep, but he followed the doctor's orders and held out until 8:30.

Merv continued to watch the Vaccarinos' house, could see shadows in the windows, but he dozed off before the meth-heads left.

When he woke at three, wet with sweat, he forgot why he was out there on the pool deck, and stumbled up to his room to sleep.

Tuesday, June 19, 2001

Warm

High 107 / Low 70

Clear

AFTER HER RUN AND MORNING NAP, KENDRA WATCHED TELEVISION, sipped a tart protein drink, snacked on a few rice cakes. The endorphins had brought her to a mood of happy anticipation, made her a little restless. Thomas was probably still asleep, and she had already finished half of her workout. Maybe she could convince him to do something today—like leave the house. They could go to the mall or to a movie. They could go ice-skating, or ride the fake waves at Splash World.

The first summer Splash World had opened, five or six years earlier, Joyce had bought her and Thomas season passes. They knew how to ride all the slides, where to catch the biggest waves, what to avoid in the snack bar. They took the public bus—the SunTran—to the park almost every morning, wearing only their swimsuits and ninety-nine-cent rubber flip-flops from the drug store. Kendra and Thomas were the same height as each other then, and they were both dark brown by the middle of June. They rode the slides together on the same mats or rafts. They made up mean secret code names for the other regulars at the park. One of the lifeguards was "Poo Eyes"; a girl from school, Bettina something, was "Devil Whore Dog." At the end of the summer, Thomas won a body-surfing competition. That was the last summer Thomas did anything other than watch TV and become weaker.

But when Thomas came down today, he was dressed, wearing long Hawaiian print surf shorts and a tight blue T-shirt. His short hair was styled with mousse—carefully mussed in the front.

"Where are you going?" Kendra asked him. She used the remote to turn down the television.

"None of your business," he said.

She stood and chased him, pinned him against the wall in the kitchen, began to tickle him. His soft, doughy stomach, and those fragile ribs.

"Tell me," she said. "Tell me where you're going."

Thomas laughed desperately. "Stop," he said. "Stop!" His breath was minty.

Kendra peeled up his shirt, wiggled her fingers into his squishy belly, felt for his navel, watched his thin muscles quiver. "Where?" she said. "With who?"

"The mall," Thomas said. "With Brooke."

Kendra stopped tickling him and took a step back. She stared at him. "That's all you had to say."

"I almost wet my pants," Thomas said between breaths. "You're not pissed about Brooke?" he asked, patting his hair. "I thought you'd still be at the gym."

"I'm not pissed," Kendra said. "Plussing as which, I'll be nice to her if she's not a total bitch to me."

"I don't trust you," Thomas said. "I'll wait for Brooke on the front steps."

Kendra watched him fix his hair in the hall mirror. Then she retired to her room, stretched out on her new Navajo rug, and began to read an article about supersets.

A few minutes later, Thomas and Brooke stood at her door. Brooke wore a mini Hello Kitty T-shirt with short shorts—an outfit that was only vaguely cool five or six summers ago, Kendra thought.

"I don't mean to bother you or anything, and I won't dare step into your room," Brooke said, "but there's something you should know."

"Petey's missing," Thomas said. "For like three or four days."

"Oh," Kendra said. She adjusted the strap of her new sports bra. "I'm reading."

"This is serious," Brooke said. "Even his mom doesn't know where he is."

"He's probably in Phoenix sniffing pens and shoplifting with his homies," Kendra said.

"The cops might call you," Brooke said. There was desperation in her voice that Kendra didn't recognize. Brooke had lost some weight. In her tired nineties Spice Girls slut shorts, her legs actually looked toned. Kendra told her so.

"Your boyfriend is missing, and all you can do is evaluate my legs?"

"He's not my boyfriend," Kendra said. "Not even close."

"How can you be such a bitch?" Brooke asked. "Petey could be like kidnapped or injured or something."

"Don't be so dramatic," Kendra said. "Plus, I can be a bitch, but I told Thomas I'd be nice to your sorry ass."

"Thanks, Kendra," Thomas said, without a hint of sarcasm.

"You guys can leave now," Kendra said. "Have fun on your date. I need to finish this article."

"What if Petey is dead or something?" Brooke said.

"Why do you even care about Petey?" Kendra said. "Plussing as how, you seem to be dating my brother."

"*Plussing as how* you speak fucked-up ignorant grammar," Brooke said. "And we're not dating."

"We're not?" Thomas asked.

"Come on," Brooke said, and the two of them left.

"Have fun on your date," Kendra called after them.

As if Petey was someone to be concerned about. As if she'd let her brain be filled up with Petey. Kendra mostly worried about Thomas. Even before she found the jockstraps and gym clothes, she knew he was weird. He never did anything except watch television. Never really had any friends until this spring when he started to hang out with Brooke, the freak. Kendra didn't care if Thomas was gay. She just wanted him to do something, any-thing, which is why when she thought about the jockstrap collection, she was oddly proud of Thomas, imagining him skulking around the locker room, waiting for just the right moment to snatch what he wanted. He was going away to college in the fall, all the way to New York. He could be full-on gay there, and nobody at home would know. Or he could start fresh and be whatever he wanted. At least he was leaving the house today. At least he was dressed in something more than his underpants.

If Franny were a cool counselor, Kendra could ask her about Thomas. They could discuss Thomas. But Franny wasn't cool. Franny would just ask how Thomas's collection of used jockstraps made Kendra feel. "They make me feel like ripping your ugly hair out and stomping on your dumb little watch, bitch," Kendra whispered. She flung the muscle magazine across her room.

Merv looked out over Splash World from his spot atop the Kamikaze. It was the highest, the busiest slide. The sun today seemed to be boring through the thick layers of sunscreen on Merv's shoulders, but the heat felt good, reminded Merv that he wasn't sitting in a cubicle under fluorescent lights, breathing processed air, cursing the guy next to him for getting the best covered parking spot—like he imagined Rusty and Jason to be doing. He gazed over at the Santa Catalina Mountains, leached of their green by the sun, but still impressive, mighty, the end of the Rockies, still enough for Merv to admire.

As the sliders plummeted down the Kamikaze, Merv looked over to the wave pool. Annie and Jeff and Ted were the lifeguards on duty. Jeff and Ted seemed to be arbitrating an argument between two little kids. Annie was on top of her chair. The pool was crowded, dotted with the bright red rafts that Splash World rented out so people could ride the manmade waves. It was mesmerizing to watch the rafts, a grid of red rectangles, rippling in unison when the series of five waves started. Five waves, the third always the biggest, then a two minute break, five waves, two minute break, five waves . . . Every once in a while, he'd see someone really catch the third wave, plow through the crowds to the shore of trucked-in sand like a real surfer.

Merv had found a group of small appliances on the front porch this morning. After the neighbor fitness girl helped his mother home last week, Merv sort of knew it was coming. The coffee maker was among the toaster, portable heater, and iron, lined up neatly on the second step, on display. His mother had been to work two days in a row, had even been sleeping well— with the help of the medication. She seemed much happier. More energetic. So Merv was disappointed when he saw the appliances. He'd ask his mother about them tonight, when she returned from work. He knew what she'd say, though. Word for word, he knew what she'd say: "I worry about fire, Merv. This is how I don't worry. This is how I can go on."

A kid pulled up on his mat and caught a good amount of air on the Kamikaze. Merv stood and blew his whistle. Yelled down at the kid: "I saw that! Once more, and you're out!"

The kid, a skinny sunburned tow-head, dropped his baggy surf trunks and mooned his little white ass at Merv. "Kiss it!" he yelled up to Merv. "Kiss my ass!"

Merv laughed, but clicked on his walkie-talkie. "Security. Security. Male Caucasian, age eleven or twelve, blond hair, red and blue flowered long swimsuit, walking from Kamikaze along sidewalk toward Lemon Drop. Indecent exposure."

"Ten-four."

"Ten-four. On it."

"Ten-four"

"Ten-four. In pursuit."

Merv watched the security team, the four who were working that day, descend upon the boy. When they reached the boy, seconds after Merv alerted them, the boy didn't put up a fight, just walked calmly with them toward the front gate, his head down. "That's him," Merv said into his walkie-talkie. It looked funny: four hulking muscleheads escorting a skinny prepubescent kid like that.

"Ten-four."

Merv felt like an asshole. The kid had shown that he had balls to pull up on his mat and catch that much air, and he had more balls to moon Merv. More balls than Merv had ever had. Merv had never even come close to having balls like that. Once, though, when Merv was sixteen or seventeen and drunk on stolen Coors, he and his buddies had spent a few hours lapping the Empress Theater and the other porno places on Speedway Boulevard, screaming "Pervert!" from their slowed cars at men sheepishly running to their cars in the parking lots. Big deal. No balls.

Every once in a while, since he quit college for good, Merv found himself curious about what went on inside those places on Speedway Boulevard. Once, he even pulled into the parking lot, but his fears and an odd guilt overpowered his horniness and he went home.

Now, as the sliders filed past Merv, and he warned each of them not to pull up their mats, he noticed something yellow in the far cove of the wave pool. Maybe nothing—a wrapper. A potato chip bag or something. Just floating there. It was gone, then back again. Hidden in the sun's sparkling glare.

When he looked at it with his binoculars, and saw that it was a yellow swimsuit, a kid floating there, nobody around him, just bobbing in the mild waves of the cove, Merv jumped from his chair.

He blew his whistle twice and yelled, "Kamikaze closed!" before he pulled back on the lever and stopped the flow of water that kept the slide slick. He grabbed a mat from a kid and rode the slide himself, experiencing that light feeling in his stomach that never failed to frighten him, all the while craning his neck to watch the yellow swimsuit over in the cove.

At the bottom of the slide, he nearly slipped, as he began to sprint toward the wave pool. "Call Nine-one-one!" he yelled at George, the guy who collected and handed out mats to Kamikaze riders. "Call Nine-one-one!"

As he ran across the sidewalks and the lawn before the wave

pool, Merv blew his whistle and shoved a few people out of the way. The lifeguards at the wave pool began to blow their whistles, too, so most of the people enjoying the wave pool started to trudge toward the shore, making Merv's access to the floating boy across the pool more difficult. "Move, move!" he yelled, pushing through the confused mass of people in the warm water, cursing himself for not having run around the perimeter instead. "Move!"

When he finally reached the cove, he couldn't see the boy. He looked all around, and finally dived under, his eyes burning in the highly chlorinated murky water. No yellow swimsuit. Up for air, another look around, then down again. This time, he spotted the yellow through the cloudiness, over near the edge, and with his lungs burning for oxygen, Merv swam over. The boy's shape appeared, fuzzy, muted and gray, like the reception of a distant Mexican television station. He grabbed the boy's arm and swam up for air.

The boy's skin was cool. Merv held the boy's head above the water and kicked over to the side where Annie was waiting. She hoisted the limp boy from the water and laid him on the bright green grass.

Merv climbed out, and yelled at Annie who was blowing quick breaths into the boy's mouth: "What the hell! Get out of the way!"

Merv pushed Annie, who toppled over, and lifted the boy. Sirens blared in the distance. Merv felt the boy's little ribs, and measured down from his sternum. He administered the Heimlich maneuver, the boy's gut feeling like a jellyfish, until finally, the boy coughed out what seemed like gallons of water and puke, ropes of mucus hanging from his mouth.

At this point, the paramedics arrived. They were sprinting toward Merv and the boy, flanked by a few of the security officers. Merv handed over the boy. A paramedic laid the boy on the grass, listened for breathing, and began CPR.

Merv stepped back. Looked around. Everything was too bright, overexposed. The grass almost glowed. The giant Lemon

Drop loomed in the background, beaming yellow. The by-standers' swimsuits melted and swirled together in an ugly pal-let. He sat down and gripped the warm moist grass.

Merv saw that the boy was breathing. An oxygen mask was strapped to the boy's face, and they were carrying him away on a stretcher. The crowd cheered. A wave of exhaustion washed through Merv. He wanted to sleep, to curl up in the grass and sleep under the beating sun. And for a moment, he was asleep, dreaming, crawling through a sickening funhouse at a carnival, dragging his dead legs as some faceless evil thing chased him through tilted rooms and mirrored mazes . . .

Annie woke him a second later: "What the hell!" she yelled.

"What?" Merv said, thinking he might puke.

"You shoved me hard!"

"Our policy is Heimlich first," Merv said. He stood, still dizzy. He brushed the grass from his butt. "You knew that."

"Why were you watching the wave pool, anyway?" she said.

"What?" Merv said, incredulous.

Annie's face was purple. "You don't trust us? You think I don't know the procedure?"

"What the hell is your problem?" Merv said. "The kid was drowning. I ran over here and saved him. Where the hell were you? Why the hell are you yelling at me? Because *you* weren't doing *your* job?" Merv started to walk away from her, felt the mud under the grass suck his river sandals. "You're not making any sense, Annie," he added, not looking at her.

"You think I don't know the procedure?" Annie said. "I know the procedure."

Merv turned and faced her again. "You're not making sense. You started CPR before expelling the water with the Heimlich."

"I know the procedure!" she yelled. "I know the procedure!"

Someone in the crowd yelled, "Bitch!"

"You're fired as of right now for so many reasons," Merv told her. He looked at his watch. "As of two fifty-three P.M. on June nineteenth, you no longer work here."

A few people in the crowd clapped, one guy cheered, yelled to

Merv that he was *the man.* Someone had rolled Raymond over to the scene. With shaky legs, Merv walked over to him.

"Raymond, do you ever have days like this?"

"I used to," Raymond said. "But I was never a hero."

Merv dreaded the paperwork.

KENDRA RECOGNIZED THE COP FROM THE WEIGHT ROOM AT THE RACQUET Club. He was one of the few guys who worked his legs. Most of the guys there only worked their torsos and walked on skinny chicken bones. This guy's quads, the way they filled his jeans as he stood in the kitchen, impressed her. He had introduced himself to Kendra and her mother as Detective Honig.

"You don't seem upset," Detective Honig said to Kendra.

The two of them sat at the kitchen table, joined by Joyce, who had brought over a glass of water for the detective.

"I'm not," Kendra said.

"Was he your boyfriend?" He took a sip of water.

"Not in a while," Kendra said. "Not ever, really."

Detective Honig stared at Kendra.

Kendra stared back. He looked pretty young. Smooth skin. No wrinkles. No gray hair, only light brown, cropped close.

"I haven't seen Petey over here in ages," Joyce said. "He used to come over all the time."

"You no longer like him?" Detective Honig asked Kendra.

"I don't hate him," Kendra said. "I'm sort of sick of him."

"Why?" he asked, jotting in his pad.

"I hate his music and I hate the smell of Magic Markers, and I hate Brooke Luter, who always hangs out with him."

"What music?" he asked.

"That pounding tired gangsta crap," Kendra said.

"She's right," Joyce added. "I hear it thumping from his house and car almost every day. Not recently, though."

A loud thud startled Kendra.

Joyce gasped.

Kendra turned around to see a small black bird through the sliding-glass door, flapping in circles on the back porch. It had flown into the glass.

"You should get one of those stickers to put on that door," Detective Honig said. "It looks like a bird silhouette, and it prevents them from flying into it."

"We need to kill it," Kendra said. "It's suffering." The squawks were shrill and pathetic. Kendra felt them in her gut.

"Don't," Joyce said, but Kendra had already jumped up and slid the door open.

Kendra stepped into the wall of heat.

The injured cactus wren peeped and squawked at Kendra. One of its wings was oddly extended, bent looking.

Kendra stomped the bird's head with her running shoe. A wet pop.

Joyce gasped again. "Kendra! Kendra, that's disgusting!" A cigarette, the first one Kendra had seen in a while, dangled from Joyce's lips.

Keeping her foot in place, Kendra looked over at Joyce and Detective Honig. "Get me some paper towels and a garbage bag," she said. The bird had stopped moving, and a small pool of blood bloomed from under Kendra's shoe, maybe staining the back porch, maybe seeping through the cracks and dripping onto Thomas's jockstrap collection. She tried hard to think about something other than the poor bird, looked out into the desert that separated her house from Petey's. Several birds were pecking at fallen fruit scattered at the base of a tall, many-armed saguaro cactus.

"The BMX meth-heads," Kendra said to Detective Honig, who now stood in the doorway. "Last week or the week before, the BMX meth-heads were at his house."

"Who?"

"Plussing as which, Thomas knows about them."

"What?" Detective Honig said. He chugged his water and jingled the ice cubes in the glass.

"My brother told me about them," Kendra said. "We saw them in Petey's driveway."

"Who are they?"

"Come out here and shut the door," Kendra said to him. "You're wasting the air conditioning."

But Joyce was already guiding him out, closing the door behind them both, a big wad of paper towel in her hand, smoke leaking from her nostrils. "How are you going to clean that up?" she asked Kendra.

"I'll scoop it with the paper towel, then I'll spray the blood off the porch with the hose," Kendra said. "Duh."

"I think it might be better if Kendra and I spoke alone," Detective Honig said to Joyce. "Is that okay?"

"Oh," Joyce said. "That's fine." She passed him the paper towel.

"Thanks," Detective Honig said, handing her the glass of ice cubes.

Joyce stepped back inside and shut the door. She took the cigarette from her lips, mouthed and gesticulated, Okay? to Kendra.

Kendra nodded.

"Kendra," Detective Honig said, "you don't seem that concerned about Petey. Should I be concerned? Am I wasting my time?"

"If that's your job," Kendra said.

"Did you and Petey fight recently?"

"We never fight," Kendra said.

"Did he fight with his mother?"

"I doubt it," Kendra said.

"Why?"

"I've never seen him even talk with his mom."

"Petey's mother described him as . . ." He flipped through his pad, ". . . as five-ten, about a hundred and fifty pounds. Is that right?"

"No," Kendra said, her foot still firmly pressed on the smashed bird. "More like five-eight, a hundred and fifteen pounds."

"Kendra," Detective Honig said, "why would you even hang out with Petey?"

Kendra thought for a moment. "We've been friends since we were little. Plussing as which, his birthday is one day after mine."

"I've written down Brooke Luter. Are there any other people I should talk to? Should I talk to your brother Thomas?"

"Thomas mostly hangs out with Brooke. He never hangs out with Petey." She wondered if the detective was gay.

"Do the meth-heads go to your school?"

"I never met them. Thomas says they live under Tucson Mall. They ride little BMX bikes." He was in the weight room enough to be gay.

"Well, my name's Nick," he said, handing her a business card with the paper towel. "Call me if you think of anything else or if you have any questions. Otherwise, I'll see you at the gym."

She wondered if someone like Nick Honig would ever date someone like her brother Thomas. "I have one question," Kendra said, and before she lost her nerve, she asked it: "Are you gay?"

"That's a strange question," he said, smiling. His teeth were white and stark in contrast to his tanned skin.

"Forget it," Kendra said. "I just wanted to know something about the guys at the gym."

"What?"

"Well, do buff gay guys mostly date other buff gay guys, or do some of them like skinnier guys or maybe even fatter guys?"

"I imagine they have all sorts of different likes and dislikes, Kendra," he said. "You think Petey Vaccarino is gay?"

Kendra laughed. For a moment she forgot she had her foot on the dead bird. "No," she said.

* * *

After she cleaned the crushed bird from the porch, Kendra sat on the edge of the pool and soaked her feet in the water, which was still refreshing despite the hot summer days. Petey had been missing for just over a week, which was a little odd, Kendra thought. When Brooke Luter had brought it up a few days earlier, it was nothing to be alarmed about, just Brooke's stupid drama. But now, after speaking with the detective, it did seem weird.

She played different scenarios in her mind: Petey had taken a bus to California and was living on the streets of L.A., sleeping in his filthy clothes under a bridge—his choice. He was hanging with the BMX meth-heads in the tunnels under Tucson Mall—his choice. He was up in Phoenix, partying with his friends, drunk on cheap beer and marker fumes—his choice.

When she tried to imagine Petey in danger, or hurt, or dead, even when she thought of realistic possibilities—like he had finally huffed too much and died and his stupid friends didn't bother to call 911—Kendra wouldn't allow herself to worry. A waste of time. Brooke Luter could be the one to get all dramatic. There was nothing Kendra could do, anyway.

The white sun was too strong, burning her face and arms, so she pulled her legs out of the cool water and walked inside the house.

On her way to the gym that afternoon, Kendra stopped at 7-Eleven to pump some gasoline into her mother's new Lexus—a business expense, a treat after leasing all twenty spaces in a new shopping center in Sierra Vista, including clinching the anchor space and leasing it to one supermarket just an hour after another had unexpectedly backed out. That afternoon, last spring, after she had tied up all the leases, Joyce had come home and hugged Kendra, told her they were going car shopping. She ended up with the Lexus. Gold, with beige interior.

Kendra normally didn't care about which car she drove—her mother's Lexus, her father's SUV-of-the-week, or the tan Volvo sedan they had given her and Thomas—but her mother had been acting strangely generous ever since Detective Honig left, and kind of forced the Lexus on her.

"This could be a very trying time for you," Joyce had warned Kendra, walking into Kendra's bedroom, as Kendra packed her bag for the gym.

"Why?"

"Petey could be anywhere," Joyce said, standing in the door-way, twirling her key chain like she was a basketball coach.

"What does that have to do with me?" Kendra said. "Plussing as how, we're not even dating or anything."

"If you're scared or sad, you know that you can talk to me or Franny about anything."

"Not likeful that I'd talk to Franny," Kendra said. She dug around her dresser drawer for a pair of socks.

"Be careful what you say to anyone about Petey," Joyce said. "And I don't think 'likeful' is a word."

"I'm sure Petey is in Phoenix or something."

"I bought a case of those chocolate protein bars you like. They're on top of the fridge." She tossed her keys to Kendra. "Take my car to the gym. I'm not going anywhere this afternoon."

"Thanks," Kendra said, confused, "but the Volvo works fine."

"Take the Lexus," Joyce said. "I insist. The air conditioner is strong. You'll love it."

The credit card swiper on the gas pump was out of order, so Kendra had to pay inside of the mini-mart. She stood in line at the counter behind two sorority girls in their matching T-shirts: DELTA GAMMA BEACH BASH!!! Each was fit: shapely legs and vague musculature in their arms. After quickly assessing their physiques, Kendra noticed what they were buying. One clutched a big bag of Doritos under her arm and carried a six-pack of Corona beer, not even Corona Light. The other held a bag of Oreos and several Hostess Apple Pies. She was sipping from a pint of strawberry milk.

Kendra turned around. She picked up a bag of honey-roasted

cashews, a Snickers, a tube of Pringles potato chips, *not* reduced fat Pringles, and her own pint of strawberry milk.

Ten minutes later, wiping her hands on the underside of the leather driver's seat in her mother's Lexus, Kendra felt as if she had just woken up. She didn't really remember buying the snack food, or consuming it, but the colorful wrappers and packaging were there on the floor of the car. She was surprised that she didn't feel sick. She started the car and drove left on Skyline, toward her home—not right, toward the gym.

The drive from Tucson to the Phoenix area was a boring two hours, especially with a barely functional stereo in the car. Each time Merv made the trip, it seemed more businesses had sprouted in the faded dirt along I-10. He imagined that soon Tucson and Phoenix would be connected, that the fast food huts and outlet malls would grow to cover the one hundred miles of desert. Picacho Peak would be obscured by an office park. A continuous stream of stores and restaurants would link the cities. Maybe just one long outlet mall. Maybe you could walk from Tucson to Phoenix and never have to leave an air-conditioned environment, picking up barely discounted merchandise along the way.

Merv had heard somewhere that Phoenix was growing at the rate of an acre an hour, that there was so much heat rising from the asphalt covering the metro area that rain clouds could no longer form over downtown. The rare rainstorm was confined to the outskirts, South Tempe or North Scottsdale, where Jason and Rusty lived.

Merv wasn't looking forward to the barbecue at Rusty's, but it was better than sitting around the house, watching his mother go crazy. The barbecue guests last time were hard-working college grads, hoping to pay off their student loans or mortgages before turning thirty, tolerating life in a retail-crowded town, and justifying their expensive cars by the number of hours they spent inside them. They babbled relentlessly about 401K's and interest rates, bemoaning the dot-com crash that had devastated most of their finances.

Merv wished that they'd just do away with the formality of grilling meat. It was too hot, and they'd all eventually end up inside, drunk, watching television until someone got motivated and made everyone else go to a bar or out for pizza or Mexican food.

Rusty sat on the edge of the pool, his feet splashing to the rhythm blaring from a boom box on the deck next to him.

As Merv walked into the shade of a ramada, where the few guests had gathered near a smoking barbecue grill, Rusty yelled, "I can't believe you made it up here. How'd your car do?"

"Fine," Merv yelled. "Turn down the music or come over here."

Merv was surprised that there were only two other guests: a woman, and a dork he knew named Walter.

Rusty continued to kick the water.

Jason introduced Merv to Melissa, who, with her short, choppy blond hair looked like Jason's last girlfriend, Janet. Merv wondered if she knew that.

Walter, who called himself "Hardcore," fanned the barbecue with a spatula.

"Rusty and I thought you wouldn't come today," Jason said. "You were sort of a dick on your birthday."

Merv pointed to the pink scar on his forehead. "After I left that night, some asshole threw a bottle at me."

"You should have stayed with us, Merv," Jason said.

"Let's change the topic," Merv said. "I want a beer."

"Your real name's 'Merv'?" Melissa asked dramatically. She wore a sports bra and drawstring shorts. She flaunted her gym-toned body, gesticulating smoothly. "Like the gay talk show host from the seventies?"

"Your real name is 'Melissa'?" Merv said. "Like Joan Rivers's ugly, no-talent daughter?"

Melissa laughed. "I sense grouchiness," she said, laughing.

"Merv's always grouchy," Hardcore said.

"I'm just envious of your self-assigned nickname, *Walter*," Merv said. "Maybe I'll call myself 'Turbo' or 'Mr. Intense' or something equally as threatening or macho as 'Hardcore.'"

Melissa laughed. "How about 'Throb'?" she added.

"Or 'Snake'?" Rusty yelled from over near the pool.

"I like 'Snake,'" Merv said. "It's tough in a sort of fifties greaser way—and there's the obvious phallic symbolism."

"My friends gave me the name in high school," Hardcore said quietly.

"Maybe it's time to give it up," Melissa said. "I gave up my Swatch watch from high school."

Hardcore, in his too-bright Hawaiian print polo shirt, baggy shorts, and unscuffed Birkenstocks, looked like he had walked into a department store and asked the sales clerk if she could help him pick out something casual to wear. For a fleeting moment, Merv felt sorry for him.

"I dress the same as I did in high school," Merv said. "I have the same pair of Air Jordans I had when I was fifteen."

"In Japan they pay like five thousand for old Air Jordans," Melissa said, "and old Levi's."

"They also sleep in tubes and pay something like twenty-six dollars for a Big Mac," Jason said.

"More like nine dollars," Melissa said. Then, without warning, she stripped off her shorts, revealing a low-waisted black bikini, and dove into the pool, splashing Rusty and his boom box in the process.

Soon, everyone joined Melissa in the swimming pool, abandoning the barbecue like Merv had predicted and hoped. The water was warm, almost too warm, Merv thought. His Budweiser was still cold, though, and he was relieved that neither Jason nor Rusty hassled him much for the bratty attitude he had copped on his birthday.

Merv watched Melissa move through the water with confidence and grace. Even when she was just fetching a beer for Walter, wading through the shallow end, she moved like she knew everyone watched her and she was used to it. He could never have a girlfriend like her, and he felt the realization in his stomach, like someone had sucker punched him. But then he wondered if he wanted a girlfriend like her, and the feeling in his stomach subsided.

Melissa babbled about signing bonuses and mortgage rates, pausing every few minutes to sip her beer, allowing Jason or Rusty to chime in. Merv thought about telling everyone about saving the boy at Splash World, how the boy's father, who was a computer salesman somewhere, had given Merv a new computer that he still hadn't figured out, but Merv kept his mouth shut and listened, bored. He decided to drive back to Tucson tonight. He didn't want to stay over.

"SHE LOOKS TOTALLY ORANGE," KENDRA SAID. "DID SHE GO TO A TAN-ning booth?"

"Be quiet," Thomas said.

"You're taping it," Kendra said, "aren't you?"

"Quiet!" Thomas said. He threw a cushion at Kendra, who sat on the other end of the couch. They were watching Brooke on the six o'clock news as she pleaded with the viewers.

". . . any information at all, please call the police!" Brooke begged, clutching her hands to her chest. The words *Peter Vaccarino's Best Friend, Brooke Luter, 17* were under her image on the screen.

"Plussing as which," Kendra said, "she thinks she's going to be discovered by some producer or director or something."

"She does not," Thomas said, turning away from the television. The Petey story was over, and the anchorman was blathering about a rise in auto theft within the Tucson city limits.

"This is serious. I mean, it's on the news," Thomas said.

"Petey's fine," Kendra said. "Brooke loves all this attention. Did she go to a tanning booth?"

"I don't know," Thomas said, standing. He stopped the VCR and hit the rewind button. "She's really freaked out about this. She was crying yesterday."

"She's such a faker," Kendra said. Kendra herself was concerned about Petey, had actually had a difficult time sleeping the night before, so difficult a time that she had slept through her alarm and missed her opportunity for a morning run. There were moments when she was angry with Petey for leaving and not telling anyone and probably having a good time, and other moments when she was sure he was dead, rotting in the wilderness or locked in a morgue with a numbered tag on his toe.

"Why do you hate her so much?" Thomas asked.

"Why do you like her so much?"

"I can tell her anything," Thomas said. "That's why. She can keep a secret."

Kendra didn't respond. She walked through the kitchen, out the sliding glass door, kicked off her running shoes and jumped in the pool. She let herself sink to the bottom of the deep end, ten feet, and sat there for as long as she could, looking up at the sun through the jiggling silver and blue water, until the little air she had in her lungs burned, until she felt like she might piss.

She took a deep gulp of air when she surfaced, then sank again, bubbles leaking from her nose, and looked at the sky through the water again, not caring about the T-shirt, sports bra, and workout shorts she wore. The water was a little too warm, not as bad as she had thought, but she loved it—the echoey muffled sounds from within herself, the blurry blueness of it all, proud that because fat floats and muscle sinks, her physique allowed her to be down there.

Kendra imagined she was the host of her own fitness television show. Each week was a new exercise, something revolutionary, that she had invented. This week was Kendra's Half-Water Workout, an amazing aerobic calorie burn without the muscle and tendon stress. "It's really not that difficult," she imagined herself saying into the camera. "It's all in the lungs. It's about expanding your lungs and pushing yourself to your limits." She imagined hordes of people practicing her method in swimming pools across the nation. She imagined being interviewed on *Good Morning America:* "I was bored with my same old workouts, so I just jumped in the pool and let myself sink. Plussing as which, my knees needed a break from running . . ."

And she remained in the pool for over an hour, bobbing up for air every few minutes, allowing her fantasies to become even cornier—Kendra videos, workout calendars, jeans, lunch boxes— until she noticed from her spot next to the drain ten feet below the surface that someone was standing on the edge, the shaky dark image breaking through the blue.

She resurfaced, and through her burning eyes she saw that it was Mrs. Hunter, smiling, wearing a bright pink T-shirt and loose tan pants cinched with a drawstring. It was odd to see her in anything but her robe, even odder to see her smile.

"Hi," Kendra said, treading.

"Hi," Mrs. Hunter said. "I'm so sorry to intrude, but your gate was open."

"No problem," Kendra said. She was a little embarrassed to be in the water in her gym clothes, like she was some sort of freak who had just jumped in the pool for no reason, but then she remembered she was talking to Mrs. Hunter, a full-fledged lunatic.

"I wanted to thank you for helping me the other day," Mrs. Hunter said. "Merv told me that you may have saved my life."

Kendra had never heard Mrs. Hunter talk this much. "You needed help, and I helped you. Plussing as which, it was no big deal."

"Well, I wanted to thank you for being so thoughtful and—" she said, stopping short. "I just wanted to thank you. You're a wonderful young girl and a wonderful neighbor."

Kendra didn't know what to say, but she continued to stare up at Mrs. Hunter, noticed that she was wearing a little makeup, just some lipstick and blush, maybe base. Kendra hadn't considered that guiding Mrs. Hunter home that morning ten days ago was a heroic act. She was sure she had done nothing else heroic in her entire life, except for maybe once, in the sixth grade, when she defended a fat girl from a few boys who were grabbing at her breasts. Kendra beat one of the boys, Brian Berger, so fiercely, breaking his collarbone, that it led to her first trip to a psychologist, which was mandated by the principal. Brian Berger had been in her algebra class just this spring, and he sat as far away from Kendra as possible every day.

"I don't want to keep you any longer," Mrs. Hunter said, "Goodbye, and thanks again." She walked off, slammed the wrought-iron gate and yelled, "Sorry!"

Kendra was mystified by the visit from Mrs. Hunter, and kept treading, happy that the sun had moved and a few palo verde trees cast shadows over the pool, providing some relief from the rays.

Her T-shirt, sports bra and running shorts were cumbersome now that she was treading, so she slipped them off—giving herself a little challenge by not allowing herself to touch the edge of the pool or swim over to the low end while doing so. She remained in the deep end, enjoying her nakedness, the freedom of movement, and started to exercise in earnest. She treaded with her arms over her head for twenty-second intervals. She didn't cheat, either, and soon her legs and lungs were burning, the deliciously familiar wash of endorphins working her system, the amazing feeling of surviving, of thriving.

After her thirty-third interval, Thomas appeared and broke her reverie. He stood on the end of the diving board and looked down at her. "You're naked," he said. "That's gross."

"Being as which you're staring at my body," Kendra said, now incorporating her arms in her treading to keep herself afloat, "you're a pervert."

"*Being as which* you have a phone call, you better get out."

"Bring me a towel and bring me the phone," Kendra said. "Duh."

"I told him to call back in five minutes." Thomas continued to look at his sister. He bounced a little on the end of the board. His pink toes hooked over the edge. "It wasn't Petey, by the way."

"Go get me a towel," Kendra said, "or I'll kick your sorry ass."

"You're so fucking violent," Thomas said, walking across the pool deck. He opened the wicker towel chest and pulled out a fresh one for Kendra. He walked back to the pool and held the towel at arm's length, his eyes closed.

"Plussing as which," Kendra said, stepping out of the water with the hot, humid air pushing against her, "stop staring at my body." She grabbed the towel from Thomas and wrapped it around herself.

"Brooke is right," Thomas said. "Your grammar is totally fucked up. And my eyes are closed. Believe me, I'm not looking at your body."

Kendra looked at Thomas, fought the urge to push him into the pool. The way he was standing there so stupidly, right on the edge, his eyes closed so tightly he looked as if he was constipated. He was asking for it. Scrawny. Lazy. Then she heard the phone ring, and said, "You're so lucky," before she ran into the kitchen to answer it.

"You know who this is?" the voice on the phone said.

Kendra sat at the kitchen table, dripping water onto the Mexican tiles. She could hear the drips. "No," she said. "Is this Petey?"

"No, it's me, Miguel."

"Aren't you like in jail or something?" Kendra asked. "Plus you're a high school dropout."

"I stopped going to school for a week, then I switched to Cholla."

"Plussing as which, you never even called me," Kendra said. "Not that I really cared." She had cared, though. Still did. And not just because she missed the sex.

"I didn't know your last name until yesterday," he said. "I looked through my sister's yearbook. Your picture is pretty."

"I haven't seen it yet," Kendra said. "Why'd you switch schools?"

"I went to live with my uncle," Miguel said. "You'd like him. He's a boxer. All fit and shit. I'm a boxer now."

"You can't just decide to be a boxer."

"I box, therefore I'm a boxer. I had a match last weekend. I won. You should have come, bitch."

"Don't call me bitch, bitch," Kendra said. "I'm sure I could still kick your ass."

"Still tough," Miguel said. "I like that."

"So why are you calling me?"

"I don't know," he said.

"I need to get dressed," Kendra said, "Plussing as which, I'm dripping water all over the place."

"I never met anyone who talked like you," Miguel said.

"I never met a boxer before," Kendra said. "A few of the guys at my gym punch bags and jump rope, but they just do it for their bodies."

"Come by and meet my uncle. Come on the Fourth of July. He'll have a keg, and we can watch A Mountain burn." Last year and the year before, A Mountain had caught on fire, providing all of Tucson with a spectacular show that lasted for hours after the final firework had been launched. Kendra watched the orange blob of burning desert grow and change shapes like an amoeba. It was miles away, to the west, but it was still thrilling to gaze at it from her bedroom, blasting Weezer on her Walkman: "Pink triangle on her sleeve let me know the truth . . ."

"Remember Petey?" Kendra asked Miguel.

"That kid was messed up bad. I once saw him fall down the stairs near the music room."

"He's missing," Kendra said. "For like two weeks."

"Probably in jail."

"The police are looking for him," she said. "He disappeared."

"So?" Miguel said.

"I was just telling you," Kendra said.

"So, are you coming on the Fourth?" Miguel asked.

"Give me the directions," Kendra said, scrambling in her mother's desk for a pen and paper.

Merv's bedroom door stuck with humidity when he tried to open it after rolling out of bed. Humidity meant crowds and clouds. If there was even a blink of lightning, it meant closing the park. If the lightning appeared before noon, it meant handing out half-off passes to disappointed sliders—a pain in the ass.

The humidity was early this year. It usually hid until late July, allowing Tucson to live up to its reputation of dry heat for half the summer. Then the clouds would blow in and loom, useless gray masses that cast shadows over half the city, doing nothing except making everyone sweat, until August, when they finally broke and roared and dumped water on the desiccated landscape.

Once, when Merv was a kid, back when his dad was alive, the monsoons rolled in by late June, dousing the city every afternoon, and the desert took on bright hues of green by July fourth. The Colorado River toads went crazy that year, invading everyone's swimming pools, croaking loudly all night as they called for mates and mated, leaving strings of eggs clinging to pool toys or skimmer baskets. Merv's dog's name was Jeremy, a midsized mix of cattle dog and shepherd named after Merv's uncle, who, like the dog, was extremely intelligent. Merv's father had taught Jeremy the dog all sorts of tricks, like opening the garage door by jumping and slapping the button with his paw, or fetching things like baseball caps and shoes from the upstairs bedrooms. Merv's mother let the dog into the pool one night and told him, "Get the toads! Get the toads, Jeremy!" Merv and his mother watched Jeremy swim after and kill several toads before they noticed him slowing down. In the neon purple light from the pool, they saw him roll onto his side and stop paddling. Merv dove in and pulled him onto the cool deck, but it was too late, Jeremy was dead, heavy as a sack of rocks, his beautiful blue eyes rolled white. At the veterinarian's office that night, they learned about the toad's poisonous skin secretions. "It's always on the news and in the papers," the vet told Merv's mother. Merv could tell the vet was angry with his mother. The next morning, Merv was awakened by his parents' arguing. He heard his father call his mother a "stupid cunt" for sending Jeremy into the pool to kill the toads. Merv looked up "cunt" in his dictionary, first with a *k*, then with a *c,* but couldn't find it. Instead of bothering his fighting parents, Merv sneaked outside and opened the lid to the skimmer. He found four of the toads that Jeremy had killed, each as big and brown as a baseball mitt, each a loose, punctured sack, swirling in the water. He pulled out the skimmer basket, and tossed the toads over the wall, calling them "stupid cunts." With the net, he fished the other dead toads from the pool until there were no traces of the horrible creatures that had killed Jeremy, the only dog that Merv's family would ever own.

Today, as Merv pulled open his shades, he was hit by a wall of white sunlight, the flash he needed to really wake up. It was only seven, and he didn't have to be at Splash World until ten today, but he was happy to be up this early. He wanted to spend a leisurely morning with his mother before she left for work at eight-thirty.

Merv's mother walked in the backdoor as he was scooping the scrambled eggs he had prepared onto two plates.

"Oh, Merv," she said, smiling. "Breakfast."

"Yes," he said. "I got up early. It's humid."

"It's beautiful. I just went for the longest walk." She sat at the table, spread her hands flat on a wicker placemat, and inhaled strongly through her nose.

"So you slept well?" Merv asked. He spread butter on the toast and joined his mother at the table. She was still breathing weirdly, deeply. Her eyes were closed.

She opened her eyes slowly and looked at Merv. "I honestly can't remember the last night I didn't sleep well."

"That's good," Merv said. He wanted to ask her if she was sleeping well without pills, but he was afraid of hearing the answer. For the last week or so, she had been so happy, so energetic, so sane. Instead, he asked her if she had seen the teenage lesbian neighbor.

"What?" Merv's mother said. "Kendra Lumm?"

"Yes, Kendra. The lesbian muscle girl."

"I don't think she's a lesbian."

"Are you blind?" Merv asked. He took a bite of toast and said, "Those muscles are her way of screaming 'I'm a dyke!' to the world."

His mother finished chewing and swallowing. "Don't be so judgmental. She's into fitness. She's very driven."

"Driven to be a man."

"Can we change the topic, please? That girl saved my life. You told me so yourself."

"Sure," Merv said, silently agreeing with his mother. "Has that other horrible neighbor kid shown up yet?"

"I thought this was going to be a nice breakfast, but you seem determined to ruin it. And, no, they haven't found Peter Vaccarino yet."

"Too depressing," Merv mumbled.

They ate without speaking for a few minutes, Merv noticing that his mother's appetite seemed to be normal—she finished her eggs quickly. "Petey'll show up," Merv said hopefully. "He's probably off having fun with his friends."

"If you watched the news or read the papers, you'd know that they have no leads," Merv's mother said.

"It's on the news?" Merv asked, incredulous.

"Yes." She wiped her mouth with a paper napkin and stood. "Thanks for breakfast. The eggs were great."

"You're welcome," Merv said. "I didn't know Peter Vaccarino was really missing. I wouldn't have called him 'horrible' or anything." Merv thought about the short breakfast, felt like an asshole, wondered why he had been such an asshole. Maybe it was the humidity. His mother seemed like she was close to normal—not quite bitchy enough, but close. If whatever medication she was on kept working, she'd be nagging him soon enough, he knew.

Merv showered, rubbed on sunscreen, spent a few minutes looking for his misplaced sunglasses (which he found next to the toaster), and arrived at Splash World early, hoping the clouds would stay where they were, in the west, and not crackle with lightning.

He liked the park in the morning when it was empty of visitors. He could smell the overwatered grass, the clean whiffs of chlorine from the pools—a nice relief from the popcorn and hot-dog fumes he was normally forced to abide at Splash World. He only heard the birds chirping and cars buzzing by on Tanque Verde Road. No screaming kids, no water pumps, no hisses or groans from the wave-making mechanism.

The security team was gathered at a shaded picnic table near the employee locker room: five big guys, led by a guy named Hank who had the thickest neck Merv had ever seen and a goofy, boyish face that looked a little more intimidating when he wore his wraparound sunglasses and security cap.

"Hey, Hank," Merv said. "Good morning, guys."

"Merv!" Hank said, standing, quickly walking over to Merv, guiding Merv to the table. "We have a whole new system of security coverage figured out. We're starting it today."

"Great," Merv said. "I'm sure it'll work fine."

"Don't you want to hear the new plan?" Hank asked, pressing on Merv's shoulder, forcing him to sit at the head of the picnic table.

"I don't have time," Merv said, wiggling out of Hank's grasp, standing. "But I trust you guys. I went to bat for you with corporate, remember?" He walked backward toward the locker room. "Don't think twice about enacting a new security strategy without my approval." While it was true Merv trusted the security team and had petitioned the corporate offices in Long Beach to give them a significant raise, citing the statistics that showed Splash World Tucson to be far below all other locations in crime rate, he couldn't bear sitting at a table with them as they discussed their new strategy, which probably didn't stray much from their former strategy.

Hank looked disappointed, but turned and began to talk to his security teammates, using a small chalkboard to show where each post would be.

As soon as Merv walked into the locker room, he wished he

hadn't. He heard faint whimpering from the toilet stall, and from the wheels he saw underneath, he knew it was Raymond.

"Can I help you, Raymond?" Merv asked.

"No," Raymond said, but then his whimpering was louder.

"Are you sure?" Merv asked, walking over to the stall. He knew it was awful, but he hoped Raymond would say no again. Then he would have asked twice, which would be enough to assuage any guilt that might build up like it had earlier at the breakfast table.

"I just can't get this tube . . ." Raymond muttered.

Merv stood there a moment, stared at the smooth gray particle board that separated him from pathetic Raymond. In his head, Merv repeated, *Please, no, please, no . . .* He remembered all the twenties Raymond had placed in his hand. He remembered how Raymond seemed to drool a lot more this summer than he had last. "Are you sure I can't help you?" Merv said into the particle board. *Please, no, please, no . . .*

Raymond sniffed, and sniffed again. "Let me just cover up a little," he said.

Merv heard the crinkling of a plastic bag, then the door to the stall swung open. "Come in," Raymond said.

Merv walked around the stall and found Raymond facing the toilet, sitting upright and high in his electric wheelchair. No slump. No slouching.

"I just need you to grab that tube on my left and put the end of it in the toilet," Raymond said. "The other end is securely in place, and I'd like to relieve myself."

Merv saw the tube, a clear length of surgical tubing, one end leading to Raymond's lap, the other coiling on the floor. "Sure," he said. "No problem."

He leaned over and grabbed the tube and placed the end on the toilet seat. "Do you actually want it in the water, or is this okay?"

"That's great, Merv," Raymond said. He sniffed. "Thank you so much. Some days my hands just don't work."

Merv could smell Raymond's breath. Like the cherry air-freshener from car washes, like he had drunk cough syrup or eaten a bunch of red lollipops for breakfast. "You all set?"

"Now, if you'd just step outside the booth, I can go."

"Oh," Merv said. "Sorry." He stepped out and lightly shut the door to the stall.

"Wait there, though," Raymond said.

"I will," Merv said, washing his hands, cursing the custodial crew for not refilling the antibacterial soap dispenser. As he was drying his hands with the stiff brown paper towel, he heard Raymond's piss hitting the water of the toilet bowl.

After a minute or so, Raymond rolled backward out of the stall and turned to face Merv. "I have this for you," he said, holding a fifty between two knobby fingers.

"I can't accept that," Merv said. "I only just picked up a small tube."

"Please," Raymond said. "It's the least I can do." A milky strand of drool connected his chin to his lap.

"I really can't," Merv said. "Really."

"Merv, there are very few things that really bother me about this degenerative muscle disease. The main one is bathroom problems. I wouldn't have accepted your help if I didn't trust you, if I didn't think you were a good person." The drool strand snapped and puddled on his lap. "I do trust you, and you never make me feel embarrassed or pathetic. Please take the money. I don't have anything else to offer."

"Do you consider me a friend?" Merv asked.

"Of course," Raymond said. "Of course."

"Friends help friends," Merv said. "I can't take any twenties from you any longer, either. You're a guest here at this park, a paying customer, and it's my job to help you enjoy your experience. Now, do you need to get into your other wheelchair so you can enjoy the beach?" Sometimes, like now, Merv couldn't believe the words that flowed from his mouth. Where had he learned to be such a phony? He knew it was wrong to accept any more tips from Raymond, but that crap about Splash World and his duties?

Raymond protested a bit more, even mentioned that helping wheelchair-bound park visitors with their catheter tubes was most likely not in Merv's job description, but Merv continued to refuse the money.

Later, after work, as Merv changed into Levi's, he discovered a fifty and a twenty in the back pocket of his swim trunks.

Wednesday. June 27. 2001

Cooler

High 98 / Low 62

Clear and Sunny

"So you're saying you don't want to talk about Peter Vaccarino?" Franny asked. She folded her plump hands on her knees and stared at Kendra.

Kendra stared back. "That's what I just said. Why don't you teach me something useful, like how to talk right."

"We've made some very significant communication progress, Kendra," Franny said. "It's okay to be proud of yourself."

"I'm talking about grammar," Kendra said. "Everyone says I have ignorant grammar, even Miguel, who speaks Mexican half the time."

"Miguel?" Franny asked. "Your boyfriend who suddenly dropped out of school back in the winter?"

Kendra lied without hesitation. "No, another one." She had made the mistake of telling Franny about him before, and Franny had spouted some confusing and annoying words about separation anxiety and sexual empowerment. "I want to talk right."

"Have you thought about why you might want to improve your grammar right now? Why today?" Franny smacked her lips, and Kendra cursed herself for noticing.

Kendra looked over to the trashcan. Taco Bell wrappers and boxes. She should have known. She had noticed a slight vinegar odor when she walked in, thought maybe Franny had douched, then wished she hadn't thought that. But the cheap hot-sauce from Taco Bell was half vinegar. Miguel had once shown her how one little packet of the stuff could clean a handful of the dirtiest pennies, turning them from a dull brown to a shiny copper in just a few seconds. "Because my grammar sucks and I'd like to not sound like a retard."

"Why today, though? Why didn't you ask about this back in May or April or even sooner? I mean, why today specifically?"

Kendra thought for a moment, wondered what Franny wanted her to say. Finally, she said, "The summer is a good time to catch up with other kids my age?"

"Could it be that you're distracting yourself from thinking about Peter Vaccarino?" Franny asked. "Not that I'm judging you. Not that it's an unhealthy response to tragedy, because it's a very healthy response to tragedy to do something positive even if it's not directly related to the tragedy."

"What tragedy? Petey's been gone for a few weeks. Big deal. He's probably having more fun than any of us who stayed here this summer." Kendra pulled her shoulders back, sat up, smoothed her denim skirt. "You want me to cry and freak out? I already told the detective everything I know about Petey."

"We'll work through this," Franny said, almost in a whisper. She placed her hand on Kendra's knee. Her fingers felt clammy, like five slugs. When Kendra felt her cold metal watchband make contact with her skin, she flinched.

Franny had never touched her before—not that Kendra could remember, anyway. She wondered how she was supposed to react. She tried to ignore it, but wondered when she would take her hand away. She hoped she could remember to wear pants next time. "I just want to improve my grammar. Okay?"

Franny finally removed her hand after giving Kendra's knee a final squeeze and sighing. The spot Franny had touched tickled, and Kendra scratched it. Franny spun around in her desk chair and rummaged through papers and booklets on her desk. As she leaned over and reached into a file drawer, her shirt shifted, and Kendra could see her flabby back. It was like Franny's fat ass extended upward farther than it should, a pink ham on either side of her spine.

Franny pulled a catalog from the file cabinet and faced Kendra again. "There are several courses this summer, some as short as three weeks." She flipped through the catalog.

Kendra noticed it was a Pima Community College catalog and asked Franny if she could even sign up for a course there. "Being as which, I'm not even a junior in high school yet."

"You might even get college credit," Franny said. "Maybe you'll meet some new friends." She handed the catalog over to Kendra. "Read through it and call me if anything looks interesting."

"I just want grammar," Kendra said. "Are we done for today? Can I go now?"

Sitting in traffic at the intersection of Grant and Campbell, Kendra drummed the steering wheel to the generic techno music on the radio and caught the guy in the convertible on the left staring at her. He smiled, motioned for her to roll down her window. He looked older, like thirty or forty. Too tan. Skinny arms. A cheesy, sun-bleached mustache. The traffic was backed up several blocks, and there was no way that Kendra could make it through the intersection on this light, so she tried to ignore him.

Then he honked. And honked again.

She looked over, and he smiled at her. Kendra rolled down her window. "What?" she said, trying to sound as annoyed as she was.

"Hello," he said.

"Are you my dad's friend or something?" she asked. "Because I don't recognize you."

"I'm only twenty-eight," he said, still smiling. His teeth were widely spaced and stark white.

"You look much older," she said.

The traffic light finally changed, but Kendra could only advance a few car lengths. His car was still next to hers.

"I'm just trying to make conversation," he said. "I thought I was lucky for getting stuck in traffic next to a hottie like yourself, but you're not very friendly."

"I'm losing air-conditioning," Kendra said, rolling up her window.

He yelled, "Bitch!" before her window was completely closed.

Kendra's first instinct was to throw something at him, but all she had with her was her cell phone and a half-eaten protein bar. Then she thought about ramming his shiny convertible with her old Volvo, scraping and denting the hell out of it as he continued to call her names. Or she could follow him home, beat the shit out of him in front of his trashy fat pregnant girlfriend right there in the driveway of his boring beige house, right there in the brutal white sun. His girlfriend would be screaming, pulling Kendra's hair, trying to get her off her boyfriend, whose mouth was gurgling with blood.

The car behind her honked and snapped her out of her fantasy. She did look up and see the asshole in the convertible's license plate: XAM 597.

She repeated it over and over, aloud and in her head: X-A-M-5–9-7, X-A-M-5–9-7 . . . until she reached the front desk at the Racquet Club, where she asked the attendant for a pen. She wrote the license plate number on the back of a tennis camp brochure.

"Thanks," she said, as she handed him back his pen.

As Kendra swam laps in the lukewarm pool, she continued to fantasize about getting revenge on the asshole in the convertible. Then her thoughts drifted to Petey, and then to Miguel, until her mother Joyce lightly bonked her on the head with a kickboard and startled her enough to take in a little water through her nose and cough.

"I have twenty-three more laps," Kendra told her, staring through her tinted goggles. She coughed again, felt the water burning through her sinuses.

"I'll be upstairs in the restaurant," Joyce said, her hand on her forehead as a visor. "Come have a late lunch with me."

"You came here to eat?" Kendra didn't much care for the club's restaurant food: greasy fries, a million different hamburg-

ers, onion rings, boring salads of iceberg lettuce and mealy tomatoes. "Gross."

"I did a yoga class," Joyce told her.

"Really?"

"It keeps me grounded."

"I'll be up there in ten minutes," Kendra said, surprised that
her mother was into yoga. "Get a table inside, and order me
three ice waters with lemon."

She sped through the final twenty-three laps, her lungs on
fire, as she fought to breathe on either side, every three strokes,
instead of only breathing on one side, every other stroke. Swim-
mers who only breathed on one side, Kendra believed, practiced
a lopsided stroke, one that led to lopsided muscle development.
Kendra had worked hard on her perfect symmetry, studied her
symmetry in the mirror. During these faster laps, though, it was
difficult to wait for the third stroke to gulp some air, and sometimes she cheated, especially after a flip-turn.

It was also during these final laps that Kendra felt the rush of
endorphins. She concentrated on the breathing, keeping her
kick strong, and really reaching with each stroke, so thinking
about anything else was impossible. No Petey, no Franny, no
Miguel, no grammar, no jockstrap collection, no asshole in the
convertible.

"Aren't you and dad afraid of running into your friends from
the eighties?" Kendra asked her mother. The lone waiter at the
little club restaurant had allowed Kendra to come into the
kitchen and pick out a tomato for her drab salad. He also mentioned that they had boneless chicken breast, which the cook
could grill. She had ordered it, and was pleasantly surprised
when she tasted it.

Her mother ate cocktail nuts and French fries with ranch
dressing. She drank cranberry juice. Kendra didn't bother protest-
ing her mother's meal choice. Hearing her mother's whacked jus-
tification would have just frustrated her more. "I'm not afraid,"
her mother told her, "but your father is petrified."

"You do yoga and drive a Lexus," Kendra said. "Not very punk rock."

"Yoga is totally punk rock—in my mind, anyway. It's your father the golf pro who's not being very punk rock."

"Do you think I'll be much different when I'm like your age?" Kendra asked. "I don't."

"You will be," Joyce said.

"I doubt it," Kendra said, knowing she would never be fat or out of shape.

"I used to style my hair with Elmer's Glue, Kendra," Joyce said. "People change."

Merv looked at his watch to make sure his clock was correct. It was nine-fifteen in the morning, and he had been torn from a dream by loud knocking and the doorbell. In the dream, he was sitting at his post atop the Kamikaze, and all the sliders were pulling up on their mats, catching huge air. Some flew over the sides, crashed, died, but no one cared, and no one listened to Merv's protests. His whistle didn't work, and neither did his walkie-talkie, and when he tried to yell for security, his voice was a quiet squeak.

Maybe his mother had forgotten something; her keys, he thought, as he pulled some shorts over his boxers and sniffed a T-shirt from the floor. He decided against the T-shirt and walked downstairs to answer the door.

Through the dust-packed peephole, he could barely see a man, dressed in a bright green polo shirt and jeans, standing in the white morning sun.

"Nicolas Honig," Merv said, recognizing the man as he opened the door. "What do you want?"

Nicolas was thicker with muscle. His hair was cut shorter than Merv remembered, too. Nicolas Honig had been a cheater in high school, but instead of getting caught and punished, the teachers looked the other way. Nicolas had been one of the few real athletes at Merv's little prep school, so none of the teachers busted him, even when he was stupid enough to leave his cheat-sheet in the blue book of his physics final exam. The worst class had been AP American history, an entire year of the teacher not only looking the other way when Nicolas cheated, but also fawning all over him for his baseball prowess. Merv hadn't tried that hard in American history and scraped by with C's, but Rusty and Jason had studied hard and sometimes fared worse than Nicolas on the tests. Merv complained directly to the headmaster about Nicolas's cheating and the faculty's special treatment, but nothing ever happened, except the American history teacher, the baseball coach who fancied himself a ladies' man and some sort of role model for all the boys, decided that the rest of the exams in American history would be take-home essay questions that would be carefully scrutinized. He had stared at Merv when he made the announcement to the class.

"Merv Hunter," Nick Honig said now. "To be honest, I was hoping you'd be at work so I could talk to your mother before I talked to you."

"She's at work," Merv said, feeling the same horrible injustice and frustration that he had felt when he was seventeen, telling on Nick. He felt it in his stomach.

"You're still working at Splash World, right?"

"What do you want, Nicolas?" Merv asked. He was ready to say goodbye and close the door.

"I need to speak to you about Peter Vaccarino."

"He's missing," Merv said. "He's been gone for a while. It was on the news."

"I know," Nick said. "I'm a detective with the Police Department and I've been assigned to the case."

"You're kidding," Merv said.

Nick pulled his badge from his back pocket and showed it to Merv. "I'm serious," he said. "May I come in?"

Merv guided Nick to the kitchen table, asked him if he wanted anything to drink while he prepared breakfast for himself. Before he sat down with the detective and enjoyed his breakfast, he ran upstairs, pulled on a clean T-shirt, and wet and flattened his hair, which had been sticking up in all directions.

"You always eat the yolks?" Nick asked Merv.

"Always," Merv said, dipping the corner of his toast into the leaking center of his fried egg. "It's the best part."

"Cholesterol," Nick said.

"Flavor," Merv said.

Nick smiled. "So, how have you been for the last twelve years?"

"Fine," Merv said, chewing. "And you?"

"Fine," Nick said. "You should have come to the ten-year reunion. It was great to see everyone. Gigi has three kids and her husband only speaks French."

"Rusty told me it sucked," Merv said. "He didn't tell me you were a cop."

"Well, I am." He traced little circles on the kitchen table with his finger. "Did you know Peter Vaccarino?"

"I spoke to him a few times," Merv said. "He had lots of loud parties and he always played his music loud, so I had to go over there and tell him to shut up."

"Was he aggressive or rude?"

"No," Merv said. "He was always wasted on something. The last time I went over there he had a bunch of those nitrous oxide silver canister things in front of him on the table and his nose was all marked up from sniffing Magic Markers."

"How do you know he sniffed pens?" Nick began to jot into a small notepad.

Merv thought he looked ridiculous, like he was pretending to be a detective. "Most of the other times I went over to complain he was sniffing them," Merv said. "That kid has some serious substance-abuse issues."

"That's what I hear," Nick said. "That's one of the reasons why it's difficult for me to justify spending any time on this case."

What an asshole, Merv thought. Nick Honig used to sell acid to half the school. He had once ripped off Rusty with some horrible mushrooms that tasted like dirt and made no one high. "If

he were an honor student and an Eagle Scout it would be easier,
I suppose."

"You're right," Nick said. "Did you ever see or hear him fighting with his mother?"

"No," Merv said.

"And his girlfriend? Kendra Lumm? Did he fight with her at
all?"

"She's his girlfriend?" Merv said, stupefied. "Are you sure?"

"Why are you surprised?"

"I thought she was a lesbian."

"They do seem like an unlikely couple," Nick said. "Have you
heard or seen them together, especially arguing?"

"No," Merv said. "I never even saw her at any of the parties."

"I should probably talk to a few more people in the neighborhood today," Nick said. He stood, poised to write in his notebook. "Any suggestions about who might be the most helpful?"

"Not here in this neighborhood. But you should find these
three nasty guys on BMX bikes. I saw them over there at the
Vaccarinos' one night earlier this summer. They come to Splash
World every once in while and we have to kick them out."

"Could you do me a huge favor?" Nick asked, pulling a business card from his back pocket. "Next time you see them, call me
immediately. Call the number on the card first, and if that
doesn't work, I'm giving you my personal cell number." He scribbled the number on the back of the card and handed it to Merv.

As Merv walked Nick to the door, he finally gathered enough
courage to ask through his tightened throat what he had
wanted to ask since he learned Nick was a cop: "So, did you
cheat your way through the Police Academy?"

"Some people change, Merv," Nick said. "Others still live at
home with their mothers."

Merv retired to his room after Nick Honig left. He hoped to
sleep for a few more hours, but he couldn't. Even after he closed
his shades and lowered the thermostat, he couldn't relax. Merv
kept thinking about what Nick had said and the anger churned

through his stomach. It was true; Merv hadn't changed, but he had tried not to think about it. He hoped others didn't notice, and reminders that they did, like the reminder from Nick today, made him question too much. He wondered when it was that he had lost all ambition. Had there been one single moment when he had fallen into complacency?

He looked around his room for anything that hadn't been there when he was in middle school. Other than his clothing, nothing much was new. The same brown lamp. The same army trunk covered with the same decals: THE SPECIALS, FISHBONE, THE UNTOUCHABLES. The same threadbare brown plaid bedspread and sheet set. He knew if he looked under his bed in the old metal toolbox, he'd find the same two *Playboys* and one *Penthouse* that he had gotten from Rusty in tenth grade, all the models with big eighties hair, all of them more familiar than any of the girls he had gone to prep school with.

Just as Merv had spread shaving cream on his face, the phone rang. He wiped his face on a towel and ran to his room to answer it.

"Hello."

"Is this Merv?" a woman said.

"Yes," Merv said. "Who's this?"

"Guess."

It sounded like Deena, and he began to think about lies he could tell her to get off the phone with her. Her final message after they stopped dating had consisted of nothing but a scream. Merv's mother had heard the message and asked Merv what he had done to Deena. "I suddenly became sane," he had told his mother.

"Sorry, Deena," Merv said now, "I'm really busy."

"This isn't Deena."

"Who is this?" Merv asked again.

"I'll give you a hint. Joan Rivers's no-talent ugly daughter."

"Hey, Melissa," Merv said, relieved and happy to hear from her.

"So, are you super busy right now?" Melissa asked.

"No," Merv said. "I have the day off."

"Good," she said. "I'm bored out of my mind here at work so I called Rusty and got your number. Entertain me."

"Entertain you?" Merv said. "I'm not very entertaining on command."

"Damn," she said. "What if I give you a few days' notice?"

"That could work," Merv said.

"I'll be there in Tucson on Friday for work. You want to show me around?"

"Is Jason coming down?" Merv asked.

"He and Rusty are going to Flagstaff, I think."

"Oh," Merv said, confused. "Sure. We can go out to dinner or something."

Later, as Merv was shopping for a new comforter and sheet set in Park Mall, he wondered if he should call Rusty and ask him what was up between Melissa and Jason, if they had broken up. Then he figured he was being conceited to think that she wanted anything but a Tucson tour guide for a few days. He could hear Rusty telling him that Jason and Melissa had a perfect relationship and that he was flattering himself to think that Melissa would be interested in him, a thirty-year-old who still lived with his mother and worked at a waterslide park.

Instead of braving the scorching parking lot right away, after he bought the bedding, Merv looked around at clothes. They all looked stupidly age-inappropriate and trendy, or like versions of the same clothes he already wore.

The suits and ties reminded him of his father, who wore at least a sport coat nearly every day of his adult life, even on the weekends during the summer. Merv remembered the horrible morning when he walked into the kitchen and discovered his father sitting at the table, a bowl of some healthy mush in front of him, wearing only dress pants and a T-shirt. Without a sport coat and a collared shirt, his father looked like he was wearing a costume. His arms were pale and thin, his knobby elbows the thickest part. At that moment, Merv knew his father was really dying, that his illness had now won the battle, and just two weeks later, Merv's father did die.

Merv placed his huge bags of bedding on a wooden bench in front of a large fountain that rudely stank of chlorine. He sat down. The mall was clogged with other Tucsonans trying to escape the heat, mostly bored-looking teenagers and senior citizens wearing ugly tracksuits in every pastel shade of pink and blue. Giant babies, grandfathers and grandmothers reduced to wearing things that made them look like giant babies. Few people held shopping bags.

It had been the summer before tenth grade when his father had died, August fourth. Toward the end, Merv would help his father walk out to the pool, wrapping his arm around his father's bony waist, guiding his steps. Merv would take a cushion from one of the chaise longues and set it on the edge of the pool deck, dust it off. Then he'd help his father sit, roll up his trouser cuffs, let his skinny legs and purple-veined feet soak in the lukewarm pool. They only went out there after dark, sometimes past midnight, which Merv appreciated because he could hardly bear to look at his emaciated father. Merv gazed up at the swarms and swirls of stars in the velvet sky and listened to his father talk.

"The air," his father would say, "the air is why I love the desert." Then he'd take a few deep, labored breaths, full of whistles and wheezes that reminded Merv of his mortality.

His father would try to talk about how Merv needed to take care of his mother, what to do with the finances, but Merv always managed to guide the conversations elsewhere—except for the night of August third, when Merv mustered up enough courage to ask his father if he was scared to die.

"I'm relieved," he had said. "I've never felt such relief, Mervy."

When Merv stepped out of the mall into palpable heat, he took a deep breath, breathed in the sun.

Friday, June 29, 2001

Hotter

High 103/Low 69

Clear and sunny

KENDRA SLEPT IN AGAIN. IT WAS NEARLY TEN BEFORE SHE ROLLED OUT OF bed, brushed her teeth, and gathered her messy hair in a pony-tail. When she unzipped her gym bag, ready to stuff her swim-suit and goggles into it, she noticed the tennis camp brochure, the asshole's license plate number she had jotted down. She considered waking Thomas then, asking him to help her track down the asshole on the Internet, but she decided to let him sleep. The sleuthing could wait.

But when she walked into the family room, she found Thomas, in his usual spot, sitting atop a cushion on the floor, watching wrestling.

"Dude, it's almost July, and you haven't done anything this summer," she told him.

"*Dude,* at least I woke up before double digits," he said, aim-ing the remote at the television, lowering the volume.

"Being as which I need your help," she said, "I won't give you any shit. You know how to find someone's address and phone number from their license plate number?"

"Easy," Thomas. "It's fifty bucks."

"I'm not giving you fifty bucks," she said.

"The service on the Internet costs fifty bucks," he said, stand-ing. He clicked off the TV. "It only takes a few minutes."

"Oh," she said. "Can you help me?"

"No," Thomas said. "Brooke and I are putting up flyers of Petey. She'll be here in ten minutes."

"You guys are retarded," Kendra said. "Plussing as which, I think people would have seen his picture on the news or in the newspaper."

Thomas stood in front of her, hands on hips, the white sun pouring through the window behind him. The way the intense light hit him softened his edges, made him look thinner, like a larger version of the chicken embryos Kendra had examined under a microscope in biology lab in the spring. Thomas didn't respond to her, just walked by and up the stairs. Kendra had thought that he would be at least a little curious about the license plate number, why she wanted to track down its owner, but apparently Brooke's latest stupid idea was more important.

Kendra forgot about her workout. She sat down at the computer and tentatively turned it on. She had never done so without Thomas or her mother there to help her, tell her where to click. But she did it, and soon, she was connected to the Internet.

She typed "lisense plate" into the search engine, which only listed websites about plates and dishes. She had scanned over one hundred hits until she realized that she had misspelled "license." After typing it correctly, she immediately found what she was looking for: PersonFinders.com.

Thomas was right; the service cost fifty dollars. Kendra ran downstairs and rifled through the phone desk in the kitchen. She thought she had seen a whole stack of Joyce's credit cards, held together by a rubber band. Pens, pencils, junk mail, a barrette, stamps, a bottle of ginkgo biloba, and finally, under a golf glove, the credit cards. Kendra pulled two Visas and a Master-Card from the stack, and ran back upstairs.

After the first Visa was denied, the second one worked, and ten minutes later, Kendra had the guy's name and address:

BRUCE ROMBOUGH
100 VISTA ESTRELLA
TUCSON, ARIZONA 85704
(520) 299–1179

She printed it out.

Seeing his name, address, and phone number on the piece of paper elicited an excited flip in Kendra's stomach. He had looked like a Bruce. And what a stupid last name: Rombough.

Kendra found Vista Estrella quickly; she had used the Internet to pinpoint the address. She felt that giddy jumpy feeling in her stomach as she drove up Vista Estrella, near the Tucson Mall, a curvy street at the base of the foothills lined with several types of densely placed cacti.

The old Volvo's air conditioning was finally kicking in when she found Bruce Rombough's address: a huge, sprawling apartment complex, waves of identical brown adobe boxes pushing up into the desert. Estrella Village. ONE HUNDRED spelled out in huge golden letters on a wall obscured slightly by cacti and palm trees. There must have been over a thousand units.

She drove around the complex, anyway, cursing PersonFinders.com for not giving her his apartment number, looking for Bruce Rombough's convertible. She thought of Petey, how he'd like to help her do whatever it was she was going to do to Bruce Rombough's car. She hadn't figured out what exactly she wanted to do to his car, but she knew it had to be good—she had to make it worth the fifty dollars she'd eventually be forced to pay her parents. Eggs and shaving cream were too easy, too common. Sugar in the tank and tire slashing seemed too common, also, too Judge-Judy—white trashy and too severe—although Bruce Rombough was an asshole. Petey could think of something, she knew, and it would be fun to have an accomplice. And Petey was never busy. After he was done with Brooke, maybe Thomas would return with her tonight, help find Bruce Rombough's car. Thomas could think of something good to do to it.

Recently, though, if Thomas went out with Brooke, he didn't return until late at night.

Kendra didn't feel like lifting when she finally made it to the weight room at the Racquet Club. Driving around the huge apartment complex in the weakly air-conditioned Volvo had drained the energy from her. She used small weights, worked her rotator cuffs, biceps, and triceps. She completed a cycle on the machines, convinced herself that maybe her body needed a break from real weightlifting, that the machines would stretch and tone her muscles.

She said hello to Rich and Will as she was leaving. They were doing some sort of torturous pec work using a bench and criss-crossed cables.

"Why don't you join us?" Rich said. His skin looked fried, too orange, but his musculature approached perfection: defined everywhere, but not bloated or veiny like most body builders. He had the thickest shoulders of anyone she knew.

"I like my tits the way they are," Kendra said. "Will needs it more than me," she added.

"Hey!" he said from his place on the bench. He stopped his repetitions and sat up, allowing the pull of the cables to spin him around. The weights slammed down with two loud clanks. "I have great pecs." He took a deep breath and puffed out his chest until he laughed.

"I'm kidding, bitch," Kendra said. "You both know I love your muscles." She smiled and waved, stepped out into the sun, but turned around and went back inside.

"I have a question for you guys," she said. "It's kind of personal."

"We're not a couple," Will said.

"Not anymore," Rich said.

"Do you guys only date other bodybuilders?" Kendra asked, speaking softly.

"No," Rich said. "Most bodybuilders are dumb as dirt. Look at Will, for instance."

"And most are fucked-up straight guys stuck in the closet," Will said. "I don't have a type."

"Bullshit," Rich said. "Your type is anyone with money."

"At least my type is old enough to vote," Will said. "At least my type doesn't have algebra tests to study for."

Rich turned to Kendra. "My last boyfriend was nineteen. Old enough to vote and drive and drink alcohol in Mexico."

"I think my brother's gay," Kendra said. "He's eighteen." She imagined him with Rich on a date. Both wore dark suits and ties. Rich opened the car door for Thomas, helped him with his jacket and chair at the restaurant. Thomas would be into either Rich or Will. They both had better bodies than any of the professional wrestlers he watched every day.

"Is he cute?" Rich said.

"Does he have a bod like yours?" Will said.

"I think he could be cute," Kendra said, "but I'm his sister so I don't really know. And he's kind of skinny."

"Some guys love skinny," Will said.

"I like skinny sometimes," Rich said.

"Rich likes to play daddy," Will said.

"Thomas likes computers and wrestling," she said, watching Rich's and Will's faces drain of their enthusiasm. "He's really funny and really smart, though. He's going to Columbia University in New York in the fall. Plussing as which, he got like a perfect score on his SATs."

"Plussing as which?" Will said. "What the fuck does that mean?"

"Apparently you and your brother had different English teachers," Rich said.

"He's cool," Kendra said, embarrassed. "Couldn't me and him meet you out sometime? Like, where should he go?"

Rich turned to Will. "We could meet them at IBT's some time next week, couldn't we?"

Will rolled his eyes, rubbed his chalky hands, but told Kendra, "Sure."

"Cool," Kendra said.

"We'll call you," Rich said.

* * *

The Pima College campus closest to the Racquet Club was nothing more than a gathering of trailers and cubic cinderblock
buildings. Kendra parked behind a Whataburger, ignoring the
WHATABURGER PARKING ONLY sign, and cut through greasy oleanders to reach the administration trailer.

"I want to take an English class," Kendra told the woman
who sat behind the first desk she encountered.

"Current student?" the woman asked. She wore white lipstick that glowed amidst her overly tanned face.

"I'm still in high school," Kendra said.

The woman spun around in her office chair and pulled forms
from three different baskets. She handed them to Kendra. "The
pink one lists all the English classes on all campuses this summer. Fill out the white one now. The yellow one goes to your
high school guidance counselor."

Kendra sat at a small desk and filled out the white form. Nothing tricky. She ran through the list of English courses and found
one that began next Monday and only lasted three weeks. It met
weekdays from eleven A.M. to two P.M. Three credits. English 107.
Kendra wondered if this would count for English next year, if she
could have a free period to mess around. Eleven to two was perfect, though. She'd spend the hottest time of the day in an air-
conditioned room on the main campus, which was perched up in
the base of the craggy mountain range in the west side of town.

Kendra handed the completed form to the woman. "What
now?"

The woman looked over the form, made a Xerox copy of
Kendra's driver's license, stapled it to another form, and put them
in a basket. She handed Kendra a small pink slip. "You gotta
pay," the woman said, "but you don't have to now. You can pay
next week, if you want."

"That's it?" Kendra said. She had thought that registering
would take at least an hour. She had imagined lines to wait in,
forms to get notarized, records to be transferred.

"That's it, honey," the woman said. "You have a lovely tan, by the way."

"Thanks," Kendra said, nervous that this woman, whose own skin was deeply sun-ravaged, the color of dried blood, was complimenting her tan. "I use sunscreen, but I guess I need more."

"Baby oil is great," the woman said. "For before and after the sun. Makes it soft and doesn't interfere with the natural tanning process."

"Thanks," Kendra said, horrified.

A few moments later, she was standing in front of tall shelves of sunscreen at a huge discount drugstore. She chose three different brands of sweatproof, waterproof SPF 45. She rubbed some on her arms and legs as she waited in line at the checkout.

"Smile!" Joyce said, as Kendra walked into the family room. Joyce blinded her with a camera flash.

"Don't," Kendra said, squinting, seeing white fuzzy blobs, flash residue.

"Too late," Joyce said as she snapped another photograph.

Kendra, pissed off and already suffering a headache from afternoon traffic, groped her way toward her mother, reached for the camera.

Joyce snapped two more, giggled and backed away. "It's my new digital camera!" she said. "I can take as many as I want because they're all free!"

"Great," Kendra said. "Stop it."

"No more toy shows," Joyce said. "I'm doing it all over the Internet."

"Finally," Kendra said. "That's cool." She sat on the sofa, pulled off her running shoes, rubbed her feet, stretched her ankles.

Joyce snapped one more photo of her, and Kendra grabbed one of her shoes. She chucked it at her mother without really thinking. Joyce ducked, and the shoe smashed a small lamp on top of a bookcase.

"I drove to the east side of town, near Mount Lemmon," Melissa said. "And then to another site all the way west out in Starr Pass, so I saw a lot of Tucson."

"You did," Merv said. "You drive all over to these people's homes? Why can't you just call them?"

"My company is totally retarded. I have to administer the surveys and make sure every single question is fully understood," she said. "You know, really tricky questions like 'Is there blood in your sputum?' and 'Approximately how many times per day do you cough?'"

They sat at a back table in Café Poca Cosa, a restaurant Melissa had read about and insisted Merv meet her at. It occupied the ground floor of a hotel downtown, a few blocks from Merv's favorite bars.

They had been served huge salads of greens, peppers, tangerines, and mangoes on wooden platters. Now Merv worked his way through cod fillet with halved Brussels sprouts, tomatoes, red onions, and a few unidentifiables.

"At least you can tell people you do research for a pharmaceutical company," Merv said. "I work at a water-side park."

"I gather you hated college?" she asked.

"I didn't really hate it," Merv said. "I just didn't go that often."

"I think it's weird how everyone is expected to go to college. I don't think college is for everyone. I mean, someone has to run the water parks, right?" She took a bite of her green corn tamale pie. A little drop of mole moved down her chin.

"I guess," Merv said, taken aback. He didn't tell her about the mole.

"I didn't mean it like that. I didn't mean it like we need uneducated drooling slobs to run the service industries; I meant it like someone may prefer working at a restaurant or a supermarket or a water park to spending years and years in college."

"I see," Merv said.

"You think I'm a snob," she said. "Don't you?"

"No," Merv said. In fact, he thought it was adorable how she was backpedaling, trying hard not to offend him. He could watch her talk for hours. He marveled at her beautiful full lips, like they were in a permanent state of kiss. She wore a white sleeveless polo shirt that accentuated her freckled, toned arms. Not overly toned like the neighbor girl's, but defined.

"What are you looking at?" she asked him, smiling, blushing a little.

She had caught him staring. "You have some mole on your chin," he said. "Just a little drop."

Melissa daubed her chin with her napkin. "This is seriously like the best food I've ever had."

"It's okay," Merv said, holding back the enthusiasm he felt for his cod, the likes of which he had never tasted. No fishy flavor or odor, just light flaky meat with a mole that hinted of pistachios.

"Just okay?" she asked.

"I'm lying," he said, smiling. "It's the best."

Merv had tried to drop the idea that Melissa was interested in him, tried to convince himself that she was just being nice to him because he was one of Jason's best friends. Here she was, treating him to dinner on her company's expense account, making him laugh, all in an effort to be a better girlfriend to Jason, to win over Jason's friend.

Or, she could actually be interested in Merv.

Merv couldn't imagine that Deena would have done anything like this. In fact, she had told Merv that she hated Jason and Rusty, said they were privileged assholes with a sense of entitlement to everything and everyone. When Merv had asked her to explain, she told him he couldn't look at them objectively because they were his best friends. The same night, Deena shoved Merv off in the middle of sex, scratching his neck with her fingernails. "You're grunting like an angry, violent animal!" she had yelled.

"We're fucking!" Merv had said. "People make weird noises when they're fucking!"

Deena told him to leave, but called him in the morning and acted like nothing had happened the night before, started babbling about how she needed to trim the hedges in front of her small pink adobe house.

"I don't think you're a snob," Merv said now to Melissa. "Not even close."

"I'm just blathering over here about nothing," she said. "I don't even know what your parents do."

"My father died when I was fifteen," Merv said. "He was an attorney. My mother works for his former partners."

"Sorry about your dad," Melissa said. "That must have been awful to lose him in high school."

"He was sick for years," Merv said. "He'd get better for a few months, then fall sick again. It sucked for him."

Merv's father actually subscribed to the same belief that Melissa held: College is not for everyone. He had told Merv many times that it was okay if he didn't go, that he himself had only gone to college and law school because his parents forced him. "Every night I spent in the library memorizing some tort bullshit, I cursed my parents," he had told Merv. "I felt the hate for them in my stomach. That's not how a son should feel about his parents."

Melissa took Merv's hand as they walked the hot streets of downtown after dinner. They looked in the windows of a few empty storefronts, talked about what downtown Tucson could be—a thriving area for work, living, and play—if only people would smarten up.

The Tap Room at the Congress Hotel was crowded with grumpy artists and drunks, and cloudy with their cigarette smoke. The jukebox played a scratchy old Hank Williams song.

Melissa sipped her Coors, looked over Merv's shoulder. "I love those curtains," she said. "Like something my dad must have had in his room when he was a kid."

Merv regarded the curtains. Smoke-stained patterns of cowboys lassoing horses and cows, hiding behind cacti, shooting Indians. He had been to the Tap Room hundreds of times, but he had never noticed the curtains that kept the little bar dark. "Not very politically correct," he said to Melissa.

"I love them," she said. "I'd like a dress made of the same material."

"Oh, you're one of those," Merv said.

"One of what?"

"One of those hipster chicks," Merv said. "Like a secret poet or a singer in a punk band."

"I played trumpet in the high school band and I hate poetry," she said. "Wow, you're really good at reading people. You have me totally figured out."

"Guess what instrument I played in high school," he said.

"None," she said. "You went to that weird prep school with Jason and Rusty and I know you didn't have band."

"Got me," Merv said. "You're smarter than you look."

"I look dumb?"

He looked at her. Adorable. Beautiful. Round face. Full lips. Skin as smooth as melting ice. He wondered why she was sitting at this table with him in this dingy bar.

"You just went from smiling," she said, "to a full-blown frown."

"I was just thinking," he said. "And, no, you don't look dumb."

They sat there, soaking up the smoke, downing two pitchers of Coors, for over an hour. Melissa told Merv about her little sister who was killed in a car accident when she was twelve. Melissa had been sitting in the backseat next to her, and all of a sudden there was a boom and her sister was dead. Just like that. "It was weird," Melissa said. "You'd think it would bring me closer to my parents, that our little family would all be closer, but I pulled away from my parents and started reading bad fantasy novels about helpful unicorns and magical elves, and my parents got a divorce a few years later."

Merv went on to tell her about his father's death, how the house was disintegrating, how his mother went crazy, was still crazy.

When they finally stepped out of the bar into the fresh air, both took deep breaths. "That was a downer," Melissa said. "How'd we ever get on the topic of death?"

"You started it," Merv said, smiling.

"I did," she said. "So it's my responsibility to change the mood." She stepped in front of Merv, and gently placed her hand on his neck, guiding him down for a kiss.

Monday, July 2, 2001

Warm and humid

High 107/Low 74

Partly cloudy

KENDRA WOKE EARLY. SHE WAS RUNNING THE HILL BY FIVE-THIRTY, sweating more than usual under the hot clouds that had draped the valley in uniform grayness. Maybe it would rain.

She ate quickly—an egg-white-and-vegetable omelet and a protein bar—and headed off to the Racquet Club, where she worked through back and biceps hurriedly and swam for an hour. She grabbed a protein smoothie before she headed to her high school to get the community college form signed.

"Look what the cat dragged in!" Mrs. Shawn said when Kendra stepped into her office. "Kendra Lumm!" Mrs. Shawn usually wore shoulder-padded office suits from the eighties, but today she was in a pink T-shirt, shorts, and tennis shoes. She looked so small, like a miniature version of herself.

"Hi, Mrs. Shawn. Will you sign this for me?" Kendra handed her the form.

"Have a seat," she said, reading over the form. "I assume you heard that Peter Vaccarino's missing."

Kendra sat. "Yes," she said. "I heard." She hadn't been in the office since April, when Mrs. Shawn had called her to discuss her progress in pre-algebra.

"You're wanting to take a class at Pima College," Mrs. Shawn said. "That's so ambitious. Are you hoping to follow your brother to the Ivy League?"

"No," Kendra said. "I just want to talk better."

"Still, very ambitious," Mrs. Shawn said. "So this is a basic grammar course? A speech course?"

"I think so," Kendra said.

Mrs. Shawn stood and looked through a pile of papers on her desk, then another on top of her file cabinet. "I have a course catalog around here somewhere."

"The lady there said it was an English course. She knew I was still in high school."

Mrs. Shawn returned to her seat. "It's so good to see you, Kendra. You've grown so much in the last year. How's your summer going?"

Kendra smiled. She got the feeling Mrs. Shawn was lonely, wanted to chat about nothing. She decided she better get out of there quick.

"And how's Thomas? Is he excited about Columbia? About moving to New York?"

"He's relaxing a lot this summer," Kendra said. "So, like, if I take this class do I have to take English next year?"

"Save your syllabus," Mrs. Shawn said. "Save all your work. I'll evaluate it in the fall. Maybe it'll count for a semester. Whatever the case, I'm so proud of you, Kendra!" She reached across the desk and squeezed Kendra's shoulder.

"Thanks," Kendra said. "Great."

"Have you spoken to the police about Peter Vaccarino yet? I gave them your name. You're one of the only people I ever saw him with. You and Brooke Luter."

"A detective came by last week or something," Kendra said. "Plus, didn't you see Brooke on the news?"

"I didn't see that!" Mrs. Shawn said. "How did she do?"

"Fine," Kendra said.

"Well spoken?"

"She was bawling and begging people to call if they had any information about Petey."

"Peter will turn up," Mrs. Shawn said. "Don't you think?"

"Yeah," Kendra lied. "He'll turn up."

* * *

The Pima Community College Main Campus was nestled in the base of the dark jagged mountains on the west side of town, a thirty- or forty-minute hot drive across the city from Kendra's house. As Kendra sat stuck in traffic at Oracle and Ina Roads, listening to an old Journey song on 96 Rock, she was actually excited. She had stopped at a huge drugstore and bought a new notebook and several new pens, along with two protein bars and a Gatorade in case her professor gave the class a break. She imagined her new class: crowded with college students, serious students, all of them paying attention and furiously scribbling notes. Wooden desks. A big one for the professor, who'd be tall, with a beard and glasses. Kendra would be speaking like everyone else by the end of the summer.

There were only two other people in the cinderblock classroom when Kendra arrived five minutes early: a middle-aged obese woman with short curly hair, and a scruffy looking college guy in cut-off shorts and a faded black Misfits T-shirt. They sat at small plastic-chaired desks on either side of the room. Kendra's father owned a similar Misfits T-shirt to the one the kid was wearing, maybe even the same one: the gory band members' faces surrounding the logo. She was familiar with the old death punk band. The lead singer had been a short guy with decent musculature. Kendra thought their music was stupid.

The guy smiled and nodded at her when he caught her reading his shirt. "You like the Misfits? Danzig?"

"My dad does," Kendra said. She sat at one of the desks between her two classmates, pulled her new notebook from her backpack and carefully placed it in the middle of the desk. She lined up her new pens to the right. The plastic seat was cool.

"Your dad?" the guy said.

The fat lady turned around. "My name's Bernice," she said. Bernice said her name with some sort of weird accent Kendra didn't recognize, but she said "My name's" with no accent.

The guy's name was Todd. "Does your dad really like the Misfits?"

"Why would I lie?" Kendra said. "I think they suck."

"I think they suck, too," a woman said. She had come in the room and sat at the desk next to Kendra's. "Even in the late seventies and early eighties, their whole morbid death punk shit was so boring. They were finely tuned for prepubescent aggressively pimply boys into grinding macabre noise and histrionically morose lyrics."

"So much for first impressions," Todd said. "People think my poetry is morbid."

"If it's not gratuitously so, that's fine," the woman said. "If it is, I'll let you know." Then she turned to Kendra. "I like your arms. So worked, but not too masculine."

"Thanks," Kendra said, taken aback. In less than a minute, three strangers had spoken to her. The new woman's arms were pretty nice, too. She wore a sleeveless white T-shirt that showed them off. She was tan, with dark brown hair and eyebrows like Brooke Shields's. Sort of exotic looking, Kendra thought. "Where do you work out?"

"At school," the woman said. "My name's Crystal."

"Kendra."

"I'm Todd," Todd said, smiling at Crystal.

"My name's Bernice," Bernice said, again using a weird accent with her name.

A man walked in. His straight thick hair hung down to his knees. It was nicely brushed. Shiny, no snarls. Kendra had seen him before. She and Thomas had seen him at the supermarket once. Thomas speculated that the guy was a Satanist or in some weird cult. The guy wore big rings on every one of his fingers and both thumbs. He swooped his hair up and let it rest on a desk before he sat at the adjacent desk in the far corner. One desk for him; one for his hair. Kendra was both disgusted and intrigued.

The hair man caught Kendra looking at him. "What are you looking at?" he said.

"Your hair," Crystal said. "Duh."

"I wasn't asking you," he said.

"I felt compelled to answer," Crystal said. "Clearly you crave attention, or you'd cut your hair."

"What do you know?"

"I know your hair must collect a lot of filth all day, especially if you're draping it all over public furniture," Crystal said.

"Ever heard of shampoo?" the hair guy said.

"Ever heard of barbershops?" Crystal said.

And then a short man in jeans and a tweed jacket quickly scampered into the room. He wrote on the chalkboard: *English 107, Poetry Writing. Instructor: Smith Boyle.* Kendra's stomach dropped. Fuck, she thought. The wrong class. She was about to leave when the instructor began to recite a poem.

"Legs dangle far/from the sheets/at noon. Like branches/dipping in the murky river/they dangle./Arms hang, trace circles on the dusty floor./Not a desert/nor asphalt/a green bucolic garden/for us/at noon." Smith Boyle then sat on the edge of his desk, closed his eyes, and drew a deep breath through his nose. Kendra noticed his patchy hair, like he dyed it. Some of it was red; some of it jet black—like Kissy, the guinea pig her class had taken care of in fourth grade. "This poem was published in the *Wild Acorn Review.* It's one of several of my poems you'll be hearing over the next few weeks. Why do I read my own poems, you're wondering, I'm sure, but it's just to illustrate what it takes to write poems. I'll take you step by step through the writing process, from the initial seed or spark, if you will, to the final syllable."

Crystal reached over and wrote, *Is this guy for real?* On Kendra's open notebook.

Kendra wrote, *I thought this was a grammer class.*

Crystal crossed out *grammer* and wrote *grammar,* underlining the *a.*

Smith Boyle continued, took roll, mentioned that the class barely squeaked by with an enrollment of only five. "I guarantee, though, that you'll all be breathing poetry over the next few weeks. Prepare to become poets!" He rubbed his little hands together—like a raccoon, Kendra thought.

Crystal wrote, *This is a joke, right? There's a hidden camera inside the fire alarm.*

Kendra wrote, *I have to switch classes.*

Crystal grabbed the notebook and wrote, *YOU CAN'T!!! THIS WILL BE FUN, I SWEAR!!! THREE WEEKS OF THIS DORK! AND THE GUY WITH THE HAIR!!*

Kendra took the notebook back and wrote, *The guy with the long hair freaks me out.* She was about to show the note to Crystal when Smith Boyle walked over.

"This is college," he said to Kendra. "This is poetry class. If it's not as sacred to you as it is to me, maybe you shouldn't take this class." His eyes were glassy, wet-looking, and unnaturally blue.

Bernice raised her chubby hand. "But, Professor Boyle, the class will be canceled if anyone drops, right?"

"I'm sorry," Kendra said. "I think I signed up for the wrong class."

"But she wants to stay," Crystal said. "We're both excited at the prospect of becoming poets under your guidance and tutelage."

At break, Kendra sat on the cool tiled floor next to the Coke machine right outside the classroom, sipped her Gatorade. She listened to Crystal and Todd argue about music, watched Bernice, who remained in the classroom by herself, rub her hand under her arm and then smell it. Kendra didn't know where the hair guy or Smith Boyle had gone. She could get up and leave, she thought. She could take a class during the next summer term, a grammar class or a speech class. To hell with these freaks. But, as she stood, about to retrieve her notebook and pens from her desk inside, Crystal walked over.

"We still have ten more minutes," she said. "You smoke?"

"No," Kendra said. "And I think I'm leaving."

"You can't!" Crystal said. "Please don't!"

"This is the wrong class," Kendra said. "I need a grammar class. I don't even know how to spell 'grammar.'"

"Just stay," Crystal said. "You don't need a grammar class. It's not like English is your second language."

"I'm still in high school. I won't get credit for this class. It's a waste of time."

"Don't you want to see what the hair guy's poetry is like? It'll be funny as hell. And I'm sure you can get some kind of credit for this."

"I hate poetry," Kendra said. "And the teacher kept staring at my legs." She had caught him several times as he babbled on about syllables and line breaks and weak verbs and other bullshit Kendra thought was boring and useless but took notes on nonetheless.

"If you drop it," Crystal said, "the whole class will be canceled."

"Sorry, but—"

"It's too late to get into a grammar class now, anyway. What're you going to do every afternoon? Watch TV? This is way better than TV."

Crystal was right. Kendra imagined herself at home, reading fitness magazines, worrying about Thomas, worrying more about Petey. She remembered what Franny had said about positive distractions. This class, along with working out, would fill her days completely. And Crystal seemed cool. Kendra had never met anyone like her before—someone who was obviously smart, used big words, knew how to make fun of people, and still wanted to be her friend.

"Plussing as which," Kendra said, "I *do* want to read the hair guy's poems."

"I wonder if they're all about hair," Crystal said.

"Me and my brother saw him in the supermarket once. My brother snuck up and looked in his cart. He said it was full of canned hams, but I think he was lying."

"Probably hair products," Crystal said. "Vile image: some poor soul shampooing the hair guy's hair! I bet he has a kidnapped woman shackled to the wall who shampoos his hair. He throws her scraps of meat—ham—and makes her wear rags!"

"Sometimes she gets cookies if she shampoos real good," the hair man said, peeking out from the other side of the Coke machine.

Kendra's first assignment was to write three haikus with a single theme or image. It took her over an hour, but she did it:

> Across the desert
> In a tan house with a roof
> Mother waits for son
>
> He sniffs marking pens
> He drinks beer with his homeboys
> He left town real fast
>
> The cop asked me why
> I did not know and still don't
> I'm sure he is good

As she was typing her poems from her notebook onto the computer, Rich called and told her that he and Will would be at I.B.T.'s on Fourth Avenue if she wanted to bring Thomas to meet them. If she and Thomas got there early enough, before eight or eight-thirty, they could enter through the back patio without I.D. hassles. Kendra told him that they'd be there, and she ran downstairs to look for Thomas.

He wasn't in his usual spot in front of the television. She heard him outside, splashing in the pool with Brooke, both of them giggling madly.

"Brooke, I need to talk to Thomas in private," Kendra said as she stood at the edge of the pool, her toes hooking over. "Being as which you should be like on the news crying about Petey or something."

Brooke swam over to the shallow end and stood. She wore a

one-piece racing swimsuit in navy blue. She was kind of toned, Kendra admitted to herself.

"If you spoke English maybe I could understand you," Brooke said.

"You have a huge green booger," Kendra lied. "Go inside and blow your nose."

"She's lying," Thomas said. "You don't have a booger."

"I have to go to work, anyway," Brooke said. She climbed out of the pool and began to towel off.

"Brooke got a job at Dillard's in the mall," Thomas said.

"Which mall?" Kendra asked.

"Park Mall," Brooke said.

"I'll make sure to not go there," Kendra said.

"You wouldn't like the clothes there, anyway," Brooke said. "No muscle dyke fashions."

"I could kick your ass so easy," Kendra said. "Plussing as which, that bathing suit makes you look fat."

"Are you ever going to stop with that fucked-up grammar? You sound like a fucking retard," Brooke said. "And I know you won't kick my ass. Thomas told me all about your therapist and your anger management problems. If you kicked my ass, your psycho ass would be in therapy for another three years. Is it worth it?"

Kendra felt Brooke's words in her gut. She wanted to jump in the pool and hold Thomas underwater for telling Brooke about her stupid therapy sessions with Franny. He'd struggle, but she'd win, and soon, not even a single small bubble would rise to the surface. She might let him up for a second just so she could tell him why she was drowning him. "Because you told Brooke, that's why!" And then she'd push him back under. Brooke would grab the skim net and thwack her with it, but Kendra wouldn't let him up. Brooke would throw rocks, scream, and finally burst into tears when she realized Thomas was dead.

Before she began to imagine how she would kill Brooke, the only witness to Thomas's murder, Kendra, embarrassed, turned around and walked into the house. She went up to the computer, finished copying her poems, printed them out, and locked herself in her bedroom, where she read muscle magazines. She did one thousand crunches to a mix CD Thomas had burned for her.

Thomas knocked on her door a few hours later. Kendra ignored him. She had been listening to a Christian call-in talk show on the radio. Listeners would call, and the host, a mild-sounding man, would answer their questions about relationships, family problems, and moral dilemmas. The host began every response with, "Jesus was faced with a similar choice when . . ."

"Kendra!" Thomas yelled. "What are you making me for dinner?"

"Make something yourself, asshole!" Kendra said.

"Come on! I'm hungry!" he whined.

She doubted that Jesus' brother ever told someone he hated that he was going to therapy for anger management problems and then begged him to make him dinner. She doubted that Jesus' brother stole and collected jockstraps and gym clothes from athletes. She doubted Jesus' brother was a lazy fag who watched wrestling all day but somehow managed to get like all A's in high school and score almost perfect on the SAT, while Jesus couldn't even talk right.

"Kendra! Please!"

"I'll make you grilled cheese with tomatoes," she finally said, as she opened the door. "But we have to go out tonight."

Thomas grinned. "And make tomato soup," he said.

"Some of my friends from the gym are going out and they want me to meet them," she said. "Plus, you have to come with me."

"Why?" Thomas said. "I rented *Blade Runner* and Brooke's coming over later."

"If they don't show up, I don't want to be waiting there alone," Kendra said. "Plus, I'm meeting them early. Like, eight."

"Where?"

"Some place on Fourth Avenue," Kendra said.

"If you make me dinner right now, I'll go," Thomas said. "But I mean, right now."

Kendra did make him dinner, and as she stirred the canned soup, she thought that was what Jesus would have done: forgiven the person who had betrayed him. She decided she'd relate the whole incident to Franny next week, starting with Brooke's cuntish behavior in the pool and ending with this nice dinner prepared for faggoty Thomas—only she wouldn't use the words *cuntish* or *faggoty* to describe Brooke and Thomas.

As Kendra parallel-parked the Volvo across Fourth Avenue from IBT's, she thought that maybe she should have told Thomas where they were going and who they were meeting. The surprise could be good, though. Or she could just play it cool, like it was no big deal, which is what she had decided on. It was a nice night, the beating sun had finally set, and the air was lighter. When they had passed the bank with the giant thermometer on its roof, Kendra noticed that it was still ninety-nine, but it had felt much cooler with the windows rolled down, cruising at fifty on Speedway Boulevard, past bright strip malls and colorful fast-food restaurants.

"Kendra," Thomas said, turning down the stereo, "this place is a gay bar."

"I know," Kendra said.

"You're a lesbian? Brooke was right?"

"No," Kendra said. "We're meeting two guys. Two guys from the gym. Rich and Will."

"Why can't we meet them at a normal bar?" Thomas said.

"Being as which they're gay!" Kendra said. "Duh!"

"Am I supposed to be psychic?"

"If we go around back, we can get in through the patio gate without getting carded."

"I'll wait in the car," Thomas said, sinking low into his seat.

"Come on," Kendra said. "You'll like them. They're both totally worked like your professional wrestlers. Actually, more worked."

"So?" Thomas said.

"So," Kendra said. "Come meet them. One might like you."

"What do you mean?"

"They don't just date other bodybuilders," Kendra said. "I asked."

"I'm not gay," Thomas said.

"It's cool if you are," Kendra said. "I won't tell anyone."

"I'm not gay!"

"What about the wrestlers?" Kendra asked, and then she took a deep breath through her nose, bracing herself. "Plussing as which, what about the jockstrap collection?"

"What?" Thomas said, not looking at her. "What are you talking about?"

"Under the back porch," Kendra said. "All those things you stole from the jocks at school."

"What?"

"Plussing as how that doesn't seem like something a straight guy would do, right?" Kendra felt her heart racing in her chest, moving up into her throat. "Plus, I mean, sorry, I guess."

Thomas swung open the car door and stepped out. He turned to face Kendra. "You can go meet your gay friends! I'm taking a cab home and I'm watching the video with Brooke, my girl-friend! The girl I fuck!"

"That's totally sick," Kendra said, confused.

"Not only are you a fucking retard, you're a fucking bitch," Thomas said.

"Just because I found your jockstrap collection?" Kendra said, her voice quavering a little on "collection." "Plus, I thought it was a snake under the porch. That's why I found it."

Thomas slammed the door and jogged off toward Speedway.

Kendra remained in the car for a few minutes, scanned the radio for the same Bible-thumper station that had amused her earlier in the evening. She settled on Joan Jett's old "I Love Rock and Roll" and hummed along until she began to cry, cursing herself for being so stupid, for telling Thomas about the jock-straps, thinking he was gay, for talking like an idiot—all that welled into the front of her mind, followed by overwhelming fear that Petey would never return, and guilt for not doing more to help find him.

It was two more songs before Kendra realized that people walking by on the sidewalk could see her crying in her car. She pulled a towel that stank of chlorine from her gym bag and wiped her face before she walked through the alley to the dusty patio and let herself into the gay bar to meet her friends.

Merv hadn't been hungry in a few days. Ever since he and Melissa kissed his stomach had shrunk. He had been grappling with his attraction to her and the notion that he was betraying Jason. He felt guilty but he also felt elated, still giddy from the date. This morning, all he could force down was a half a piece of toast smeared with peanut butter and a small glass of orange juice. His mother had noticed and offered to make him pancakes or waffles, but he had refused.

He hadn't been sleeping well since the date, either. The night of the date, he didn't get home until two in the morning, and he didn't fall asleep until after four. His mind raced, and soon it was time for work. The other nights were similar. Last night, he had almost gone into his mother's medicine cabinet in search of a sleeping pill.

This morning, his mother had seemed so alert, so happy, offering pancakes, leaving early for work. It made Merv nervous. He knew she had to be taking sleeping pills or maybe something else, but he was sure that Dr. Grossman had only prescribed her enough for a few nights.

After Merv arrived at Splash World and parked his car under the half-shade of a palm tree, he watched as Raymond in his wheelchair was lowered on an electronic platform from a public bus. He wondered what drove Raymond to come to Splash World every day, all day. He wondered where he lived, if he had any family, and friends other than Splash World employees.

Merv's problems seemed trivial compared to Raymond's, and the guilt in his stomach twisted in response.

Merv walked across the expansive parking lot, waded through the palpable heat rising from the asphalt, and greeted Raymond.

"What a nice welcome," Raymond said, hitting his wheelchair's joystick, making the whole thing jerk to a stop as Merv approached.

"You're here so early," Merv said.

"I usually head over to Starbucks for a cup of coffee," Raymond said. "Would you like to join me? You look sort of tired this morning."

"I am tired," Merv said. He looked at his watch. "And I will join you."

"If you would be so kind as to retrieve my cap from the bag hanging behind me, I'd appreciate it," Raymond said.

Merv unzipped the bag and found the cap. He placed it on Raymond's head, adjusted the bill for maximum shade. He noticed a line of drool slowing squirming down Raymond's neck, pooling on the collar of his mint green polo shirt. "How's that?" Merv asked.

"Perfect," Raymond said. "Thank you."

"I'm usually afraid of coffee," Merv said, as they headed down the sidewalk toward Starbucks. "But this morning, I need some. I can't be falling asleep atop the Kamikaze."

"Like that rancid twat Annie you had to fire after she nearly killed that little boy," Raymond said.

Merv was startled by Raymond's statement. He suddenly felt a weird allegiance to Annie, but all he could manage was, "What?"

"She didn't know the procedure and she almost killed that boy with CPR."

"We don't know that she almost killed him," Merv said.

"But she didn't follow Splash World procedure," Raymond said. "You told her so when you fired her. I was there. Remember?"

The white sun hit Merv in the face as they passed a giant square bank building. He felt his skin burning almost instantly and wished he had applied sunscreen before taking the stroll with Raymond. He didn't feel like questioning Raymond for calling Annie a "rancid twat" even though he thought it was weird, totally out of character. He was too tired. He kept seeing white twinkles in his peripheral vision, and his left eye kept twitching. Maybe he was too tired to work, too tired to be responsible for the safety of all the sliders on the Kamikaze today.

All the Starbucks employees knew Raymond and greeted him as he rolled into the shop. Merv noticed the two women behind the counter arguing. "You had him twice last week," one said. "Bullshit," the other said. He figured they were arguing about who'd be lucky enough to make Raymond's coffee and collect the tip from the tip cup. Merv figured Raymond's tip would be generous.

Merv and Raymond sat at a small table by the window, which looked out onto crowded Tanque Verde Road. When Merv was a kid, Tanque Verde was just two lanes, a few feed stores and 7-Elevens, the way to Mount Lemmon. Now there were six lanes at some points, and faux-Southwestern-style strip malls for miles.

"What would you like?" Merv asked Raymond. Merv stood, ready to head to the counter and order.

"No, no. Sit down," Raymond said. "They come to me. I have them trained."

"Wow," Merv said.

"Phyllis or Nancy," Raymond said. "Two young women with two names for older women. You don't meet too many young Nancys or Phyllises, do you?"

"No," Merv said. "You're right."

Phyllis walked over. She was thin, wearing low-rise jeans and green vintage Adidas that almost matched her Starbucks apron. Her bare arms were stained with coffee and various syrups. "You went to Green Fields," she said to Merv.

"I did," Merv said, studying her face, looking for someone familiar. "Did you?"

"I was in sixth grade when you were a senior," she said. "My name's Phyllis Green."

"I didn't really know the sixth graders except for that Adam kid with the red hair," Merv said.

"He's in medical school now," Phyllis said. "Isn't that weird?"

"Yes," Merv said. "Wow."

"Did you hear that Mrs. Hendricks and Dr. Lewis got married and moved to Hawaii?"

"No," Merv said. "I don't really keep up on Green Fields news. I haven't been out there in years."

"It's totally different," Phyllis said. "They built a real gym my sophomore year and—"

"I'll have the usual," Raymond said loudly, cutting her off. "I want the bagel toasted today. And whatever Merv wants."

"I want whatever has the most caffeine," Merv said. "I don't care what it tastes like."

Phyllis nodded and walked off toward the counter.

"Sorry to interrupt your class reunion," Raymond said. "I don't have much patience for that sort of thing."

"I should remember her, but I don't," Merv said. "There were only like one hundred and fifty kids in the entire school."

"Obviously private?" Raymond asked.

"Yes," Merv said.

"I knew you came from money," Raymond said. "I'm sorry. That sounds so vulgar." Raymond unfolded a paper napkin with his twisted hands.

"My dad was an attorney," Merv said. "He liked Green Fields more than I did."

"Why didn't you like it?" Raymond asked. He spread the napkin on his lap.

"I liked it okay," Merv said. "I just never really got into studying or sports or anything like my friends did."

"And that's why you're at Splash World?" Raymond said.

"I like my job," Merv said, suddenly sickened by the concept that decisions he had made fifteen years ago when he was a sophomore in prep school—watching television instead of studying for an algebra quiz, not joining the soccer team, eschewing Model U.N. for a ski trip to Colorado—were still affecting him today. Rusty and Jason had studied for algebra, played soccer, and acted as the two delegates from Libya in Model U.N., and their lives weren't any better than Merv's—not really. They had accomplished more, he guessed, but neither was too psyched about his job. Neither liked living in Scottsdale.

"I know you do," Raymond said. "It's probably others' perceptions of your job, your position in life, that you don't like. Am I right?"

"You are," Merv said. "Sort of."

Phyllis served them their coffee. Raymond's had a super long straw extending from it. Phyllis placed the coffee in the drink holder on the arm of his wheelchair and directed the straw to his mouth. Raymond held his mouth open for the straw like a baby bird, and caught Phyllis's finger with his lips. She nonchalantly wiped it on her apron, and then served Merv his coffee, and Raymond his bagel, which was cut into small bite-sized pieces, each topped with a tiny dollop of cream cheese.

Merv took one sip of his bitter coffee and felt it burn his stomach. The bagel pieces, the aroma of coffee and baked goods, Phyllis's spit-wet finger, no sleep, empty stomach—it all melded together into a nauseating swirl, and Merv grabbed the edge of the table.

"What's the matter?" Raymond said. "You look like you're going to faint."

"I haven't been sleeping or eating well," Merv said, and he went on to tell Raymond about Melissa and the date, even told him about his mother's mental problems, his father's death.

Raymond awkwardly fed himself the bagel pieces, dropping a few on his lap and on the floor. He chewed almost robotically. Milky white drool spilled from both corners of his mouth. "You need to start with this Melissa problem," Raymond said. "Call Jason or Rusty, whichever one isn't dating Melissa, and talk to him. You three know each other pretty well. He'll be able to help. Half the fear is the fear of the unknown. Make the call. Right now. I have a cell phone in my pack."

"I don't know Rusty's number at work," Merv said.

"Do you know the name of the company?"

"Yes," Merv said.

"Get my goddamned phone and call information," Raymond said. "Don't be so helpless."

"It's long distance," Merv said.

"It's a cell phone," Raymond said. "Now get it and dial four-one-one."

Merv did. He was relieved when Rusty's voice mail picked up.

"It's Merv. I need to talk to you. I'll call you later. I'm at work all day, but I need to talk to you."

"Don't you feel a little better," Raymond said.

"Yes," Merv said, and he reached across the table and wiped the drool from Raymond's chin and neck with a wad of paper napkins.

Merv had to leave Starbucks quickly, without Raymond, when he looked at his watch and realized he'd been sitting and talking for over an hour. The call to Rusty did help to assuage the guilt and fear churning in Merv's stomach, even if all he did was leave a message. The message meant he had to call him later, and having any plan of action was better than having none at all.

Two of the meth-heads were riding their little bicycles around the dirt on the edge of the parking lot, weaving through the tall palms. From where Merv stood, across the lot, one of them looked naked—skinny, pink, like an alien just hatched from a slime-filled egg. Merv began to walk toward the entrance gate, toward the meth-heads.

They began to ride toward him. The one with the purple gums grinned and sped and aimed his little bike directly at Merv. The other, the one Merv had thought was naked, but who was actually wearing what looked like women's panties, followed closely. Merv pretended not to see them as they pedaled furiously in his direction, but he felt the fear in his already shaky stomach. Merv imagined one of them pulling a knife from his pants, ripping a gash in Merv's side as he rode by. Or they could both just jump off their bikes, grab onto Merv, bite and claw him like vampires. Just as they passed him, Merv hopped onto a little island of landscaping, grasping a few branches from a greasy oleander.

They shrieked—high enough pitched and psychotic enough to really startle Merv—and brushed up against him before they rode off. They smelled like piss and burning plastic and one of them left a wet spot on the shoulder of Merv's T-shirt.

Merv could still smell them, or thought he could still smell them, when he dialed the police station from the office inside Splash World.

"How tall was the one in the panties?" Nick Honig asked Merv.

He and Merv sat at a picnic table under a few palms. Nick sipped an iced tea. A stream of people had already begun to flow into the park, and Merv was dreading his day atop the Kamikaze.

"He was on his little bike," Merv said. "I'm not sure."

Nick closed his notebook. Sighed heavily, looked away. Merv could see he was annoyed. "Can't you answer any question?"

"You told me to call you when I saw them again," Merv said. "And I called you."

"Next time," Nick said, "look for distinguishing characteristics, watch them to see where they go."

"I told you," Merv said, "they rode behind Taco Bell. I did watch them." Both of the meth-heads' spines had been visible as they pedaled away, vertebrae pushing up against pink skin like a row of tents. One of them wore old army boots, painted orange and green and purple. The other wore tattered sneakers. Merv couldn't remember which wore which, so he didn't mention them to Nick. Fuck Nick, anyway. Ungrateful fuckhead.

"How many times total have you seen them?" Nick asked. "An estimate."

"Ten or twenty," Merv said. "Usually in the mornings." Merv checked his watch. He needed to go climb the eighty-six steps and open the Kamikaze. "Look, you'll know these guys when you see them. Super skinny, sunburned, long greasy hair, fucked-up teeth and gums, and their stupid little bikes. It's not like there's hundreds of guys in Tucson who fit that description." He stood.

"How 'bout you don't tell me how to conduct this investigation," Nick said, "and I won't tell you how to run your little water slides."

Merv muttered, "Sure," and walked off toward the Kamikaze, the whole way trying to conjure better comebacks to Nick's rudeness: *How 'bout you . . . I know it's tough, but how 'bout . . . How 'bout you try as best as you can with your limited resources to catch a few skinny drug-addicted retards on children's bikes, and I'll get back to my work. I saved a kid, you know. I breathed life back into him after I pulled him out of the water. You can't even catch a few derelicts who hang out in the same places all the time, and I saved a kid from drowning. And one was wearing panties! If you can't find a tweeker in panties on a kid's bike, then maybe you should turn in your badge. . . .*

Merv caught himself nodding off behind his sunglasses a few times before lunch. Once, he nearly fell out of his chair, startled from a dream about Phyllis from Starbucks and Rusty making fun of him about something indeterminable. They were in class, which was being held in the suit department at a department store, and there was a test. Of course, Merv hadn't known there was a test, and no one would tell him what it was about.

At noon, he radioed Sean, the guy he had hired to replace Annie, to take his spot overseeing the Kamikaze. His dull headache, burning eyes, and exhaustion were too much to handle, so he went into the employees' lounge, put his head on the cool table, and slept for a few minutes until he was shocked awake by a falling dream.

That was it. He bummed a cell phone from one of the lifeguards and called Rusty at work again. This time, Rusty answered: "This is Russell."

"This is Merv."

"Merv!" Rusty said. "You dog. Melissa said she had a great time the other night."

"She said that?" Merv said. "When?"

"Last night we met for drinks."

"And what about Jason?" Merv asked. He felt the bile seeping up his throat. His heart raced.

"He was at home, working on some spreadsheets," Rusty said. "Melissa really likes you. I told her you were a mentally challenged registered sex-offender and that—"

"He doesn't care?" Merv asked.

"What? Who?"

"Jason doesn't care?"

"Care about what?" Rusty asked. "Are you high?"

"I'm not high," Merv said. "I'm at work and I'm totally tired. I've slept like five hours in like three days."

"Like your mom," Rusty said.

"She's actually sleeping fine now," Merv said. "But what about Jason and Melissa?"

"I think they're both sleeping fine," Rusty said.

"No!" Merv said. "Does Jason know that Melissa and I went out?"

"I guess," Rusty said. "So?"

"Aren't they like a couple?" Merv asked.

"No," Rusty said. "Jason was the one that told her to call you."

The fear and the guilt in Merv's stomach drained. His heart slowed. "You're kidding."

"What's your problem?" Rusty asked. "You seem really fucked up."

"I thought they were a couple," Merv said.

"Are you in like eighth grade?" Rusty asked. "Melissa said all you did was like kiss once."

"I just thought they were a couple," Merv said.

"It's not like you had sex," Rusty said. "God, you're weird."

"Well, I really liked her but I thought the whole time that she and Jason were a couple but she was really cool and I really liked her—"

"You already said that," Rusty said. "Why don't you go and get some sleep and call Melissa later. You should come up to Scottsdale this weekend and relax."

"Maybe," Merv said, yawning.

After he hung up with Rusty, he radioed a few people and told them he wasn't feeling well, that he was going home early.

Merv woke at ten P.M., confused with the darkness, but refreshed. He dug around his child-size desk until he found Melissa's number. He called her.

"I thought you had fallen off the face of the earth," Melissa said. "And I wasn't about to give in and call you."

"Sorry," Merv said. "I've been busy and really tired."

"So?" Melissa said.

"So," Merv said.

"Yes?"

"Yes?" Merv said.

"I'm fine," Melissa said. "I had a great day. Thanks for asking."

"Sorry," Merv said. "I just woke up."

"Rusty says you might come up here this weekend."

"I might," Merv said. He sat on his bed and slid his feet into his river sandals.

"Well, if you do, we should go out for dinner or something. I know some good places. Do you like Thai food?"

Merv wasn't sure if he'd ever eaten Thai food, but he said, "I love Thai food."

"That's good," Melissa said. "How do you feel about cats?"

"I'm allergic," Merv said.

"Bad," Melissa said. "I have three."

"Oh," Merv said.

"And dogs?"

"I love dogs," Merv said.

"Bad," Melissa said. "I'm afraid of all dogs, especially small dogs. The color orange. What do you think of the color orange?"

Merv thought for a second. "I'm neutral."

"It's my favorite color," Melissa said. "Maybe we should quit this game. Next thing you know, you'll be telling me that you hate the Rolling Stones."

Merv did hate the Rolling Stones. The song "Waiting on a Friend" had been playing on the radio when his mother knocked on his bedroom door to tell him that his father had died. But even before that, Mick Jagger and the others had sort of scared him. They were reckless, all of them with crazy, loose-looking eyes. And they were ugly. Really ugly. "No comment," Merv said.

"Good boy," Melissa said. "Smart boy. And when I show you my collection of vintage Stones concert T-shirts, you'll pretend to be impressed, you'll even let me talk about how much they mean to me, how much they've always meant to me."

"I will," Merv said. "And I'll nod and smile."

"Perfect," Melissa said. "And now I have to go. My kitties are calling me."

"Goodnight," Merv said.

"Call me this weekend even if you don't come up here, okay?"

"Will do," Merv said.

KENDRA HADN'T GOTTEN HOME UNTIL AFTER TEN LAST NIGHT. RICH AND
Will had kept her at the bar for only an hour or so, but when
she left, she didn't feel like going straight home, so she drove
around Tucson for a while, stopping at an A-frame taco shack
on Grant Road for a fish burrito. She could only take one bite.
The fish was batter-dipped and deep-fried before it was smoth-
ered in green sauce and cheese and rolled into a tortilla. A fat-
bomb that close to bedtime was not a good idea. She had
thought the fish would be grilled. The burrito had just been an
excuse to avoid home for a little while longer, anyway. She
didn't know what to expect from Thomas, and the uncertainty
scared her.

She figured anyone weird enough to steal and label sweaty
gym clothes was capable of just about anything. Kendra knew
she was twice as strong and nimble as he, but it was his brain
that scared her. He was smarter, a lot smarter. Kendra had accepted that early on, when she eavesdropped on her sixth-grade
teacher, Mrs. Burkelle, as she suffered through a parent-teacher
conference with Joyce. Mrs. Burkelle had been Thomas's teacher
two years earlier, and she said she was surprised at how different
Kendra was from Thomas, that she had never seen such a difference in scholastic performance among siblings. From her spot
outside the open window, Kendra heard her teacher say, "When

Thomas was in my class, he was reading at an eleventh-grade level. Kendra's reading at a third-grade level. She's a very physical girl."

"And?" Joyce said. "Is there anything wrong with that?"

"There wouldn't be if she were more on track academically than she is," Mrs. Burkelle had said. She had often told Kendra to "get on track." The phrase was meaningless to Kendra. She mostly ignored Mrs. Burkelle, her greasy hair, flappy arms, and the huge armpit-sweat stains that blossomed in every garment she wore.

"And she still doesn't quite understand fractions," Mrs. Burkelle added.

"So, what would you like me to do?" Joyce asked. And then the special worksheets started. Every night, after Kendra finished her real homework, she and Joyce would sit down at the kitchen table with a stack of worksheets. Kendra thought the worksheets were stupid; she wasn't learning anything new. They consisted of basic word lists, words like *cat, dome, dinner, fog. . . .* Kendra was supposed to read each word aloud three times, then use it in a sentence. "I saw a cat. . . . I saw a dome. . . . I ate dinner. . . . I saw fog. . . ." At the bottom of each worksheet was a small section labeled *Fun Time* that was often just one short list of words on the right and a list of the same words in different order on the left. Kendra was supposed to draw lines from each word to the same word in the other list. *Cat* to *cat, fog* to *fog, dome* to *dome* . . . The worksheets lasted about a month before Joyce declared them "a fucking waste of my time and yours." She told Kendra that she was sorry that she had agreed to do them and that her teacher, Mrs. Burkelle was "a horrible lazy cunt," and went on to say, "Never tell anyone I said that. She kind of scares me."

Kendra had expected to see Brooke's Honda in the driveway when she pulled up the night before, but it wasn't there. Both a relief and a stressor. She had figured that if Thomas were home, she might have to deal with him. If he wasn't, then he and Brooke were together, perhaps having sex, the thought of which had triggered simultaneous waves of fury, despair, and nausea in Kendra.

When Kendra finally walked in, Joyce was standing in the kitchen, photographing some toys with her new digital camera. She had set up a backdrop by draping a light blue towel over a chair and placing the items on the seat. "Hey, Ken," she had said. "Is Thomas with you? I need him to help me download these photos onto my computer."

"No," Kendra had said, and she walked up to her room.

She didn't fall asleep as quickly as she usually did. She worried about Thomas. She had never seen him as angry as she had earlier that night. She should never have brought up the jockstraps under the porch. Stupid. He'd never talk to her again. He'd head off to college and that would be the last she'd see of him. Kendra's mind had continued to race, and just like she knew she would, she imagined Thomas and Brooke together, having sex. The Brooke in Kendra's imagination was fatter and more hideous than the real Brooke: flabby tits, hairy stomach, dirty toenails. Thomas was thinner, smaller, milky white in pallor. As the clock ticked on, the two of them became uglier, weirder.

Her alarm went off at five-thirty, but she just smacked it and slept until nine, when she finally awoke to the sun streaming through the window, hitting her face, making her upper lip and forehead sweat, even in her air-conditioned room.

Thomas was making scrambled eggs when Kendra walked into the kitchen. He was dressed in surf shorts and a sleeveless T-shirt that showed off his skinny arms like he was proud of them or something. Kendra was about to make fun of him, but stopped herself. All she said was, "Hey."

Thomas didn't respond, just scooped the eggs from the pan onto a plate with a spatula. The eggs were brown, overcooked.

"Your eggs stink," Kendra said. "You burned them. That causes cancer."

Thomas looked at her and took a big bite of his brown eggs. He continued to stand there at the counter, shoveling the brown eggs into his mouth, chewing loudly.

Kendra prepared herself some scrambled egg whites with a few shakes of Parmesan cheese, a bowl of oatmeal, and a grapefruit sprinkled with a little organic brown sugar.

Thomas tore through his breakfast and had finished rinsing off his plate before Kendra sat down at the table to eat her own meal. Fine, Kendra thought. He could behave like the baby he was. Most people would have given him tons of shit for his perverted collection of jockstraps and gym shorts, but not her; she was too nice. The fact that she had worried about him last night, that she didn't sleep well, and that he had caused her to cry in her car really pissed her off. If he wanted to ignore her for the rest of the summer, he was welcome to do so. He and Brooke could hang out all the time if they wanted. They could play their stupid splash-and-tickle games in the pool, they could watch their boring videos, or paste flyers about Petey all over the city. They could fuck like dogs for hours on end. Kendra resigned herself not to care. It seemed like when she did try to do something nice for Thomas, like warn him against Brooke the whore or set him up with a totally hot guy, the type of guy any fag would love, Thomas shit all over her. To hell with him and his stupid sleeveless shirt and stick arms. Jock-collecting weirdo.

She was about to microwave her oatmeal again when Brooke appeared at the glass door and startled her.

"Fuck," Kendra said.

Brooke knocked lightly and walked in. "Where's Thomas?" she asked. She didn't shut the door and Kendra could feel the heat spilling in.

"I don't know," Kendra said. "Plus, shut the door."

"We're going to Phoenix today," Brooke said, sliding the door shut behind her. "To talk to some of Petey's friends there."

"Big whoop," Kendra said. "Who cares?"

"He's been missing for over two weeks."

"Maybe I should go on the news and cry," Kendra said. "And being as which you're my brother's girlfriend, why are you spending so much time looking for Petey?"

"I'm not Thomas's girlfriend," Brooke said. "Didn't we already have this stupid conversation?"

And then Kendra just said it—even though she felt like it might be wrong to do so, she just said it: "He told me last night that you two were fucking."

"Liar," Brooke said, more dramatically incredulous than usual. "Thomas!" she yelled.

"Ask him," Kendra said. "Plus, he thinks you're a couple."

"Thomas!" Brooke yelled again.

He came galloping down the stairs. "Sorry you had to deal with Kendra," he said to Brooke. "I didn't hear your car."

Brooke pointed to Kendra with her car key. "This ungrammatical muscle dyke says you said you and I are fucking."

"I never said that," Thomas said. He stared at Kendra, his brow and mouth pinched tight.

She stared back. "You said it last night," Kendra said. "Outside of—"

"Shut up, you liar," Thomas told her. Then he walked over to Brooke and guided her out. He didn't shut the door, and heat poured in until Kendra stood and slid it closed.

When Kendra walked by the small cardiovascular workout room at the Racquet Club and spied Hetta, she had to take a second look. It was weird to see someone that fat on a StairMaster. It was like Hetta was wrestling with the machine. And Hetta had it set on a pretty intense level. She wore an oversize T-shirt emblazoned with an image of Winnie the Pooh. It draped over her black stretch pants. She was drenched in sweat, her face red and purple, her hair stringy in its wetness.

Good for her, Kendra thought, and she imagined Hetta as a special guest on her fitness show: "My friend Hetta . . . my neighbor Hetta went from three hundred and forty pounds to one hundred and twenty-five pounds in just three months. Tell us how you did it."

"Well, Kendra," Kendra imagined her saying, "I followed your program very closely, that's all!"

"And you did my special water workouts?"

"Of course, Kendra," Hetta said. "Those were my favorite. Several months ago, when you told me in the supermarket that I should lose weight, I shouldn't have been pissed off. I should have thanked you!"

As Kendra walked up the stairs to the weight room, she wondered how much Hetta actually weighed. Two hundred easy. Probably like two twenty.

It wasn't until Kendra was into her third set of bench presses, still speculating about Hetta's weight-loss and fitness programs and goals, that she fully calmed down from the incident with Thomas and Brooke. It was odd for her to ever feel stressed in the weight room. The smells, the other people working out, the grunts, the clank of dumbbells and barbells—the most comfortable place in the world for Kendra.

Smith Boyle began the class by reading more of his poetry aloud to the class. More confusing shit about limbs, arms, legs, feet. Lots of feet. Something about the space between toes.

Crystal slipped a note to Kendra: *If this doggerel is his attempt to compensate for his short stature, thinning hair, yellow teeth, and most-likely microscopic cock, he's failing miserably.*

Kendra smiled at Smith Boyle, and wrote, *What's doggerel?*

Bad poetry. A handy word for this class.

My poems suck, Kendra wrote.

I'm sure they're not as bad as his shit, Crystal wrote. *Did you party last night? Your eyes look totally shot.*

No, Kendra wrote. She was sort of offended.

". . . so that's how I worked the image into the last stanza," Smith Boyle said. "It was quite a puzzle—a conundrum, if you will—but I figured it out by turning my focus back toward the central symbol of the box, the canister, the vessel."

Could he be any more disgusting? Crystal wrote.

". . . the revision process because it's sometimes when the best things happen to my poems. I had an editor from the *Bent Penny Poetry Journal* tell me once that my poems were 'too polished'—as if that's possible. I stopped sending her my poems after that remark. Can a red Mustang convertible be too polished? How 'bout some thigh-high boots? Or an apple? Well, I come from the school of polished poetry . . ."

Yes, Crystal wrote, *he can be more disgusting.*

In an attempt to stifle her laughter, Kendra snorted loudly, spraying her notebook with spittle. "Excuse me," she managed to say between laughs and fake coughs, as she hurried out of the classroom into the restroom down the hall.

She leaned her shoulder against the hand dryer and allowed herself to fully laugh, proudly feeling the intense ab workout she had subjected herself to earlier with every gasp.

"You're totally busted," Crystal said, rushing into the restroom. "I told him I had your inhaler in here." She patted her bag.

"This class is a waste of time," Kendra said. "He talked for like an hour about that dumb poem."

"He gave us a five-minute break," Crystal said, "and we're supposed to read our haikus to the class when we get back."

"Fuck," Kendra said. "Being as which mine suck, I totally don't want to."

"I can't wait to hear the hair guy's poems," Crystal said, grinning. "It'll make this whole class worth it."

The hair guy's haiku series was about a pool hall. Kendra actually thought it was pretty good. She could experience the pool hall he evoked with his poetry: smoky, dark, the clank and smack of balls, the purple glow of the jukebox in the corner . . .

"One pool hall cliché followed by several more," Crystal said after raising her hand. "Generic drivel."

"I like to start a critique by pointing out the strong points of the piece," Smith Boyle said. "I personally appreciated the basic yet evocative language."

"I thought they were lovely," Bernice said. "I think Tim's a real poet."

"My name's Jim," the hair guy said.

"The poet isn't supposed to speak while we're discussing his or her work," Smith Boyle said. "Kendra Lumm, what do you think of Jim's series?"

"I could imagine the pool hall real clear," Kendra said. "Plus, I think it was a good idea."

"I agree with Crystal," Todd said. "I think it pretty much sucked because of the clichés."

"I never said it sucked," Crystal said, "and now that I think about it, Jim may have been using all those clichés ironically."

"What?" Boyle Smith said.

"Perhaps Jim is bored with the traditional way in which poetry is interpreted, so he's stacking one tired cliché on the next as a subversive act," Crystal said. "He can satisfy the morons who can't recognize the clichés and also satisfy the intellectuals who are forced to face the clichés head-on."

"I guess I'm a moron," Bernice said. Kendra could tell that Bernice was outraged because she had sort of squeaked the words out and breathed heavily through her nose.

"I'm not sure I follow you, Crystal," Smith Boyle said, stroking his short beard.

"What's there to follow?" Crystal said. "I'm attempting to give Jim the benefit of the doubt."

"Thanks," Jim said. And then under his breath and from behind his hair, Kendra heard: "Cunt."

Kendra read her poems last. By that time, she was tired, had a headache from the buzzing and flickering fluorescent light above Smith Boyle. She was ready for a nap or something, and no one had much to say except for Crystal, who seemed to have memorized the series after just hearing it once.

"Kendra's language is so basic," Crystal said, "but her ideas are so complex."

"Huh?" Todd said.

"That's bullshit," Jim said.

"The last line, for instance," Crystal said. "*I'm sure he is good.* The word *good:* Is there another word in the English language that is at once so basic and so complex?"

Crystal's ideas about Kendra's haiku series, though confusing, allowed Kendra to forget her headache and boredom for a moment.

"The first line, too," Crystal continued, "is at once basic and complex. If people hear *Across the desert* without realizing its profound and obvious biblical allusions, then what are we doing here?"

"That's bullshit, too," Jim said.

"Jim," Smith Boyle said, "please try to be as polite and diplomatic as the others."

"And stop with the profanities," Bernice said. "If I had wanted to hear cuss words, I would have gone to the movies."

"I thought poetry was about freedom of expression," Jim said. "I didn't realize we'd be censored."

"Poetry is about freedom of expression," Smith Boyle said, "but when we're critiquing others' work, we need to adhere to certain guidelines or the process breaks down . . ."

As Smith Boyle and Jim argued about freedom of expression, Crystal wrote in Kendra's open notebook: *Let's make a list of the food Bernice would consume during a typical two-hour cuss-filled movie. 1) Giant tub of popcorn, extra yellow butter-flavored oil.*

Kendra wrote: *2) Footlong hotdog 3) large lickerish*

Your spelling is horrible, Crystal wrote, *4) 5-pound honey-glazed ham, sneaked into the theater in her pants.*

I know my spelling sucks. Sorry.

That's ok. F. Scott Fitzgerald couldn't spell, either.

Kendra didn't know who F. Scott Fitzgerald was. She figured he was a president or a poet. Crystal was the first person she had met who was probably smarter than Thomas. She wondered why Thomas—if he truly wasn't gay—couldn't date someone as cool as Crystal. Then she answered herself: Because he's a skinny-armed professional wrestling fan, that's why. Plussing as which, he's as weird as shit and never really leaves the house or does anything except for lately helping Brooke do her stupid Petey-finding bullshit.

* * *

After class, Kendra braved the white afternoon sun and heavy traffic and drove up Oracle Road toward 100 Vista Estrella, Bruce Rombough's apartment complex. She drove a few slow passes through the parking lots, looking for his car, but had no luck. She didn't want to go home, though, so she drove around the entire complex: hundreds of stucco buildings, each consisting of at least eight units. She parked in the shade under a corrugated metal shelter, and stepped out of her car into the heat.

She walked through the unlocked wrought-iron gate closest to her parking spot into a cluster of buildings. Kids splashed in a fenced pool in the center of a lawn so green it looked artificial. A few people cooked hotdogs on a cement barbecue. A familiar eighties song blared from an open window: ". . . my thoughts, I confess, verge on dirty . . ." The whole scene was much less depressing than Kendra had imagined it would be, and she took a seat in a grubby plastic lounge chair by the pool. The afternoon sun felt good on her arms and legs, but Kendra knew it was bad for her, remembered the sun-ravaged woman at the Pima College office, and dragged the chair into the shade on the west side of the pool area.

Kendra watched the kids in the peanut-shaped pool play Marco Polo, and noticed the one who was "it" was cheating, peeking through his squinting eyes. He swam after a skinny little girl in a bright pink swimsuit, the smallest of the bunch, whose long hair was so light, she almost looked bald when she surfaced from underwater. "You're cheating, Bradley!" the little girl yelled, clinging to edge in the deep end. "I can see you looking!"

The kid, Bradley, continued to swim at her. The little girl stretched and grabbed a flip-flop from the pool deck. When Bradley reached her and surfaced to tag her, she smacked him in the face with the rubber sandal.

"Shit," Kendra said aloud. She was glad, though, that the little girl had hit Bradley the cheater. He deserved it.

Blood burst from Bradley's nose and settled in a red cloud around him in the deep end. He sank, his eyes big and white as he went under. The little girl clambered out of the pool, stood at the edge and screamed as she watched Bradley. A few other kids swam away from the blood.

"Is he like really drowning?" Kendra asked. "Or is he faking it?"

No one answered her. In fact, three kids, including the little girl who had slapped Bradley with the flip-flop, gathered their towels and ran out of the pool area. The two other kids in the pool area remained in the low end, staring at Bradley, mouths agape.

Bradley surfaced, flailed a little, and sank again.

Fuck, Kendra thought. She hurried to the edge of the pool and looked down at the kid. A bloody nose. Big deal. What a spaz. A weak cheater. He had been going after the smallest kid in the bunch.

Kendra kicked off her running shoes, and jumped into the pool feet-first. Underwater, she wrapped her arm around Bradley's plump belly, which felt surprisingly slimy, and pulled him toward the shallow end. He kicked and squirmed, but she easily brought him to where he could stand.

Bradley stood there, staring at Kendra, two lines of bright blood and snot streaming from his nostrils and thinning as they hit the water in front of him.

"You're welcome," Kendra said to him. "Being as which I just saved your life, you should thank me."

"I know how to swim," Bradley said.

"He does," said one of the other kids, a girl with curly red hair and more freckles than not.

"I swim every day," Bradley said.

"You were like freaking out and bleeding all over the place," Kendra said, stepping out of the pool, wringing her T-shirt, then her hair. "Plus, your nose is still bleeding."

"I know how to swim," Bradley repeated.

"Whatever," Kendra said.

Kendra walked back toward her car, holding her running shoes with two fingers. The bright green lawn was warm, moist and squishy on her bare toes. When she reached the gate, she turned around and yelled to the kids in the pool: "Do any of you have the last name Rombough?"

"I know how to swim!" Bradley yelled back. He was out of the pool, holding a towel to his face.

Now that she was drenched, Kendra had no choice but to head directly home.

Brooke's car wasn't in the driveway, which was a relief to Kendra. Thomas and Brooke were probably still in Phoenix. Stupid waste of time. Kendra had no idea who Petey's friends in Phoenix were. She had met a few guys who had come down once back when Petey was a skater who never skated, but she hadn't met anyone from Phoenix since Petey decided to be a wannabe white gangsta.

As Kendra walked into the highly air-conditioned house in her still-wet clothes, she shivered. Joyce was standing at the kitchen table, again photographing toys with her new digital camera.

"You missed your appointment with Franny," Joyce said. "You know, if you don't show up, the insurance doesn't pay. That's almost a hundred dollars."

Shit, Kendra thought. She had forgotten. Once poetry class was finally over, she had thought she was free, was excited to be free. "Being as which I saved a little fat kid from drowning, I missed my appointment."

"What?" Joyce said. She had been arranging a set of small *Laverne and Shirley* dolls on a white towel. "Really? Where?"

"At this pool," Kendra said, crossing her arms, shivering. She felt the goose bumps on her forearms.

"What pool?"

"At these apartments," Kendra said. "Kind of near Tucson Mall."

"Who lives there?" Joyce asked.

"Lots of people," Kendra said. "There's like ten thousand apartments there."

"I mean who do you know who lives there?" Joyce asked.

"I don't know anyone there," Kendra said. "Plussing as which, I'm freezing." She jogged up the stairs, ignoring Joyce's further questions.

A few moments later, after Kendra had showered and dressed in a T-shirt and shorts, she joined Joyce at the kitchen table.

"Check this out," Joyce said, handing Kendra a photograph. "I found it in a box in my closet."

Kendra looked at the old photograph of her parents. Her father sported a tall spiky Mohawk and wore a leather jacket covered in metal studs. Her mother also had a Mohawk, although it was shorter and less spiky than her father's. Joyce's eyes, circled in thick eyeliner and eye shadow, appeared to be sunken into her skull, but her pupils, just like her husband's, were huge, shiny black pucks. Her skin was washed out and pale, like watery milk. "Neat," Kendra said.

"That was at the Clash," Joyce said. "In Phoenix, years and years ago. I think I was pregnant with Thomas and I didn't even know it."

"What drugs were you on?" Kendra asked. She and her mother had openly discussed her mother's teenage drug use back when Kendra started junior high. Kendra had never even smoked pot. She didn't want to trash her lungs. No other drug even vaguely interested her, although there was a period when she considered steroids—until she saw the muscle chicks suffering from the weird man-face phenomenon.

"No comment," Joyce said.

"Come on," Kendra said. "Tell me."

Joyce smiled coyly, and sat down across from Kendra. "At the Clash, your father and I were on acid. I took three hits; your father, more than that."

"Maybe that's why Thomas is so fucked up," Kendra said. "Plussing as which, he's so skinny."

"Thomas is not fucked up," Joyce said. "When I found out I was pregnant, I stopped everything, even beer."

"He's kind of strange," Kendra said.

"In fifth grade, his I.Q. was tested at 151," Joyce said. "He's a genius."

"He's still weird," Kendra said. She studied the picture again. Her parents looked their age—about nineteen or twenty, Kendra guessed. No lines on their faces, both of them grinning madly. In the photograph, her mother was carrying an old metal lunch box. Even though Kendra had sold hundreds of old lunch boxes with her mother, she couldn't make out which one it was. "What lunch box was that?"

Joyce grabbed the photo and studied it. "You won't believe this, but it was one called Hometown Airport. Super rare. I didn't know that then. Everyone called me 'Heroin Girl' and they thought I kept my drug kit in there."

"Where's the lunch box?" Kendra asked.

"I lost it at a show," Joyce said. "I could sell it now for over a grand, I think."

Joyce had told Kendra about her experiences with pot, cocaine, mushrooms, acid, speed, and even homemade opium that she and her friends had boiled out of poppies that grew alongside the Old Nogales Highway, but she had never mentioned heroin.

Joyce caught her wondering, and said, "I never did heroin, Kendra. God! Nothing with a needle."

"How did you know I was thinking that?" Kendra asked.

"You're easy to read."

Kendra was vaguely offended. "I am not."

"Oh, yes you are," Joyce said. "For instance, I know you're pretty worried about Peter Vaccarino, but you won't let on."

"Big whoop," Kendra said. "Plussing as which, I'm not *that* worried." Kendra stood, walked over to the refrigerator and looked for something to eat.

"It's perfectly fine to be worried," Joyce said. "That's one of the reasons why I'm glad we have Franny for you. That's one of the reasons why you need to schedule another appointment with her this week. See if she can squeeze you in somewhere."

"I'll just go next week," Kendra said, settling on a cup of yogurt. She walked back to the table. "I'm busy this week, being as which I have tons of homework in that poetry class."

"I thought you were taking a grammar class," Joyce said. She was fiddling with the digital camera again, aiming it at Kendra, then toward the stairs.

"Me, too," Kendra said.

"Do you like it?"

"Sort of," Kendra said—and she meant it.

Because of his nap the afternoon before, Merv woke at four-thirty, fully rested and refreshed. His stomach felt fine. The burning worry was gone, and he was starved, so after he dressed, he crept downstairs, carefully placing each of his steps so as to not wake his mother. Instead of starting his car in the driveway, which was right below his mother's window, he put it in neutral and released the emergency brake. He rolled down the driveway and started it in the street.

The eastern sky was beginning to glow orange, draining the landscape of its darkness and repainting the desert with fresh colors—reds and purples instead of the browns and grays Merv was used to. The long shadows seemed to outline everything in black like special effects in a bad Krofft television show from the sixties or seventies. It was hotter than Merv had imagined it would be, so he rolled up his window and turned on the air conditioner. He felt his car lose a little power as it kicked in.

Merv saw only a few other cars along the way. One was full of what looked like high school girls. When he was stopped next to them at the light, they seemed to be arguing about something. One girl in the backseat was crying, and the girl in the front passenger seat kept turning around and yelling at her. Merv guessed that they were ending their night of fun, that the girl in the front seat was angry with the girl in the back for trying to steal her boyfriend. They all had been drinking, having purchased the beer with a third-rate fake I.D. at Lim Bong Liquors or some other shady establishment kept financially afloat by underage drinkers. Then they had gone to a party at Front Seat Girl's boyfriend's house. Late in the evening, after everyone was good and wasted, Front Seat Girl discovered Backseat Girl with her boyfriend in the bathroom—only he wasn't really Front Seat Girl's boyfriend; she only had wished he was, and Backseat had known this. She had no right to be making out with him—no, blowing him—in the bathroom. Slut. Now she was crying to try to turn the tables, but Front Seat Girl was not buying it. No way. Cry all you want, whore. I will kick your ass.

Or maybe Front Seat Girl was a total bitch, always picking on Backseat Girl, trying her best to exclude her from everything. Backseat Girl's parents had tried to instill in her enough self-esteem to brush off that kind of juvenile bullshit, but tonight she finally cracked: Front Seat Girl had made her cry, embarrassed her in front of the rest of the girls. Her parents had told her these girls were no good, going nowhere, more concerned with boys and parties than their futures. Merv saw her parents—generic, like the parents on any sitcom, the father in a fancy sweater, the mother's hair perfect—sit her down and lecture her. She didn't care, though; she wanted these girls as her friends, even if it meant forgoing homework and her future for beer and boys. . . .

When Merv finally stopped imagining different stories about the girls, he found himself parked at Splash World. He couldn't remember driving there, really, and this frightened him a little. He had been lost in the girls' world for several miles, even though they had turned at the intersection where he had first spotted them. For all he knew, he had sped through every red light and had run over several pedestrians. And the crumbs on his lap and the wrappers on the passenger seat: he barely remembered stopping at 7-Eleven and choosing the tiny waxy chocolate doughnuts and the orange juice. When he looked at the little plastic digital clock stuck to his dash, he saw that it wasn't even five.

He sat in the small office next to the employee locker room and sifted through some papers: biohazard reports, safety records, attendance logs. He was supposed to enter the attendance logs into the old, green-screened computer, but he had been procrastinating since the end of May. It was the most boring part of his job at Splash World, a task that only took five minutes per day if he did it every day, but he didn't.

He clicked on the computer, waited for its familiar and annoying hum, and started in on the pile. As he worked his way through the papers, past May and into June, he noticed that the attendance this year was consistently high. Last year there had only been three days above four thousand, but Merv counted ten already, and he had only made it to June fourteenth, not even a third of the season.

As he entered the impressive numbers, he kept hearing faint laughter and screams, like kids in a nearby playground. But it was only five-thirty, so he thought he was imagining it. When he heard someone clearly yell, "Dude!" he decided to go outside and have a look around.

He followed the shouts and laughter past the Kamikaze and Lemon Drop to the wave pool, where, in the same small cove where he had rescued the boy earlier in the summer, he spotted the BMX meth-heads splashing around. He crouched behind a wall of fake rocks and watched. The tweekers were bathing, washing themselves with small bars of hotel soap, the white wrappers floating in the water around them. Their bicycles were propped against the fence that separated the park from the back corner of its parking lot. Their clothes were strewn on the lawn, as was a large Navajo blanket that Merv guessed they all used as a towel.

Merv jogged back to the office and dug through the desk for Nick Honig's card. Nick had written his cell phone number on the back. After a few minutes of searching, Merv just called the police station, knowing that Nick probably wouldn't yet be there.

"May I speak to Officer Honig?" Merv asked the guy who answered the phone. "Nick Honig?"

"*Detective* Honig," the guy corrected, "is off for a few days. Should I patch you through to his partner's voicemail?"

"There are these guys Detective Honig's looking for," Merv

said, suddenly out-of-breath with a charge of adrenaline, "and they're here, swimming."

"Is this an emergency?" the man asked.

Merv thought for a second. "No," he said. "Not really. But Nick really wants to talk to these guys."

"Should I patch you through to his partner's voicemail?" the guy repeated.

"It seems like a shame that you can't send someone down here to get these guys," Merv said. "They *are* trespassing. I'm at Splash World."

"I know," the guy said. "We have caller I.D."

"Oh, yeah," Merv said. "I guess you would. So are you sending some officers down here?"

"I will," the guy said. "What's your name?"

"Merv Hunter. I'll wait for them at the front gate."

"I'm patching you through to Honig's partner's voicemail. His name is Gardner."

Merv left a message for Gardner, then hurried outside to wait for the officers. The sun loomed in the eastern sky, already burning Merv's face. He hadn't yet slathered himself with sunscreen and he had left his sunglasses in the office, so he stood in the narrow shadow of a parking lot light post and thought about the tweekers. He was convinced now that they lived somewhere nearby. He wondered how they had gotten into Splash World and how they had gotten their bikes in. If the cops didn't find anything, he'd dispatch his security team to find their entrance. There was one guy on security each night until four in the morning. Merv figured the meth-heads had determined when they could enter the park undisturbed.

He imagined them sleeping under bushes, curled together like new puppies. They survived on packets of ketchup from McDonald's and taco sauce from Taco Time. They snatched their clothes from the thrift store donation bins in supermarket parking lots—although it looked as if they rarely bothered with their appearance. Their bikes, Merv guessed, were stolen from rich kids in the foothills who were too lazy or stupid to lock them up when they went into 7-Eleven for a Slurpee or a game of Street Fighter 3. The tweekers didn't make their own meth; they just delivered it on their bikes to kids like Petey Vaccarino. Petey was foolish to invite them into his rich little world. They saw everything he had, and maybe they killed him for it. Either that, or they brought him into their world, and Petey, because he had some money, was living in a meth lab out in a tract home near Marana, watching TV all day, getting high, getting thinner, scratching his pink skin furiously.

Merv waited for almost a half an hour before he went back into the office and called the police again. A different operator answered.

"I've been waiting for you guys forever," Merv said. "I'll be in the office at this number if anyone decides to show up."

"Name?" the woman asked.

"Merv Hunter," he said. "At Splash World. I called earlier about trespassers, some guys Detective Honig's been looking for."

"I see it in the log," she said.

"Well?"

"Well what?" she asked.

"Are any officers coming out here?"

"It's not logged as urgent," she said.

"What?" Merv asked.

"It's not logged as urgent."

"Okay," Merv said. "Forget it."

"Sir," the woman said, "is it urgent?"

"I guess not," Merv said. "I tried."

The officers didn't show up until after noon. Merv had been talking to Raymond on the fake beach, the warm waves lapping over his ankles. Raymond had been complaining about his physical therapist. "An honest-to-goodness sadist, the guy is," Raymond said, and then a uniformed officer tapped Merv on the shoulder.

"You're like six or seven hours late," Merv said to the guy. "My security team found the hole under the fence that they used to crawl into the park."

"Who's 'they'?" the officer asked.

"The meth-heads that Nick Honig's been looking for," Merv said. "They were here early this morning, swimming in the cove over there." He pointed to the cove.

The officer sighed and took out a notepad. "Did your security team mess with the hole they were using to get into the park?"

"Ask them," Merv said. "They're in the office behind the main snack bar near the entrance."

The officer took down Merv's name and thanked him for the help. "I'll have Detective Honig call you next week."

"Sure," Merv said, and he turned back to Raymond. "You were saying?"

"There were some intruders here this morning?" Raymond asked, letting his wraparound sunglasses slide a bit down his nose.

"Just some kids," Merv said. "Homeless, drug-addicted kids."

"There should be shelters for kids like that," Raymond said.

"I'm sure there are," Merv said. "These kids ride around on lit-tle bikes. They were hanging out with a kid in my neighborhood way up in the foothills, and now that kid's missing."

"I saw that kid on the news!" Raymond said. "Did you know him?"

"He lived—I mean *lives*—across the wash from me. He's a drug addict, too. A little shit with a loud stereo and horrible taste in music."

"I thought there was something fishy," Raymond said. "The reporter didn't seem to have much to say about him. Ordinarily when there's a kid missing, the reporters say things like 'He was an honor student' or 'She played on the softball team last year,' but with this kid, nothing except a description."

"If they said he was a spoiled drug addict who plays his car stereo way too loud and terrorizes the neighborhood," Merv said, "no one would care about him."

"There was a strange woman making a plea for information," Raymond said. "A friend."

"Was she muscular?"

"Not really," Raymond said. "No."

"Then I don't know her," Merv said. He looked at his watch. Time to head back up to the top of the Kamikaze. "I'll see you later, Raymond." Merv began to walk away, but Raymond called to him.

"Hold on!" Raymond said. "Could you get my sunscreen from my pack?"

"Sure," Merv said.

"The sun seems extra strong today."

Merv dug in the pack hooked onto the back of Raymond's wheelchair. He saw the big wad of money, held together with yellow rubber bands. Hundreds of dollars, probably thousands. A few magazines—*Playboys*, which elicited a grin from Merv, who was happy that Raymond still had that sort of interest. The old-fashioned tube of sunscreen was at the bottom. It was a white tube, a French brand Merv had never seen before.

"A little on my nose and face," Raymond said. "And I'm sorry about the magazines."

"That's cool," Merv said, as he applied the sunscreen to Raymond's warm face. "I have a few under my bed at home, I think." The sunscreen smelled like limes.

"I forgot they were in there until you started to rifle through," Raymond said. "Could you get my forearms, too?"

Merv rubbed sunscreen into Raymond's clammy thin arms, which were splattered with freckles and moles. Raymond hummed, breathed loudly through his nose.

"I have the sun cream shipped from a small shop in Paris," Raymond said. "It's the only stuff that doesn't make me feel waxy or greasy."

"It seems pretty good," Merv said, "but have you had any of these moles checked out?"

"I spend half my life with doctors, Merv," Raymond said. "They've been monitoring my moles for years. Nothing ever comes of it."

"Good," Merv said, and he thought he was finished. He wiped his hands on his trunks.

"And my neck," Raymond said. "Please."

"Sure."

Later, Merv floated in the pool at home. A kickboard with his can of Budweiser atop of it floated next to him. It was eight o'clock and the sun was finally beginning to set, lighting the sky with fiery oranges and bursts of purple and red. The beer was cold, the pool water was perfect—not too warm yet.

He wondered about Peter Vaccarino, if he was dead. Mrs. Vaccarino was probably catatonic by now. Mr. Vaccarino, Merv thought, lived in Orange County. They had divorced when Merv was in grade school. He remembered his parents gossiping about it. He used to see Mr. Vaccarino's car, an old silver Mercedes convertible, parked in their driveway once or twice per week, but that had stopped a few years ago when he moved away from Tucson.

The police had really fucked up. They could easily have caught the tweekers. Merv wished they had. He had enough to think about at work without always having to keep his eyes open for them. Nick Honig would be pissed. He'd look like the asshole he was if anyone found out he had missed the perfect opportunity to question the tweekers.

Merv kicked over to the water jet in the deep end. Too weak. He knew he should get out, turn off the pump, and backwash—release some of the pressure. When he was younger, he used to backwash the pool, then jump back in the water and press his cock against the strong water jet. He'd come right there in the pool. No one else used the pool, anyway. One time, though, when Merv was in high school, he looked up and saw his mother staring at him through the kitchen window. She didn't say anything, but he knew she saw him pressed up against the side of the pool, maybe even saw his face when he came. He wondered if she knew what he was doing, if she really knew he was a pervert. If he got home from school before she got home from work, sometimes he'd sneak a *Playboy* out to the pool and prop it up on a rock so he could look at it while the water jet worked him. He'd wrap the magazine in a towel and skulk back up to his room after he was finished. Now he couldn't even be bothered enough to get out and backwash the pool—and it needed it.

Still wet, Merv walked into the air-conditioned house and shivered. Even though he was hungry, he turned around and went back outside. He lay on a lounge chair and finished his Budweiser as the warm breezes dried him. This was the perfect time of the day. The humming cicadas died down, the sky was lit in blazing smears of color, and the sun was gone. It was still hot, but not prohibitively so, and he let the heat envelop him.

When he finally went inside—all dry, even his swim trunks—his mother had returned from work. She stood at the stove, stirring pasta.

"I was thinking maybe we should drain the pool," she said to Merv.

"Why?" Merv said. "It's clean. I checked the pH yesterday and it was perfect."

"It costs money to run that pool, Merv," she said. "A lot of money."

"Not that much," Merv said. The air conditioning was too cold. He wrapped the towel around his shoulders like a shawl.

"The water bills always double over the summer," she said. "And the electricity bills double, too."

"Maybe if you didn't set the air conditioning to thirty below," Merv said, sitting at the table. "There's some white sauce left in the fridge if you want to use it."

"A girl named Melissa called a few minutes ago," she said. Then she stared intently into the boiling pot of pasta.

"Shit," Merv said. He wasn't sure if Melissa knew he lived with his mother. Now she knew for sure, and she'd know he had been hiding it.

"She said to tell you to call her tonight."

"Shit," Merv repeated.

"Is she problematic like that last one?" She still didn't look up from the pasta.

"Aren't you burning your face?" Merv asked. "It's all red."

"I'm opening my pores."

"That's gross," Merv said.

"I've got nothing better to do," she said.

Two or three times a year, she lapsed into this routine. Next, Merv knew, she'd mention that she hadn't been on a date in fifteen years, that she didn't have any friends.

"Whose fault is that?" Merv said.

"Mine," she said. "No wonder a nice man won't take me on a date."

"Burning your face won't help you find a date," Merv said. Her face was almost purple. "You'll get blisters."

"I told you, I'm opening my pores," she said. "This way, I do two things at once: cook dinner and work on my complexion."

At least she was speaking. At least he hadn't seen any unplugged appliances today. At least she hadn't been wandering around the neighborhood before sunrise. And then he realized something. If Peter Vaccarino had been abducted and murdered, then he should make sure his mother wasn't wandering around the neighborhood at dawn. "Have you been out walking lately?"

"No," she said.

"Good," Merv said. "Until they find Peter Vaccarino, I don't want you out there by yourself."

"Kendra Lumm would protect me," she said. "Not that there's a huge demand among criminals for crazy middle-aged women with fat thighs."

"Don't say that," Merv said, angry.

"They are fat."

"I'm talking about the 'crazy' part," he said. "Don't call yourself crazy."

"Face it, Merv," she said. "I'm crazy."

"Shut up," he said.

"Less crazy now that I'm sleeping, but I'm still crazy."

"Well," Merv said, "don't go out on walks by yourself. That muscle girl can't protect you from guns."

She dumped the pasta into a colander in the sink, leaned into the last burst of steam. "Mush," she said. "This pasta is all mush. I overcooked it."

"Maybe if you focused less on your pores and more on the pasta, that wouldn't happen."

Merv remembered a time he had walked into the library back when he was a senior in prep school. He had heard Rusty and Jason talking about his mom to a sophomore girl named Katy, who ended up following Rusty to Johns Hopkins and eventually became sort of a stalker. The three of them had been sitting on the deep red couches in the magazine section and they didn't notice Merv standing next to the glass display of kachina dolls nearby.

"She's fucking nuts," Rusty had said.

"Everything in their whole house was unplugged and the cords were taped down," Jason said.

"Why?" Katy asked, braiding a thin strand of her shiny black hair.

"I told you," Rusty said. "She's fucking nuts."

"Last week I called there," Jason said, "and she answered the phone. She didn't say anything. She just picked up the phone. I had to say 'hello' like ten times before I heard her sigh. Then she just put down the receiver and walked away. I couldn't call back all night. She left it off the hook."

"Poor Merv," Katy said. "His father's dead and his mom's crazy. Do you guys think I should take AP physics next year?"

Merv had appreciated how Katy had tried to change the subject, but Jason wouldn't let go: "Have you been in their downstairs bathroom? There are pills all over the counter," he said. "Like a hundred bottles."

"I got a B in it," Rusty said. "But I got a five on the AP."

"Did you take it at the same time as calculus?" Katy asked.

"One time last year when I slept over," Jason said, "she made me spaghetti for breakfast. And it wasn't leftovers."

It had been then that Merv walked out. He had forgotten why he had been looking for Jason and Rusty anyway.

Wednesday, July 4, 2001

Hot and dry

High 111 / Low 82

Clear

SMITH BOYLE DIDN'T ASSIGN ANY EXTRA HOMEWORK FOR THE FOURTH OF July, but Kendra sort of wished he had. Even though she had only been in class for a few days, it had begun to occupy her mind. Listening to her classmates and professor talk about her poetry was gratifying, even when they criticized it. Jim, the hair guy, had hated everything Kendra wrote. He had called her sonnet "utter crap." Crystal defended her, though, always conjuring something intelligent to say about Kendra's poems that both lauded Kendra's talent and insulted Jim or Smith Boyle. The assignment for the fifth was to rewrite one of the other assignments. Kendra would work on her haikus again, include more natural details.

She planned on sequestering herself in her room for the two and a half hours she normally spent in class at Pima College. She'd work only on the haikus, think of only the haikus. After, she'd head down to South Tucson to Miguel's uncle's place for the barbecue. If that party sucked, she might head to a party Crystal had told her about in Barrio Viejo near downtown.

Hetta was on the StairMaster again when Kendra passed by the small cardio room at the Racquet Club. She was soaked in sweat, her light blue T-shirt transparent in its wetness. She was really pounding away on the machine, making the whole thing rock from side to side. Her face was flushed, the color of bubblegum. Maybe a doctor had told her that she needed to exercise, Kendra thought. Maybe her obesity was a huge health risk. Maybe she had high blood pressure and diabetes. Or, maybe her husband finally smartened up and told her to lose some of that blubber or he'd walk out on her fat ass.

About an hour later, as Kendra was working her rotator cuffs, Hetta walked into the weight room and started to do curls with tiny dumbbells. To Kendra, this was really odd, amazing even. Hetta had changed out of her sweaty cardio clothes. She wore a giant pink T-shirt over black stretch pants. Like Franny, Hetta had wings of flab that draped and flopped from her triceps. At least Hetta was working out, though, even if she was doing her curls wrong—swinging her elbows. Kendra doubted that Franny had ever worked out.

Kendra put down her weights and walked over to Hetta. "Hi," she said.

"Hello," Hetta said, and then she pointedly looked away.

Kendra thought for a moment. What would Franny suggest she do? Should she ignore Hetta like she had done to her, or should she try to talk to her, maybe show her how to do curls correctly? "How are you?" Kendra finally asked her.

Hetta didn't look at her. "Fine," she said.

"I could show you how to do curls the right way," Kendra said. "Seeing as which you're moving your elbows too much."

"No, thanks," Hetta said. She racked the two seven-pound dumbbells and walked away. Kendra watched her wide ass jiggle under the stretch pants until she disappeared around the corner.

I tried, Kendra thought. Bitch. Fat bitch. She could wreck her elbows. Kendra decided that she'd ignore Hetta from now on, even if Hetta's health kick stretched into the fall.

But she spotted Hetta again in the locker room. Kendra had gone in there to change into her swimsuit and Hetta was stuffing her towel into her gym bag. Kendra locked eyes with her for a moment, but neither of them said anything. If Kendra had only finished her workout a few minutes earlier, she could have caught a glimpse of Hetta getting out of the shower—an image that both repulsed and intrigued her. How would all that blubber arrange itself on one frame? Hetta's hair was wet and she was wearing jeans and a fresh T-shirt, so she had indeed been in the shower. Kendra felt funny showering at the club, and often just waited until she got home. She wondered how Hetta got over the embarrassment, especially with her gross body.

Later, Kendra sat on her bed in her highly air-conditioned room and studied her first haiku:

> Across the desert
> In a tan house with a roof
> Mother waits for son

She changed the second line to read, *In a tan house with cactus.* More natural. More nature. She puzzled over the other two lines, but soon decided that neither could be improved.

She read her second haiku, tried to do what Smith Boyle had said: "Read it like it stands alone, then read it like it's a part of an organic series."

> He sniffs marking pens
> He drinks beer with his homeboys
> He left town real fast

She couldn't change it. It did stand alone, and it also did seem like a natural part of the series. The series was about Petey, after all, and he sniffed marking pens and drank beer with his homies, and he did leave town real fast. Crystal had liked it. Smith Boyle and Bernice had said good things about it. Bernice said it was "sad," and Smith Boyle had praised its casual and natural use of the vernacular, which Crystal told her meant *slang.* Kendra couldn't remember what Todd had said.

The cop asked me why
I did not know and still don't
I'm sure he is good

She couldn't change the third haiku, either. Smith Boyle had said something about using contractions consistently, so she thought about changing the second line to I *didn't know and still don't,* but it didn't seem to matter or affect the poem. Besides, Crystal had remarked that *did not* was a lot more powerful than *didn't.* And there was no way she'd change the last line, not after Crystal had defended it so ferociously and had made Smith Boyle agree with her.

Despite her intention to only think about her haikus, Kendra began to wonder about Crystal. She was cool, made Kendra laugh. She seemed to know Kendra, and it felt weird. The best thing about Crystal was her ability to dish out shit to Jim, Smith Boyle, and Todd. She controlled the class. Everyone was afraid of her, although Jim tried hard to conceal his fear. It seemed like Crystal knew more about poetry than Smith Boyle did. She could make anyone in there look stupid or feel smart with just a few words. She wished Crystal were in her classes in high school. Maybe Kendra wouldn't be so bored and dread it so much if she were.

She looked through her clothes, tried to find something to wear to the party. It was too hot for jeans, and she always felt slutty in short-shorts, so she settled on a pair of red floral surf trunks. She was about to walk down the hall to Thomas's room and dig through his drawer of T-shirts, but then she remembered that he was pissed at her. He had a few sleeveless ones that might look good with her surf trunks, but she didn't dare enter his room. He'd freak out if he knew she'd been in there—although she hadn't seen him today. She wondered what he and Brooke were doing for the Fourth. Considering Brooke had no friends other than Thomas and Petey, and Thomas had no friends other than Brooke, they probably didn't have many options. Kendra had two parties to go to. If Thomas hadn't been such an asshole lately, she might have invited him along. It would have been good for him to meet new people, to see that there are other people in Tucson besides Brooke to hang out with. Tough shit. He and Brooke could spend a shitty boring evening together. They could rent a stupid video, eat popcorn, and get fat together.

Kendra settled on a sports bra and a Penn T-shirt, a gift from her mother, who had bought Kendra a T-shirt from every college she and Thomas had visited last summer. Before she pulled on the T-shirt, though, she rifled through her desk until she found a pair of scissors, and she cut off the sleeves.

She flexed a little in the mirror. Her arms looked great: cut, but not overdone. She turned around and examined her triceps—the V was perfect, as was her ass, she thought: tight and pronounced.

The traffic on Speedway Boulevard wasn't that bad until she hit the Campbell Avenue intersection near the University. When she stopped at the light, she was careful not to look around at the people in the other cars. She didn't want another Bruce Rombough incident. She turned up the stereo and sang along to a Garbage song: ". . . Do you have an opinion? A mind of your own?" In the road ahead, she could see waves of heat squiggling up from the hot asphalt. Why, she wondered, was everyone out this afternoon? Fireworks weren't starting for another five or six hours and it was hot as hell.

When she finally managed to break through the congested intersection, traffic moved quickly. She passed through some poor neighborhoods of spray-painted faded shacks and broken-down cars, before she found Miguel's uncle's place: a big old adobe house, painted a terra-cotta color, built on the eastern edge of A Mountain. She pulled into the dirt parking loop in front of the house and found a place behind one of several shined SUVs. A mural of Guadalupe adorned the waist-high wall that separated the driveway from a cactus garden that was dense with giant prickly pears, pads the size of platters, a few reaching over and shading the walkway of red gravel.

She heard Mexican music from inside the house, the same type of fast carnivallike music that the guy in the taco truck played when he pulled into the parking lot at school. Accordions, guitars, drums. She knocked on a side door. It looked like an old church door, like the ones Hetta ripped off from poor people in Mexico and sold to Kendra's neighbors. Joyce had bought one, and Kendra had listened intently as Thomas chastised her for doing it. Kendra had felt justified in hating Hetta then, but never brought it up with Franny—it would have been a waste of time, anyway. Franny would have made her question Hetta's motives, and speculate as to whether Thomas's tales of Hetta exploiting the poor were founded.

No one answered the door, so she pressed the doorbell, which was hidden behind snarls of cat's claw. She heard the bell ring, but still no one answered. She tried to see inside through a small rounded window, but that, too, was obscured by the thick cat's claw. Finally, she just walked inside, hoping that Miguel would be right there so she wouldn't have to introduce herself to anyone.

It was cooler, but not as cool as Joyce kept her house. The crude Mexican tiles were so polished and shiny they looked wet. She stood in what appeared to be a small study, the walls lined with sloppily laden bookshelves. Several old manual typewriters occupied the top. A colorful and childish painting of a fisherman, a few fish in his net, hung alone on the one bare wall.

Kendra walked through the room and followed voices and the smell of marijuana down a hall, walls crowded with children's school photographs, until she pushed through a swinging door into the kitchen, where five fat Mexican guys in cowboy boots and western snap shirts sat around the table, passing a bong and laughing.

One guy stood when he saw her. He hitched up his Levi's and said, *"Mamita, qué rica estas!"*

A few other guys agreed with whatever it was that he had said. Two of them whistled at Kendra.

"Um," she said, "is Miguel here?"

"Come and sit with us," the standing guy said. "Smoke some

pot." He walked over and put his arm around Kendra's shoulder. His hand felt clammy against her skin. "My name is Jorge, and this is Manuel, José, Juan, and another Manuel. The pot's good."

Kendra stiffened. Wanted his hand to be off her shoulder. The pot smelled like dog shit. They were all staring at her, sizing her up. A few laughed lightly. "Where's Miguel?" she asked, taking in the colorful dishes and mugs stacked in the glass cabinets.

"You don't want to hang out with us?" Jorge said. "You too good for us?"

Kendra twisted out of his grasp. "I hate the smell of pot," she said. "Plus, where's Miguel?"

"Want me to help you look for him?" Jorge said. "We can start in the bedroom." He pumped his hips.

The other guys laughed. Two high-fived each other. Kendra quickly walked out, through a living room of rustic leather furniture and onto a sunny patio that was busy with people of all ages. She deeply breathed in the hot fresh air.

Miguel stood by a huge smoking grill, spatula in hand. Kendra could smell that he was using mesquite to cook the steaks. He was shirtless, shiny with sweat. He had bulked up a little, and looked totally toned. Formidable pecs and shoulders. Arms and abs nicely cut.

He smiled at her and waved her over with a pair of black-tipped tongs. Two little kids ran in front of her with water balloons, nearly tripped her. A group of Latina chicks, all sitting in lawn chairs with cans of Budweiser in their hands, sized her up as she walked past them to Miguel.

"Have you been abusing steroids, or what?" Kendra said to him. "Plussing as which, your nose looks totally the same and all your teeth are there."

"No one's broke my nose yet," Miguel said. "Your hair looks different."

"Your body looks different," Kendra said. "You're all buff and shit."

"Dude," he said. "I train like every day. All I eat is protein. A minute ago, my uncle caught me with a Budweiser, and he knocked it out of my hand."

"I don't lift as much as I used to," Kendra said. "I was getting too big."

Miguel stepped back a little, fanned the smoke out of his face. "You look good, bitch."

"You look good, too, bitch," she said.

"I know," Miguel said.

"I know I look good, too. Being as which I'm starving, make me a steak. Well done."

"You still talk all fucked-up."

As soon as he had said it, Kendra felt her stomach twist and her throat bunch up.

"Being as plussing as how . . ." he said. "I forgot about it. It's funny. I like it. It's original."

It's retarded, Kendra thought. I sound like an idiot, and even Miguel, whose first language is Spanish, can recognize it.

Soon after Miguel had plopped the charred steak onto her paper plate, one of the Latina chicks in the lawn chairs called her over. Kendra walked to her, chewing the piece of steak she had just put in her mouth. The mesquite grilled steak was good—lean, not too burned.

"How do you know Miguel?" one asked her.

"From school," Kendra said, between chews. "Catalina Foothills."

The woman motioned that Kendra sit in a lawn chair, and she did. She felt five sets of eyes roaming over her body for the first few minutes, but the chicks actually ended up being friendly and funny. Most were Miguel's cousins; one, Andi, was his older sister.

"That boy looks for any excuse to take his shirt off now that he has a body," Andi said. "He walks outside to get the mail, he takes off his shirt. He helps my mom with groceries, he takes off his shirt. He pours a glass of orange juice, he takes off his shirt."

"I don't mind," one of the others said.

"Me, neither," another said.

"You're his cousin," Andi said to her. "You're fucking gross."

"It's okay to think your cousin's hot," she said.

"I think he's hot," another cousin said. "I wouldn't do him because he's my cousin, but he's still hot."

"You all are fucked up," Andi said. "I never think any of my cousins are hot."

"That's 'cause they're not hot."

"Franco's hot."

"Franco's fat."

Kendra sipped her beer, which quickly grew warm, and slowly ate her steak, as she listened to them complain about their husbands, all of whom had gone to Hooters the day before and gotten so drunk, they called their wives for rides home. Kendra soon gathered that their husbands were the five guys inside the house getting high. She wondered which poor woman was married to Jorge, and if they had any kids.

Miguel spent most of time talking about boxing with his uncle, who seemed to ignore Kendra, except for the few times when he shot her dirty looks: squinted eyes and curled lip. He was bald and buff, and he wore a wife-beater and black jeans. His head was shaped like a lemon, vaguely pointed. It glistened with sweat in the sun.

When his uncle went inside to get some more steaks, Miguel pulled Kendra into the driveway and kissed her.

It was the first time in a while that she had kissed anyone. Miguel was a good kisser. Not too aggressive, not too invasive with his tongue. Soft, big lips, especially his bottom lip. She tasted beer on his breath, which wasn't that bad. Petey was the worst kisser. He'd immediately stick his skinny tongue in her mouth and twirl it around. Sometimes, if he was really wasted, he'd clank his teeth against hers and ruin everything.

As she kissed Miguel in the shadow of A Mountain, she tried to remember the last time she had kissed Petey. She couldn't remember. She couldn't remember the last time they had had sex either. Maybe ninth grade. Maybe the summer before ninth grade. The idea of sex with Petey now was ridiculous. She was sort of disgusted when she thought about it. At least she had made him wear condoms every time. Her mother had given her a big box from Costco when she was thirteen. Joyce had given a box to Thomas the same day. Kendra doubted Thomas had ever needed to use one, despite his claims that he and Brooke were fucking. She imagined that if she dug around in his room, she'd find the box, unopened.

Miguel pulled away and looked into Kendra's eyes so intently it was briefly disarming for her. "My uncle thinks that after you and I fuck tonight, my energy will be down for the fight I have next week."

"Plus," Kendra said, stepping back, "what makes you think we're fucking tonight?"

"Come on," Miguel said. "I'll show you my bedroom. It's really cool. I got a king-size bed."

"We're not fucking," Kendra said. "Not even close."

"Then why'd you come today?"

"You invited me to a barbecue," Kendra said. "That doesn't mean we're going to fuck."

"Could you at least blow me?" he said, half-smiling.

Kendra wished Crystal was there with her, wished Crystal could answer for her. "No," Kendra said. "Plussing as which, I'm leaving."

"Wait!" Miguel said, grabbing her shoulder, tightly. "Hold on, bitch."

"Let me go, bitch," Kendra said, stepping away from his grasp. "Asshole."

"What's your problem?"

"I have another party," Kendra said. "Being as which this is bullshit."

"You can't even talk right," Miguel said. "Are you mentally retarded? Do you ride the short bus to school?"

"I'm glad you switched schools," Kendra said, her heart racing away. She walked to her car. "You're a dick!"

"Yeah," Miguel said, grabbing his balls. "Fuck you, bitch. I got girls lined up to fuck me."

"Whatever," Kendra said, easing into her hot car. She'd normally roll down all the windows and let it cool a bit, but not now. She slammed the door, closed herself off from Miguel's ranting and macho displays of crotch-grabbing.

A few moments later, Kendra found herself in a Taco Bell parking lot, staring at a huge poster of a burrito, the sauce glossy, the beans a perfect brown; the meat, lettuce, tomatoes, and onions all in colors too bright for food. She had been gripping her steering wheel so tightly that her forearms ached.

When Miguel had made that crack about her being retarded, she should have smacked him, been the first to break his nose. She imagined him reeling back from her punch, flipping over the wall adorned with the Guadalupe painting, and landing in the cactus garden. All the initial pricks from thorns would be nothing compared to those he got when he tried to get out. She'd be laughing at him, wouldn't even offer him a hand. She might dump her warm beer on him. The alcohol from the beer would sting.

The fantasy stopped quickly, though. She knew that with his new body and his boxing, he could easily kick her ass, and this enraged her even more. There had been a moment, when Miguel grabbed her shoulder, that she was truly frightened. She didn't realize it until now, but he had actually scared her.

She stepped out of her car into the heat, and began to pace on the grubby sidewalk in front of Taco Bell. She vacillated between plans of driving back to the barbecue and beating the shit out of Miguel and feelings of relief that he had not beaten the shit out of her. She wished she were at the club, swimming laps. She needed to swim about a mile and clear her head. Franny's plan of thinking pleasant thoughts never seemed to work. Kendra could think about swimming, but, in order to truly calm down, she needed to actually swim laps.

"Hey!" a woman yelled. Kendra turned to see a Taco Bell employee, an older woman with short gray hair, holding open the door. "You all right?"

"What?" Kendra said, confused.

"If you're high," the woman said, "you need to move along, or I'll call the cops."

"What?" Kendra said, still confused.

"You're out here talking to no one and marching back and forth. You're scaring away potential customers."

"I'm not high."

"In or out," the woman said. "And if you come in, I'll need you to buy something."

A wave of embarrassment pushed Kendra back to her car. She started it immediately, not really noticing the pounding heat, and drove north on Grande Boulevard. It was pathetic to Kendra that even the old lady in her brown Taco Bell uniform had thought she was crazy. She didn't remember talking to herself as she paced in front of the restaurant.

The moment at Taco Bell recalled to Kendra a few stories her mother had told her about her own teenage years, back when she was known as "Heroin Girl" or "Death Girl." Kendra wondered how her mother could have possibly tolerated always being stared at, always being talked about, all that speculation and gossip. The attention. That sort of attention would drive Kendra crazy. Kendra imagined that everyone who went to high school with her mom thought she was a freak. She sported a blue Mohawk and had her nose pierced—and this had been the early 1980s. When Kendra had looked through her mother's yearbooks with her, she had seen how everyone else was dressed and how they wore their hair. Nearly every girl had big, fluffed-up hair and big earrings. Even her mother's few friends didn't look as weird as her mother. Their hair was spiked up and one of them wore a dog collar, but their hair could be combed down and the dog collar removed. Joyce couldn't really comb down her Mohawk and she'd always have that hole in the side of her nose. In her senior portrait, Joyce wore a chain from her nose piercing to her ear. "That's the one thing I regret," Joyce had said. "I liked the Mohawk and the nose ring, but that chain was kind of stupid, kind of like 'Look at me, I'm so rad,' you know?"

"I guess," Kendra had said, even though she really didn't understand how the chain was any worse than the haircut or the pierced nose it was linked to.

Her father had looked totally normal in high school. Kendra had looked through his yearbooks, too. He had short hair and wore polo shirts. He had grown up in a small West Texas ranching town and there had only been seventeen kids in his graduating class. He won a golf scholarship to the U of A, and moved to Tucson when he was eighteen. His freshman roommate turned him on to punk rock, and by sophomore year, Kendra's father was singing lead vocals for UPS, which secured gigs as far away as Los Angeles and Omaha. There was a photograph of him in *Sports Illustrated* when he was a junior because he showed up for the PAC-10 Tournament of Champions with spiked purple hair, wearing a Circle Jerks T-shirt.

Even though it was still early, Kendra pulled over at a drive-in restaurant, Mariscos Chihuahua. Her own cell phone had no reception there, so she called Crystal's cell phone from a pay phone in the parking lot. The black receiver was too hot to hold directly, so Kendra used her T-shirt as a buffer. "The barbecue was a bust," she told Crystal.

"Good," Crystal said. "Come over here now. This party is so boring already."

"Should I bring anything?" Kendra asked.

"Bottled water," Crystal said. "All they have here is shitty beer and I'm totally sick of it."

Kendra pulled into the nearest 7-Eleven and carried ten bottles of water to the counter. Hanging out with Crystal was just what she needed, and she felt the giddy excitement in her stomach.

As she drove the narrow streets of Barrio Viejo, admiring the candy-colored adobe houses, looking for 122 Simpson Street, Kendra wondered what Petey was doing for the holiday. Was he drunk or high? Was he already passed out? She remembered two or three years ago when Petey and his friends went down to Nogales and smuggled back tons of fireworks. They had shot them right there in Rancho Sin Vacas from the end of Petey's driveway, and several neighbors had gathered to watch. There were neighbors Kendra had never seen before, even kids her own age, all of them oohing and aahing at Petey's illegal fireworks display. For the finale, Petey lined up ten or so pretty big rockets, and as he lit them, he caught his sleeve on fire. While the rockets were exploding in the sky, raining blue and red sparks over the desert, Petey was flapping his arm violently. Kendra had laughed. He had looked so stupid, fluttering and flailing like he was. Then one of the neighbors Kendra had never seen before ran over to him and doused his sleeve in Diet Coke. Petey wasn't burned in the slightest; the guy made him check. All the neighbors had clapped for Petey, and he bowed for them when all the rockets had finally been shot.

The party was crowded when Kendra arrived. The stereo was blasting the Ramones, and the whole place—an ancient adobe house with elaborate tilework, walls adorned with colorful masks, and Mexican pigskin furniture, was dense with cigarette smoke. Everyone, girls and guys, seemed to be dressed the same way: dirty low-rise Levi's, vintage sneakers, and shaggy hair. Kendra spotted Crystal right away. She was sitting at a small table, talking to a guy with mussed hair and thick plastic-rimmed glasses.

Kendra plowed her way through, hefting two plastic bags full of bottled water, and said hello.

"Thank God you're here," Crystal said, grabbing a bottle from one of Kendra's bags. "I'm so thirsty."

"I brought a lot," Kendra said.

"Brad and I are the only ones here who aren't smoking tonight," Crystal said. She put her hand on the guy's shoulder. "This is Brad."

"Hi," Brad said.

"I'm Kendra," Kendra said, extending her hand. His hand was rough and callused. She opened a bottle of water for herself.

"You guys want to go up on the balcony and get some fresh air?" Crystal asked.

"I need to find Gerry," Brad said. "I'll meet you up there in a few minutes."

Kendra followed Crystal up the tiled stairs, past more shaggy-haired, dirty-jeans-wearing guests, all of whom seemed to be smoking. A few stopped Crystal, kissed her on the cheek, chatted briefly. Kendra couldn't hear anything, though, because the Ramones were louder on the stairs: ". . . I wanna be sedated . . ." The music reminded Kendra of her birthday parties when she was a real little kid. Her mother used to play the Ramones for Kendra's guests, and they'd pogo around the house, dancing like crazy. The kids would talk about it in school for weeks afterward, and by the third grade, invitations to Kendra's birthday parties were the most sought-after. That fizzled by fifth grade when everyone pretended to hate dancing and someone started to spread the rumor that Kendra's mother practiced witchcraft.

Up on the small balcony, where the air was hot but not smoky, Kendra told Crystal about her slam-dancing birthday parties.

"Your mom sounds so cool," Crystal said. "I don't even think my mom knows who the Ramones are."

"I think she still has videotapes," Kendra said. "All these little kids jumping up and down to Black Flag and the Sex Pistols. Plussing as which, I've seen—"

Crystal cut her off with sort of a karate-chop action. "Okay, I don't want to be mean or anything," she said, "but what's with that 'plussing as which' stuff?"

"I don't know," Kendra said, embarrassed.

"I can't decide if it's cool or totally fucked-up."

"It's fucked-up," Kendra said. Her throat was tightening. Suddenly, her stomach felt hollow, like she was starving and nauseated.

"Then why do you always say it?"

Kendra breathed deeply to loosen her bunched throat. She didn't want to cry. "I can't help it."

"We could do aversion therapy!" Crystal said.

"What?"

"I'll pinch you or pull your hair every time you say it," Crystal said. "You'll be cured in a week or so."

"Really?" Kendra said.

"Oh, my God!" Crystal said. "I have a much better idea for aversion."

"What?" Kendra said. She wasn't sure what aversion was, but she didn't want to be pinched or have her hair pulled.

"It's a secret," Crystal said. "If you say it tomorrow in class, I'll do it then."

"Just tell me," Kendra said.

"It will gross you out."

Later, they went back into the party and mingled. Two girls from Catalina Foothills High School approached Kendra. Kendra didn't immediately recognize them, but they recognized her. One babbled quickly, said she had been in Physical Science with Kendra last semester, that she had always admired how Kendra didn't take shit from anyone, and that she wanted to be as fit as Kendra but she couldn't quit smoking long enough to run a single lap. They chatted a little about what classes they were taking in the fall, what teachers they hated, what guys they hated. Kendra wished she could recognize them, but she couldn't. Amy and Erica. They each sported the same sloppy haircut like everyone else at the party, but they were wearing short plaid skirts instead of dirty Levi's. "Isn't your brother like a genius?" Amy asked.

"Yes," Kendra said. "But he's a dork."

"Did he really get a perfect score on the SAT?" Erica asked. Kendra thought she might recognize Erica. She had a little dimple on her chin. From art freshman year.

"Did you used to have long hair?" Kendra asked her.

"Yes," Erica said.

"We were in art together," Kendra said. "With that skinny nervous teacher."

"Mrs. Irving!" Erica said. "She smelled like vitamins all the time!"

"You know Peter Vaccarino, right?" Amy said. "He's missing, you know. I saw it on the news."

"I know," Kendra said. "I had to talk to the cops."

"Do they think he was abducted?" Erica said, grabbing Kendra's arm. "But who would abduct him?"

"Some pervert," Amy said.

"He was involved with drugs," Erica said. "Maybe some dealer was pissed off at him."

"I heard he's addicted to glue," Amy said, then she turned to Kendra. "Is he?"

"More like marking pens," Kendra said. She wanted to leave. She didn't want to talk about Petey.

Kendra and Crystal walked down the dark cobbled street to the edge of the neighborhood. They stood at a small grotto, the Wishing Shrine. The smell of melted candles and incense filled the air. People had pinned photos of babies and soldiers to a statue of a woman. A few of the votives were burning, and the ground glittered with pennies. "I never knew this was here," Kendra said.

Then, to the west, before Crystal said anything, the sky erupted with colorful fireworks over A Mountain. They were within a few miles, so they could hear the whistles and booms.

"If I were a lesbian," Crystal said, "I'd totally make out with you now."

"Me, too," Kendra said.

"Sometimes I wish I were a lesbian," Crystal said. "Life would be so much easier. I could borrow clothes from my girlfriend."

"Plus guys are dicks," Kendra said.

"What do you think of Brad?" Crystal asked.

"He seems nice," Kendra said. "Cool." Actually, she thought he was boring and that his eyeglasses were stupid. He spoke only about Japanese animation. Crystal could do way better. Kendra watched as the sky bloomed with greens, blues, and purples. Sparks burst into smaller and smaller sparks, streamed through the night in dying ripples.

"I could just ask him out, I guess," Crystal said. "Let's go back to the party."

"I think I might go home," Kendra said. "I'm tired."

"You're not even going to stick around to see if A Mountain catches on fire?"

"No," Kendra said. "I'll see it on the news if it does."

The Fourth of July was always a busy day at Splash World, so, following company policy, Merv doubled up the work-force—twice as many lifeguards, slide operators, food service workers, security officers. It made Merv's job easy, though, and most of the employees were happy to be there, earning time and a half. Instead of sitting atop the Kamikaze, Merv spent the day walking around the park, checking on his employees, making sure they took breaks when they should, handing out cold bottled water from a wheeled cooler he pulled along the walkways.

Merv walked over to Raymond, who sat in his usual spot on the shore of the wave pool, hiding from the sun under a big white cotton hat and huge wraparound sunglasses. Two young kids, a boy and a girl, were standing next to his wheelchair, talking with him.

"You're a busy man today, Merv," Raymond said. "I haven't seen it this crowded all summer."

"The biggest day," Merv said, squatting next to his wheel-chair. "And no clouds yet. We'll be here until sunset."

"I don't know if you noticed, but I'm taking my antisun measures more seriously," Raymond said. "I'm even preaching to these two kids who aren't wearing any sunscreen."

"I'm already tan," the little girl said. "I never get sunburned." She was tan, the color of butterscotch, which was accentuated by her yellow swimsuit. Her hair was bleached into near white-ness by the sun.

"I get sunburned," the boy said, "but I forgot my sun lotion at my house. And you're drooling." He pointed to Raymond's mouth.

The kid was right; Merv could see a little drop of drool shining on the edge of his lower lip.

"Merv," Raymond said. "You know where the sunscreen is in my pack. Get it out for us, will you?"

"Sure," Merv said, understanding as he did so that Raymond had not wanted the kids to see his magazines or wads of cash.

"I want you to use it all," Raymond told the kids. "Both of you," he said specifically to the little girl. "Just because you get tan doesn't mean you don't need sunscreen."

The little girl took the tube from Merv. "This is different sunscreen than my mom's at my house."

"It's the best in the world," Raymond said. "Now run along."

The two kids did, settling under a veranda nearby. "It smells good!" the girl yelled.

"Like candles!" the boy said.

"You know them?" Merv asked.

"I just met them," Raymond said. "The little boy wanted to know if he could ride in my wheelchair." Raymond let his sunglasses slide to the edge of his nose and looked up at Merv. "Any special lady for the fireworks?" Raymond asked.

"No," Merv said. "Maybe this weekend, though." The water from the wave pool ebbed over his river sandals. It was warmer than he had thought, not refreshing in the slightest. "What about you?" Merv asked, immediately feeling bad for doing so.

"No," Raymond said. "No date tonight and no date this weekend." He sighed, sniffed deeply.

Merv opened the little cooler. "You want a bottle of water?"

"No, thanks," Raymond said. "Unless you have a long straw."

"I don't," Merv said. "Sorry."

"No problem," Raymond said. Merv noticed the drool was now a thin line connecting Raymond's chin to his chest.

At noon, Merv had lunch with Hank, the head of security. He ordered in a large cheese pizza, and they ate it straight from the box at Merv's desk in his little cramped office, using old safety re-ports as plates. He described the three meth-heads to Hank, told him how the police were searching for them, how he had seen them many times in the parking lot, and yesterday, bathing in the wave pool.

"We'll need someone here from four to eight A.M.," Merv said. "At least until the police catch them."

"It's dumb that the cops haven't apprehended them," Hank said. "I've seen them, too. A million times. They're in the park-ing lot all the time, riding their tiny bikes."

"I know," Merv said.

"At least now I have a reason to subdue them," Hank said, rub-bing his big hands together, grinning in a way that made Merv a little nervous.

"I'm not sure about the legality of that," Merv said. "Just call the cops if you see them in the parking lot again."

Hank ate a slice of pizza in three bites, chewed it quickly, then said, "I'll call the cops if I see them anywhere. And I'll as-sign someone to the four to eight shift, starting tonight."

Hank gobbled through several more pieces of pizza as he told Merv about his new security strategies. Merv was only half-listening. He was trying to think of an excuse to call Melissa. He knew he had to call her tonight about the weekend, but he felt like calling her now. She'd be home, probably just watching bad daytime television, lounging on her couch with her cats.

When Hank finished the pizza, he finally left. Merv sat there, the one fluorescent light buzzing over his head, his ancient computer humming. He wished he had a funny story to tell Melissa, or a legitimate-sounding question to ask her. He could call her now and tell her he was coming up to Scottsdale for the weekend, but then he'd have no real reason to call later tonight.

When Nick Honig knocked on Merv's open door, Merv jumped. "You scared the shit out of me," Merv told him.

Nick stepped inside, took a seat without Merv's invitation. Nick had on khaki shorts and a blue T-shirt. He wore white tennis shoes with white socks—pulled up. Merv thought he looked like a dork. "You saw them again?" Nick asked.

"Yes," Merv said. "And I called the police and they didn't show up for several hours."

"I was out of town," Nick said. "Las Vegas with my wife and kids."

"They were here," Merv said. "Bathing in the wave pool."

"I left Vegas early," Nick said. "My wife wants to kill me. I left her there with the kids."

"Oh," Merv said. Who the fuck cares? he thought. He wondered who would be stupid enough to marry Nick Honig. "My security team has been alerted, and as of tonight, we'll have twenty-four-hour coverage."

"Great," Nick said. "I've got a whole new angle on the case, but I nevertheless want to talk to the meth-heads."

"Did you talk to Brian at the front gate at Rancho Sin Vacas?" Merv asked. "He might have seen them that night."

"I've scoured that neighborhood," Nick said. "Done background checks on everyone."

"Anything interesting?" Merv asked. He wondered what criminals were living in Rancho Sin Vacas. The muscle girl's parents were likely criminals, the father with tattoos covering both arms. When Merv was a kid, the muscle girl's parents used to host giant parties with punk bands playing in their pool area.

"Not since your dad's suicide fifteen years ago," Nick said. "Your neighborhood's squeaky clean—not that I'd be at liberty to tell—"

"My dad died of liver disease," Merv interrupted. "He didn't commit suicide." Merv remembered how withered and empty his father had looked those last few days.

"Oh," Nick said. "Sorry. I thought . . . maybe there was a mix-up in the background check or something."

"I want to see the report," Merv said, his voice cracking a little. "I have a right, right? I want to see the background report and the coroner's report. I want to see them all." Merv felt his face flush with heat. His stomach burned. He could barely breathe.

"I'm sure there was a mistake," Nick said. "It happens all the time."

"Don't bullshit me," Merv said. "I'm not stupid. You said he committed suicide. You said it!"

"I could be wrong, Merv," Nick said, holding up his hands. "I've made mistakes before. I'll double check. I'll look through the papers this afternoon. Call me tonight, if you want. You have my cell number?"

"Give it to me again," Merv said, sliding a pen across the desk. "I saw my dad every day. He was sick. He was skinny and pale and weak. His eyes were yellow. I talked to him the night before he died."

"I'm sure there was a mistake," Nick said, standing. He left his cell phone number on the desk. "Call me later and we'll straighten it out."

"This sucks," Merv said. "This really sucks."

"I have to go," Nick said. "Like I said, it's probably a mistake."

When Nick left the little office, Merv slammed the door. He sat back down in his chair.

It made sense. His dad was dying, anyway. He was in pain. But someone should have told Merv—someone other than Nick Honig.

He dialed his mother at home. Instead of letting the machine pick it up, she actually answered.

"Did dad kill himself?" Merv asked immediately.

"Merv?" she said.

"Did he?"

"What?" she said. "Why are you asking now?"

"Did he?"

"This isn't the best time to talk," she said. "I'm swamped here."

Swamped with what? Unplugging appliances? Taping down cords. Her excuse meant "yes." Merv slammed down the receiver. Nick Honig. Fucker. Why'd he even have to bring it up? Those discussions Merv had had with his dad during his dad's final days now seemed false. Everything his dad had said was said with the knowledge that he was about to kill himself.

* * *

Merv spent the remainder of his shift in his little office. He didn't feel like talking to anyone. He played an old typing-test game on his computer for a while, then he jotted a list of questions to ask his mother:

1. When did Dad decide he was going to kill himself?
2. Did you know?
3. Why didn't you ever tell me?
4. Why didn't you tell me then?
5. Why didn't you tell me later?
6. What was the exact name of the disease Dad had?
7. How did he kill himself?
8. Who else knows?
9. Did his suicide mess up the insurance?

After number nine, he crumbled the list and tossed it.

At seven-thirty, after walking the grounds with Hank, making sure all the pumps were turned off, Merv packed up his bag in the employee locker room. He heard whimpering from the stall and knew it was Raymond. He squatted and saw the wheels from Raymond's wheelchair. Not today, Merv thought, almost said aloud. Raymond could deal with his own piss tube or whatever it was. Or someone else could help him. There were still ten or twenty other employees milling around the grounds. Someone would hear him, help him. Merv slammed his locker and walked out into the sun.

"Why didn't you just tell me?" Merv asked his mother. She stood at the kitchen counter, chopping a carrot with a knife that looked better suited for carving a turkey. He sat at the kitchen table, his arms crossed over his bare chest, having just come in from a few minutes in the pool.

"What would have been the point?" she said. "It was a horrible time."

"I was there," Merv said. "Remember?"

"He was sick," she said. A slice of carrot rolled off the counter onto the floor. She squatted to retrieve it. "And he was in pain."

"I know that," Merv said. "I just don't get why you didn't tell me."

"You were fifteen," she said.

"What about when I was older?" Merv said. "I had to hear it from Nick Honig."

"Who?"

"This asshole I went to school with who's now a cop. He's in charge of Peter Vaccarino's case."

Merv's mother crunched through some carrots. She looked at the blade on the knife. "This knife," she said, "is warped."

"Who cares?" Merv said. Crazy. She was crazy. "Are you on new medication?"

"Did the police officer tell you about the prostitutes?" she asked, popping another carrot slice into her mouth.

"What?" Merv said.

"Your father and the prostitutes," she said. "I used to throw you in the car and drive down to Miracle Mile to look for him. Don't you remember?"

"No," Merv said.

"And sure enough, I'd find his car parked outside a motel or a marital aids store," she said. "You don't remember?"

"Marital aids store?" Merv said. "What the hell are you talking about?"

"Your father used prostitutes all the time," she said. "Black ones and Mexican ones and white ones and fat ones and skinny ones. One I found him with had missing teeth. Like a pirate. I'd take you with me to find him. You were little."

"I don't remember that," Merv said. "And you never answered my question about medication." He didn't remember going with her to look for his father—although he didn't remember much from his early childhood. The memories seemed to start around third or fourth grade. He couldn't remember kindergarten at all. He had gone to a school called Lulu Walker Elementary, he knew that—he had gone there through fifth grade. He knew the school was on Roller Coaster Road, that there were giant cement pipes in the playground that the sixth graders painted fresh every fall. But the memories of Lulu Walker only became clear when he thought of fourth grade, back when Mrs. Freund was his teacher. Her name was pronounced like "friend," but she was a bitch, always yelling, always complaining that last year's students were much better.

"He was arrested a few times," Merv's mother said. "I thought the police officer might have told you since he told you about the suicide."

"He didn't," Merv said. "Thanks."

"The doctors are sure he caught hepatitis from one of the hookers," she said, examining the blade again. "I wouldn't let him near me in bed after the second round of gonorrhea."

"This is getting too personal," Merv said.

"A minute ago you were complaining no one told you anything," she said.

"There's a difference between telling me he committed suicide and telling me he was fond of Miracle Mile hookers," Merv said.

"Well," she said, "that hepatitis killed him—or it would have if he hadn't killed himself. That, or AIDS. He claimed he didn't have it, but if anyone did, it was him."

"And what about your medication? Are you on anything new?" Merv asked. She seemed so matter-of-fact about the suicide and the hookers. And her eyes looked too wide.

"I didn't know I was required to tell you every time Doctor Grossman changes my medication," she said. "If he changes my medication."

"You're not," Merv said. "But you seem weirder than usual."

"And you left the television plugged in last night," she said.

"Most people do," Merv said.

Merv walked back outside and jumped in the pool. It was dark, and he could hear booms from fireworks in the distance. He didn't bother to look for any of them, even though he knew that the Westward Look Resort was launching some from only a few miles away. He didn't turn on the purple light, either. He swam in the dark, warm water, expelled all the air in his lungs and sank to the bottom. Perfect silence and darkness, even if it lasted only a minute or so. Merv had a theory about holding his breath under water. The time doing so didn't count. Everyone was allotted a certain amount of time on earth, and if you were underwater, the life-clock stopped ticking. It was free time to think or just space out. He had forgotten to ask his mother how his father had killed himself, and if she knew before he did it. Pills, and yes, she knew, he guessed.

Melissa's voicemail picked up and Merv sighed. He said, "Hey, this is Merv. I'm coming up to Scottsdale this weekend, I decided. I hope you're having a good Fourth of July. I'm having a shitty one. See you soon." Whiner, Merv thought as he hung up. In a mocking baby voice, he repeated aloud, "I'm having a shitty one."

Friday, July 6, 2001

Hot and humid

High 106 / Low 81

Cloudy

KENDRA RAN THE HILL EARLY; SHE WAS OUT THERE AT FIVE. THE QUAIL were going crazy, cooing, and a few other birds were trying out their calls. The humidity was thick, and the orange clouds in the sky cast a shadow over the desert, screwing with Kendra's sense of time. She didn't care, though. She ran the hill faster than usual, and was back inside, showering, before six.

As she climbed out of the club's pool at seven, she spotted Hetta shuffling toward the little cardio room. Kendra wondered again what had inspired Hetta, but didn't bother to pop her head into the cardio room to say hello. She'd ignore Hetta, as planned.

"She's there like every day," Kendra told Franny later. "Plussing as which, she really works out. Sweats gallons."

"And how does her presence make you feel?" Franny asked. Franny had eaten at McDonald's today. Kendra could smell the grease, and the wrappers in the trashcan confirmed it. Two Big Macs and a Super-Sized fries. Her drink was dripping sweat beads onto her desk.

"I don't care," Kendra said. "I'm just glad she finally listened to me."

"You think her exercise regime is the result of the comments you made to her last spring?" Franny asked.

"She never exercised before," Kendra said.

"What are some of the reasons she could be exercising—other than your comments last spring?"

"She's really fat," Kendra said. "Plus, she eats really unhealthy food, like I saw in her grocery basket."

"And?" Franny said.

"And she doesn't want to be a fat pig anymore," Kendra said. "I don't know what you want me to say. Plussing as how I don't really care about her."

"We can change the topic, if you'd like," Franny said, wringing her chubby hands. Kendra eyed her thin little watch band. It pinched in the fat on Franny's wrist, and looked as if it would snap. "How's your English course?"

"Retarded," Kendra said. "It's a poetry class taught by this dork who reads his crappy poetry to the class every day. And there's this one guy with hair down to his knees."

"Why don't you switch classes?" Franny asked.

"My friend Crystal's in there," Kendra said.

"You haven't mentioned her before," Franny said, smiling in a way that looked phony to Kendra.

"Because I just met her in the class," Kendra said.

"What's she like?" Franny asked. More of that bullshit smile. Like she really cared what Crystal was like. Half of the sessions with Franny were like this: Franny fumbling for anything to talk about, to kill the forty-five minutes. The other half consisted of Franny leading Kendra to obvious conclusions. Kendra hadn't done anything wrong in a while, months, really. Maybe Joyce would let her quit going to Franny's at the end of the summer.

"She's cool," Kendra said. "And smart."

Franny stared at Kendra and tilted her head a little, like she wanted Kendra to elaborate. Kendra didn't. Instead, she stared back, looked for McDonald's residue on Franny's lips. At least Franny hadn't been smacking her lips today. Or maybe she had been, and Kendra hadn't noticed. Kendra cursed herself for thinking about it, but realized she was lucky that Franny hadn't brought up Petey's disappearance.

* * *

Smith Boyle scolded Kendra and Crystal for laughing in class. "I don't understand how two poets like yourselves, who write meaningful and important poems, could be so disrespectful to your classmates," he said.

Bernice had farted, and both Kendra and Crystal had heard. Smith Boyle had been discussing one of his own poems, a sonnet written to his grandmother. Todd was sitting right next to Bernice, but he didn't laugh. How could he not? Kendra wondered.

"I'm sorry," Crystal told Smith Boyle. "I heard something funny."

"Me, too," Kendra said. "I'm sorry. Your poem about your Nana is great."

Bernice craned her neck and looked over her shoulder at Kendra and Crystal. She glared at them, shook her head like she was disgusted.

"Don't give me that look," Crystal said to her. "You're the one who farted."

"What!" Bernice said. "I did not!" She turned around to look at Crystal again, her mouth agape.

"You did, too, liar," Crystal said. "Kendra and I both heard it."

"It doesn't matter," Smith Boyle said. "Let's get back to sonnets."

"I heard it, too," Todd said. "Sorry."

"I heard it," Jim grumbled from behind his hair. "It was high-pitched. What'd you eat?"

Bernice stood, gathered up her two notebooks, and marched out the door.

"Happy now?" Smith Boyle said. "You've driven her out."

No one said anything. Kendra bit her tongue, tried not to laugh.

"You know," Smith Boyle said, "it takes a lot of courage to take a poetry-writing class. Your emotions are right there on the page, you're taking a huge risk. In order to have an effective workshop, we all have to trust each other. I'm going to go try to find Bernice, and you all better treat her with respect when we return." He left the room.

Kendra and Crystal laughed, Kendra so hard that her abs actually hurt.

"We better respect her," Crystal said between laughs, "or she'll fart again."

Todd turned around and looked at Crystal. "She's really nice," he said. "Her husband died last year."

"So?" Crystal said. "What does that have to do with her flatulence?"

"What's flatulence?" Kendra asked.

"Farting," Jim said. "And you chicks are evil."

"Because we laughed?" Crystal said. "It was funny. We were the only ones with balls enough to laugh. You guys are pussies."

"We're mature," Todd said. "We care about other people's feelings."

"Speak for yourself, dickhead," Jim said to him. "I don't care about feelings; I care about poetry."

"Fuck you," Todd said. "You fucking freak."

"I thought you cared about other people's feelings," Jim said in a breathy, girlish voice.

"Fuck you," Todd repeated. "And your poems are stupid."

"And yours are generic," Jim said. "To quote Crystal, they're *boring morbid drivel.*"

"I said they were *juvenile* morbid drivel," Crystal said. "Don't misquote me."

"This whole class is fucked," Todd said.

Kendra agreed, but she loved it. She'd never met a group of people who talked like they did, argued so openly, who said what was on their minds. She couldn't recall a time in any class when her adrenaline was pumping so high, when she laughed so hard.

Smith Boyle stormed back into the room and began to dramatically pack up his books. He was red-faced and breathing heavily through his nose. After he clicked his briefcase shut, he said, "I'll see you all next class. Class dismissed for the day."

"We still have two hours," Jim said.

"She's gone," Smith Boyle said. "And I'd be surprised if she comes back."

"What about our sonnets?" Jim said.

"I can't teach right now," Smith Boyle said. "I'm way too upset. One would think that a room of adults could handle . . . forget it." He walked out, leaving everyone staring at each other.

"What a baby," Crystal said. "He probably just doesn't want to discuss our sonnets because they all suck."

"Mine's good," Jim said.

"I bet," Crystal said. "More prancing unicorns and magical elves?"

Kendra watched the tiny dust motes swirling in the sun that poured through the window. She sat in a small café near the university and waited for Crystal, who was up at the counter ordering an iced mocha. Kendra didn't drink coffee or any variant of it. Caffeine made her nervous and nauseated, and messed with her energy level when she worked out.

"I can't believe that idiot let us out of class early," Crystal said, as she sat down with Kendra. "All that fuss over a fart."

"Plussing as which, he didn't give us a new assignment for the weekend," Kendra said.

"*Plussing as which?*" Crystal said. She dug in her pack and pulled out a large red envelope, which she slid across the table to Kendra. "Open it."

"Why?" Kendra said.

"Open it," Crystal said.

It wasn't sealed, but Kendra couldn't see anything inside when she opened it. "It's empty," she said.

"Look closer," Crystal said.

Kendra did, and she saw a hair, a very long hair, looping around the bottom. "A hair," Kendra said. "One of Jim's hairs?"

"You're right," Crystal said. "Now touch it."

"No," Kendra said.

"Touch it!" Crystal said. "I stayed after class the other day

and found it. Whenever you say any of your weird ungrammatical things, you have to touch it."

"That's sick," Kendra said. "Why'd you get it?"

"To make a voodoo doll," Crystal said. "I make voodoo dolls
of everyone I hate."

"Now I have to touch it?" Kendra asked, a little frightened by
Crystal's voodoo doll revelation. She had thought Crystal was
so normal.

"It's aversion therapy," Crystal said. "Originally, I was thinking you should have to lick it."

"I don't think touching the hair will make me stop talking all
fucked-up," Kendra said, reaching into the envelope, far
enough down that she knew she was touching the hair.

"The act of having to carry around the envelope and reach in
there every time will make you think twice before you say
'plussing as which' or whatever again," Crystal said. "Keep that
red envelope in your notebook. I'll get another hair for the
voodoo doll."

Crystal was as weird as the others in the class, Kendra
thought. Kendra wasn't about to carry around the red envelope
wherever she went and touch the hair every time she was ungrammatical.

"I can see you're not buying it," Crystal said. "As an added
aversion, why don't you imagine running your fingers through
Jim's entire head of hair every time you have to open the envelope." Crystal took a big sip from her drink. "No! Imagine running your fingers through Jim's hair after making hot passionate
love with him!"

"That's really sick," Kendra said, laughing.

"It'll work," Crystal said. "I swear. I learned all about it in my
psych class last semester. There. I've cured you of your horrible
grammar problem." She took another sip from her drink.

"I wish," Kendra said. "I'm getting some carrot juice."

Later, taped to her bedroom door, Kendra found a postcard featuring two kittens. On the back:

Kendra, I was wondering if you wanted to have lunch on Saturday. My treat of course, in appreciation of your helping me that morning. Sincerely, Ellen Hunter.

The crazy lady from across the desert. "Oh, God," Kendra said aloud. "Joyce!"

She dropped her pack on the floor and ran down the stairs, looking for Joyce. She couldn't remember if Joyce's car had been parked in the driveway. "Joyce!"

Joyce walked into the kitchen from the dining room. She carried a phone, had her hand pressed over the receiver. "I'm talking to a Japanese client!" she said. "It's hard enough to decipher his bad English without you yelling at me."

Kendra held up the postcard. "Did she come by?"

"Who?"

"Mrs. Hunter?"

"Who?" Joyce said.

"Our neighbor!" Kendra said. "She's only been our neighbor since forever!"

"I don't know," Joyce said. "Is that all you need?"

"Who taped it to my door?"

"Probably Thomas," Joyce said. "Ask him about it." She turned around and walked back into the dining room. Kendra heard her apologize to the Japanese client. Kendra would not ask Thomas about it. Besides, she rarely saw him anymore. He was always out with Brooke, taping up those stupid *Have you seen Peter "Petey" Vaccarino?* flyers everywhere. Kendra had seen them on telephone poles all over town next to signs for yard sales or advertisements for weight-loss systems. The photo of Petey barely looked like him, especially in black and white, Xeroxed onto bright yellow paper. Kendra had looked closely at one of the flyers before she walked into the café earlier in the afternoon. It was taped to the side of a U.S. mailbox. The photo made him look older and bald—or going bald. She almost ripped it down when she read the final line of print under the photograph: "We miss you, Petey!" Who was *we,* she had wondered. Petey's mother and

Brooke? Brooke and Thomas? Thomas had once announced that Petey was by far the stupidest person he had ever met. This came after Petey was taken to the hospital in an ambulance after having sniffed pens and downed a bottle of cough syrup—in school, during biology.

The drive up to Scottsdale was uneventful. Merv spent the two hours scanning the radio stations for songs he liked and thinking about his father.

Once, in eighth grade, Merv had had a party, a boy-girl party where everyone swam and ate chips and drank soda. Merv's mother ordered pizza. Merv's father was out by the pool the whole time, spread out on a chaise longue, hiding his eyes behind aviator sunglasses. Kristin Rippon, the girl Merv had a crush on, mainly because of her breasts, pulled Merv aside by the diving board.

"Your father is creeping me out," she had said.

"Why?" Merv asked. Even though she had been swimming, Merv could smell something nice on Kristin, kind of a citrus smell, maybe shampoo or sunscreen, that made its way through the bleachy scent of chlorine from the pool.

"He's staring at us," she whispered loudly.

"Who?"

"Me," she said. "And Susan and Julie. All of us."

"But he's wearing sunglasses," Merv said. "How do you know what he's looking at?"

"Can't you just tell him to go inside?" she said, wringing out her blond curls, giving Merv a nice view of her breasts, which were bigger than any other eighth grade girl's. They were the size of grapefruits, barely contained in the floral bikini she wore. A brown mole the size of a lima bean sat on her right breast, bordering her cleavage. "It's weird with him out here. And Julie has a bottle of vodka in her bag."

Merv walked over to his dad and asked him to go inside. He

said that everyone felt weird with him out there, that they couldn't relax and be themselves.

"I understand completely," his father had said, standing up. "I'll be out in a while to grill the burgers, though, but I won't say a word."

"Thanks, Dad," Merv said.

The kids took turns adding the vodka to their cans of Mountain Dew or Sprite, hiding behind a kumquat bush, and by the time Merv's father came back outside to cook the hamburgers, everyone had a nice buzz. Merv's father no longer wore his sunglasses, and Merv noticed how he ogled the girls in their swimsuits. As Merv sat at the glass table and ate his hamburger, he saw how his father's eyes were trained on Kristin's breasts, Julie's ass, and all of Rebecca. Merv was glad that none of the girls noticed or complained.

Merv never did get to bury his face in Kristin's breasts, not in eighth grade, and not during the following five years. Rusty dated her for all of junior year, but they broke up that summer when he found out she cheated on him with a guy in France.

That one party in eighth grade was the only time he had ever seen his father behave in a questionable way; it was the only time he had seen his father as a sexual being. And, as Merv drove up to Scottsdale on the boring brown-and-gray stretch of I-10, he decided that it was completely normal that his father had been checking out all the girls in their bikinis. Merv did it all the time at Splash World. It made the days fly by, sitting up there on the Kamikaze. And most of the hot girls at Splash World were like thirteen or fourteen. By the time they reached high school, most girls were too cool for Splash World.

There hadn't been any porno in the house other than Merv's own under-the-bed magazine stash, as far as Merv could remember, and he had never heard his parents fighting about prostitutes or infidelity. Maybe his mother was making it up, maybe the whole prostitute story was just a delusion, part of her psychological problems.

* * *

By the time Merv reached the vast sprawl of Phoenix—strip malls, prefab houses, and pavement—he felt a giddy excitement in his stomach. In less than an hour, he'd see Melissa again. Merv reminded himself that they had only been on one date, shared one little kiss. But there were no red flags. She didn't seem whiny or psycho. She didn't mind that Merv worked at Splash World—or didn't yet let on that she minded. She was already friends with Jason and Rusty. She had a good job, a great sense of humor, a killer body. When Merv pulled into the parking lot of a 7-Eleven to get a Gatorade, he had to wait in the car for a few minutes while his erection subsided.

Inside the 7-Eleven, a tall guy with a round, babyish face and round glasses was yelling at the clerk, a tired-looking woman with stringy long hair and dangling feather earrings. "I gave you a ten!" the man yelled. "Are you stupid or something?"

"You gave me a five," the woman said, impassively. She blew a strand of hair from her face.

Merv headed back to get a Gatorade from the refrigerated shelves. He grabbed a roll of peppermint Life Savers as well, reading the label, stalling before walking to the counter where the disgruntled man was yelling louder: "A trained monkey can make change! You owe me five dollars!"

"I gave you the correct change," the woman said, monotone.

The man was dressed for golf in goofy plaid pants and a bright pink polo shirt. His hair was parted neatly on the side. Like a father from a fifties sitcom. Merv noticed that every time the man spoke—or yelled—he stood on his tiptoes. "Look, you trashy bitch, I gave you a ten!"

"A five," the woman said. "I don't even have any tens in the register." She opened the drawer to show the man, and Merv thought the argument would end.

"You stupid, stupid bitch!" the man yelled. "This fucking store always rips me off, every fucking day!"

"I work here every day," the woman said. "This is the first time I've seen you."

Merv hoped the woman had pressed whatever secret button it was that alerted the police. Merv watched in what seemed like preternatural speed as the man picked up a huge jar of pickles from on top of the glass-encased hot-dog rotisserie and smashed it on the floor with a loud pop and splash. Pickles glided across the slick floor in all directions.

"Please leave," the woman told the man. She was still calm, seemed unfazed. "Now."

Adrenaline skipped through Merv's chest, tightened his throat. "Yes, leave," he cracked. "Leave her alone."

The man turned around and looked at Merv, who stood clutching his Gatorade and Life Savers halfway down the candy aisle. The man's lips were bright red, and big. Liver lips. Maybe he was wearing lipstick. He began walking toward Merv, his rubber-soled boots squeaking in the yellow pickle juice. "You work here?" the man asked Merv.

Before Merv could say no, the man grabbed Merv's neck and shoved him into a shoulder-high cardboard Pez display. As Merv toppled backward, all he could think about was how clammy and warm the man's hand had felt.

He landed hard, broke his fall with his wrists, his right one especially.

The man ran out of the store, the door chiming as he jolted it open.

Merv stood and ran after the man. He nearly fell again as he slid through the pickle puddle, but he made it through to the door and out into the heat to see the man run into traffic on Indian School Road.

In the white afternoon sun, cars skidded, swerved, screeched. A glossy red pickup truck sideswiped a small Asian sedan in an effort to miss the man. A gargantuan black SUV didn't stop in time, and Merv heard a double thump and watched as it carried the man on its silver grill several yards before coming to a halt and tossing him into the asphalt, then under its front tires.

Merv heard several more crunches and skids, but didn't see any more collisions. He only watched the man's blood pooling around his head. The man's round glasses still clung to his face—they weren't even slightly askew.

Nearly two hours later, after giving nine or ten statements to the police, Merv sat behind the steering wheel in his ovenlike car, and said, "I hate fucking Phoenix." When he turned the key, pain shot from his wrist up to his elbow. It was more intense when he went to shift into reverse and finally back out of the 7-Eleven parking lot.

"That is so psycho!" Melissa said, molding the bag of frozen peas around Merv's wrist. "I can't believe it."

"It was totally weird," Merv said. "I wish I had stopped at another 7-Eleven." He couldn't stop imagining the man's face: those too-red flabby lips, his round glasses.

"How many accidents altogether?" Melissa asked, finally sitting next to Merv on her big white couch.

"I have no idea," Merv said. "At least like five or ten."

"You look totally pale," she said. "Are you all right? Are you going to puke?"

"I'm freaked out," Merv said. "I forgot to turn on the air conditioner in my car. These peas feel good."

Melissa stood and began walking to the kitchen. "I'm so retarded. I'll get you some water right away."

"Thanks," Merv said. He looked around her apartment for the first time. Adobe walls, two high bookcases packed with books, a third with CDs. When Melissa walked back through the arched doorway, Merv noticed the flowers painted above it. This was an old building, a building with character—not what Merv had expected from Scottsdale, especially after seeing where Rusty and Jason lived. They lived in giant cubes of soulless apartments with cement stairwells and numbered parking spaces. Rusty called his building a "swingles complex."

Melissa brought a bottle of Evian and a tall blue-rimmed glass of ice. She poured the water into the glass and handed it to him. "I'm sorry."

"For what?" Merv said. He chugged the water, felt the chill as it went down and into his stomach.

"For not getting you water sooner," she said. She sat again, put her hand on Merv's leg. "We need to get your mind off that accident."

"Well," Merv said, "it's good to see you."

"You, too," Melissa said. "My cats are locked in the bedroom."

"You didn't have to do that," Merv said, smiling.

"I know," she said. "I wanted to. Now, let's see that wrist."

Merv's wrist was red and puffy, the thickest part of his forearm, as swollen as it was before applying the bag of frozen peas. "I've only been icing it for a few minutes," he said.

"It might be broken," Melissa said. "We should get an X-ray."

"It'll be fine in a while," Merv said, and he leaned over and kissed her cheek. She kissed him back, and soon Merv dropped the bag of frozen peas and found himself in her bed, frantically trying to remove her clothes, his wrist throbbing, two cats staring at him from their perch on her dresser. One hissed.

"You're crying," Melissa said, looking into Merv's eyes, her chin resting on his chest. "That's so sweet."

Merv was crying, or actually his eyes were watering, but not as part of any emotional or spiritual catharsis elicited by the sex they had just shared, but because of the cats and his allergies. His throat was itching, too, as were his inner ears. "The cats," he said. "Sorry."

"At least Chauncy stopped hissing," she said, closing her eyes.

Merv had been thinking constantly about Melissa since their first kiss, been fantasizing about sex with her. The frenzied anticipation that drove him the last twenty minutes had been much like what he felt the time he lost his virginity. But now, with the pain from his swollen wrist coursing up his arm, and the cat allergies taking over, he just wanted her off him, wanted the bag of frozen peas, and wanted to get those X-rays. He kind of wanted to go home, too. "I'm sorry," he finally said after thinking about how to phrase it, "but my wrist is killing me. Could you maybe get off me?"

She opened her eyes. "Um, sure." She rolled over and quickly began to dress.

"I feel weird," Merv said. "I mean, I'm sorry. It's my wrist."

"I'll get the peas," she said.

The radiologist pointed to a hairline fracture in Merv's ulna and others in two smaller hand bones. After the nurse practitioner showed Merv how to adjust the Velcro brace and prescribed some Percocet for the pain, he was finally allowed to leave.

"You were in there for like two hours," Melissa said, when Merv found her in the waiting room, sitting on an orange vinyl chair, flipping through an old dog-eared *People* magazine. A nearby television was tuned to a loud baseball game. She tossed the magazine aside; it toppled off the end table and, along with several other magazines, cascaded to the floor. She didn't bother to pick up the magazines, and began quickly marching toward the exit.

"Wait up," Merv said, grabbing her shoulder with his good hand. "Are you pissed off or something?"

"I'm just bored," she snapped, "and I did a lot of thinking while you were in there. As much as I could with that stupid baseball game blaring on the television."

"Okay," Merv said, a little confused. "Are you hungry? Why don't I buy you an early dinner or something?"

"Are you okay to drive with that brace?" she asked. "I was thinking that maybe you should stay with Rusty or Jason tonight. Because of the cats."

"The cats," Merv repeated, although he knew that wasn't the real reason she didn't want him staying at her apartment. "You seem really pissed off about something."

"I'm not," she said. "Let's go." She guided him through two sets of tinted automatic doors into the white sun.

Merv had left his sunglasses at her apartment and could barely see in the intense glare. It was like a wall of flashbulbs. "What's your problem?" he said. "I mean, gee, I'm so sorry that some psycho at a 7-Eleven shoved me into a Pez display and broke my wrist. I'm so sorry that I'm allergic to cats."

"Your wrist and allergies didn't seem to bother you while you were fucking me," Melissa said.

"What the hell?" Merv said, confused and offended.

Melissa began to walk faster toward her car. "You know exactly what I'm talking about," she said.

He followed the vague blob that was Melissa through the intense glare, jogged a little to catch up, wondering what he had done wrong.

Merv had to knock on the window to get her to unlock the passenger side door. She had turned up the stereo—some weird African music—and the air conditioning was blasting, already beginning to cool. After snapping on his seatbelt, which hurt his wrist, he lowered the volume so he could speak, but Melissa beat him to it: "I can't believe we already had sex," she said.

"Why?" he said.

"Just the same old pattern," she said. "I have sex before I'm even sure if I like the guy, before I can trust him to be different."

"It seemed like the natural thing to do at the time," Merv said.

"And then to shove me out of bed when you were done," she said, backing out too quickly, skidding a little when she braked and put the car into drive.

"In case you haven't noticed," Merv said, bracing himself on the dashboard, "I have a broken wrist."

She took a deep breath. "You know," she said, "this is my problem. I'm just freaked out that we had sex so soon, that's all. I'm disappointed in myself, that's all. You didn't do anything wrong. Not really."

"Okay," Merv said. He wanted to stop at a pharmacy, but didn't dare ask her to do so. He counted five pharmacies before they reached her apartment. They seemed to be as ubiquitous as 7-Elevens and other convenience stores.

"You can drive, right?" she asked, as she parked her car in the shade of a palo verde tree.

"I guess," Merv said. "I left my sunglasses in your apartment. And my car keys."

"Where are they?" Melissa asked. "I'll get them." Before he answered, she opened her door.

Merv got out of the car, too, and standing there in the one-hundred-plus heat, he wanted to scream. Not at Melissa specifically, but he wanted to scream: at his father, at the dead freak who pushed him over at the 7-Eleven, at his mother, at the two-hour drive back to Tucson, at Melissa's cats, and at Melissa. Instead, he quietly said, "On the coffee table."

Monday, July 9, 2001

Hot

High 103/Low 78

Sunny and clear

KENDRA STOOD OUTSIDE HER POETRY CLASSROOM AND READ THE NOTE scrawled in jittery writing that was taped to the door:

> *Dear Poets:*
>
> *Because of the atmosphere in the class Friday, and because you do not respect poetry or your fellow poets, I have decided to cancel the class. You can optain a refund in the business office in the Building G West.*
>
> *Sincerely,*
> *Smith Boyle, Poet*

"Shit," Kendra said aloud. She then noticed Jim was standing behind her, eating through a sandwich.

"Shit is right," he said. "But at least I won't have to deal with any of you assholes anymore." He walked off, but the odor of the onions from his sandwich lingered.

Kendra wondered if Crystal had already been there and read the note. She sat against the side of the Coke machine and waited for a moment until she heard Crystal and Todd coming down the hall. She stood. "It's canceled," she said. "The whole class."

"That fucking sucks," Crystal said. "I need three credits."

Crystal wore an old AC/DC T-shirt, sleeves cut off and shoulders adorned with safety pins. She and Todd looked at the note.

"I need the credits, too," Todd said. "I'm supposed to graduate in December." His face was red, badly sunburned.

"How old are you?" Crystal asked him.

"Twenty-seven," he said.

"You *do* need to graduate," she said. "That's old."

"Thanks a lot," he said.

"I was trying to graduate this spring and save my parents another thirty-five grand," Crystal said. "This sucks."

Crystal and Todd looked expectantly to Kendra, as if they wanted her to say something about graduating, how the cancellation had ruined her grand plans. She didn't really have any plans, so she just said, "Yeah, this sucks." Then she looked to Todd and said, "You're totally sunburned."

"I went tubing on the Salt River," he said.

"That river is squirming with bacteria and sewage," Crystal said. "You should get a tetanus shot."

"It wasn't that bad," Todd said.

"My dad took my brother and me a few summers ago," Kendra said. "My brother got really sick and plussing as which, my dad had to pull over on the way home and let him shit next to some cows on a ranch in Oracle."

"The hair," Crystal said. "Do you have the envelope with you?"

"Um," Kendra said. "Not sure."

"What the fuck are you talking about?" Todd said.

"None of your business," Crystal said.

"See you next Tuesday," Todd said, over his shoulder, as he began to slowly walk away.

"Fuck you," Crystal said to him.

"We won't see him next Tuesday," Kendra said.

"See you next Tuesday," Crystal said. "C-U-N-T. He's a fucking eighth-grader."

"Oh," Kendra said, laughing a little. "I get it."

"I'm taking you out to lunch," Crystal said. She grabbed

Kendra's shoulder and guided her down the hall. Todd had walked the other way. Halfway to the stairs, Crystal looked back and yelled, "Nice to meet you, Todd. Bitch!"

"Last night, I decided the hair thing is stupid," Crystal said.

"Good," Kendra said. "Can I throw the envelope away now?" The two of them sat in a booth in the deliciously air-conditioned El Presidio Grill, on Speedway Boulevard, tucked into a corner of a strip mall. It was dark and the vinyl from the booth seat was actually cold on Kendra's legs.

Crystal pulled two small homemade cloth dolls from her purse and placed them on the table. "I heard you say 'plussing as which' once today, so I'll make the dolls kiss." One of the dolls was clearly meant to represent Kendra. It was a girl doll with blond yarn hair and arms that were cut and sewn to make them look muscular. The other's body was longer, as was its hair: Jim. Crystal made them kiss.

"That's creepy," Kendra said, and she meant it. Voodoo dolls, or whatever they were, scared her. She and Thomas had watched some sort of pseudodocumentary on cable once, where voodoo witch doctors in Haiti cast spells on people. The witch doctors used dolls and potions and chants. Kendra remembered one woman, a victim of a curse, clutching her side and writhing in the dirt among a bunch of flapping and squawking chickens. The woman was screaming loudly while her sisters kneeled beside her and prayed until the curse subsided.

"Did you feel anything when they kissed?" Crystal asked. "I got one of your hairs from the back of your desk the other day. It's tangled in with the yarn."

"That's really creepy," Kendra said. She wanted to grab the dolls and tear them up, but she was afraid she might cause herself harm or something.

"It'll cure you of your bad grammar in no time," Crystal said. "You'll be thanking me." She grabbed the dolls and stuffed them back into her purse.

"Why do you even care what I say?" Kendra said.

"Because I'm your friend," Crystal said. She lifted the menu and studied it for a moment, zigzagging her finger over the list of entrees. "Lots of protein choices for you."

Kendra wasn't hungry. A nervous knot in her stomach wouldn't allow it. The dolls were weird. Crystal was weird. The fact that she took the time to make them was weird.

"Kendra," Crystal said. "What's wrong? The dolls are a joke."

"I know," Kendra said, but Crystal's comment didn't help her regain her appetite, and she opted for a spring salad with light vinaigrette dressing and no croutons.

When Kendra finally arrived home—after nearly two hours of listening to Crystal talk about some guy she liked—all she wanted to do was sleep. It wasn't even five yet, but she was exhausted. Before she had gone to Pima College for her canceled poetry class, Kendra had worked out hard. She ran her hills in the morning, swam her laps, but she also hit a treadmill and pounded out three miles in just under twenty-one minutes—only a few feet from where a sweat-glistening Hetta was working away on a StairMaster. Hetta had definitely lost weight, but Kendra didn't say anything to her, and, as usual, Hetta said nothing to Kendra.

As soon as Kendra stretched onto her bed, Joyce knocked twice and walked into her room. "That neighbor lady, Mrs. Hunter, wants you to call her as soon as you can," she said. "She wants to take you out to lunch tomorrow. She told me you saved her life."

Kendra sighed. "Oh, God," she said. "Why can't she just leave me alone?"

"Be nice, Kendra," Joyce said, easing onto Kendra's bed. "The poor woman is probably lonely."

"I know." Kendra rolled over, hid her face in the pillow. "I'll call her."

"I'm grilling chicken breasts for dinner," Joyce said. "Would you like one?"

"Yes," Kendra said. "Two, please." She rolled over again. "What's her number?"

* * *

"Kendra! I'm so glad you called," Mrs. Hunter said. "I was just about to give up on you."

"I've been busy," Kendra said. "I was taking a class at Pima, but it got canceled today, so I'll be less busy."

"Great." A few seconds passed before Mrs. Hunter broke the silence. "I was hoping to take you out to lunch tomorrow or maybe even dinner tonight."

"My mom's making me chicken breasts tonight," Kendra said. "Plussing—" She stopped herself. She thought of the stupid dolls Crystal had made. She thought of Crystal making them kiss. She thought of actually kissing Jim, seeing him without his shirt, his scrawny chest draped with his gross hair. "And tomorrow for lunch would be great. I'm not very busy."

"I'll pick you up at noon sharp," she said.

After she hung up, Kendra gently placed the phone in its cradle on the wall. She felt a wave of happiness rising in her chest, like the day when her math teacher told her that she could move out of remedial math and into pre-algebra. "Really?" Kendra had said to her teacher, Mr. Goldwynn. She had been waiting for him for several minutes in his cramped little windowless office behind his classroom. The faded photographs of his ugly family were depressing. Both of his children, a boy and a girl, who looked to be around nine or ten in the photographs, were cursed with his wide-set eyes and giant forehead. His wife had looked like a chimpanzee.

"Your scores have been excellent, and your attitude is super," he had told her when he arrived, clutching a manila folder stuffed with worksheets. "I've already sent a note home to your parents."

This wave of happiness was better, though: She had stopped herself from her retarded grammar—and she had said what she meant without it. Crystal was right. Crystal was smart. Her psychology voodoo dolls worked. She called her and told her so.

"I knew it," Crystal said. "I didn't want to say anything before, but I've used the same methods to cure my friends at school. Smoking, a broken heart, even trichotillomania."

"What the hell is trichotillomania?" Kendra asked.

"Eating your hair," Crystal said. "There was this chick in my philosophy class freshman year, and she'd sit there during lecture and discussion and pluck her hair, then bite off the meaty end— the little chunk of scalp—like she was eating an artichoke."

"That's totally sick," Kendra said.

"She did it symmetrically, too. She had the same size bald patches on either side of her head. She wore bandannas and wigs."

"I knew this guy who used to eat the skin around his fingernails," Kendra said. "Not his fingernails, but the skin. He'd peel off strips with his teeth. His fingers were always bloody."

"Halfway through the semester," Crystal said, "she started going at her eyelashes and eyebrows, so I made a voodoo doll of her. I went up to her after class and I said, 'Look, your hair-eating's making me sick and it's having a negative effect on my grade, so I made a voodoo doll of you. Whenever I see you plucking or eating, I'll jab a pin in the doll." Kendra could hear Crystal take a sip of something. "She told the professor and the dean, and I denied it. I was like, 'I don't even know her. Who are you going to believe? Some hair-eating freak, or me?' The chick stopped eating her hair. I only had to jab the pin in the doll once."

"That's so cruel," Kendra said, laughing.

"It worked, though. I mean, at least in class she never plucked and ate her hair. She should thank me. I saved her thousands on psychiatric bills."

It was then that Kendra realized that she didn't even know where Crystal went to college; that in a month or two, Crystal would be leaving. She sprawled on her bed before she asked.

"Sarah Lawrence," Crystal said.

"Where's that?"

"Outside of New York City."

Kendra felt a confusing anxiety well in her chest. "My

brother's going to Columbia in the fall," Kendra said. "That's in New York City. Near Harlem."

"I know where it is," Crystal said. "Duh."

"When do you have to go back?" Kendra asked her.

"Like, at the end of August or something," Crystal said. "Or maybe the beginning of September."

"Oh," Kendra said.

"You should come visit me and your brother in the fall," Crystal said. "Is your brother cool?"

"He's a dork," Kendra said. "But he's really smart."

"Is he cute?"

"He's my brother," Kendra said. "I don't know. He's skinny and totally out of shape, plussing as which, he has this bitch girlfriend."

"What did you say?"

"I said he has this bitch girlfriend," Kendra said. "Brooke Luter."

"No, before that," Crystal said.

"He's skinny and out of shape?"

"You said, 'plussing as which,'" Crystal said.

"I did?"

"Time to make the dolls kiss one another."

"Can't I have a free pass?"

"No," Crystal said, and then she made wet exaggerated kissing noises into the phone. "I have them right here, and I must say that the Jim doll looks as if he wants a lot more than a few kisses from the Kendra doll. His hips are moving in a funny way."

"Shut up!" Kendra said, giggling. "Please stop."

"Weird grammar equals hot pumping love from Jim and his long, luxurious hair."

The two chatted and laughed on the phone for almost another hour, until Joyce called Kendra down for the barbecued chicken breasts.

Kendra's father sat at the table in a sweaty t-shirt, already eating through a pile of mashed potatoes. His face was ruddy. He smiled at Kendra and waved at her with his fork, as she walked down into the kitchen.

"You shouldn't eat all those carbs this late in the day," Kendra said. "You'll get all mushy—or, in your case, mushier."

"I'm not that mushy," he said, pushing his chair from the table and lifting his T-shirt to expose his pale belly. A detailed tattoo of the Grim Reaper stretched up from his hip to next to his navel. The Reaper's face was misshapen and warped where her father's belly was most blubbery. The tattoo always scared Kendra. As a kid, she had tried hard to avoid seeing it whenever they went swimming. His arms were adorned with spiders and snakes—even a snake swallowing a rat on his right forearm—but these had never frightened her. It was the skull face of the Reaper with his blank, empty eyes that worried her. When she learned what the Reaper represented, she thought her father was asking for it, that he'd be killed any day. She still thought that.

"Be nice to your old father," he said now. "I had a rough day today. Seven old geezers from New Jersey who did nothing but complain about the heat and argue with me about my grip suggestions."

Kendra joined him at the table. "You look sunburned on your face," she said. "Did you use sunscreen today?"

"Every single day," he said. "And a visor."

"You need to reapply often," Kendra said, "or you'll get cancer and your face will rot off. I saw it on television. This chick had no nose, just two plastic straws stuck into a hole."

"Thanks for the tip," he said. "I was thinking that I need to quit the golf business and go back into music. Dark clubs. No sun. While I'm still young."

"I don't think so!" Joyce yelled from the back porch, where she was forking a few barbecued chicken breasts onto a plate. "You had your chance, but you blew it by knocking me up." She walked into the kitchen, allowing the heat to follow her until she slid the door shut behind her.

"I think you had something to do with that," he said. "A trap."

Joyce leaned down and tongued his ear.

"See what I mean?" he said to Kendra. "The slippery se-
ductress."

"You're both gross," Kendra said, although she sort of liked
that her parents were still into each other. Petey's dad had left
years ago, and his mom seemed like an empty shell. Mrs. Hunter
was alone, too, and she was an oddball. "And I want two chicken
breasts."

Kendra retired to her room after finishing her chicken. She had
grabbed two CDs from her father's shelf in the family room and
listened to the Damned's heavy guitars as she flipped through
fitness magazines on her bed. She read an article about the evils
of high-fructose corn syrup, another that ranked elliptical-orbit
trainers.

When she looked at her clock, it wasn't even seven o'clock, so
she doffed her headphones, grabbed her car keys, and bounded
downstairs. Maybe Crystal would meet her at the mall or they
could go to a movie.

Thomas stood in the kitchen by the refrigerator, sipped a can
of Mountain Dew, and glared at Kendra.

"What?" she said to him. She had decided she'd no longer tol-
erate his attitude. He was the jockstrap-collecting perv, not her.
She had just been trying to be nice when she brought him to
meet her friends from the gym.

"I hate you," he said.

"I saw you got rid of your weird jockstrap collection," Kendra
said. She had crawled under the porch to check a few days earlier. "Pervert."

"If you mention it to anyone, I'll fucking kill you," he said.
He crunched the empty Mountain Dew can in his hand as if to
punctuate his threat.

Kendra laughed. "How? You have like no muscle tone," she
said. "I guess you and Brooke, the girlfriend you never have sex
with, could gang up on me." She picked up the phone to call
Crystal.

"Don't tell anyone about it," he said.

"You could strangle me with one of your stolen jockstraps, I guess," Kendra said. "Or you could get Brooke to fart near me. How is that cow?"

"Just don't tell anyone about it," Thomas sort of whined. "Okay?"

Kendra ignored him, dialed Crystal's number.

On her way to pick up Crystal, Kendra saw a little girl sitting with her mother on a cement bench at a bus stop, making her doll wave at passing traffic. At the stoplight, Kendra watched as the little girl turned her doll to look at each car she waved at. When the girl's mother grabbed the doll from her and stuffed it in her bag, the little girl began to wave to cars herself. Good for you, Kendra thought. Your mom's a bitch. It's bad enough that you have to sit at the hot bus stop and breathe in the poison exhaust from traffic, but that See-You-Next-Tuesday should let you have a little fun. Kendra honked and waved at the little girl before the light turned green.

Later, as she sped down River Road with Crystal in her passenger seat, Kendra thought about the little girl at the bus stop. "People are so fucking awful," she said.

"You just figured that out?" Crystal said.

"In general," Kendra said. "People are mean."

"Maybe it's evolution," Crystal said. "Maybe it's genetic. We're coded to be assholes."

"You're not an asshole," Kendra said. "Some people aren't."

"I've certainly been an asshole," Crystal said. "I'm sure those losers from poetry class think I'm an asshole. You've been an asshole, I'm sure."

"I have," Kendra said, making a sharp right up toward Vista Estrella.

"Why the hell are you turning here?" Crystal asked.

Bruce Rombough's car twinkled in the dying orange light of the day. The car had clearly just been washed and waxed. Even the tires shone so much they looked wet. Kendra imagined Bruce

Rombough at the carwash, complaining to the greasy kid who worked there that there were still spots on his car, that they better wax and buff it again. She imagined him giving the kid a measly dollar tip, the kid mumbling something about how now he could afford a bag of Fritos.

"We could do the traditional sugar in the gas tank or tires slashed," Crystal said, from where she stood on the curb. "But that's not creative enough."

"I could scrape something in the side of it," Kendra said. She stood, brushed the dust from her ass. "I'm not sure what he deserves."

"I have to piss," Crystal said. "I could do it in a cup and we could dump it all over his car." She walked over to Kendra's car, opened the back door and dug around.

"I don't think there are any cups back there," Kendra said. "I'm not a pig."

"I found this," she said, standing, holding an empty Gatorade bottle. "You are so a pig."

Kendra stood watch next to her car. Crystal squatted in the backseat and pissed in the plastic bottle. "I got a little on your seat," Crystal said. "Just a few drops." She handed Kendra the bottle through the open window. "Give me your keys."

"Why?" Kendra asked.

"I'll drive getaway."

"All right," Kendra said. The bottle was warm in her hands. "Your pee is really dark. That means you're not drinking enough water. You're dehydrated or you have shitty kidneys. I read all about it and it made me drink way more water."

"Just give me the keys," Crystal said.

Crystal started the car and let it idle while Kendra walked back to Bruce Rombough's car. "What should I do?" Kendra said to Crystal.

"Are his windows all the way rolled up?"

"They're cracked open a little," Kendra said, "but not enough to pour into."

"Get over here," Crystal said, stepping out of the idling car, carrying the newspaper they had used to choose a movie. "You drive."

Crystal rolled a funnel from the newspaper and proceeded to carefully pour the piss into the window on the driver's side of Bruce Rombough's car. About halfway through the bottle, the alarm sounded—a nonstop obnoxious honking, so loud it startled the girls, causing Crystal to drop the bottle and newspaper, and run to Kendra's car.

"Go!" Crystal screamed, as she got into Kendra's car. "Go!"

Kendra skidded as she bent her Volvo around the corner, nearly sideswiping a Dumpster. Adrenaline flushed up from her gut and made her giggle furiously. Crystal was hunched over, ducking, also laughing. Kendra could barely see through the tears in her eyes when she reached the intersection at River Road, so she pulled into a strip mall and parked in front of a dry cleaners.

Crystal looked up. "Why'd you park here? If anyone saw us, we're dead."

"I can't drive," Kendra said, then she began laughing again. Her abs hurt like she was doing inverted crunches.

"You're a very lucky girl," Crystal said. "I don't do revenge pisses for all my friends. Only the ones I really like."

Because of his broken wrist, Merv wasn't permitted to work in any life-saving capacity at Splash World. That meant he spent his day strolling around the park, checking on his lifeguards and the other employees. He packed a wheeled cooler full of ice and bottled water and pulled it behind him. The lifeguards at the wave pool teasingly called him "Water Boy." All day, people asked him what he did to his wrist, and by noon, when Raymond asked him, he had distilled the story down to one sentence: "A psycho in a 7-Eleven in Phoenix shoved me over a Pez display before he ran into traffic and killed himself," he said. And then he added, "Honest."

Raymond pawed at his sunglasses until they slid to the tip of his nose. He rolled his eyes up to meet Merv's. "You saw him die?" he asked.

"Saw and heard," Merv said.

"And aside from your wrist, you're all right?"

"Yeah," Merv said. "You want a water?"

"Not unless you have an extra-long straw," Raymond said.

"I forgot," Merv said. He had meant to tape a few straws together for Raymond. He still felt a little guilty for ignoring him last week when he heard him whimpering in the bathroom stall. "I'm sorry."

"No problem," Raymond said. "I hydrated myself quite a bit this morning."

Looking down at Raymond, Merv noticed the ice-blue paint on the cement shore was peeling in several spots. The trucked-in sand gathered in the exposed areas. For the last few summers, the paint had endured the high foot-traffic until September, when the spots began to appear. They always drained the pool in October, and repainted it before Halloween. As Merv looked around and saw spots of peeled-away paint all over the shore, he decided they might have to close the wave pool for a few days and repaint sometime soon. The guys at the corporate office in Long Beach would be happy, though: The peeling paint was testimony as to how much park attendance had gone up—without any major promotions or other marketing efforts.

Before he could respond to Raymond, Merv's walkie-talkie beeped. It was Hank. "Can you meet me at your office?" he asked. "We have a problem."

"I'll be there in a minute," Merv said. "What's going on?"

"I just need you to get here as soon as possible," Hank said.

"I'll be there in a minute," Merv said. "Out."

"I'll catch you later," Raymond said. "Sounds serious."

Merv jogged across the park to his office, pulling the wheeled cooler behind him. To circumvent groups of people on the sidewalks, he veered onto the bright grass, leaving tracks. He had never heard Hank sound so panicked.

"We have a problem," Hank said, when Merv finally reached the small office building.

Merv was out of breath, and his wrist hurt from swinging it as he ran. He felt a little dizzy from the run and from the Percocet he had taken the night before. "What's up?"

"Come into your office," Hank said, holding the door open.

Inside, one of the BMX meth-heads, the one who wore a dog-collar, sat the floor, his hands behind his back. He was spitting blood onto his lap. David, another member of the security team, stood next to the bleeding kid.

"I found him in the parking lot, trying to break into a Lexus with a screwdriver," David said. David's neck was as wide as his head. The SECURITY T-shirt he wore could barely contain his linebacker shoulders. "I tackled him. Now he's bleeding from his mouth and he won't say anything. His hands are cuffed."

"Let me think a second," Merv said. "Did you call the police yet?"

"No," Hank said. "Can we talk outside for a moment?"

Outside, around the corner, under a giant palm, Hank grabbed Merv's shoulder. "This kid could sue the fuck out of Splash World. David's not authorized to tackle anyone. He's not authorized to cuff anyone—not even those plastic riot cuffs."

"Where'd he get the cuffs?" Merv asked.

"All my security guys have them," Hank said.

"Why?"

"For situations like this," Hank said.

"But you just said you're not authorized to use them," Merv said.

"The kid doesn't know that," Hank said. "That's my point."

"Wait," Merv said. "What?"

"The meth-head," Hank said. "He doesn't know that, but if the police find out and arrest him, he'll get an attorney from the state and that attorney will certainly know it."

"But they've been looking for this guy and his two friends for a while," Merv said. He leaned against the rough-barked palm. "Shit."

"Think of all the paperwork," Hank said. "I think we should just let him go."

"Fire David," Merv said. "He shouldn't have tackled the kid—or cuffed him. He's bleeding all over my office. He probably has AIDS."

"I can't fire David," Hank said. "Let's just let the kid go and forget this shit."

"Fire him," Merv said. "That's step one. Let the kid go and don't let him know that anything David did was illegal. And then get someone from housekeeping to bleach the shit out of my office. And make sure David didn't get any blood on him. And if he did, don't fire him. That'd be another lawsuit. If he did get blood on him, he has to go to the hospital—"

"Hold on," Hank said.

"Wait," Merv said. "Don't fire him at all. He'd sue Splash World, too."

"So we let the kid go?" Hank said. "And nothing else?"

"And get housekeeping in there," Merv said.

"That's what I wanted to do in the first place," Hank said, walking back to the office.

"And meet with your entire team," Merv yelled, "and let them know what they can and *can't* do. And take away those stupid riot cuffs."

Merv sat in the grass under the palm, listened to the dry fronds high above him crinkle in the slight wind. To hell with Nick Honig and his stupid investigation, he thought. And then he thought of Petey and Petey's mother. If those meth-heads had anything to do with Petey's disappearance . . . Merv already felt the guilt in his stomach. He could call Nick, tell him the truth: one of his security guys caught the meth-head but illegally tackled him and cuffed him, so they had to let him go. Nick would understand. He'd undoubtedly been in similar situations. And if the kid was illegally apprehended, he'd probably be useless for the investigation; they'd have to let him go, too. It hadn't been Merv who fucked up. It was Hank and David. They were the ones responsible for messing with the investigation, they were the ones responsible if Petey was alive, in some dungeon somewhere, being tortured by a bunch of tweekers with purple gums and scabby skin.

Just after Merv stood and brushed the grass from the seat of his shorts, the bleeding meth-head walked up to him. He spit a gob of blood and something else onto the grass in front of Merv. "Happy now?" he said.

"What?" Merv said.

"Happy now?" the kid said. "Your musclehead assholes beat the shit out of me. Happy?"

"No," Merv said. "No, they didn't beat the shit out of you and no, I'm not happy."

"He knocked out my tooth on the pavement, asshole," the tweeker said, lifting his puffed lip so Merv could see. The kid's other teeth were brown, growing from purple gums. His sun-bleached hair had a green tint, which made Merv think that he'd been sneaking into the wave pool or some other pool at Splash World. His pink chest was speckled with scabs and sores, and blood stained the front of his shorts. He looked like something from Michael Jackson's old "Thriller" video, a zombie who had just dug himself out of his own grave, ready to wander the streets in search of victims.

"Why don't you just leave?" Merv said. "Before I call the police."

"I'm leaving, dickhead," the kid said. "This place sucks . . ." He walked off. ". . . during the day." He laughed.

Merv called Nick Honig after the two people from housekeeping finished in his office. He was happy to smell the bleach fumes and to see that both the workers were wearing yellow rubber gloves that stretched up to their elbows.

He told Nick Honig that a member of the Splash World security team caught one of the BMX meth-heads, but mistakenly let him go.

"No problem," Nick said. "I'm working on another lead that's more promising."

"Great," Merv said, feeling a wave of relief wash through his gut. "I thought he had really messed up your investigation."

"I'm pretty sure we can find those meth-heads whenever we want now," Nick said. "I'll bring them in for questioning later this week after I explore this new lead a little further."

"Let me know if I can do anything," Merv said. He really meant it, too, which surprised him.

Merv spent the remainder of the day pulling the water cooler around the park, chatting it up with patrons. He tried not to think about Melissa, wanted to dismiss her as another psycho he should never have dated—not that they really ever *dated*. One date, really, and that cracked-up day in Scottsdale over the weekend. He hadn't called Rusty or Jason after he left Melissa's place, didn't want to deal with their questions. After picking up his prescription, he just drove home to Tucson, stopping about ten times to drink and piss. The Percocet had made him kind of stoned, and he had been afraid of falling asleep behind the wheel, even in the bright daylight with his radio blasting classic rock. Led Zeppelin at full, distorted volume wasn't enough to quell his fears of dozing off—he had even sung along with Robert Plant, making his own voice as high and as full of lust: ". . . you better lay your money doooooooown . . ."

He was surprised that Rusty and Jason hadn't called him yet. Although, he figured, maybe Melissa was embarrassed about the whole incident and hadn't called them yet. Rusty and Jason probably figured that he and Melissa had been having so much fun that they had forgotten to call. Merv would call Rusty tonight and explain the whole thing.

As Merv washed his sweaty and stinky wrist brace in the sink in the locker room, Raymond called to him from the stall again: "Merv, is that you?"

Merv turned off the water, shook his brace, and said, "Yes." He knew Raymond must have looked through the crack where the panels met on the stall walls.

"Could you help me a minute?" Raymond said. "Nothing that embarrassing, I swear."

"No problem," Merv said. He walked over to the stall and the door swung open.

"I dropped my sunglasses on the floor," Raymond said. "Could you get them for me?"

"Of course," Merv said. He crouched down and picked up the glasses, which had landed next to the base of the toilet. "I'll even wash them off for you. That's not the cleanest place for sunglasses to land."

As Merv rinsed them in the sink, Raymond rolled out of the stall. "Thank you, Merv."

"No problem."

"I'm sorry about your wrist," Raymond said.

Merv dried the sunglasses with a paper towel, and handed them to Raymond, who struggled to put them on his face. Merv put them on for him, even squatted down to make sure they weren't lopsided or uneven. "All set," Merv said.

"I bet the girls love those dimples of yours," Raymond said.

Merv laughed nervously and said goodbye.

Traffic was horrible. Merv had forgotten about the construction on Swan Road that cut northbound traffic to one lane, and he ended up trapped in a line of cars that stretched for miles into the Santa Catalina foothills. In his rearview, he could see the brown blanket of smog perched above the city of Tucson.

It was an hour and ten minutes before he walked into his house to find his mother stretched on the sofa, her bare feet resting on the coffee table. She was watching a loud sitcom and giggling along. She didn't even turn her head to acknowledge Merv's presence.

"Hello?" Merv said to her. "I'm here. Your son Merv is home."

"Your mother Ellen is busy watching TV and resting her legs," she said.

"Did you make dinner?"

"No," she said. "Did you?"

"I just got home!"

"Just in time to make something," she said.

Merv dropped his bag on the couch next to her. "What kind of pills are you on?"

"None of your business," she said. "The relationship I have with my psychiatrist is between me and him."

As he walked into the kitchen, Merv said, "Well, maybe you should mention to him next time that your attitude needs an adjustment."

"I prefer to talk to him about how I raised a son who's thirty and still lives at home," she said. She turned up the volume on the television. The tinny laughter was deafening, so Merv didn't bother to respond.

"I cut out an article about the guy in Phoenix who attacked you," she yelled into the kitchen. "I taped it to the fridge. They mention you by name."

"Did they find a copy of *The Catcher in Rye* in his pocket?" Merv asked.

"Why?" she asked.

"All psychos carry *The Catcher in the Rye*," Merv said. "I bet if I looked through your purse, I'd find a copy."

"Imagine what it would be like if you were actually funny," Ellen said impassively.

Merv didn't want to read the article. He preferred not to know the man's name or anything else about him. It was bad enough that he had seen the guy get hit by an SUV. If he knew the guy's name, that he had kids and a wife or something, that would make the memories of it all the more horrific. He grabbed the article from the refrigerator door, crumpled it, and tossed it in the trashcan under the sink. The only part of the article he had read was the headline: DISTURBED PRESCOTT MAN KILLED IN PHOENIX TRAFFIC.

Munday, July 16, 2001

Hot and humid

High 104 / Low 77

Cloudy, with chance of showers in

the afternoon

WHEN ELLEN HUNTER CALLED KENDRA THIS MORNING AND ASKED HER TO meet for lunch downtown at Café Poca Cosa, Kendra didn't hesitate to accept the invitation. Last week's lunch with Ellen had actually been pretty fun. They had eaten at The Ovens on Campbell and River Road, and Ellen had complained about her son and deceased husband the entire time. Kendra learned that her son Merv was thirty and that he had never graduated from college. She had known he lived at home, but she had assumed Mrs. Hunter—Ellen—had liked him living there. Wrong. "I'm sick of the men in my life disappointing me," she said. "My dead husband cheated on me like crazy. With hookers. Nasty hookers. He got hepatitis from one. That's how he died."

All Kendra could say was, "Wow."

"'Wow' is right," Ellen said. "My psychiatrist says I'm supposed to be angry with him now, even though he's dead. It's healthy. I should have let him have it when he was alive. I should have packed me and Merv up and hit the road the first time I caught him screwing a whore."

"Yeah," Kendra said. She couldn't wait to call Crystal and tell her about it all.

"And Merv . . . he's like a giant five-year-old," she said. She bit into her small pesto pizza, pulled a seed from her teeth and continued: "Actually, he's more like a fifteen-year-old. He stopped maturing when his father died—my psychiatrist backs me up on this theory."

Ellen had gone on to tell Kendra about the guy she should have married, her high school sweetheart in Prescott, a guy named Gerard whose sense of humor, Ellen felt, was perfectly tailored to hers. "With one goofy expression, he could nearly make me laugh hard enough to wet my pants." He was a baseball player, recruited by the Baltimore Orioles his sophomore year at the University of Texas, where he had won a scholarship—not for baseball, but for debate. "Some dumb redneck frat boy in Austin ran him over and killed him. He was on the sidewalk, just minding his own business, walking to class, and this drunk idiot swerves up and kills him. The kid's father was an oilman, rich, and he didn't even serve any time." She put down her fork and leaned across the table, closer to Kendra. She whispered, "I was in a full-on nuthouse for a year and a half. A drugged zombie. The week I got out, I met Merv's father, the man who would eventually choose skanky whores over me and leave me broke with a big house and a fifteen-year-old son to take care of."

Ellen's stories hit Kendra in the gut. Kendra's mista salad and catfish no longer looked appetizing. She sipped her ice water.

"I'll shut up for a minute or two today," Ellen had promised when she called Kendra this morning. "I feel like I didn't let you get a word in last week, and I'm sorry."

"That's okay," Kendra said. "Plus, I had fun."

Now Kendra was speeding down Broadway Boulevard under a cloudy sky. The air was sticky and thick, and the shadiness was odd, giving the city a veneer of dinginess and gloom. Everything from bus stop benches to adobe buildings looked dirtier—brown and gray.

As she slowly passed under the bridge into downtown, Kendra glimpsed the BMX meth-heads in a dirt lot to the right, the three of them, straddling their little bicycles, staring into the oozing noontime traffic like they were looking for a specific car. They were sunburned pink, and two wore T-shirts or rags wrapped around their heads. The third wore a ball cap with flaps down the back. She nearly pulled off the road, but the way they were standing, their skinny, twisted torsos, scabby skin, and fucked-up teeth: they scared her. They knew where Petey was, she was sure of it, but they scared her.

When she arrived at Café Poca Cosa, she pulled her cell phone from her bag and dialed 911. She was quickly connected to Detective Honig.

"This is Kendra Lumm," she said. "I saw them! I saw the guys who were with Petey the night before he disappeared."

"The skinny guys on bikes?" Detective Honig asked.

"Yes," Kendra said, her voice cracking with excitement. She took a deep breath, but it didn't quell the adrenaline coursing through her system. "Right on Broadway in a dirt lot right near downtown. Plussing as which, I could totally identify them, if you want." She said it. She said "plussing as which," and she wanted to punch something.

"I'm working on another lead," Detective Honig said. "But I appreciate your vigilance."

"You don't even want to talk to them?" Kendra asked.

"Not yet," Detective Honig said. "But I'll be calling you tonight or tomorrow about this other lead."

"Wait!" Kendra said, sensing that he might be ready to hang up. "The BMX wastoids are right there on Broadway. I passed them like two minutes ago and they weren't moving."

"Like I said, I appreciate your call," he said. He sighed and then added, "As a matter of fact, maybe I'll send someone down there to talk to those guys. What are the cross streets again?"

"Broadway and that underpass before you get into down-town," Kendra said. "If you're coming from like El Con Mall."

"If you're heading west?" Nick said.

"If you're heading into downtown."

"But you can head into downtown from any direction."

"Like from El Con Mall!"

"That would mean you're heading west."

"Okay then!" Kendra said. "You know these are the guys me

and Thomas saw Petey with the night before he disappeared, right?"

"Right," Detective Honig said. "I've got another call. Thanks again." He hung up.

Kendra clicked off her cell phone and threw it into her bag. "Fucker!" she yelled. "Fucking moron." She stared through her bug-spattered windshield at the white adobe wall in front of her. A crack ran from the ground all the way to the roof. A brown liquid dripped from the crack and traced a path downward from about the crack's midpoint. Probably some nasty poison, Kendra thought, but she didn't care. She thought for a few more moments about Petey and Detective Honig's lame investigation, then she picked up her cell phone again. She called Crystal.

"Make the dolls kiss," she told her. "I said it again. Make them kiss. Make them fuck. Whatever."

"I should have asked for another detective," Kendra said to Ellen, taking in the bright green ceiling and purple walls.

"They would have just referred you back to Honig," Ellen said.

A waitress came by and placed two generous salads in front of them. The salads were served on large wooden planks and consisted of lettuce and a bunch of vegetables and fruits Kendra had never before seen: something bright red and shredded, a long tan-colored root of some sort, a baseball-sized spiked fruit that had been cut open to expose its pink juicy center, all sprinkled with what looked like bleached pumpkin seeds. Kendra didn't know where to start on the salad. She didn't know what piece of silverware to use, either, so she waited for Ellen to make the first move.

Ellen went for the spiky, opened fruit, picked it up with her hands and bit into the center. "I love these," she said.

"What is it?" Kendra asked.

"I don't know," Ellen said, "but I love them. They taste like a cross between a kiwi and a tangerine."

"My brother has this friend, Brooke, and she says that the

cops would be working way harder at finding Petey if he were some honor student or Boy Scout."

Ellen licked the juice from her lips. A large drop worked its way down her chin and splattered onto the table. "Probably true," she said. "Personally, I think the kid just ran away in search of more fun. He's probably drunk or high or whatever he wants to be right now." Ellen didn't wipe her chin.

"I used to think that pretty much," Kendra said. "Until today when I saw the guys on the bikes." She went to work on the leaves of lettuce with a fork, careful to avoid the weird white seeds and other mysterious ingredients.

"I'm sure he'll turn up," Ellen said. "He'll be throwing those noisy parties again before summer's over."

"Maybe," Kendra said. She resigned herself to blame Detective Honig if Petey wasn't okay, if he didn't show up soon.

"So let's talk about something more cheerful," Ellen said. "What classes are you taking in the fall?"

"I don't know," Kendra said. "Math and stuff."

"I was lousy at math," Ellen said. "I was good in English and art. I used to paint watercolors of the desert, good ones."

Kendra couldn't concentrate on the conversation. She was thinking about Petey, and her eyes wandered over the expanse of the bustling restaurant. From the outside, it had looked like a soulless and dingy hotel, maybe designed in the seventies, just a big dirty cement cube in the middle of a parking lot. But Kendra liked the restaurant, which occupied the majority of the ground floor. It was bright, and the walls were adorned with punched-tin luminarias and reviews from magazines and newspapers from all over the world. The waitresses wore intricately embroidered Mexican peasant skirts and moved through the sea of tables and ficus trees, hoisting trays big enough to hold the giant portions of exotic fare. Kendra's mother had told her to try the mole, that it changed every day, and once, when she had been there, one of the ingredients had been crushed beetles from a certain mountain in southern Mexico.

If Petey did surface, she'd kill him for making her worry.

* * *

Kendra had been planning on just grabbing her gym bag and heading to the club, but when she pulled up to her house, she noticed two police cruisers in her driveway, parked next to another strange car, a tan American sedan. Her immediate thought was that she was busted for vandalizing Bruce Rombough's car. Maybe some neighbor of his had leaned out of his apartment and caught it all on video, maybe they'd show the video on the news tonight. Maybe Crystal had already been apprehended. Crystal *was* the one who had left the Gatorade bottle at the scene of the crime. Crystal was an adult and would be really busted, sent to real jail with real criminals, big lesbians with crew cuts and hairy arms. Kendra would be sent to a juvenile detention center. She'd passed one on the highway north of Tucson in Oracle. There were signs along the way that warned drivers not to pick up hitchhikers.

Kendra would lie to the cops, tell them that she had forced Crystal to piss in that Gatorade bottle and dump it into Bruce Rombough's car. She had threatened to kick Crystal's ass if she didn't. Or maybe she'd say that Bruce Rombough actually wanted them to dump piss in his car, that he was a pervert who had been paying the girls to piss on him and his possessions. The car had been the coup de grâce, his ultimate erotic fantasy fulfilled.

Kendra parked in the street and walked slowly through the dense humidity up the hill to her house, calming herself with logical thoughts: If she were busted for the pissing incident, her parents would probably think it was funny. She'd probably have to pay for Bruce Rombough's car to be cleaned. Even if she were brought in front of a judge, it was her first run-in with the law. A fine. Tops. Same for Crystal—unless she had been arrested before. They got Kendra from the license plates on her Volvo. She could lie and say she just met Crystal that day, that she told her that her name was . . . Camille or something.

Kendra paused halfway up the driveway, stood in the gravel,

and pulled out her cell phone. She called her house, and Joyce answered.

"What's going on in there?" Kendra asked before her mother even finished saying hello.

"You'd never guess the shit that's going on," she said. "But they want to talk to you, too. Where are you?"

"The driveway," Kendra said. "I'm not busted or anything, am I?"

"No," Joyce said, "but they need to talk to you. I've called your cell phone like twelve times."

"I had it turned off for lunch," Kendra said, now rushing up the driveway. "Is this about Petey?"

"They think Brooke has something to do with his disappearance," Joyce said. "Brooke Luter. Thomas's girlfriend."

"That whore," Kendra said, jogging to the front door. "I knew it." She opened the door and nearly bumped into Joyce, who was standing in the foyer, talking into the portable phone.

"I never trusted her, either," Joyce said. "She always dressed so provocatively."

"You mean like a spent old whore," Kendra said. "Being as which we're like a foot apart, we can hang up the phones." Kendra clicked off her phone, then said, "Fuck!"

"What's your problem?" Joyce asked.

"I said 'being as which,'" Kendra said.

"So?"

"I'm sick of my fucked-up grammar."

"I think 'being as which' is okay," Joyce said. "It sounds okay to me."

"It's not," Kendra said. She clicked her phone back on and called Crystal. She left Crystal a voicemail: "Make them kiss again. I fucked up." She clicked off her phone and dropped it into her bag, finally closing the front door behind her. The air conditioning was on high, Kendra could tell. The cooling sweat on the back of her neck actually gave her a welcome chill.

"Make who kiss?" Joyce asked.

"Just some dolls," Kendra said. "Where are the cops?"

"I need a cigarette bad," Joyce said. "But don't let me."

Four uniformed officers and Detective Honig were talking to Thomas on the back porch. They all sat around the glass-topped table. Through the kitchen window, Kendra could see that Thomas's face was ruddy, streaked with tears. His head was down, but he looked up and mumbled a few words to the officers every few minutes. Kendra couldn't make out anything anyone was saying—the hum of the air conditioner was too loud.

"Get over here," Joyce said. "Now!"

"Why?" Kendra said.

"I just don't think it's right to be spying on them."

"Don't you even care what they're asking him?" Kendra said.

"I'm not about to interfere with police business," Joyce said. "Now come over here and sit down."

Kendra didn't move from her position at the sink. She watched as all of the officers scribbled into small pads. One held a microphone to Thomas. "I always hated Brooke," Kendra said.

"Get away from that window!" Joyce said. "Now! You're going to get us all in trouble. You're making me nervous as hell."

Kendra cupped her hand above her brow and leaned over the sink, which was full of dirty dishes, closer to the window. Just as she did so, Thomas looked up, and their eyes met. He abruptly stood and pointed at the window. "Bitch!" he yelled. "Fucking bitch!" All the officers looked at her. She smiled and held up a glass, like she was just getting a drink.

About ten minutes later, Thomas walked into the house. He was no longer crying, but his eyes were bloodshot and his face still held a red flush. "They want to talk to you now, cunt," he said to Kendra. "And, Mom, they said you have to go out there and tell them it's okay to talk to Kendra because she's not eighteen."

Joyce and Kendra stood. Joyce grabbed Thomas's shirt and

pulled him close. "If you ever call your sister a cunt again, you'll be going to Pima Community College instead of Columbia!"

"That's okay," Kendra said. She was sort of frightened by her mother's outburst. "I've been called worse."

"Well, your brother will never call you it again," she said. Then she pulled Thomas even closer. He turned his head to the side, looked at the floor. "Will you?"

Thomas didn't answer.

"Will you?" Joyce repeated. Kendra noticed how her mother's top lip twitched.

"That's okay," Kendra said. "They're waiting for us out in the heat."

"Will you?" Joyce said again, this time louder, her lip twitching even more, like someone was tugging an invisible string that had been attached to it.

"No," Thomas finally said, squirming loose from his mother's grasp, and fleeing up the stairs.

Then she turned to Kendra: "If he ever calls you that again, I want to know about it." Her eyes were wide, bugged.

"Fine," Kendra said, sliding the door open. She leaned out into the heat and asked Detective Honig why they couldn't talk inside.

"We can," he said. "I guess. Where's Thomas?"

"Up in his room," she said.

"So it's private?"

"Yes," Kendra said.

All the cops sat around the kitchen table. Joyce had carried three chairs in from the dining room, one by one, to accommodate them. Kendra observed that none of the cops had offered to help her. Joyce had also served them ice tea, and she stood at the kitchen counter while Detective Honig questioned Kendra about Brooke Luter. Kendra noticed the circles of sweat that spread from Detective Honig's armpits, darkening his red polo shirt. The other officers, who looked alike in their uniforms, all sporting the identical buzz cut, and slight beer-bellies, said nothing, only took notes. One held a microphone between Kendra and Detective Honig.

"She's a bitch," Kendra said. "She was always hanging out with Petey even though he didn't really like her."

"How do you know he didn't like her?" Detective Honig asked.

"He told me the only reason he hung out with her was because she paid for everything and bought him beer and cigarettes." Kendra thought for a moment, tried to remember Petey's exact words. "He said something like 'Brooke's okay as long as she brings me beer or Taco Bell.' She was always bringing him Taco Bell."

"Did he say anything else about her?"

"Not really," Kendra said. "She was always over there. At first, I was pissed and told him that if he hooked up with her, I'd kick both their asses, but then I told him to go ahead and hook up with her if he wanted. I don't think he ever did. He wasn't that desperate and he was always wasted, anyway."

Kendra watched as a weird sneer played at Detective Honig's upper lip. He drew a breath deeply through his nose, puffed his chest, and let it out with a half whistle. "And what about Thomas?"

"What about Thomas?"

"Did either Thomas or Brooke say anything about whether or not they were having sex?"

"Hey!" Joyce said from over in the kitchen. "That seems like a personal question. Kendra, you don't have to answer it."

"Mrs. Lumm," Detective Honig said, "we have some information about Brooke Luter that might make you understand why we're asking these questions, but we wanted to ask the questions first so Kendra's answers aren't influenced by the information in any manner."

"If this is about Petey," Kendra said, "I totally want to cooperate." She knew Brooke was a phony—all those stupid posters, her little display of tears on the news, her fake concern. Kendra had known it was all bullshit. And before Joyce could protest any further, Kendra said, "Thomas said they fucked but Brooke said they didn't."

Detective Honig looked over to Joyce. "You see, that's very important information for us. Very important." He placed both his palms flat on the table, then brought them together, touching his fingertips together, making a small steeple from his hands. "When did Thomas say they fucked?"

"A few weeks ago," Kendra said.

"And when did Brooke dispute that?"

"Like, the same day," Kendra said. "I think."

He looked over to Joyce again. "Just so you know, neither Kendra nor Thomas is in any kind of trouble. This phase of the investigation involves the woman who calls herself Brooke Luter." He turned back to Kendra, stared intently into her eyes. Kendra noticed that his right eye was bluer than his left, which was greener. "And what's your opinion about their sex life? I realize this is just your opinion."

"I doubt they had sex," Kendra said. "I hope they didn't have sex."

"Doubt or hope?" Detective Honig asked.

"Both," Kendra said.

"It seems a little odd that you're asking a sixteen-year-old girl to speculate about her brother's sex life," Joyce said. "It seems weird."

"Brooke Luter is thirty-four years old," he said. "Her real name is Nativity Funsett. She grew up in a small town in west Texas, graduated from Bennington College in Vermont, and proceeded to set herself up in six different cities, always pretending to be a high school sophomore. She was arrested twice for fraud, twice for petty theft, and in Oregon she was charged with but not convicted of statutory rape."

Kendra couldn't contain herself and began to chuckle, repeating Brooke's real name: Nativity Funsett. "I knew she was a loser," Kendra said. "Thirty-four!"

"In Indianapolis, she got straight A's and was head cheerleader," Detective Honig said. "And she was twenty-eight then."

Joyce stood at the counter, her mouth agape, one hand on her hip.

"One kid thought she was a substitute," Kendra said, "and she got really pissed off."

"Is she crazy?" Joyce asked. "I mean, she must be crazy, right?"

"She does look thirty-four," Kendra said. "I knew it. I knew she was a liar. And she always wears the dumbest clothes. Slutty clothes."

"You didn't know she was thirty-four," Joyce said to Kendra. "No one did. Thomas didn't. I hope." Then she looked to Detective Honig. "Did Thomas know she was thirty-four?"

"He seemed pretty surprised when we told him a few minutes ago," Detective Honig said. "Genuinely surprised."

"How'd you catch the freak?" Kendra asked. She was dying to call Crystal. "I hate her. I knew she was psycho. I knew she was weird."

"Someone recognized her on the news," Detective Honig said. He stood, as did the other four officers. "We'll be in touch, but let us know if anything related to Peter Vaccarino or Brooke Luter comes up."

"You think she has something to do with his disappearance, don't you?" Joyce asked.

"I can't say," he said.

"I bet that whore kidnapped him and made him have sex with her," Kendra said. "She was so desperate for sex, always wearing those shorts way up in her cellulite ass like a hooker."

"Kendra," Joyce said, "that sort of editorializing is unhelpful and annoying, so shut up."

Detective Honig rolled his eyes. "When does Thomas leave for Cornell?" he asked Joyce.

"Columbia," Joyce said. "Not until the end of next month."

He put his heavy hand on Kendra's shoulder. "And you'll be around all summer?"

"Yes," she said. "And if you want any more information about Brooke Luter, just call me. I was in art class with her last semester.

She sucked at art but always argued to get A's on her lame projects. She always painted flowers."

"Thanks," Detective Honig said.

Kendra had swum thirty-one laps, reached the point where she felt like she could swim forever, felt the weird false happiness from the endorphins light up her brain. Thinking of Brooke Luter, she actually caught herself laughing under water. Her face hurt from grinning. And instead of dwelling on Brooke as the spent whore idiot she was, at around lap number twenty, Kendra began to concentrate on how Brooke might be involved in Petey's vanishing. Moving through the water, breathing symmetrically on either side every third stroke, really reaching and pulling, Kendra couldn't come up with anything. It didn't make sense that Brooke would have abducted or killed Petey— unless he knew she was a thirty-four-year-old psycho bitch who had been to high school like ten times. She wondered if Detective Honig had thought of that. Probably.

At lap thirty-one, someone tapped her on her head before she ducked into a flip-turn. Kendra stood in her lane and was face-to-face with the lifeguard. "Lightning," he said from his position on his hands and knees on the deck. "You have to get out of the pool. Sorry."

"No problem," Kendra said. She removed her goggles and wrung out her hair, before she pushed up on the deck and sprung out of the pool. Just as she did so, lightning blinked in the east. Finally, she thought, her feet burning on the textured cement, even on this cloudy day. It better rain. She stepped into her flip-flops, and walked to the locker room, where she changed into workout clothes.

The weight room was nearly deserted. Kendra shared it only with an old guy who was lifting very small weights with horrible form. His skinny pink legs made the old-style gym shorts he wore look like a skirt. He was doing curls with eight-pound dumbbells, allowing his elbows to pop out to the sides with each repetition. Kendra wanted to talk to him and show him how to properly execute a curl, but she didn't bother. Instead, she picked up a pair of twenty-five-pound dumbbells, stood a few feet from the old guy, and sped through a set in perfect form. If he wanted to watch her and learn, he could; otherwise, he could continue with his inefficient—and perhaps dangerous—curls, and never progress.

"You got nice muscles for a girl," he said to her after he finished a pathetic set of only five repetitions—Kendra had counted.

"Thanks," Kendra said, unsure if he was insulting her.

"You work out a lot, I bet," he said. "I used to have muscles like you."

"Great," Kendra said, although she doubted that he ever had musculature even vaguely close to hers. You didn't get musculature like hers with sloppy form. She hadn't really wanted to work her biceps with free weights today, anyway—she was just being nice to the old man. She had wanted to work a quick circuit on the machines in the room adjoining the free-weight room, mainly to stretch and tone.

Before she went in there, though, she stopped and used the phone by the drinking fountains. She had called Crystal right after the police left, but Crystal hadn't answered. She was dying to tell her about Brooke, but again Crystal's voicemail picked up and Kendra left a message: "It's like six and I totally have to tell you something really weird and really funny. Where are you? And why aren't you answering your cell phone? I'm at the gym for like another hour. Call me on my cell!"

Hetta sat on an ab machine, rocking back and forth. Waste of time, Kendra thought when she saw her. Get your fat ass back on the StairMaster before you start trying to have abs.

Hetta looked directly at Kendra but didn't even hint at acknowledging her.

Kendra spoke, though, partially to spite Hetta and partially so she could talk about Brooke. "Did you see all the police cars at our house this afternoon?"

"No," Hetta said, not glancing at Kendra again.

"There were three," Kendra said. "Five cops total, including a detective. Detective Honig."

Hetta said nothing, only kept rocking back and forth, pushing the padded bar with her blubbery gut.

"They were there about Petey," Kendra said. "Peter Vaccarino, and they think this one girl Brooke Luter has something to do with his disappearance. She's thirty-four, but pretended to still be in high school and she was in my art class and—"

"Isn't it obvious that I'm busy?" Hetta said, still not looking at Kendra. She adjusted the elastic that held her sweaty ponytail in place.

Kendra wanted to say, You're wasting your time, you fat cunt, but she remembered Franny, all the bullshit she had to go through back when she told Hetta that the food in her supermarket cart was all crap. She also remembered how Joyce freaked out when Thomas used the word *cunt* earlier. She imagined Hetta calling Joyce and telling her, then Joyce calling Franny and scheduling like a million appointments for Kendra. Instead, after thinking for a moment, Kendra said, "I thought you might be interested in what's happening in your own neighborhood. Sorry to interrupt your workout."

Hetta stopped rocking, stood and wiped the sweat from the padded bar and seat with her towel. She quickly walked out of the room, leaving Kendra with the entire circuit of machines to herself.

Kendra walked between two rows of pink adobe bungalows, hidden in the middle of Barrio Volvo near the University. She had never noticed the bungalows before even though she had driven down this street hundreds of times—sometimes when she went to see Franny she forgot to get cash for the garage and had to find a parking spot in the neighborhood. The hot wind picked up dust and rattled the tall palms. A page of newspaper looped through the sky above the last bungalow, number twelve, Crystal's brother's place. Crystal had finally called her just as Kendra opened her locker back at the club.

Kendra knocked on the door, which unlike the doors on the other bungalows, was painted bright blue, the color of a cartoon sky.

"Come in!" Crystal yelled from inside.

Kendra turned the knob and pushed hard, finally put her shoulder into it, to get the door open.

"The humidity makes it stick," Crystal said. She sat on an Oriental rug that covered shiny red Mexican tiles, books and papers spread on the floor in front of her. "Get yourself a glass of water. The kitchen's through there." She indicated with a tilt of her head.

Instead, Kendra moved a few papers aside and joined Crystal on the rug. "Where's your brother?" Kendra asked.

"He and his girlfriend went to get some burritos at Sanchez," Crystal said. "I had them get you a chicken one with the sauce on the side."

"Perfect," Kendra said. "I'm starving."

"I was thinking about that thirty-four-year-old chick who your brother was dating," Crystal said, "and it's really fucked up. How come no one knew? Did she look totally young?"

"I thought she looked old," Kendra said. "So did a bunch of other people."

"What kind of freak wants to go to high school again?" Crystal said. "High school sucked. A stress pit."

"The detective said she went to like six different high schools after she graduated from college," Kendra said. The rug was beginning to itch her legs, so she moved to the couch, a deep, soft sofa, slipcovered in a white canvas. A small air-conditioning unit hummed away in the window, and Kendra's new spot afforded her a nice cool blast. "All over the country."

"And you know her?"

"Of course," Kendra said. "She always hung out with Petey

and then my loser brother. She was at my house like a thousand times."

"You think she's psycho?" Crystal asked. "Like, really fucked up?"

"She actually didn't seem psycho until I heard she was thirty-four," Kendra said. "I mean, she was a bitch and I know she wanted to fuck Petey, but she didn't seem psycho."

"Check this out," Crystal said. She held an open book up to Kendra. She tapped a black-and-white photograph of a lamp with her pointer finger.

"What?" Kendra said. "A lamp."

"The shade's made of human skin," Crystal said.

Kendra grabbed the book and looked closer at the lampshade. It didn't look especially like human skin. It was stitched together kind of sloppily, but it looked normal. She flipped to the cover of the book: *Encyclopedia of Serial Killers,* then closed it. "That's fucking sick."

"Some guy in like Illinois in the fifties skinned a bunch of people," Crystal said. "He made a belt out of nipples, but there's no picture of it."

"Shut up!" Kendra said. "That's so sick."

"They modeled the killer in *The Silence of the Lambs* after him," Crystal said, taking the book from Kendra, leafing through it. "The one who almost kills Jodie Foster at the end."

"I remember," Kendra said. She had watched the movie a few years earlier, late one night on cable. Thomas had told her it was great, and he watched it with her, made popcorn. By the end, Kendra had noticed that Thomas was clutching the couch cushion so hard that the blue veins on his arms surfaced. When Jodie Foster finally shot and killed the straggly-haired serial killer, Kendra said, "Thank God," aloud and Thomas teased her: "It's only a movie, you baby." Kendra locked her window that night, something she had never done before. She was thankful that she wasn't fat, that a flesh-hungry serial killer like Buffalo Bill wouldn't be interested in her.

"My brother's girlfriend is in a criminal psychology program," Crystal said. "That's why they have all these fucked-up books."

Kendra wanted to change the subject. The photograph of the lamp and the memories of Buffalo Bill hit her with nervous pangs. It was stupid, she knew. The books in front of Crystal on the rug were full of vile photographs of crime scenes and dead people, Kendra thought, and she didn't need to see any more, not with Petey missing. "I like your hair," Kendra said. "Did you get a trim?"

"No," Crystal said. "I washed it like I do every day."

"It looks different," Kendra lied. It looked exactly the same. Dark brown, thick, shiny.

"Maybe the humidity," Crystal said. She stood, toed the books and papers to the side, and stretched her arms upward. "I wish it would rain."

"Everyone does," Kendra said. "Did you work out today?"

"I lifted," Crystal said. She pushed the sleeves of her pink T-shirt up, and flexed her biceps like a circus muscleman. "I want muscles like yours."

"Mine are too big," Kendra said. "I look like a dyke."

"No, you don't," Crystal said. "Want some water? It's purified."

"Sure," Kendra said. After Crystal walked out of the room, into the kitchen, Kendra stretched her leg and kicked the books farther to the edge of the rug. "I'm only using the machines at the gym," she said loudly. "No free weights for a while."

"I never see anyone with a good body using the machines," Crystal said from the kitchen. "It's all old people and fat ladies." She walked back into the room with two tall glasses. She handed one to Kendra.

Crystal's brother Ron was tall, maybe six-four, with the same dark hair and skin as Crystal's, only his eyes were light blue. His arms were totally worked, thick with muscle, but hairy. Too hairy. The hair distracted from the muscles, Kendra thought. His legs were the same way, and she could see a bunch of hair curling over the crewneck collar of his T-shirt.

Jen, Ron's girlfriend, caught Kendra checking him out, and grabbed his meaty arm. For the rest of the evening, Kendra noticed that Jen was almost always touching Ron, but always watching Kendra. A cat-sprayer, Kendra thought. She felt like saying, "Um, I'm not into your boyfriend. I might be if he like waxed his whole body and did more cardio, but I'm not now, so you can stop your territorial pissing."

Jen was thin, but not fit. Skinny fat. No tone. Legs like giant hot-dogs, calves nearly as big as thighs, or thighs nearly as small as calves—whatever, they were gross. Her arms, though thin like her legs, had that sort of draping flesh. Her bleached hair was cut bluntly at her shoulders and tucked behind her ears to show off a pair of giant hoop earrings. Her face was pretty in a generic way, Kendra thought, although her facial features seemed to be erased with a thick coat of base and no other makeup that Kendra could make out. Tits, though. Jen had tits, and she showcased them with a tight, peach-colored T-shirt. They were real, too, as far as Kendra could discern. They sat in the right place on her chest and weren't over-the-top big like most fake boobs Kendra had noticed.

They sat around the living room and ate the burritos. Crystal dripped some sauce on the white sofa, and Jen's eyes bugged with indignation. Kendra watched as Jen's gaze closely followed Crystal's attempt to wipe the red sauce from the canvas with her paper napkins. Finally Jen stood and marched into the kitchen, returning with a bottle of soda water and a roll of paper towels.

"You're just grinding it in," Jen told Crystal. "Move."

"Sorry," Crystal said, standing, walking her plate to the kitchen. "God."

"These slipcovers are a bitch to clean," Ron said. Then he laughed nervously.

Kendra was glad about the sauce fiasco. Crystal had told Jen and Ron about Petey's disappearance and about Brooke Luter being thirty-four, and Jen had babbled about it all, using psychology and criminology terms that Kendra didn't understand, and pulling out her books between bites of her burrito.

When Jen started to talk about serial killers who had stalked and killed teenage boys, and the things they did to them, Kendra wanted to smack her. She did not need images of cannibalistic psychos chopping up Petey and storing him in their refrigerators. She did not need to know about botched lobotomies on victims in attempts to turn them into sex zombies. And she certainly did not need to see photos of Gacey and Dahmer, their victims, and the blood-spattered crime scenes.

"They *are* a bitch to clean," Jen said. "I knew we should have bought them in cranberry."

"You said you wanted white," Ron said.

"I did want white," Jen said. "I didn't know your sister would drip enchilada sauce on them. Now I wish we had bought the cranberry ones. If they were cranberry, it wouldn't matter if your sister dripped enchilada sauce on them, now would it?"

"I'm right here!" Crystal called from the kitchen. "Stop talking about me in the third person!"

"Stupid bitch," Jen mumbled. She looked over to Kendra with a surprised expression, like she had forgotten Kendra was there. "You didn't hear that," she said to Kendra.

"I heard it," Ron said, standing and walking toward the kitchen. "I never complain about your crack-whore sister or her mongrel children."

"Heather is not a crack-whore!" Jen said.

"Meth-head, speed-freak, whatever!" Ron walked into the kitchen.

"Heather has had some substance abuse problems," Jen said to Kendra. "It's a disease. Addiction is a disease." She daubed at the sauce stains some more.

"I know," Kendra said, wishing she could just leave, drive home with her windows rolled down, let the heat bake her in her car, remind her that she was alive, a survivor in this heat. Or maybe it would actually rain. Maybe she could stay up late and listen to the rain, smell the creosote released into the cooled night air by the moisture.

~~~~~

Merv dug around in the small storage room, looking for the boxes of half-off passes. His wrist was hurting, making the search difficult.

The clouds over the Santa Catalina Mountains were dark, the color of ashes. He knew there would be lightning soon enough, and he had to find those passes to hand out to the people stupid enough to come to Splash World today. This morning Merv had hung the huge warning signs on the chain-link fence by the entrance booths: THE PARK CLOSES IMMEDIATELY FOLLOWING THE FIRST FLASH OF LIGHTNING. HALF-OFF COUPONS DISTRIBUTED BEFORE 2 P.M. ONLY. THANK YOU. ENJOY YOUR DAY AT SPLASH WORLD. Merv never adhered to the 2 P.M. policy. He would hand out coupons no matter what time the park closed because of lightning.

He rummaged through boxes of promotional flyers from years past—Teen Night, Fourth of July '99 Concert with Al Perry and the Cattle, Free Cap Night—squishing a bunch of silverfish with his thumb, before he found the coupons. They were bundled with rubber bands like ransom money and hidden inside a large plastic trash bag in the corner behind a few hoes and rakes. Stupid. Whoever put them there should be fired.

He walked over to the entrance gates and handed stacks of coupons to Jeff and Rita, telling them to keep the extras in the booths. Merv noticed that both booths needed a paintjob. The original red had faded into a dull brown, and was bubbling and chipped in some places.

Back at his desk in his messy little office, Merv found Melissa's business card under a box of stale Fig Newtons. He deliberated for a moment but then called her.

"You've reached the voicemail of Melissa Birnbach. Please leave your name, number, and the time you called, and I'll return your call as promptly as possible. Thank you."

Merv didn't leave a message, but he called back after a few minutes, when he finally figured out what to say. "Hey, Melissa, it's Merv here. I just found your card and I thought I'd call and say hello and see how you were doing. I hope you're doing well. I'm okay. My wrist is getting better, but it's not healed yet. We'll close early today because of lightning, I'm sure. But maybe you could call me. At my house tonight or here if you get this message soon." He left her the direct number to his desk at Splash World.

To distract himself from waiting for Melissa to call, Merv began to clean off his desk. Old newspapers, food wrappers, a few dead batteries, junky sunglasses he no longer wore, ancient floppy disks from the previous manager—he threw them all away, used the plastic trash bag where the coupons had been stupidly stored. The only things on his desk now were his outdated computer, a cup of pens and pencils, the telephone, and a yellow pad of paper, on which he wrote, *Booths need to be painted.* And as soon as he wrote it, the phone finally rang.

"This is Merv Hunter," he said.

"Great," a man said. "This is Doug Simone from Splash World, Torrance."

Merv couldn't remember a Doug Simone. He had met a bunch of the corporate guys a few summers ago when they passed through Tucson. Whenever he had a question or a request, he talked to a woman named Cindy at Splash World in Las Vegas. Whenever they spoke, Merv could hear her fingernails clicking on the keyboard in front of her. The first time, he had thought it was a bad connection. It was the second or third call when Merv finally figured out she was typing—at a superhuman pace.

"Hi, Doug," he said now.

"We looked over the figures for June," he said. "Over the top, Merv, over the top."

Merv didn't know what Doug meant, whether Doug was pleased or upset. "Oh?"

"You're up thirty-one percent from last year, and our analysts had projected an eight percent drop," Doug said. "Over the top, Merv."

"Great," Merv said. "I thought it seemed busier last month."

"You've outdone Albuquerque and San Dimas," Doug added. "And Vegas."

"Great," Merv said. He doodled on the yellow pad, drew a bunch of lightning bolts shooting from the note he had written himself. Then he began to draw a hand with long, hooklike fingernails.

"We'd like you to come out here for a few days, have a look around," Doug said. "Have you been to L.A. before?"

"Yes," Merv said. Only once. The summer after they had graduated from high school, Merv, Rusty, and Jason had driven eight hours in Jason's mom's new BMW for a week at Rusty's aunt's place in Santa Monica. Rusty's aunt lived in a huge Spanish-style home with a maid named Lucy who didn't speak English and never changed the expression on her face: morose. Rusty's aunt seemed lonely; her own children had moved away years before, and she was divorced from her husband, who had been a big studio executive until a string of his films bombed and he became the pariah of Hollywood. "I mean how many stupid Scott Baio sex comedies can you make before you start losing money?" Rusty's aunt had said, giggling. "Idiot." She seemed overly enthusiastic about having the boys visit, horning in on their conversations and plans, doling out unsolicited advice—especially to Merv, whose own college plans paled in comparison to Rusty's and Jason's.

Merv had liked Santa Monica, but he ran out of money after three days and had to borrow from Jason and Rusty, who were sick of lending him money and told him so. He had thought it better to ask to borrow money in small amounts at a time, until Jason freaked out at a bagel place in Venice. "Merv!" he had yelled. "Why can't you just fucking plan better and bring enough money for once in your pathetic life!" He opened his wallet, extracted forty bucks and handed it to Merv. "Is this enough for the last three days? If it's not, let me know now and I'll give you more, but I don't want to hear your crying poor mouth anymore." Merv had said it was enough, but on the last day he pulled Rusty aside and hit him up for twenty, begged him not to tell Jason.

"Perfect," Doug said presently. "I'll have Cindy call you with the travel arrangements. Next week's good, I assume."

"It's fine," Merv said, "but why? I mean, why do you want me out there?"

"Just to have a look around," Doug said. "Check things out. We'd like to talk to you about how you manage such a stellar park."

When Merv hung up, he still didn't know why Doug wanted him out there in Torrance. He wasn't even sure where Torrance was in relation to L.A. He guessed that corporate Splash World was going to offer him a raise, or maybe a thank-you bonus for June's profit increase, but they could do that over the phone.

The lightning flashed just after three o'clock. Melissa had never called. Merv had waited in his office for a few hours. At least he had thoroughly cleaned. His office had never been as clean as it was now. He must have tossed twenty pounds of paper. He had even wiped the thick dust from the top of his bookshelf, vacuumed the dull beige carpet, and sorted through two drawers of employee files, culling the ones older than six years and shredding them.

His wrist ached and itched inside the brace, so he ripped off the Velcro straps and let it cool for a few minutes, holding his wrist up to the air-conditioning duct on the wall behind his desk.

He stood at the exit area and distributed the half-off coupons to the throngs of people leaving. "It's dumb," one little kid told Merv. "The lightning is like a hundred miles away." The kid was a sunburned towhead, maybe six years old.

"I'm sorry," Merv said. "It's the law."

"It's a dumb law. Like the law about the tags on mattresses."

Merv laughed, handed the kid a coupon.

"Gee, thanks," the kid said before he walked off, his rubber flip-flops slapping the sidewalk.

"Funny kid," Raymond said, rolling up to Merv. "Do I get a coupon?"

"Of course," Merv said. "Good for a year from today's date."

"I have a season pass, Merv," Raymond said. A long strand of white drool attached his chin to his lap. It looked like yarn. Merv wondered how Raymond couldn't notice it. He wished he had a napkin, and checked his empty pockets.

"Oh, yeah," Merv said. "I guess you would have a season pass."

"Before I get on the bus, could you help me for a moment in the restroom?" Raymond asked. As he spoke, the line of drool jiggled. He jerked his head upward to look Merv in the eye, and the drool stuck to his neck.

"I have to hand out these coupons," Merv said. "Aren't the lifeguards in there?"

"They weren't there a moment ago," Raymond said. "I wouldn't ask if it weren't close to being an emergency. I'm terribly sorry."

"No, no, that's fine," Merv said. "Let me give these coupons to Rita in the booth, and I'll meet you there." He was already rushing over to the booth, weaving through disappointed park guests, feeling guilty for troubling poor Raymond. He thought about his father when he was sick and feeble—he wondered if he had ever had to ask strangers or acquaintances for bathroom help.

When he finally made it to the employee locker room, sweat was coursing down the back of Merv's neck. George, a lifeguard, was coming out, and Merv asked him if Raymond was in there.

"Yeah," George said.

"Did you help him?" Merv said.

"No," George said. "He had drool all over his neck and he looked really pissed off."

"Did you ask him if he needed help?"

"Ah, no," George said.

Asshole, Merv thought. He walked past George and went into the locker room.

The place smelled of bleach, which Merv appreciated. Last

summer it had wreaked of piss, until Merv fired the maintenance guy in charge of the restrooms and hired a guy named Holden who sort of shuffled around the park all day and never said anything, but took pride in his job.

"In here," Raymond said from the stall. "As usual. It's not locked."

Merv pushed open the door to the stall with his left hand and found Raymond parked in front of the toilet, a large wad of toilet paper in his lap. Raymond breathed heavily, each exhalation a chunky wheeze.

"I would have asked George for help but he ran out as soon as he saw me," Raymond said. "Perhaps he had a bus to catch."

"Maybe," Merv said. "You need me to help with that tube again?" He squatted down to Raymond's level.

"Yes," Raymond said. He breathed a few times. "But I need help with the other end. It seems to have slipped off. I'm so sorry. I wouldn't normally ask for this sort of help from someone other than a healthcare professional, but this has never happened before. I'm so sorry. Really, I feel so embarrassed and—"

"That's fine," Merv said. Fuck, he thought. "Don't worry about it. Just tell me what I need to do."

"It's a condom catheter," Raymond said. "It slipped off my penis. It's just like a normal condom, only thicker rubber." He pawed at the toilet paper in his lap, pushing it onto the floor with his gnarled hands, exposing his penis, which was pink and glistening, and hard—curved slightly to the side, but definitely hard, poking upward from his rolled seersucker trousers.

This is wrong, Merv thought. This is really fucked-up. "Hey," Merv said. "Um, I'm not sure I can—"

"You're startled by my erection," Raymond said. "It happens when I have a full bladder, that's all. It's nothing sexual, I assure you."

Merv looked down at his own feet, then closed his eyes for a moment. He wanted to jump up and run out of there. He took a deep breath through his nose, felt the burn of the bleach fumes.

"Am I even authorized to do this?" Stupid, he knew, but he didn't know what else to say.

"You're uncomfortable," Raymond said. "I'm sorry. If it makes you feel any better, I can't feel anything down there. I haven't felt anything for years. I'll give you one hundred dollars to help me out here, Merv. I'm really quite desperate or I wouldn't ask you to do such a—"

"That's fine," Merv said. "You don't have to pay me." He quickly grabbed the condom end of the catheter with his injured right hand. The catheter was the color of a life preserver, Day-Glo orange. He took another deep breath, and grasped Raymond's penis at the base with his left index finger and thumb. It was clammier than he had expected, and he felt a heave's worth of bile work its way from his stomach to his throat. He slid the condom over the bulging head and down the shaft.

"That's perfect," Raymond said. "Could you now put the other end over the edge of the toilet so I can go?"

Merv did, and as soon as he left the stall, he heard the urine trickling into the bowl. He hurried over to the sink, ripped off his wrist brace, and scrubbed his hands, hitting the soap dispenser so hard that it fell off the mount. Pearly pink soap spilled all over the wall and sink. A few globs spattered on Merv's leg. I don't get paid enough for this shit, he thought. Not nearly enough. He put the brace back on his wrist and left the locker room before Raymond managed to roll out of the stall.

Wednesday, July 26, 2001

Cooler

High 97/Low 68

Cloudy, with chance of afternoon

thunderstorms

KENDRA HAD BEEN WAITING OVER A WEEK FOR THE BROOKE LUTER STORY to appear in the paper. Before she ran the hill in the morning, she'd stop at the bottom of her driveway, skin the plastic bag off the newspaper, scan the front page, then the metro section. Nothing for ten days. She promised herself that she'd call the offices of the *Arizona Daily Star* if the story wasn't in there by Friday, but there it was today, occupying the bottom corner of the front page: DERANGED WOMAN MIGHT BE KEY TO FINDING LOCAL TEEN. A mug shot of Brooke—Nativity—who had her hair in pigtails. In the photo, Nativity was grinning, her eyes wide and feral-looking. Kendra sat right down on the gravel and read the entire story.

Mrs. Shawn from the high school was quoted as saying, "Brooke Luter was a top student and a real leader. It's a shame she's not really sixteen." She went on to say that Brooke had expressed interest in applying to small liberal arts colleges, perhaps in New England.

A girl named Martha Martinez, a sophomore who Kendra didn't know, said, "Some people thought she looked old. One guy called her 'The Substitute' and teased her. Most people thought there was just something wrong with her." Yeah, Kendra thought, she was a bitch.

The article didn't convey much information about Petey, just that he was missing and that Brooke was his friend. There was no mention of Thomas, either, but the reporter wrote that the police were investigating the possibility of pressing statutory rape charges if Brooke had engaged in sexual activity with boys under the age of eighteen, the legal age of consent in Arizona. Brooke's mother, back home in Holliday, Texas, had no comment for the reporter except, "Not again."

Kendra rolled the newspaper up and tried to fit it back into the plastic bag. She couldn't, and the bag ripped. "Fuck it," she said, and placed a rock over the newspaper. "Like it'll rain." Even though the dark clouds had sat over the Santa Catalina range to the north of Tucson for what seemed like weeks, Kendra hadn't noticed a single drop of rain. Just hot, dusty wind in the afternoon and oppressive humidity that made these morning runs twice as challenging.

On her third run up the hill, Kendra saw three skinny coyotes run into the arroyo. The one in the lead was carrying what looked like a dirty diaper. They had probably knocked over trashcans. A few nights earlier, she had seen one drink from the swimming pool and nose around by the filter pump before she whistled from her bedroom window and it dashed into the desert.

Kendra thought about taping the article about Brooke to the refrigerator, but after she finished carefully clipping it from the front page and from page nine, and highlighting the section about sexual conduct with minors, she decided it was too mean. Since the police had questioned him, Thomas had barely left his room. Kendra had actually only seen him twice: Once, he had been walking out of the bathroom, and the other time, he had been sitting on the tile stairs, eating a small pizza from the box that rested on his lap. He was shirtless and paler than usual. His arms looked thinner, too. When he saw Kendra that time, he closed the pizza box and marched up the stairs. She had heard him slam his bedroom door.

Kendra neatly folded the clipped article and placed it in an envelope that she marked "Joyce," and left on Joyce's desk. Like

Kendra, Joyce had expressed concern that the newspaper hadn't mentioned anything about Brooke. She had even set her VCR to tape both the six and ten o'clock news, but the story hadn't surfaced there either. She and Kendra had been talking about it in hushed tones for several days.

Kendra folded the rest of the newspaper and placed it on a kitchen chair. She checked her watch: 6:34. Too late to go back to bed. Too early to call Crystal.

When she returned to the kitchen, Thomas was sitting at the table, munching through a bowl of Froot Loops. He looked up at Kendra and said, "Hi." His eyes looked more sunken, the circles that surrounded them like dark bruises.

"Hi," Kendra said. "Why are you up so early?"

"I just all the sudden woke up," he said. "I don't know why."

Kendra walked over to the refrigerator and pulled out a small carton of egg whites, a yellow pepper, and some nonfat cheese. "You want an omelet?" she asked Thomas over her shoulder.

"No, thanks," he said. "I'm having cereal."

"The protein will give you more energy," she said. She began to chop the yellow pepper. She dropped the seedy core in the garbage disposal.

"I'm sorry I called you a cunt," he said.

Kendra didn't turn around. An odd sense of embarrassment welled in her chest and prevented her from doing so. She didn't know how to respond, and she knew it must have killed Thomas to apologize. She unhooked a frying pan from where it hung above the stove and placed it on a burner. "Are you sure you don't want an omelet? Last chance. Cheese and yellow pepper?"

"No thanks," Thomas said. "Did you hear what I said?"

"Yes," Kendra said, pouring the egg whites into the pan. "You don't want one."

"No," Thomas said. "Before that."

"I guess," Kendra said. "Plussing as which, it's no big deal." Fuck, she thought. Damn. Tell Crystal later, tell her to make the dolls kiss.

"Mom thought it was a big deal," he said.

"I heard her call this guy who cut her off on River Road a cunt before," Kendra said. "I don't know why she freaked out on you."

"Do you think Brooke—or Nativity—has anything to do with Petey's disappearance?"

Kendra finally turned around. Thomas looked so small at the table, like a little kid, a sick little kid. At least he was wearing a T-shirt, so she didn't have to see his ribs. "I don't know," she said. She didn't know. But she figured the police would find out if they hadn't already.

"I don't think she does," Thomas said. "She was crying all the time about him. Like, really crying, and she spent hundreds of dollars at Kinko's making those posters. Not that she couldn't have been doing that as a smokescreen of sorts."

"I have a question," Kendra said. "And don't get pissed, okay?" She sprinkled some of the shredded cheese onto the egg whites in the pan. "Did you ever even think Brooke might not be seventeen, or sixteen, whatever she said she was?"

Thomas didn't answer immediately, so Kendra continued to look into the frying pan. She took a spatula from the drawer and checked the edge of the egg whites to see if they were ready to fold. They weren't.

"I just thought she was smart," Thomas said, "so I didn't really care about the other stuff. She knew tons about philosophy and literature. She was always quoting Kant and talking about postmodernism, but she would also squeal with delight whenever Weezer came on the radio and get drunk with Petey and talk shit about other girls at school."

"She liked Weezer?" Kendra said.

"My point is that she did like normal teenage bullshit, but she was also smart, so I liked her."

"That's because she went to college already," Kendra said. She carefully spaced the slices of yellow pepper in the pan. "Plus, she was thirty-four."

"I know that now," Thomas said. "Duh."

Kendra folded the omelet. "I just thought she was a bitch," she said. "Sometimes I even forgot she looked weird and dressed like a slut from two summers ago because she was such a bitch."

"She dressed like everyone else," Thomas said.

"If everyone else was a slut from two summers ago."

"You were just jealous because she started hanging out so much with Petey," Thomas said, walking over to the sink with his bowl and spoon.

"Yeah, right," Kendra said. "He was always huffing anyways." She flipped the omelet. Lightly browned. Perfect. She took a deep breath through her nose, enjoying the smell of the peppers, and she quickly asked, "So did you and her really have sex or what?"

"I'm sick of that question," Thomas said. He turned on the water and began to wash his hands at the kitchen sink, using blue liquid dish detergent instead of the bar of soap that sat in its colorful ceramic dish on the windowsill.

"Why don't you use the soap?"

"It smells like ass," Thomas said. He rinsed, turned off the water, and dried his hands on his Bermuda shorts.

Kendra called Crystal just after noon. Crystal didn't seem that interested in the Brooke article. In fact, she told Kendra that her mother had brought the newspaper to work with her, so she couldn't read it. "Maybe I'll read it on-line later," Crystal said.

"You should," Kendra said. "You want to watch the news later? Then we can go to the movies or something."

"It's too hot to leave the house," Crystal complained. "I swear, if those fucking clouds don't break today, I'll puke."

"I ran this morning and it was really gross," Kendra said. "The weight room at the club smells like feet. I could barely do a few sets before I got nauseated." She had seen Hetta there again, walking briskly on a treadmill, reading a fashion magazine. "Come over, though. I'm bored."

"You come over here," Crystal said. "I'm totally bored. Besides, your brother freaks me out."

"You've never even met him." Kendra pressed the phone to

her shoulder with her ear and began to retie her running shoes, tightly.

"I saw him peek out of his room when I was upstairs," Crystal said. "He looked all pale, like he's been stored in formaldehyde all summer." She giggled.

Kendra thought for a moment. Crystal should not even talk about brothers, she thought. Hers was a spineless wuss with a bitchy girlfriend who ordered him around. Plus he was too hairy. "Your brother's girlfriend is a bitch," Kendra said.

"And?" Crystal said. "What the hell does that have to do with anything? Your brother's girlfriend was arrested for impersonating a high school student."

"Oh," Kendra said. I'm retarded, Kendra thought. She finally finished with her laces—they were sufficiently tight, maybe a little too tight.

"I just decided I'm busy all day," Crystal said. "Why don't you call me in a few days when you're not being so snippy and weird."

"I'm not being snippy and weird," Kendra said.

"You are," Crystal said.

They never settled the matter, and after they hung up, Kendra felt a worried pit opening in her stomach, like Crystal was blowing her off for good. Her brother's girlfriend had been a bitch, though. And Crystal knew it. Crystal doesn't even know Thomas, Kendra thought. He was a little pale, but anyone whose girlfriend was just arrested for pretending to be someone she wasn't, and anyone who had to talk with cops for like an hour and always got calls from cops, anyone like that might be pale and sick-looking.

The knowledge that Thomas would be living in a dorm full of normal freshmen at Columbia scared Kendra. She imagined them all teasing Thomas, his roommate requesting a new room, telling everyone that Thomas smelled, that he masturbated all the time. He'd accuse Thomas of stealing his dirty underpants and jockstraps. All of Thomas's dorm-mates would be like the football players at Kendra's high school who were indicted after three sophomores complained of bizarre and inhumane hazing rituals at training camp last August. One kid said he had to run a lap with a frozen hotdog stuck up his ass. She imagined that they'd do that kind of shit to Thomas at Columbia—all those mean smart people, like Crystal. Smart and mean and dangerous.

She assuaged her fears by convincing herself that at least half the freshmen there had to be dorks like Thomas. Not many meathead football players scored well on their SATs or earned high grades. She imagined for a moment that Thomas would actually be popular at Columbia, the least dorky of the kids in his dorm.

She had wanted to, but she didn't call Crystal again that afternoon. She had hoped that Crystal would call and apologize and maybe suggest that they watch the news and go to a movie together after all, and every time the phone rang, she jumped for it.

Kendra's stomach twisted nervously when a commercial for shampoo and conditioner reminded her that Crystal still had those fucking voodoo dolls. She envisioned Crystal playing with the dolls all day, making them have sex, poking them with forks, boiling them, stomping on them, microwaving them, wiping them on a dirty toilet seat. She remembered the Haitian woman from the documentary on television, how she writhed and squealed in pain on the dusty ground with a bunch of dirty chickens.

She called Ellen Hunter at five-thirty and asked her if she wanted to watch the news with her. "Of course," Ellen had said. "Why don't you come over here, though. I just got home from work and I've got my feet up."

Instead of walking on the street, Kendra decided to cut through the desert that separated her house from the Hunters'. There was a little path, maybe made by javelinas or coyotes, which wound around cacti and bushes. The arroyo was clear and when she stepped into the deep sand, Kendra realized she should be running in it every morning. Loose sand would be a great workout, a welcome break from the monotony of running the hill.

When she was younger, she and Thomas had followed it up to the very base of the mountains, where it became a lot rockier. There actually had been little pools of stagnant algae-laden water up there, each one swarming with water beetles that looked like little rowboats. It was difficult to estimate how far it was to the base of the mountain where the arroyo began, and it probably wasn't safe running in the desert alone, especially that early in the morning. There had been rumors in the neighborhood that homeless guys lived in the arroyo, and once, when she and Petey were in sixth or seventh grade, they discovered some faded and water-damaged porno magazines next to a rotten mattress and some empty beer cans. They had been convinced that a murderous pervert lived there, surviving on jackrabbit meat and prickly pear fruit, and when they returned a few days later, the magazines were gone and there were more beer bottles.

"Merv's in California," Ellen said when she opened the door, "so I'm blasting the air conditioner. I don't have to hear him complain about electricity bills."

When Kendra stepped into the Hunters' foyer, she felt it, and said, "I think your air conditioning is better than ours."

"Ours is old, but Merv never lets me use it," Ellen said. "He claims the evaporative cooler works just as well, so we run that."

They sat on the sofa in front of the television, which was tuned to Channel Four. Ellen had already poured Kendra a tall glass of ice water. "I remembered what you said about high-fructose corn syrup," Ellen said, "and I've gotten rid of all the Pepsi and Sprite in this house. Water only for me now, too."

"It's in ketchup and salad dressing and lots of other things," Kendra said. "I read an article that said it was the main reason why everyone in our country is so fat."

"Speaking of fat, Hetta came by the other night," Ellen said. She took a sip from her own glass of water, and carefully placed it back on the ladybug coaster on the coffee table in front of her. "She was trying to sell me some Mexican pottery, and she said she's lost fourteen pounds this summer."

"I've seen her at the Racquet Club like a million times this summer," Kendra said. "She hates me."

"Why?"

"A long time ago, like last year or something, I saw her in the supermarket, and I told her that all the stuff in her cart was unhealthy."

"It probably was," Ellen said. "Everyone in that family could stand to lose a few pounds. You know, our tax dollars end up paying for fat people."

Kendra and Ellen continued to talk about fat people throughout the newscast, ignoring the reports of a perpetual lawsuit against the school system and a new parkway until there it was: Brooke's mug shot, the same crazy eyes, excited grin, and pigtails. Kendra leaned forward, put her elbows on her knees. Ellen turned up the volume.

". . . earlier this week police arrested Ms. Funsett in her foothills apartment, charging her with fraud, corrupting minors and . . ."

In a moment, it was over, and the newscaster, a perky brunette whose speech pattern, Kendra and Thomas had noticed years ago, was such that she stressed the final word in every sentence, was offering suggestions on how to prepare pets for the impending monsoon season.

"This sucks," Kendra said. "They didn't even say how long she'll be in jail."

"I doubt she'll do any time," Ellen said. "All she needs is a mediocre attorney, and she'll get off."

"They better put her in jail," Kendra said. "She's a liar."

"Who'd she harm?"

"My brother, for one," Kendra said. "And everyone at school she lied to, and she lied to the police."

"Maybe Peter Vaccarino found out she was thirty-four, so she paid him off and he left town," Ellen said, clicking off the news. "But if she doesn't have anything to do with Peter's disappearance, she'll get off, I'm sure of it. I mean, legally, what law did she break? Her attorney could say she's a victim of our youth-obsessed culture."

Kendra didn't respond right away. She sat there for a few seconds, breathed in deeply through her nose, and stood. She wanted to tell Ellen to fuck off, that she didn't know shit and she should shut the hell up. But she didn't. She merely said, "Thanks," and walked out, thinking that Franny would be pleased that she didn't freak out on Ellen.

The clouds draped over the mountains were darker, swirls of gray and purple, but Kendra didn't allow herself to think it would rain. That would jinx it. The more she and the rest of the city wanted rain, the less likely it was to happen.

Even though he knew he was only a few miles from the Pacific Ocean, Merv couldn't figure out which way was west and which was east. He was driving a rental car, a red American sedan with no real acceleration power but hypersensitive brakes, on Hawthorne, and it was a little after one P.M., so the sun's position didn't help. He was already late for a meeting at Splash World in Torrance, and the traffic was thick. His wrist, wrapped tightly in its brace, throbbed. He needed to loosen his grip on the steering wheel and mellow out.

He pulled into a strip mall and walked into a nail salon. "Which way is west?" he asked the wiry girl sitting on a stool behind the counter. She was chewing gum, her jaw looping to the left.

"I don't know," she said, impassively. She looked through a movie star magazine.

There were several women behind her, either working on nails or having their nails done, but the girl didn't bother to turn around and ask any of them.

"Could you ask someone?" Merv said, pointing behind her with his finger. The thick fumes in the salon, the same smell as plastic burning, were nauseating. Merv felt a little dizzy, and he had only been in there for a moment. He wondered how the women could abide them.

"Sure," she said, but instead of turning around, she punched a few numbers on the phone in front of her and made a call. The phone at the desk of a technician, a woman sitting not more than six feet from the skinny receptionist, rang, and she answered it.

"Which way is west?" the receptionist asked. She twirled the backing to her earring, looked up at Merv. "Okay," the receptionist said. "And can you do a two o'clock on Tuesday?" She opened the appointment book in front of her. "Gina's free till two-thirty, I think." She smiled at Merv, mouthed something, and held up her finger. "French," she added. "Thanks." She finally hung up, but she didn't say anything to Merv.

"Did you find out which way was west?" Merv asked her.

"She didn't know," the receptionist said.

Merv was incredulous, and he spoke up, "Do any of you all know which way is west?"

"To the Four-o-five?" One woman in the back asked.

"No," Merv said.

"To the Ten?" another asked.

"No," Merv said, "like, to the ocean."

Several women pointed to Merv's right, even the receptionist. "Thanks," Merv said. He walked out of the salon to his rented car, muttering curses.

Today's tardiness was the first snag in an otherwise trouble-free trip. He had arrived at LAX on Monday afternoon, picked up his rental car soon after, and was in his hotel in Marina del Mar before dark, eating a steak dinner from room service, relaxing in bed, flipping through the channels. Later, he walked along the pier in Santa Monica, watched the giant Ferris wheel spinning in the sky, enjoyed the cool, wet ocean breezes and a few thin slices of greasy pizza and a beer.

The next day, he had driven south on PCH to Rancho Palos

Verdes, where he met Canton Stone, the man who owned all six-teen Splash Worlds. Canton lived in a palatial white home atop a grassy hill that afforded him views of the Pacific and the L.A. sky-line. Roseanne Barr was his neighbor, and, as Canton bragged as he showed Merv around his house—through room after room of polished tiles, high ceilings, and furniture that looked too un-comfortable in its modernity to actually use—Roseanne's views weren't half as good as his. Canton was tall, with dark brown hair and big horse teeth so white they glowed. He spoke with a slight redneck twang. Merv didn't ask about Canton's family, but he saw from the many photographs that adorned the walls that Canton had a few kids who looked a lot like he did, and a wife, a sunbaked blonde who wore her hair like a shih tzu, a ponytail spouting from the top of her head—styled the same way in every picture Merv saw.

Doug, a stout, pale guy, whose eyes looked both sad and furi-ous in their bulging droopiness, arrived soon after Merv; he rolled up in his gold Mercedes, and the three of them sat at a glass table by Canton's pool, where a maid, who was dressed casually in shorts and a polo shirt, brought them lunch: lobster salad sandwiches, mixed greens, beer. Merv was nervous, could feel the sweat gathering on his upper lip. He was polite but found it diffi-cult to make small talk with the two men. Merv wasn't a big fan of lobster, either, but, as Canton and Doug jabbered about bud-gets, projections, and a guy named "Sammy," Merv finished the entire salty sandwich, losing quite a bit of it to his lap because of the awkwardness of his wrist brace.

"Okay, Merv," Canton finally said, after daubing his mouth with a checkered napkin. "Here's the deal. We think you're do-ing a super job, as you know, the best job actually. Tucson's out-doing every other park in terms of profit, in terms of everything. You know, you've got the lowest employee turnover and the fewest lawsuits of any Splash World?"

"I didn't know that," Merv said, surreptitiously brushing off the crumbs and blobs of lobster salad from the napkin on his lap.

Canton grinned, stared intently at Merv. "Just super."

"So," Doug said, "we hired this guy, a really bright guy. Harvard M.B.A. and M.A. from the School of Education at Stanford—"

"Where'd you go to college, Merv?" Canton asked.

"I went to the University of Arizona for a while, but I dropped out," Merv said, quietly. He stared down at his empty plate, traced lines with his finger in the frost and droplets on his beer bottle.

"Me, too!" Canton said. "I lasted one semester at KU! I got all F's!" He grinned madly, gripped Merv's shoulder with one hand, and put the other up for Merv to high-five, which Merv did—with his left hand. "Doug here went to college and graduate school and all that bullshit, and now he works for me."

"I sure do," Doug said dryly. "Someone has to keep you out of jail and make sure you don't go bankrupt."

Canton laughed, kept squeezing Merv's shoulder. "Well, Merv here is living proof that management skills can't be taught in some classroom by some pompous windbag professor who smokes a pipe and wears tweed jackets." He finally released Merv from his grip, then patted his back, more forcefully than Merv expected.

"Apparently your limited college experience at Kentucky University was different from my experience," Doug said. He turned to Merv. "This guy we're bringing in will work with you to develop a management training curriculum."

"Great," Merv said.

"He'll basically be picking your brain," Doug said.

"Why'd you drop out, Merv?" Canton asked. "Me, I thought it was dumb to be paying for school when I could be making money, which I did."

"I'm not sure why I dropped out," Merv said. "I wasn't really ready for school, I guess."

"My wife's all over our kids to go to college," Canton said. "You know how much we pay to send them to this little snotty private school over the hill? Over fifty grand a year for the two of them!"

"Wow," Merv said. The tuition for his own private school

his senior year was eight thousand, but that was twelve years ago.

"When I wrote the tuition check and handed it to the head-mistress, I said, 'Do I get a blowjob with this?'" Canton said. "Just kidding."

Doug pulled his chair closer to the table. "So, Merv, you and this guy—his name's Jacob, real nice guy—will be developing a whole training regime for managers."

"My son got the lowest SAT scores in his class," Canton said. "I've spent over a hundred K on his education and he brings home a nine-fifty. Doug here has a boy who goes to public school in Santa Monica and he scored a fifteen-ten."

Doug rolled his eyes, crossed his arms across his chest.

"Wow," Merv said, trying to sound as neutral as possible.

"So, we figured this Jacob would shadow you for a few weeks in Tucson," Doug said, leaning toward Merv. "Then you'd both come out here and we set you up in our Long Beach headquarters."

Merv felt his forehead burning, wished he had remembered to pack sunscreen. "For how long?" he asked.

Before Doug answered, though, Canton said, "My wife wanted to send the poor kid to SAT camp this summer, somewhere in New Jersey, and I told her—"

"I'm sure Merv would prefer to hear the details of his assign-ment," Doug said.

"That's okay," Merv said. "My friend Rusty's mom sent him to SAT classes and they really helped."

"Your position in Long Beach would be a permanent one," Doug said. "Assuming you accept it."

Merv's stomach dropped. He tried to contain himself, but he felt the muscles in his face pulling into a grin.

"Full benefits, a relocation allowance, and—" Doug said.

"Tell him his salary, Doug," Canton said. "What the hell's wrong with you?"

"You'd start at seventy-five," Doug said, "but there are bonuses," he added.

"How much are we paying that Harvard kid?" Canton asked Doug.

"I don't think that's appropriate to discuss in front of Merv," Doug said. "Do you?"

"Why the hell not?" Canton asked.

"Privacy issues," Doug said.

Merv didn't really care what they were paying the Harvard kid.

Canton turned to Merv, squeezed his shoulder again. "So, what do you think? We uneducated trash need to stick together. I'd love to have you out here."

"It sounds great," Merv said. He'd never been to Long Beach, wasn't even sure where it was, but he already imagined his beachfront apartment, learning to surf, sitting on his deck, sipping beer, watching the girls go by. And it would never be too hot out. There'd always be a cool ocean breeze.

He didn't allow himself to pollute his expectations by thinking about his mother, barely surviving in Tucson by herself, alone with her psychological problems. Merv would figure it out some other time. For now, he anticipated calling Rusty and Jason, bragging a little. He knew one of them would call Melissa, who had never returned Merv's call. What would she care, anyway? She wouldn't be jealous or regretful. She probably wouldn't care in the slightest, Merv figured.

The nail salon was actually only a few blocks from Splash World. Now, when he saw the tangle of light blue tubular slides up on the right, Merv let out an excited, "Yes!" He was supposed to meet with the manager and the security team, and he was hoping to drive down to Long Beach afterward and check out the town, his future home.

When Merv arrived at the entrance booth, the girl behind the glass was reading a fantasy novel with a unicorn on the cover. She barely looked up from it when Merv knocked lightly.

"I'm here to meet with Janice Bening," he said.

"She's in the back, the little brown building next to the Lemon

Drop," the girl said. "Let me stamp your hand." She put down her paperback.

After she stamped his hand, Merv walked through the park, noting its dingy appearance. Bees swarmed around every trashcan he passed. The cans all needed to be emptied. Graffiti, both fresh and faded, covered every bench, and the sidewalks were stained with spilled soda and spotted with chewed gum. Even the few palm trees that stretched into the gray sky somehow looked dirty, their fronds more brown than green.

Janice Bening greeted Merv at the door, shaking his right hand with the grip of a longshoreman despite the wrist brace. Pain shot up his arm, and he nearly succumbed to his immediate instinct to hit her.

Janice's office looked a lot like Merv's had before he cleaned it: cramped, papers piled on every surface, a lamp with a crooked shade illuminating her desk. Merv sat on a black vinyl chair.

"How has your trip been so far?" she asked.

"Great," Merv said. Until you rebroke my wrist, bitch. "I met with Doug and Canton yesterday at Canton's house."

"Who's Canton?" she asked. She rubbed her chin with her thumb and finger like she had a beard.

"The owner of Splash World," Merv said. "The guy who started it all."

"Oh," Janice said. "Him. I've never been to his house."

"A great view of the Pacific and the lights of L.A."

"I've never been to his house," she repeated. "So, what can I do for you?"

Merv thought it had all been planned, finalized with Doug. "I guess Doug and Canton wanted you to show me around."

"What kind of a name is Canton, anyway?" she asked.

"Not sure," Merv said. "Maybe a family name."

"And Merv for that matter," she said. "What kind of a name is Merv?"

"My mother always liked it," he said. "Maybe you could start by showing me the slides, we could talk about the traffic on each one."

"Traffic?" She twirled a pen, spun it in her fingers like a miniature baton. Merv's dad used to do the same thing. Merv could never get it down.

"The number of customers who use the slides every day," Merv said.

"We don't keep track of that specifically," she said.

"What about in general?" Merv asked. "In general, which ones are the busiest?"

"I don't know," she said. She stared at Merv blankly, impassively. After a moment, a smirk curled at the side of her mouth. "The big yellow one is popular."

"The Lemon Drop?" Merv asked.

"Yes," she said, "that one."

The meeting with Janice's security team wasn't any more enlightening. The team members who happened to be there that afternoon consisted of two skinny Korean brothers, a zitty fat guy whose knees were scabbed over, and a jittery woman who couldn't seem to stop nodding. The scalp where she parted her hair was badly sunburned, a valley of white flakes and pinkness in her dark head of hair. Merv had known he was fortunate to have the security team that he did in Tucson, but he didn't know how fortunate until that afternoon. It was as if Janice had gone to the mall or the airport or some crappy swap meet and picked out the biggest losers she could find to make up Splash World, Torrance's security team. He was sure the jittery woman was on drugs and that the Korean brothers couldn't subdue a toddler if their lives depended on it. And the fat guy? Could he even run if he had to? Not with those messed-up knees.

By the time Merv drove back to the 405, it was just past five, and the traffic was thick, barely moving. All six lanes were jammed, except for the carpool lane where cars appeared to actually be creeping along. It took Merv nearly thirty minutes to go two and a half miles to the next exit, where he turned around and got back on the 405 heading north, the opposite way. The traffic didn't bother him, though. He felt oddly proud to be having a typical L.A. afternoon in his rental car, listening to unfamiliar radio stations, checking out the people in the cars around him. Long Beach would have to wait, though. Besides, he wanted to make a few notes about Splash World, Torrance, and fax them over to Doug before he left for Tucson in the morning.

"Can you pick me up at the airport at eleven tomorrow?" Merv asked his mother. He spoke quickly because he was on the hotel phone and he didn't want to run up the charges for Splash World, Inc. He sat at the small desk in his room, a sheet of hotel stationery and a hotel pen in front of him.

"At night?" she said.

"In the morning."

"I work, you know," she said. "How's L.A., anyway?"

"Fine," Merv said. "Can you pick me up or not?"

"You missed all the excitement," she said. "Kendra's brother was dating this woman who pretended to be sixteen but was really in her thirties."

"I don't care," Merv said. He sighed.

"The police think she may be connected to Peter Vaccarino's disappearance. It was on the news tonight. Kendra came over."

"Wow," Merv muttered. He rolled his eyes. "Should I take a cab? The company will pay for it."

"I'll be there," she said. "Give me the details."

Merv did. He looked at his watch after he hung up. He had been on the phone for nearly four minutes.

Friday. August 3. 2001

Humid

High 99 / Low 72

Overcast with chance of

afternoon thunderstorms

KENDRA WALKED BY CRYSTAL'S BROTHER'S PLACE ON HER WAY TO Franny's office. It was hot, as usual, but humid. The clouds hadn't really broken. A few days earlier it had rained a few drops, enough so she could smell the steaming asphalt for a few moments, but that's it. The lightning was starting fires all over the Santa Catalina Mountains—at night Kendra could see patches burning orange. There was no danger to houses—yet. A few summers earlier, a lost hiker, a moron, had lit a fire, hoping to attract help, and in the process he burned hundreds of acres of desert and half a foothills neighborhood. Last night, Kendra had sat at her window and worried about the possibility that the fires would burn their way down to Rancho Sin Vacas.

Now she was worried that Crystal's brother or his girlfriend, the bitchy Jen, would see her walking by. She always felt stupid walking in Tucson, somehow exposed, especially in the summer, but the lot was full, and she was lucky to find a legal parking space in the neighborhood.

Franny's office was nicely air-conditioned, and the coolness had an immediate soporific effect on Kendra, who tried to ignore the distinct smell of Kentucky Fried Chicken that was nauseating her. She had smelled it even before Franny led her into her office, and sure enough, in the trashcan there was a red-and-white grease-stained box, the Colonel's cartoon face glaring back at her.

"You have a lot of big changes coming up," Franny said to Kendra. She tilted her head slightly, and looked Kendra in the eye.

"Like what?" Kendra said.

"For one," Franny said. "Thomas will be leaving for college."

"He doesn't talk to me anymore, anyway," Kendra said, which was a lie. He had been talking to her lately. Ever since that morning when he apologized to her, he'd been much more talkative. He no longer brought up the jockstrap collection, either. He seemed bored, more bored than usual. He still watched professional wrestling on television, but since Brooke was arrested, he rarely left the house. Kendra wasn't sure why she'd lied to Franny about Thomas. It was probably just instinct, but now she'd have to dig out of it, lie more, and try to figure out what response Franny was fishing for.

"I'm sure you'll miss him," Franny said. "He's part of your support system, part of your daily life."

Kendra thought for a moment about home without Thomas. It didn't seem like it would be that different. Crystal's departure would suck much more, but she didn't feel like bringing it up with Franny. Instead, she asked, "If some guy stole a bunch of jockstraps and underpants from all the jocks at school, and this same guy labeled all of them with the names and when he stole them and then he hid them under the back porch, don't you think he has to be gay?"

Franny tilted her head again. She opened her mouth like she would speak—that sickening gooey smack sound!—but she hesitated. She finally said, "Can you think of another reason besides sexual gratification why someone would do that?"

"I thought about revenge," Kendra said, "but why would he save all them and label all of them?"

"It sounds like this person had a very specific goal in mind," Franny said. "Did these athletes tease him at school perhaps?"

"Maybe," Kendra said. She couldn't remember any of them

specifically teasing Thomas, although she imagined they must have. How could they not? Thomas was a freak with a future. They were all headed nowhere, maybe to the U of A if they were really lucky. "I guess."

"Maybe his project is about control," Franny said. "This is his way of feeling like he's in control around these athletes. I don't think it necessarily means he's gay."

In Kendra's opinion, this was the first time Franny had ever said anything worthwhile, anything logical. Kendra actually smiled at her, until she caught herself and said, "That makes sense."

"So Thomas is leaving," Franny said. "How does that really make you feel?"

"I'm happy for him," Kendra said. "He worked hard to get into Columbia and all those other colleges. He gets to live in New York City." She tried to figure out what else Franny would want her to say and finally settled on, "But I'll miss him."

"And your friend, Crystal? She should be leaving in a few weeks, right?"

Yes, Kendra thought. Duh. "I'm going to call and e-mail her a lot."

"That's very positive that you're thinking ahead like that," Franny said. "And maybe you could visit her and Thomas sometime."

"If my mom lets me," Kendra said.

Franny babbled for a few more minutes about positive steps Kendra could take to prevent problems when the two key members of her support system finally left. Letters, e-mails, phone calls. Kendra was also supposed to become involved in two new activities in the fall, one for Thomas leaving and one for Crystal leaving. Each activity—an organized sport, yearbook or newspaper staff, student government—would not only help Kendra avoid spending time missing Thomas and Crystal, but each would provide an opportunity to meet new friends, possible new members of her support system. Kendra thought all of it sounded stupid, classic Franny advice, but she smiled and nodded just like she had learned to do early on. She thought about Thomas feeling like he controlled the jocks by stealing their underwear, how every time he saw one of them, he'd think, I have your smelly jockstrap, asshole. When they teased him, shoved him, whatever, he'd always have that collection in the back of his mind.

"And there's the possibility that Peter may never be coming home," Franny said, apropos of nothing that Kendra could discern. The statement snapped Kendra out of her brief musing. Franny put her hand on Kendra's knee, which instinctively twitched. "How will that be?" she asked Kendra.

"I don't know," Kendra said. She didn't know. Sometimes it bugged her, made her a little sad, but lately she'd been thinking more about Crystal leaving. She and Crystal had only argued once, a week or so ago, when Crystal said Thomas was weird, but that was it. Crystal called the next day and they hung out at the mall, sinfully ate Cinnabons, acted like nothing had happened the day before. They had even driven back up to Bruce Rombough's giant apartment complex, looked for his car to vandalize again—Crystal brought a big bag of Gummi Bears and they were going to moisten them and stick them all over the hood, spelling out *Dick Mobile*. They didn't find Bruce Rombough's car, but just being there in the parking lot elicited a mad giggling fit from both of them. Crystal nearly choked on a Gummi Bear.

"It must be difficult," Franny said. Her hand still rested on Kendra's bare knee.

Kendra didn't know what to say—as usual. This routine of trying to figure out what Franny wanted to hear was exhausting. And her hand on Kendra's knee didn't help. "I just hope he's okay," Kendra finally said softly, in an attempt to portray earnest concern.

"We all do," Franny said, squeezing Kendra's knee. "We all do."

Joyce was photographing toys in the kitchen when Kendra returned from her appointment. An old doll called Chatty Cathy was propped up against a white box, with a white sheet draped over two kitchen chairs as a backdrop.

"How was Franny?" Joyce asked her, looking up from her small digital camera.

"She's still stupid and fat," Kendra said. "She ate a bunch of Kentucky Fried Chicken and I thought I was going to puke all over her gross office."

"No," Joyce said. "How was your session?"

"Fine," Kendra said. "When can I stop going? I mean, I haven't really done anything wrong in a long time."

"You'll stop when the insurance runs out," Joyce said. "It shouldn't for a while."

Kendra sat at the table, slid a *Barney Miller* board game aside and leaned on her elbows. "I wish it would rain."

"We all do," Joyce said.

"Any news about Brooke?"

"None that I've heard," Joyce said. She moved the doll from its spot and replaced it with the *Barney Miller* game. "I haven't heard anything from the detective in a while."

"You think Petey's dead?" Kendra asked.

Joyce snapped a photograph of the game and looked at its image in the small screen, squinted at it, and snapped another. "I hope he's alive. I hope he's happy. But I don't know, he's been gone a long time."

"I know," Kendra said. "I keep thinking he'll just show up and he'll have like a bunch of new tattoos and maybe like some dumb gold tooth, and he'll have a bunch of stories about where he was and what he was doing." She laid her palms on the cool table.

"He very well could," Joyce said. "I sold an entire C mall in Marana yesterday. Can you believe it?"

Kendra didn't know what a C mall was and she had no idea her mother was trying to sell one in Marana. It sounded like good news, though, so she said, "Great."

Kendra and Crystal had planned on swimming laps at the Racquet Club. Kendra was going to teach Crystal how to do flip-turns, but a few minutes after they jumped into the pool, lightning blinked in the north, and the lifeguard asked them to get out.

So they grudgingly changed out of their swimsuits and into shorts and T-shirts, and got the last two treadmills in the upstairs fitness room. Hetta was in there, walking briskly on another treadmill, arms swinging stiffly, like some sort of stupid toy robot.

As Kendra and Crystal adjusted their treadmills, Kendra said, "That fat chick on the corner treadmill in the purple shirt is my neighbor."

"I saw her give you a dirty look when we walked in," Crystal said. "I'm going to set it on eight and try to run more than four miles in thirty minutes."

"Running fast on treadmills freaks me out," Kendra said. "I have to concentrate so much, I can't ever relax."

"Is the fat chick the mother of that kid who disappeared?" Crystal asked. She punched in her weight, and Kendra saw: 128. That was about what Kendra had guessed.

"No," Kendra said. "She's just some dumb bitch who sells Mexican shit like rugs and pots to everyone. Her whole family's fat."

"Did they ever find that kid?" Crystal said.

"His name's Petey Vaccarino," Kendra said. She started her treadmill on six, a pace of ten-minute miles—slow, barely worth running and not walking. "And he hasn't shown up yet."

Crystal started running, too, only much faster than Kendra. Even though Crystal was now wearing her headphones, blasting vintage Joan Jett, and Kendra knew she couldn't hear her, Kendra kept talking. "Everyone thinks I should be all freaked out and sad about Petey," Kendra said. "I can't be, though. I mean, if he's dead, that would suck, but I've been thinking about it a lot and I don't really miss him. I'm more curious than upset." She said it. It made sense. Crystal hadn't heard a word of it, but she didn't care. It made sense. It was okay not to miss Petey. She didn't wish anything bad for him; she just didn't miss him, and she was curious as to where he was, if he was okay. She didn't need Franny to validate these feelings.

Kendra hit the stop button and stepped off the treadmill. She indicated with her thumb to Crystal that she was heading over to the StairMasters.

After their workout, Kendra and Crystal drove back to Kendra's house so they could change. Whit, a friend of Crystal's, a guy she had dated when she was in high school, had recently opened a bar on the southern bank of the Rillito River at Campbell Avenue and River Road. He was throwing a private party for his friends tonight. He was a little older, Crystal had told Kendra. "Like twenty-five. His dad is the biggest beer distributor in Arizona. He's dumb as dirt, but pretty cute and pretty rich."

Kendra and Crystal rummaged through Kendra's closet, searching for clothes that would make them look older. "How old was he when you dated him?" Kendra asked.

"He was twenty-two or something," Crystal said, holding up a pair of jeans. The tags were still attached. "These are cute."

"And you were like sixteen?"

"Seventeen," Crystal said.

"That's not that bad," Kendra said.

"I can't believe you've never worn these jeans." She tossed them on the bed. "You should study at the U of A library this fall," she said. "You could get an older boyfriend easy."

"What makes you think I want an older boyfriend?" Kendra said.

"I know from experience that high school guys suck," Crystal said. "So do college guys, actually."

Kendra settled on a simple linen sleeveless top in white and a pair of wrecked low-rise jeans that she rolled up and wore with leather flip-flops. The white shirt made her look tanner than she was.

Crystal wore a Marc Jacobs sundress in mint green cotton. Like the jeans, the tags were still attached. It was left over from a shopping trip to Scottsdale that Kendra had taken with her grandmother the summer before.

When they walked downstairs, Kendra saw Thomas sitting on the floor in front of the television, an open bag of chips and a two-liter bottle of Mountain Dew by his side. He looked up and smiled at Kendra and Crystal who stood in the kitchen, and he said, "Hello, ladies."

"Thomas," Kendra said, "this is my friend Crystal."

"Hi," he said.

Crystal smiled tightly at Thomas, quickly looked away. Kendra saw the gesture and couldn't figure out if Crystal was shy or rude. Rude. Snobby. Crystal had never acted shy before, and she had said that Thomas was a freak.

"We're going to a party," Kendra said to Thomas. "Do you want to come with us?"

Thomas sprang up, stepped on the bag of chips with his bare foot. A loud crunch. "Really?"

"Get your shoes," Kendra told him.

"I'll be ready in a minute," he said. He dashed past the girls and jogged up the stairs, grinning.

"What the hell is your problem?" Crystal said to Kendra in a loud whisper.

"No problem," she said.

"Why'd you invite him?"

"He needs to get out more," Kendra said. "He's bored."

"Why do we have to take him out? I mean, Whit thinks it's just going to be you and me. It's like a smallish party."

"I'll drive," Kendra said. She walked over to the refrigerator and took out a bottle of water. She held it up and asked Crystal if she wanted one.

"I still can't believe we're taking your brother with us," she said. She sat at the kitchen table, rested her chin in her palms, and pouted.

Thomas bounded down the stairs. He was wearing the same giant Bermuda shorts and stretched-out T-shirt. On his feet he wore vintage black suede Adidas and tube socks, pulled up high over his calves. He looked stupid, Kendra thought, but she was pleased, especially when she saw Crystal's face twist into a clear expression of indignation.

Kendra soon learned that Whit's bar, which was called 'ney's, occupied a small adobe building that used to be a Mexican restaurant where Kendra and Thomas had eaten quite often as children. The waiters there had known Thomas and Kendra, had always served them tall glasses of *horchata*—cinnamon sweet-rice milk—immediately after they sat down. Thomas ordered the same thing every time, a cheese quesadilla, but Kendra always tried something new.

Tonight they parked in a dirt lot, and as they walked across the street toward the bar, Thomas said, "Where's Molina's?"

"Gone," Kendra said.

"It's *'ney's* now," Crystal said. "Whit's bar."

"That sucks," Thomas said.

"It does not suck," Crystal said.

"We used to eat there a lot when we were kids," Kendra said. "They had the best *carne seca*."

"I ate there," Crystal said. "It was okay-ish."

There were about twenty people in line to get into the bar. Crystal said hello to a woman wearing leopard print pants, then she immediately leaned into Kendra and whispered: "That chick I just waved to," she said, "is a total whore. She's only like twenty-two or twenty-three, but she looks like she's in her fifties, don't you think?"

"She does," Kendra said. There was something wrong with the woman's skin. Her face looked like it had recently been molded from clay.

"That's what years of cocaine abuse and rampant promiscuity will do to you," Crystal said.

"Why is there a line?" Kendra asked her. "I thought you said this was a small party." It was hot, in the nineties even now, a few hours after the sun had finally set. The clouds hadn't broken and the mountains were still burning orange in several spots.

"I don't know," Crystal said. "Maybe Whit decided to make it a bigger party."

"How are we getting in without I.D.?" Thomas asked.

"It's a party," Crystal said. "Duh."

Thomas put his hands in the pockets of his giant shorts and turned away.

When they finally reached the front of the line, a doorman with a polished shaved head and decently developed arms asked Crystal for her driver's license.

"Why?" she said.

"You look about sixteen," he said. He was chewing gum.

"I'm a guest of Whit's," she said. "I dated him for almost two years."

"Sorry," he said. Then he asked Kendra for her license.

"I don't have it," she said.

"You work out at the Racquet Club, right?" he said.

"Yes," she said.

"You used to be way more buff, right?" He placed his hand on Crystal's shoulder and gently moved her to the side so he could get a better look at Kendra.

"I've cut back," Kendra said. "A lot. More cardio, more reps, less weight."

"You look great," he said. His lip curled into a smile on one side. He had dimples.

"Look, stop hitting on my friend and get Whit out here so we can settle this and get out of the heat," Crystal said. "It's too hot for this shit." She stood on her toes and craned her neck to see over the bouncer's shoulder. "Tell him Crystal's here."

"I can't do that," the doorman said. "Whit's not here."

"I seriously doubt it," Crystal said.

"He's not coming until two," the doorman said. "That's when the after party starts. You can come back then." He looked over to Kendra again. "Are *you* coming back at two?"

"I don't know," Kendra said. "That's pretty late."

"I don't think we'll be returning," Crystal said. She turned and began walking toward the car. She stopped after a few steps and looked back over her shoulder. "She's only sixteen, you pervert."

"I'm only eighteen," he said. "I just turned eighteen." He smiled at Kendra. He was kind of goofy looking with his glistening head and prominent ears, but Kendra liked his thick eyebrows and dimples, especially the dimple on his chin. His forearms, which were crossed over his chest, were amazingly defined, even in the dull light outside the bar. She liked it when guys didn't neglect their forearms. So many guys had huge biceps and triceps and undefined forearms.

"Happy birthday," Kendra said, smiling, then she followed Crystal.

"Our phone number spells 'turf bag,'" Kendra heard Thomas tell the guy. "That's T-U-R-F-B-A-G, if you want to call her. Her name's Kendra, and she doesn't have a boyfriend." Thomas jogged up to them.

"Are you a fucking lunatic?" Crystal asked him. "You just gave that musclehead your phone number? He looked like he just got out of prison."

"He was okay," Kendra said.

"He looks like Goldberg," Thomas said. Then he clarified: "A wrestler."

Crystal walked faster to the car. "If you think anyone else at Columbia is into watching wrestling on television all day, you're retarded," she said without turning to face Thomas.

"Why would I think that?" Thomas said.

After two unsuccessful attempts to buy beer, the three of them ended up on the seventh hole of the La Paloma golf course, where Kendra and Thomas's father taught lessons and served as the resident golf pro. The sprinklers had just shut off so the grass was deliciously wet and cool. Kendra didn't care that she was staining her linen shirt, she sprawled on the moist lawn and looked up at the night sky. The clouds obscured the stars, but the glow of the moon lit the night in a sinister purple color.

Thomas stretched out on the green up near the hole, whistled to himself.

Crystal stood a few feet from Kendra, arms crossed over her chest.

"Why are you standing?" Kendra asked her.

"This dress was six hundred dollars, remember?"

"I seriously don't care," Kendra said. "My grandmother bought it, and she's totally rich. Plussing as which, I can have it dry cleaned easy."

"I thought I cured you of that!" Crystal said.

Kendra was briefly embarrassed, but then she said, "I swear, I've only said it a few times since the dolls, and I've told you every single time."

"Hold on," Thomas said. He peeled off his T-shirt, balled it up, and threw it at Crystal. "Sit on that."

"Thanks," she said. She grabbed it from the ground, shook it out, and spread it like a beach towel before she sat down next to Kendra.

Kendra leaned up on her elbows, looked at the lights of Tucson below. From where they were in the foothills, they had an ample view of the city. Every few moments a bolt of lightning would strike somewhere in Tucson, and the three of them would try to guess where it hit.

"Bruce Rombough's car," Crystal said. She and Kendra giggled. "He was in it, in the front seat, masturbating with a really specialized porno magazine, like one featuring naked fat ladies stomping on bugs, and now he's a smoldering pile of charred flesh!"

"Perfect!" Kendra said. After the next bolt, a wild zigzagging branched one that seemed to hit closer to where they were, Kendra said, "That one hit Jim the hair guy, who was on his back porch brushing his long flowing hair and the lighting struck his hairbrush. He was stupid, using a metal brush. It zapped his hair, which burst into flames. He's running around his porch right now, wishing he had a pool to jump into."

"Have you ever smelled burning hair?" Thomas said.

Neither Kendra nor Crystal answered him. When Kendra

looked over to him, she noticed his pale skin in the moonlight. His scrawny frame was easily visible, and she hoped Crystal wouldn't make fun of him.

"This is nasty," Thomas said, "but when I study, I sometimes drop chewed-off fingernails onto the light bulb on my desk lamp, and when they burn, they smell like burning hair."

"Don't do that at college," Crystal said. "That's my tip for the night."

Kendra liked closing her eyes after seeing lightning. That way she could see it again, the bolt's image perfectly burned into her eyes—like a camera's flash. She thought of the bouncer, was sort of proud that he had flirted with her and not Crystal, was even prouder that she had flirted back a little. She couldn't remember seeing him at the Racquet Club, though. Or maybe she had seen him and just dismissed him as gay. She wondered if he was still in high school, if he played football, what his name was. At least Thomas had given him the phone number.

After several minutes of silence, Crystal broke with, "I'm really pissed at Whit."

"This is much better than some dumb party full of pretentious Tucson elite," Thomas said.

"*Tucson elite*," Crystal said. "Now there's an oxymoron." She turned to Kendra. "You better study harder next year, so you can go away for college, or you'll be stuck here forever."

"I like it here," Kendra said, and a ground-rumbling clap of thunder punctuated her proclamation.

Merv asked the lifeguards if they had seen Raymond lately, but they hadn't. "I hope nothing happened to him," Merv said. "I don't even know his last name."

"Maybe he finally got sick of it here," George said. "Or maybe he just got sick of having to leave early because of the lightning every afternoon."

In a sense, not seeing Raymond was a relief for Merv, but he felt sort of guilty about it. It was liberating to know that he wouldn't have to help Raymond with his piss tube or see him pathetically struggle to accomplish the simplest tasks, like taking a sip of a drink or adjusting his visor. But Raymond was someone who would understand the significance of Merv's new job. Raymond was someone who would be impressed.

He determined that the last time he had seen Raymond was two or three weeks ago, the day he helped slide the condom catheter back on his penis. When Merv realized this, he felt guiltier, thinking that perhaps poor Raymond was too embarrassed to show his face around Splash World. Merv should have stuck around after helping Raymond instead of hurrying to wash his hands and then dashing out of the locker room like he had. He should have played it off as nothing, treated Raymond the way he hoped people had treated his father when he was an invalid.

It was Jacob's second day of shadowing Merv, and the guy had said barely a single word. He took a lot of notes, though, on long yellow legal pads. He wrote furiously, in large letters, and he noisily flipped the page every minute or so. Yesterday, Jacob had worn a seersucker suit and leather-heeled shoes that clomped and crunched behind Merv as they walked along the sidewalks of the park. Today he wore the same shoes and a light khaki suit. He was a tall guy with a face that looked as if it was formed with precision: strong square jaw, dimple-tipped nose, eyes the color of swimming pool water, dark hair cut short and molded into a sort-of ramp in the front. Several female employees had asked about Jacob. Rita, who worked at the ticket booth and whom Merv had long ago dismissed as a sexless goth misanthrope, had even asked Merv, "Is that hot guy you were with single?" But before Merv could answer her, she asked in a suddenly disappointed tone, "Or gay? I bet he's gay, isn't he?"

"I don't know and I don't know," Merv had told her.

"Find out," she said.

Why? Merv thought. As if a handsome Ivy League genius

would be even vaguely interested in a dumpy and grouchy ticket booth worker with a stupid pierced nose and frizzed-out crow-black hair.

Merv and Jacob drove a few miles in Jacob's rental car to El Presidio Grill. Jacob told Merv that he was only in Tucson for a few weeks, so he was hoping to take advantage of the few good restaurants that it had to offer. Jacob had rented a giant SUV with an air-conditioner that blasted cool air immediately after turning it on. Merv caught himself wondering what kind of car he would buy for himself when he moved to Long Beach. Something with a good air-conditioner like this one—it gave him goose bumps as they drove past strip mall after strip mall on Speedway Boulevard.

"Doesn't this city have any zoning ordinances?" Jacob asked. "Everything looks like shit."

It was the most Jacob had said to Merv since he arrived in Tucson.

"Speedway's not a really good example of Tucson," Merv said. "Some parts are nicer."

"Look at that," Jacob said. He pointed to a giant half-inflated ape that was meant to attract customers to a sale at a used car lot. It sagged and flapped in the hot wind. "They didn't even bother to take it down after it popped."

"Maybe it just needs more air," Merv said. "The mountains here are beautiful," Merv said. "You can't deny that."

"You're right," Jacob said. "I went hiking in Sabino Canyon over the weekend. I must have seen a hundred lizards."

They were approaching Magic Carpet Golf, and Merv dreaded Jacob's assessment of the giant, garishly painted but faded tiki heads and spiders that had all begun to crack and crumble. Then Merv asked himself why he should be embarrassed. Magic Carpet Golf was cool in its own creepy way, and if Jacob couldn't appreciate it, fuck him.

Jacob didn't comment on it. Instead he asked, "How far are we from Arizona State?"

"Like a hundred miles," Merv said.

"I mean the University of Arizona," Jacob said. "My best friend from high school went there, you know. He loved it."

"It's just about five miles west," Merv said. "Or maybe ten." It figured that Jacob didn't even know where his best friend went to college, Merv thought.

"Where in L.A. are you thinking about living?" Jacob asked, craning his neck as they passed a Lexus dealership.

"Long Beach," Merv said.

Jacob curled his lip and raised his eyebrow.

Merv wondered where in the L.A. area Jacob was planning on living, but he didn't want to give him the satisfaction of asking. He sensed that Jacob wanted him to ask, wanted to brag about how wonderful whatever neighborhood he chose was.

Since he returned from California, Merv had been looking on the Internet for information about Long Beach. There was a huge aquarium there, lots of parks, and a revitalized downtown full of art galleries, cafés, and converted lofts. He had even called about a few apartments that weren't that far from the beach and weren't that expensive—not much more than Rusty and Jason paid for their apartments in Scottsdale.

Merv had called Rusty last night. "The fact that you're thirty and have never rented a place yourself is really fucking pathetic," Rusty had said.

"Shut the hell up," Merv had said. "Just answer my question."

"It's usually like first month, last month, and a security deposit," Rusty said.

"How much are security deposits?"

"How the hell should I know? Sometimes one month's rent, sometimes less, like five hundred or something."

"So," Merv said, "I might need like thirty-six hundred to move into a place. Shit."

"My friend in New York is paying sixteen hundred for a tiny box that's in a shitty neighborhood over a mannequin factory. He gets glue fumes through his vents. And he had to pay a ridiculous finder's fee."

"So, twelve hundred a month isn't that bad, is it?" Merv said.

"I called the guy and it has wood floors and Mexican tile in the bathroom and the kitchen."

"How big is it?" Rusty asked.

"One bedroom," Merv said.

"No, retard. How many square feet?"

"I don't know," Merv said. "I didn't ask."

"Melissa's right," Rusty said. "She said you were 'a little off.'"

"What the hell does that mean?" Merv said. "When did you talk to her?"

"Yesterday."

"She freaked out for no reason!" Merv said. "I had a fucking broken wrist, and she totally freaked out on me."

"She said you fucked her, then used her as a chauffeur to take you to the hospital," Rusty said. "And she said you were mean to her cats."

"What?" Merv was incredulous.

"Dude," Rusty said. "I have to go. The pizza guy's here."

Merv had called Melissa after he hung up with Rusty, but her voicemail picked up. "This is Merv," he said. He tried to sound as friendly and innocuous as possible. "Please give me a call. I'd really like to talk for a second . . ."

Halfway through his sweet-potato enchilada, Merv decided that he liked Jacob more before he began to speak. The guy wouldn't shut up. He babbled about curriculum planning, management theory, several computer programs that he found helpful, tax breaks . . . Every once in a while, when Jacob took a bite or a sip, Merv was able to mutter a word or two. Mostly Merv blocked out Jacob and tried to make a mental list of things he needed to buy at the supermarket tonight: milk, tortillas, bananas, orange juice, dishwasher detergent . . . His mother usually went to the supermarket, but she had been working late this week, on a "tedious real-estate case," so Merv had told her he would go. "It might be good for you," she had said. "You'll need to learn to buy your own groceries."

"I know how to buy groceries," Merv had said. "You act like I'm five years old."

"No," she had said. "I act like you're thirty and you've never lived anywhere but here."

Merv had been apprehensive about telling her about his job offer. He had imagined she would try to make him feel guilty that he was leaving her. He had thought he would see the appliances unplugged with their electrical cords taped down to the countertops, and he had thought that the muscular neighbor girl would bring her home every morning. None of that had happened, though. His mother was pleased, told him she was proud of him, that a change was just what he needed, that L.A. was full of opportunities. "I'll visit you a few months after you're settled."

Merv was oddly upset by her enthusiasm. He had immediately felt relief, but after he thought about the conversation, he realized that maybe his mother was eager for him to move out.

The lunch with Jacob ended promptly after forty-five minutes were up. On the way back to Splash World, Jacob turned down the radio in his rental SUV, and said, "You know, Merv, I'm really not too psyched about moving to L.A., if you want the truth. I like Boston. I like New York."

"Then why'd you take the job?" Merv asked him.

"It's practically the exact position that I trained for in graduate school," Jacob said. "Plus they're paying me a shitload. I'll have business school paid off in nineteen months, then I can move back to the East Coast, back where I can take subways and cabs and not have to drive so much."

He turned up the volume again, and sang along to Oasis: ". . . Where were you when we were getting high . . ." He tapped along on the steering wheel, too. Merv rolled his eyes and tried to ignore him. What an asshole. Merv had noticed that in the last hour of nearly constant babbling, Jacob had never mentioned any family or friends—most likely, everyone who had encountered him throughout his life had thought he was an asshole. He had no friends, and his family, back in their perfectly manicured town of high taxes and aesthetic sensibilities, were sick of him—Merv was sure of it. When Jacob started to loudly sing along to the Police's "Roxanne," Merv faked a coughing fit in hopes that he'd cease. He didn't.

When Merv arrived home, he turned down the thermostat and began to make fajitas. He chopped up four chicken breasts; green, yellow, and red peppers; a few onions. He figured he'd cook the chicken now—in a pan with a little olive oil—and wait for his mother to get home before he cooked the vegetables.

"I can't believe it," she said, when she arrived home about an hour and a half later. She dropped her purse on the kitchen table, dramatically breathed in the scents of Merv's cooking. "I didn't think you knew how to use the stove."

"Very funny," Merv said.

"Chicken?" she asked.

"Fajitas," Merv said proudly. He dropped the vegetables into the pan and turned up the heat.

"Now that you cook, I might actually miss you when you move to Los Angeles," she said.

"What's your problem, anyway?" Merv said. He had been anticipating a joke like that, and it pissed him off. "I'm making you a nice dinner and now you're insulting me." He stepped back from the stove when the oil started to spit and pop.

"I'm just kidding," she said. "Lighten up."

"I think you're genuinely excited for me to move out," he said. "You're excited for yourself, not me."

"Why can't I be excited for the both of us?" she asked. She began to rummage through her purse and pulled out a cell phone. "Look what I got today at lunch."

"A mobile phone," Merv said. "Who cares?"

"You're not *excited* for me?" she said.

When had his mother turned into a sarcastic teenage bitch, Merv wondered. "I think Doctor Grossman needs to adjust whatever medication you're on," he said.

"I've never been happier," she said.

"Because I'm leaving, right?"

"That's part of it, if you want the truth," she said. "I'm looking forward to having the house to myself, to doing my own thing."

"You act like I've been this tremendous burden all these years," Merv said. "Which is bullshit. I would have moved out a long time ago if you were even vaguely sane."

"*That's* bullshit," she said. "You've always been afraid of leaving home, ever since you were a kid. You wouldn't even let us send you to camp. You called home about a million times every time you went on one of those weekend ski trips in high school."

Merv lifted the pan off the stove, didn't care that the pops of hot oil burned and speckled his arm with red dots. He dumped the chopped peppers, onions, and chicken into the sink. He pressed it all down the drain into the garbage disposal with a spatula, rinsed off the sizzling pan with water, allowed the steam to burn his face and neck. He turned on the disposal, waited a moment for it to really kick in and grind. He walked past his mother to the family room, where he flicked on the television.

She stood and turned off the disposal, then quickly walked into the family room and sat next to Merv on the couch. "Have you finished being dramatic?" she said. "If there's more, just let me know so I can go upstairs and go to sleep."

Never before now had Merv felt the urge to hit his mother. He felt it in his hands, like they had minds of their own. This impulse, the impulse to punch her directly in the jaw, frightened him, and he tucked his hands, which were both tightly fisted, under his thighs. "Shut up," he told her, looking at her jaw, the tiny white hairs that shone in the last of the day's light pouring through the window. "Just shut the hell up."

"Don't tell me to shut up," she said.

"Shut up," Merv repeated.

She said something else, but Merv couldn't hear her. He just watched her mouth contort, saw flashes of her dental work, a small strand of saliva spanning her lips. Again, he focused on her jaw, imagined it giving when he punched it, cracking, hanging slack from her face.

He walked outside and sat on the edge of the pool, soaked his feet, watched the lightning flash over the city. "I wish it would rain," he said to the purple sky. "Please, just rain. It's August, you fucker. Rain already." Then he remembered: Tomorrow was the anniversary of his father's death. August fourth.

He and his mother had visited his gravesite every August fourth for fifteen years. They always bought two roses, a white one and a red one, and placed them on the brown, crunchy grass in front of his small marker. He had been cremated, and Merv and his mother had sprinkled half of his ashes in a park in Chandler, the town southeast of Phoenix where he had grown up. The other half was here in Tucson, buried in a small urn at the cemetery on Oracle Road, not too far from where his father used to pick up hookers—if he had picked up hookers. Based on her behavior lately, Merv wondered if he could trust his mother.

He doubted she would go to the grave tomorrow, doubted she'd even remember the significance of the date. If she did remember, she'd probably choose not to go to the cemetery, anyway. Merv would go. He'd wake early and go before work, maybe stop and buy a few roses at a twenty-four-hour supermarket along the way.

He looked up at the sky again and said, "I demand that you rain."

Thursday. August 16. 2001

High 88 / Low 65

Severe thunderstorms

KENDRA WAS DREAMING ABOUT AN OUT-OF-CONTROL AMBULANCE. SHE was in the back, on a gurney, and there was no driver. The ambulance was speeding on a twisting coastal mountain road and she couldn't wriggle from the restraints that held her to the gurney. She could see over the front seat, but she couldn't reach the steering wheel. As in most of Kendra's nightmares, no one could hear her scream, but this time it wasn't because she had no voice or that she had forgotten how to scream; it was because of the blaring siren.

The ambulance finally careened off a cliff, flew through the air for a moment, then plummeted. Kendra woke before she crashed into the vast gray ocean below.

She heard sirens and looked at the clock: 5:57. The sirens sounded like babies screaming, then sirens again. It took her a moment to realize it was just a bunch of coyotes yipping and howling.

There was no way she could sleep with the noise. She hadn't run in the morning in weeks, and last night, she was out with R.T., the bouncer from the bar Crystal had taken her to the other night, until past one. She figured, though, that since she was up, she might as well go for a run. Maybe the coyotes would quiet down and she could sleep afterward.

Last night had been her third date with R.T. He picked her up in his big black pickup truck and they drove to the Sanchez Burrito Company on First Avenue. They ate their burritos on the covered porch and watched the rain drench the city. Big, cold drops, the first real ones of the monsoon season, pounded down, filled the street in minutes. "I knew it!" R.T. had yelled. "I knew this morning that today would be the day!" He stuck his arm out in the rain. "It's cold, too!" he said excitedly.

"Finally," Kendra said.

"Finally is right," R.T. said. "We should go hiking tomorrow up in Sabino Canyon. Those swimming holes will fill up." He sat back down beside Kendra, kissed her on the cheek, pulled her close. "How about it?"

"Sure," she said. R.T. was the first guy she was with who was stronger than she was. Miguel, now that he boxed and trained, could probably take her, but when she used to mess around with him, she could pin him and hold him down—which she did. They had wrestled quite a bit, and she had always won. There was no way she could take R.T., and she wasn't quite sure how she felt about it. Sometimes, like when they were kissing in his truck, she loved it, allowed herself to fall limp, feel weak. It was the concept that bugged her. She didn't like knowing that he could take her if he wanted to. Crystal had warned her that she didn't know him that well and that she should be looking for red flags—"Anything that might make you think he's an asshole."

"Like what?" Kendra had asked.

"I don't know," Crystal said. "Like, if he comments on some chick's nice tits or he wears ugly shoes. Don't put up with any of that shit."

So far no tit comments, and his shoes were old-school Adidas like Thomas and Petey wore. R.T. did play football. He was a linebacker for Canyon del Oro High. He also played the tuba in the school band, but only during basketball season. The only red flag was his musical taste: contemporary country. Kendra's parents would disapprove highly if they found out, they'd freak out and lecture R.T. every chance they'd get, give him shit. Kendra herself pretty much hated all country music except for Johnny Cash—an exception she had inherited from her father. Country was stupid, especially now since she had actually heard a fair amount in R.T.'s truck. Every song was about love or stereotypical redneck things like honkytonks, cowboys, even trucks.

R.T. was Kendra's first real boyfriend, and Gene and Joyce had greeted him the second time he came to pick Kendra up. She was mortified when she discovered the three of them chatting at the front door. She plowed through her parents, grabbed R.T.'s hand, and tugged him toward his truck, which was parked in the driveway. "Nice to meet you," he said over his shoulder to Gene and Joyce.

When Kendra came home that night, Gene was waiting up, sitting at the kitchen table with his headphones on. "So," he said, doffing his headphones as Kendra walked into the room, "how was your date with the skinhead?"

"He's not a skinhead," Kendra said. "I think."

"He has a shaved head," Gene said. "Didn't you notice?"

"Duh," Kendra said.

"A Nazi motherfucker," Gene said with a serious tone. "Kids like him make me sick."

Kendra bought it for a second, then realized he was joking. "Dad, did anyone ever tell you that you're retarded?"

"Just my teachers and professors," he said, and he put his headphones back on.

Kendra tied her shoes and slipped into the cool, moist air. It was still raining a little, but she didn't bother putting on any extra clothes—she wore her usual running shorts, sports bra, and tank top. The creosote released by the rain smelled holy and important, and Kendra breathed it in, allowed it to energize her.

The coyotes were still going crazy, sounding like the sirens in her dream. She jogged down the driveway, leaned against the mailbox, and quickly stretched her calves and thighs, before she headed toward her workout hill.

She stopped when she rounded the corner and saw the water rushing over the street. The arroyo had filled overnight, so high that the small drainage tunnel under the street couldn't accommodate the flow. Kendra ran to the edge of the water and looked up the arroyo: a brown, gurgling river cutting through the desert as far up into the mountain that she could see through the drizzle. The water had carved a deep canyon, and a tall rotting saguaro had toppled. It was half submerged in the flow. "Shit," Kendra said. The arroyo had never filled this much. It rarely flowed at all.

The coyotes were still howling and shrieking, only now Kendra was closer.

She was careful not to get too close to the edge of the newly formed canyon—she imagined the ground giving away, dropping her into the rushing arroyo and sweeping her underwater, but she wanted to see what the coyotes were fussing over. She walked through the desert, cutting through mesquite and prickly pear, forging closer to the high-pitched sounds of the frenzied coyotes.

She spotted Ellen on the other side of the arroyo, wearing a bright yellow raincoat and standing atop a large rock. When Kendra pushed away a few wet palo verde branches, she saw the coyotes: a pack of ten or twelve, skinny and small, but swarming just below Ellen at edge of the flowing arroyo.

"Hey!" Kendra yelled to Ellen, thinking that Ellen might be in one of her zombie states like she had been when Kendra discovered her earlier in the summer. "Hey!"

Ellen looked across the brown water to Kendra. "Go home!" she yelled. "Call the police."

Kendra ducked under the last branches, scraping her arms and back. When she finally made it through to the other side of the palo verde tree, she saw that the coyotes were biting at something, fighting with each other.

"Go home!" Ellen yelled. She waved Kendra away.

"Why?" Kendra yelled.

"Turn around!" Ellen yelled, still waving her arms.

Kendra didn't turn around, though. She watched the coyotes nosing into a large tangle of branches and shrubs that had snagged on the side of the flowing water. The coyotes were after something black. Kendra squinted, stood on her toes as best she could in the moist earth, got a slightly better view. Black jeans. Black basketball shoes with white stripes. She knew then that it was Petey, but she continued to look, walked closer, stepped over saltbush and spiky yucca.

His leg, the jeans torn away, his sock and shoe still on, was the only part of him she could see. The flesh was pink and black, like barbecued chicken, and the coyotes, in their hysterical square dance, seemed to be taking turns picking at it, occasionally snapping at each other.

The coyotes woke Merv at around five-thirty. He had gone to bed early, though, before ten, enjoying the sound of the rain battering the roof, allowing it to lull him to sleep within minutes of hitting the pillow.

Last night was one of the first pleasant nights he had spent at home since he announced to his mother that he was leaving in September for his new job in Long Beach. They hadn't fought last night, even laughed together as they ate pizza in front of sitcoms. She hadn't made any of her sarcastic remarks, and when Merv walked upstairs to his room, he could still hear her laughing at something on television.

He had finally talked to Melissa yesterday, too. She had never returned his calls, so he called her again from work. She actually answered, and didn't hang up right away after Merv spoke. "How are you?"

"I'm fine," she had said in a bitter voice. "Merv."

"Great," Merv had said. "Melissa."

"Is that the only reason you called?"

"No," Merv said. "I guess I wanted to talk some."

"About?"

"So, what's new?" he asked. He pretended not to notice her rudeness, managed to keep his voice pleasant and enthusiastic.

"Nothing much," she said. "I'm taking tennis lessons."

"My wrist is still a little messed up," Merv said.

"Oh," she said, then nothing else.

Merv could barely hear her breathing. He let a few moments pass before he said, "It's been like a month or more, and I still can't figure out what I did to piss you off so much."

"I freak out if things move too fast, and I let them move too fast," Melissa said.

"Why'd you tell Rusty and Jason that I was mean to you and your cats?" Merv said. He lost his happy tone.

"You were," she said.

"What? How?"

"I think screwing someone then making them drive you all the way across town like five seconds after you come is mean," she said. "And you tried to scare my cats."

"That one was hissing at me the whole time we had sex," Merv said. "And besides, you wanted to have sex as much as I did."

"I just don't think you handled yourself like a gentleman," she said.

"And how would have that been?"

"Maybe if you called me and asked me to meet you at the hospital then we would have never had that awful sex," she said. "Maybe if you had gone straight to the hospital instead of coming over."

"Awful sex? You seemed to like it at the time," Merv said. He was incredulous.

He had resigned then, gave up. He knew at that point that he wasn't getting anywhere with Melissa. He briefly felt like he should apologize, but he remembered that he had done nothing wrong. Before they hung up, Melissa did congratulate him on his new job. "It'll be great for you to have your own place and be on your own," she said.

Merv was sick of hearing that from everyone. It was as if all along everyone had thought he was a pathetic loser for living with his mother, but no one had told him until recently.

The rain and the agreeable time he spent eating pizza and

watching television with his mother calmed him after talking to Melissa. He was glad to have finally spoken to her, though, even if she was still weird and unreasonable. He had tried, made his points, stuck to them.

Waking to the howling and screeching coyotes this morning, though, was frightening—his immediate thought after rubbing the crusties from his eyes and sitting up was that the coyotes had awoken his mother. She was probably wandering the streets with a toaster in her arms, maybe stopped, staring blankly at a rock or a mailbox.

After Merv pulled on a pair of shorts and tied his tennis shoes, he tiptoed down the hall, gingerly placing each step. He carefully turned his mother's doorknob, but sure enough, when he peeked in, he could see that her bed was empty, already neatly made, not the slightest wrinkle in her comforter.

Merv stood on the diving board and looked through the morning drizzle for his mother. He spotted her in seconds because of her bright raincoat. He was relieved that she was wearing it, and she didn't seem to be clutching any small appliance. She was standing down by the arroyo, which was flowing harder than Merv had ever seen it flow. In fact, between the coyotes' howls and squeals, he could hear it flow, like a real river, a faint but full rumbling.

Merv hopped over low-lying chaparral and prickly pear as he worked his way down the hill to his mother. He could see the neighbor girl, too, Kendra, standing on the other side of the brown water, and coyotes swarming in front of his mother. "What the hell?" he yelled.

His mother turned around. "Go back and call the police!" she yelled.

He kept working his way down the hill, though, and he squatted to pick up some rocks to throw at the coyotes. "Git!" he yelled at the coyotes, but they didn't seem to notice.

"Go back and call the police!" she yelled at him again.

"Tell them we found Petey!" Kendra yelled.

He finally made it to his mother, joined her on the rock and looked down at the coyotes, all of which seemed unfazed by his presence or the presence of his mother and Kendra.

When he saw Petey's head—a patch of light hair attached to a black and pink dirty skull, the skin pulled back from the mouth, exposing the teeth in a sickening grin—he threw a rock at the feasting coyotes. It hit one on the back, and bounced into the gurgling water with a thunk, but the animal didn't even look up from where it was chewing at Petey's neck. He threw the other two rocks, but the coyotes kept shredding and nipping at the corpse.

Tuesday, September 18, 2001

Hot and dry

High 102 / Low 71

Sunny and breezy

THE REALIZATION THAT PETEY WAS DEAD, SEEING HIS ROTTEN ARM LIKE SHE had that morning last month, wasn't enough to cause Kendra to grieve. She had gone to his funeral, looked through a few photographs of the two of them from when they were kids— Kendra in pigtails and a Popsicle-stained striped shirt, Petey on Rollerblades—but nothing caused the feelings of loss that she knew she should feel. She had lied to Franny a few weeks ago, even forced a few tears—induced by not blinking, but Kendra knew there was something wrong; she should be much sadder about Petey's death than she was.

She felt far worse for all the people killed in New York and Washington last week, all of their families. They occupied her thoughts more than Petey. She imagined the people on the flights that crashed into the towers, their lives stolen by those fuckers. She watched in horror last Tuesday morning before school as people jumped from the towers, as the towers crumbled. All those families. All those smart people with important jobs.

She knew it was horrible to think, but Petey wasn't very smart. He would have never had an important job, never do anything worthwhile. He had been a pen huffer, a wannabe gangsta white kid who would have spent his life with two Sharpies up his nostrils if he could have. He would have never worked in the World Trade Center or the Pentagon, probably didn't know where they were located, probably couldn't find New York or Washington, D.C., on a map. Kendra hadn't really known much about the Twin Towers or the Pentagon until last week, she admitted to herself, and if she didn't do better in school this year, stay on the right track, she probably wouldn't ever have an important job, either. But that realization didn't help her muster up any grief because she knew—as crass as it was, and as much as she hated herself for thinking it—Petey had been a loser, a wastoid.

Thomas had called the morning of the eleventh, crying and freaking out, telling Kendra that he wanted to leave Columbia, come home to Tucson, go to the U of A, never go back to New York. Gene and Joyce were on the other two phones in the house, and they calmed him down, told him to hold tight, appeased him by saying that they'd personally drive across the country and pick him up if he really decided to leave and didn't want to fly. "I'm never fucking getting on another plane as long as I live," he had told the three of them that morning. "No fucking way."

He had called every night since, sometimes just talking to Kendra about nothing. She knew he was sick of talking about the attacks, so she didn't mention them unless he did.

"How's R.T.?" he had asked last night.

"He's cool," Kendra said. "Busy with football and an SAT prep class."

"You been to any of his games?"

"Not yet," Kendra said. "Next week. Hey, Crystal's gonna call you. I gave her your number."

"Why?" Thomas asked.

"She wants to hang out. She's all freaked out about the attacks, too, even though she wasn't as close as you." She immediately felt bad for bringing up last Tuesday. "Sorry," she added quietly.

"Everyone's freaked out," Thomas said. "But everyone's nice to each other, too. It's really weird but nice. Even the people at McDonald's are nice."

"You shouldn't eat that shit," Kendra said. She told him then that she was glad that he had decided not to drop out and come home. "This sounds really gay," she said, "but I'm proud of you for staying in New York. I think it's sort of brave." She knew Franny would eat it up when she told her what she had just said to Thomas, but she actually meant it, and it scared her a little.

Hetta admitted to killing Petey two days after Ellen had discovered his body that rainy morning. She had run him over the night he was partying with the three BMX tweekers. The boys were all on bicycles, and Petey had been wearing mostly black clothes, was trailing behind the tweekers, who were about a hundred yards ahead of him. Hetta said she passed the three guys on their bikes, and was calling the cops on her cell phone to report them, when she hit Petey with her giant Range Rover. She had paid the meth-heads all the money she had on her—$340—to bury Petey's body and keep quiet. She even drove home and returned to them with three shovels and told them to wrap his body in a Navajo blanket she pulled from her backseat. She had replaced her Range Rover a few days later with another Range Rover. When she confessed, she said she couldn't bear to look at the small dent on the hood.

Kendra had stopped herself from fully delighting in Hetta's crime when she heard the news from her mother. She didn't know how she was supposed to react. She was shocked, but not really—Hetta was a bitch, horrible, Kendra always knew. She was happy that Hetta was in huge trouble, that she was being held in jail, but not that happy—Petey *was* dead after all.

"I have to admit," Joyce said after she told Kendra, "I never really liked Hetta, but I didn't think she was capable of this sort of thing. Did you?"

Kendra had just shaken her head. She had been imagining Hetta in a dirty jail cell, having to piss in one of those grimy exposed metal toilets. She fantasized that Hetta's cellmate was a giant tattooed muscle dyke, whose sexual aggression was surpassed only by her flatulence. The muscle dyke wore a thick man's watch, suffered from man-face after years of steroid abuse, and made Hetta her bitch. She only addressed Hetta as "fat bitch."

When Kendra talked to Franny about it a few days later, she had been totally honest, only skipping the daydream about Hetta's life behind bars.

"I was really happy that that bitch got busted," she had said. "I know I'm not supposed to hate her or anything, but I really do, and not just because she killed Petey. She was a bitch to me all summer whenever I saw her at the Racquet Club."

"Why do you suppose she wasn't very friendly this summer?"

"Because she was still pissed at me for telling her not to buy all that crappy unhealthy food a long time ago?"

"Perhaps," Franny said, "you were a reminder of Peter. Maybe seeing you made her feel more guilty and remorseful."

"Good," Kendra said. "I hope it did. I hope she's feeling guilty and remorseful as she rots in jail."

"You know," Franny had said. "Your response is valid. It's okay for you to be angry with Hetta for killing your friend."

"Duh," Kendra said. Then she paused, disappointed and a little frightened that she had just said "duh" to Franny. "Sorry."

She talked to R.T. for a few minutes this morning when she first woke up, turned on CNN, and fixed herself a bowl of oatmeal and scrambled egg whites. She settled in front of the television, but turned it off after a few minutes. The media had begun to portray sad personal story after sad personal story about the attacks on the Twin Towers and the Pentagon. Kendra felt guilty for turning the television off, though, thought maybe she wasn't honoring the victims or the victims' loved ones, so she clicked it back on and watched a woman who had lost her husband and brother bravely work through an interview. When the commercials started, she clicked off the television without any guilt, put her dishes in the sink, grabbed her backpack, and walked out the back door into the morning heat.

She looked across the desert and saw Mrs. Vaccarino getting into her car. Something fell out of Mrs. Vaccarino's purse, a lipstick maybe. She tucked her hair behind her ears and crouched down to retrieve whatever it was she had dropped. She looked under her car, then reached under. When she stood, she noticed a dark streak of car grime on her white sleeve. She leaned against her car and pressed her palms against her face for a moment before she went back inside—to change her shirt, Kendra presumed.

It was witnessing the gesture, Mrs. Vaccarino briefly hiding her face in her hands after staining her white shirt, that triggered something deep inside Kendra, made her sit on the back steps and cry for Petey. Had he ever even noticed his mother doing anything like that?

Kendra wasn't going to school today.

Merv had just finished pumping gas at the Shell station on the corner of Oracle and Ina; he had filled his tank and was ready to get on I-10 and drive the eight hours across the desert to L.A., when he saw the man standing outside the supermarket across the parking lot, tending the small florist stand. From where Merv stood, about a hundred feet away, the man looked familiar. Merv wasn't even sure what caused him to turn that way, but the guy was definitely familiar—the way he handed a bunch of red and orange flowers to a woman, his neatly parted graying hair. Maybe he was a former teacher, or a long-ago friend's father, Merv thought.

Merv decided to drive by and get a better look, and when he realized the man at the florist stand was Raymond, standing, moving his arms without any difficulty, he slammed on his brakes, frightening a woman pushing a shopping cart full of groceries with the squeal of his tires. "Sorry," he said to the woman who was now sneering at him, shaking her head in a dramatic display of disbelief and indignation.

When he turned to Raymond, Raymond was gone.

Merv pulled into a parking space, got out of his car, and began to quickly pace in front of his car, watching the waves of heat squiggle up from the pavement that separated him from the florist stand where Raymond had been standing and working. A faker, Merv thought. A pervert. A fucking sick fuck. And suddenly Merv was frightened, ashamed, felt his stomach strangle itself, felt like everything was falling away. He leaned against his car, but it was too hot, so he climbed back inside and cranked up the air conditioner. He sat there in the parking lot, hoped the wave of weakness and nausea would pass through him. His mind raced: Peter Vaccarino, Hetta killing him, Peter's skinny body all black and pink, the tweekers, the terrorist attacks, moving to L.A., moving to L.A. . . . He quickly opened the door and puked the two McDonald's hamburgers he had eaten for lunch onto the asphalt.

He started his car and turned east on Ina, toward Rancho Sin Vacas.

It was three in the afternoon—she might still be at school—but he decided he'd wait for her in her driveway if she wasn't there.

Kendra was there, though. She answered the front door wearing polka-dotted green boxer shorts and a white tank top, and said, "I thought you were moving to L.A."

"I was," Merv said. "I mean, I am. Today. Like, right now."

"You look pale," she said. "You want some water?" She gestured for him to come inside, but he didn't budge.

"I want you to look after my mother," Merv said, staring into her green eyes.

"Um," Kendra said, leaning against the jamb, "she's my friend. We'll look after each other."

"That's all I needed to hear," Merv said. "Thanks."

"Do you want a bottle of water for the road?" she asked.

Merv rested his hand on Kendra's shoulder, squeezed it a little. "Yes, please," he said. A bottle of water was exactly what he needed.

Acknowledgements

Thanks to Hilary Bass and Jin Auh for their patience and guidance.

Thanks to the students and faculty at Bennington College for allowing me the time and space to write this novel.

Thanks to Lauren and Steve Trainotti for welcoming me into their home.

A big thanks to Matt Frank and Diana Ossana who offered critical and amazingly helpful advice and edits.

Jim Conley, thanks for the New York crash pad.

Ely Teragli, thanks.

Elaine Wing, thanks as always.